Kingston Kate

Also by Elizabeth Waite

SKINNY LIZZIE
COCKNEY WAIF
COCKNEY FAMILY
SECOND CHANCE
THIRD TIME LUCKY
TROUBLE AND STRIFE
NIPPY

Kingston Kate

Elizabeth Waite

LITTLE, BROWN AND COMPANY

A *Little, Brown* Book

First published in Great Britain in 1998
by Little, Brown and Company

Copyright © Elizabeth Waite 1998

The moral right of the author has been asserted.

*All characters in this publication are fictitious
and any resemblance to real persons, living or dead,
is purely coincidental.*

A CIP catalogue record for this book
is available from the British Library.

ISBN 0 316 64362 9

Typeset in Plantin by
Palimpsest Book Production Limited,
Polmont, Stirlingshire
Printed and bound in Great Britain by
Creative Print and Design (Wales) Ebbw Vale

Little, Brown and Company (UK)
Brettenham House
Lancaster Place
London WC2E 7EN

A Childhood Memory

IN 1930 OUR Sunday-school summer outing was a trip from Tooting to Hampton Court Palace and gardens. The charabanc was outside our church hall by nine o'clock. Twenty-eight excited children scrambled aboard and squabbled over who was to have the seats by the windows. Eight already harassed Sunday-school teachers accompanied us. After a short coach ride, which took us over Vauxhall Bridge, we arrived at the Embankment. There we boarded what seemed to us an extremely big riverboat, which would take us all the way down the mighty river Thames to disembark at Hampton Court Bridge.

It was a beautiful sunny August day. The whistles blew, wisps of steam could be seen coming from the funnel and then we were going downriver, passing under Chelsea Bridge and on to Putney, Hammersmith and Richmond, under Chiswick Bridge and through Teddington. By then we had left behind all the sights and sounds of busy

London and were steaming slowly through Kingston upon Thames.

To me, an eight-year-old child, it was like entering another world. Green fields, tall trees and tiny villages all set alongside the river. Cottages that were so pretty it had us London kiddies gasping with envy. Music was being played on board our boat and the sound brought folk to their cottage doors and men came to stand in the doorways of the inns. Children lined the towpath waving to us, and we all waved back and, to this day, I remember thinking how lucky they were to live in such a clean and wonderful place.

From that day's outing, all those years ago, has come the setting I have used for this book. Littleton Green and its inhabitants are purely ficticious, though I haven't the slightest doubt that such a place did exist albeit under another name. Whether or not the same could be said today is an entirely different matter.

Of one thing we can always be sure, no one can take our memories away from us.

Chapter One

'DON'T CRY, KATE, it's nowhere near as bad as it seems.'

Kate Kearsley dashed away her tears, fell to her knees and laid her head in her mother's lap.

'Why have you got up? How ever did you manage to wash and dress yourself? You should have stayed in bed, you really should have,' she said, her voice no more than a whisper.

Hilda Kearsley wriggled to sit in a more comfortable position on the side of the bed, put her hand into the pocket of her long dark skirt and drew out a white handkerchief which she used to dab at the tears still dribbling down Kate's cheeks. 'Your father's been good for a long time, Kate. Try to remember that.'

'That doesn't in any way excuse him. Just look at your face! One eye is almost closed up. He must have been well and truly drunk last night. He's usually far more clever – doesn't leave a mark on you where it shows.'

'Oh, pet, I'll bathe me eye. The swelling will soon go down.'

'Mother! Stop being so forgiving. Why can't you see him for the bully he is rather than keep making allowances for him?'

Kate was distressed to see the state her mother was in and so angry with her father that all she could think of was it was a damn good job he'd had the sense to leave the house so early that morning, otherwise she would not have been responsible for her own actions. The way she felt she could easily do him an injury. What a business, she thought bitterly, inwardly shuddering at what her mother had endured this time.

She had long given up trying to fathom her own father. When he was sober he was a lovely man; a wonderful father and a good provider and that was as it should be seeing he owned his own boat yard. She knew full well she was the apple of his eye and, to be truthful, she adored him in return – most of the time. He had never laid a finger on her. But there was a dark side to him which frightened her and with the demon drink inside him it was a different story. She would lay in bed with only a thin wall between her and her parents' room and try not to imagine what was going on in their bedroom.

It was so unfair to her mother.

Why does she let him get away with it? Why can't she stand up to him? Tell him enough is enough. I suppose she must do just that from time to time, Kate reflected, because there would be weeks, even months sometimes, when everything between her parents would be fine and life enjoyable, even happy. Then her father would go off on a drinking spree, neglect his work and give no thought to anyone but himself. Whatever it was that took over within him, it was always her mother who he took it out on. She had to bear the brunt.

Kate shivered, raised herself to a sitting position and did her best to smile at her mother. 'I'll make a fresh pot of tea and boil you an egg with some thin brown bread and butter. Could you manage that, Mum? I'll lay it out nice on a tray and bring it up here to you. Come on now, lift your legs up an' I'll settle all the pillows behind your shoulders.'

Hilda took one of her daughter's hands in hers and gently squeezed it.

'You're a good girl, Kate, you shouldn't have to be living this dull life with just your father and me, let alone take on problems that are none of your concern. You'll be eighteen in a few weeks' time, you must start giving a thought to what you want to do with your life. If only your brother . . .' her voice trailed off and Kate knew she was overcome with emotion.

Kate had made the tea, covering the pot with the pretty blue cosy her mother had hand-stitched. She was buttering bread, warm from the oven, when the door to the kitchen opened and Hilda stood there. The stairs had been too much for her and, as she drew in a deep, rasping breath, the tears came.

Kate dropped the knife she had been using and ran to her mother's side. 'You shouldn't have come down. Here, sit here.' She pushed the big high-backed wooden armchair until it was against her mother's knees, then helped her to sit back in the chair. She didn't know

3

what to do. Her mother never cried, at least she couldn't remember ever seeing her do so before. But she was crying now; great sobs which left her gasping for breath.

Kate busied herself pouring tea into willow-pattern cups and when Hilda's sobs finally subsided, and she was quiet, she placed a cup and saucer on the end of the hob within her reach and patted her shoulder.

'Try and sip that before it gets cold. Are you warm enough?' Touching her hand, Kate realised she was freezing. 'Hang on. I'll only be a moment,' she murmured, making for the stairs. She came down carrying the big double patchwork quilt that had been on her parents' bed. 'Here, let me wrap this around your shoulders and tuck it in tight round your knees.'

Her mother's hands were shaking so badly, that she couldn't hold the cup.

'Shock. I'll have to leave you and go for the doctor.'

'No! Please, Kate! I'll be all right. I'm just cold. No doctor, please.'

'We'll see,' Kate said, as she crouched down at the grate. Opening up the top of the range she piled a shovelful of coal onto the glowing embers, adding two small logs which caught quickly, cracking and flaming and giving out a warm glow.

A little later they were both dipping fingers of bread into their soft-boiled eggs and drinking their tea.

Kate sighed deeply as she watched her mother put a hand to her side and flinch more than once; her ribs must be badly bruised. Why, oh why, did her father have these terrible outbursts? He was so big. A powerfully built six-footer with brown eyes, craggy features and a deep voice.

4

Her mother wasn't small. In fact, as she herself had often told Kate, she was too tall and large-boned to be called a beautiful woman. But she certainly did have character; graceful in all she did, with her head held high on a beautiful neck, loving and kind, mindful of those less fortunate than herself. She was not a commonplace woman; any emotion she showed was both deep and true.

Kate had heard the bare bones of the story that had been so tragic for her parents, but she thought it should never have been allowed to fester and eat away into their lives like some horrible incurable disease. She had only been two years of age when it had happened.

'Kate, dear, I do wish you would try and stop worrying. A few days and I'll be right as ninepence, you'll see.' Hilda's voice held a note of pleading.

'Yes, till the next time.'

'Don't harp on it, please. Your father will be really sorry when he sobers up.'

'True, but as I said, only until the next time.'

'You were deep in thought when I broke the silence, what were you thinking about?'

'Nothing really. Daydreaming I suppose.'

'That's not quite true, is it?'

Kate looked her mother directly in the eye. 'No. If you must know I was thinking about David. My brother who no one is allowed to mention. A subject that is entirely forbidden in this house.'

Hilda turned her glance away from her daughter as tears welled up in her eyes. She felt totally confused. She turned her head back to look at her daughter.

'Old story,' she said. 'Best forgotten.'

5

'Oh, no, Mum! No. That's more than half the trouble. Dad blames himself, you blame him as well. I know you do. I just can't understand why you've never brought it out into the open. Talked about it. Surely losing a son is best not forgotten? All these years you've both lived with the heartache of that day and it doesn't get any better, does it?'

'No, I can't say that it does. Sixteen years ago it was. Do you remember anything about it?'

'Not really.'

'No, you were only just two. Your grandma took you off to live with her for a while afterwards. A Sunday it was. Summer. A really lovely day. Crowds of people on the riverbank, families, lots of kiddies. Folk had brought picnics. There were loads of small boats on the river. Your father couldn't get his near the bank and David so badly wanted to get into it and be with his dad. I tucked up my skirt and petticoats, picked him up and waded out – it wasn't too deep where we were sitting – and handed him into your father's arms.' Hilda put a hand to her face and covered her eyes as if trying to blot out the memory.

Kate felt the urge to wrap her arms around her mother, hush her, soothe her, tell her everything was all right. But it wasn't, was it? Once in the early hours of the morning she had heard her mother round on her father and cry out, 'David was my son, too, you know. I've felt his death every bit as badly as you have, but I haven't spurned my responsibilities, nor have I tried to drown my sorrow with alcohol.' Her voice, so full of sadness, had made Kate miserable for days.

Now that her mother had started to talk, she sat quietly

and listened. It was probably the best thing that could have happened, her bringing up the subject of David. Kate knew full well that the tragic consequences of that day on the river were never very far from her mother's mind.

'David was such a beautiful child,' Hilda said, still speaking very quietly. 'I stood on the bank and watched your father steer the boat until it turned at a bend in the river. David was waving to me, his eyes alight with excitement, his curly hair blown about in the breeze. Half a mile down the river they were when your father saw that little girl in the water being swept away by the current. He didn't hesitate for a moment. No doubt about it, he saved her life. David must have been frightened when he saw his dad go into the water. He stood up, he shouldn't have but he didn't understand what was happening and he fell over the side. There was some barbed wire on the riverbed. His little feet were still tangled in it when your father got to him. Your dad couldn't save him.'

'Dad wasn't entirely to blame.'

'Most of the time I would agree with you and I do know the guilt of not having saved his own son still plays heavily on his mind, but I just cannot bring myself to forgive him. Not altogether I can't.'

'Didn't Dad hurt his back saving that child?'

'Yes. He damaged his spine. That's why he's not able to lift heavy objects, some days he has a job to straighten up. It's made working very difficult for him.'

'Poor Dad,' Kate mumbled.

'To tell the truth, Kate, you're right. Poor Dad. That boat yard has been his pride and joy since he was a mere lad. Left to him by his father and by his father before him.' Hilda broke off and shrugged. 'I suppose neither of us have coped all that well.'

Kate was thrown off balance by her mother's admission. Now her loyalties were divided. Her father had to rely on his employees to do boat repairs that he would much prefer to tackle himself. Frustation probably had a lot to do with his bouts of drinking which, in turn, led to his horrible temper. Still, it was wholly unfair that he should offload his frustrations onto her mother. There was no reason in this world for him to treat her so badly.

'Mum, I think we've talked for long enough, you look ready to drop. I'll fill the hot-water bottle and take it up, remake your bed and then I'll come down an' help you up the stairs, see you into bed and you can stay there for the rest of the day. How does that sound?'

Hilda nodded her agreement, smiling at Kate in gratitude.

With a lump in her throat Kate removed the sheets from the bed and fetched clean ones, smelling of lavender, from the linen cupboard on the landing. There wasn't a photograph of her brother anywhere in the house, at least not to her knowledge. She kept trying to imagine what he had looked like as a child. What would he look like now? He'd be a man. She tried to put him from her mind as she went back downstairs to tend to her mother, but still her thoughts were full of him.

David had been just four years old when he died. Such a small boy to be the unwitting cause of so much grief.

Chapter Two

KATE LET GO of the shafts of the wheelbarrow she was pushing and opened the front gate which led to the towpath. She was off to make her monthly visit to Melbourne Lodge; a visit she looked forward to with great pleasure. This small barrow was lined with brown paper to protect the fine linen that lay in the bottom, the top protected by a white starched cloth. By a long-standing arrangement her mother repaired the fine linen and quality shirts that belonged to the Collier household.

At times it didn't seem right to Kate that her mother should have to do this kind of work while her father squandered his money. To outsiders Fred Kearsley was a prosperous businessman. Only those close to him knew his weakness for gambling and drinking.

That was her mother all over. A fierce streak of independence made her refuse to beg her father for more housekeeping money. Besides which, she let it be known that she hadn't enough to do to fill the hours of the day and the offer to repair fine linen was as much a hobby as a means of earning money. In addition, she was a very fine needlewoman.

Kate closed the gate behind her and glanced upwards. Her mother, who was standing at the bedroom window, raised her hand to wave goodbye. She watched her daughter set off along the towpath with mixed feelings.

Kate was a beautiful young woman. In fact, that was the one thing that she and her husband were entirely in agreement about, and because she was such a lovely, trusting young girl they feared for her. Tall and slim but shapely, laughing, sparkling, full of spirit, seeing good in everyone, she had so far led a sheltered life. She should have had brothers and sisters as companions to grow up with instead of spending all her time with adults.

Kate's hair was her crowning glory. She had her father's colouring; Fred had a thick head of reddish hair, now shot through with grey. Kate's hair was also thick and heavy, and almost reached her waist. It was the exact colour of a rich ripe chestnut, and unruly was the best way to describe it. No matter how many slides or combs she used it had a will of its own, refusing to be restrained. Dangling ringlets always seemed to escape to bob free about her cheeks and ears. Beneath that mop of hair she had arched eyebrows, deep-brown eyes, cheeks and skin that were like a soft ripe peach and full lips that were always smiling. Oh yes, one look at Kate and men were impressed.

Letting out a deep sigh Hilda closed her eyes. Things couldn't go on as they were, she told herself. Life had held out such promise when Fred Kearsley had brought her home, as his young bride, to this lovely hamlet of

Littleton Green, not very far from the market town of Kingston upon Thames. Bramble Cottage had taken her breath away on sight. Fred had carried her over the threshold and she had immediately fallen in love with it. It had been like a real-life fairy story she had thought then.

Born in Bermondsey, she had been one of nine children, all of them brought up in a two-bedroomed flat, the like of which folk, who had never been outside this beautiful part of Surrey, would not believe. Seven brothers but only one sister. Five of those great strapping brothers had worked in Covent Garden. It was there they had met Fred Kearsley. He had gone to Bermondsey to purchase a quantity of leather for the inside upholstery of a boat he was building and had been directed to Covent Garden as a place where he could kill spare time and also get a good breakfast. Her brothers had brought him home and Hilda's fate had been sealed from the moment he set eyes on her.

Suddenly she felt dizzy. 'I feel so sick,' she murmured out loud. She moved back to the side of the window and leaned her head against the wall, one hand covering her mouth, the other wrapped across her sore ribs. Outside, a weak February sun showed up the frost still lingering under the hedges in the front garden. Beyond, standing beneath the huge oak tree, she could see the big wooden picnic table that Fred, with the help of his neighbours, had constructed a good many years ago. Around another mature tree he had built a seat. Her blue eyes filled with tears, and she ran her fingers through her tangled hair. They had had such happy times out there when David had been little.

11

Beyond the towpath lay the river. The dear old Thames. Always moving, always busy, it had a life of its own and a good many men depended on that river for their livelihood.

God in heaven, she and Fred had loved each other so much during those first five years of their married life. Why had everything had to go so wrong?

Hilda stared at the floor. Where had the time gone?

Moving away from the window she crossed the room to her chest of drawers, knelt and opened the bottom drawer. She took out two silver-framed photographs. She brought one of a small, smiling, curly haired boy to her lips and kissed the glass. The other photo was of Fred and herself. He had been twenty-five and she seventeen on the day in 1901 that they were married.

What a year that had turned out to be. In January she had become a bride, two weeks later Queen Victoria had died and come October, David had been born.

Angry at herself for harping back on matters that no amount of tears would alter, she put the two silver frames right at the very back of the drawer, underneath the clothes and shut it again.

She stared out of the window again for a few seconds, then made for the bed. 'I'll have to have a lie down,' she muttered to herself. Last night Fred had been brutal, hurting her far more than she had admitted to Kate. Things between them were getting worse, not better, and if she wasn't careful one night he might end up doing her a really serious injury.

I should do something about the way we live our lives, she chided herself. But what? With her head resting back against the pillows, her eyes closed and she thankfully dozed off. Even so, there was a frown on her wan haggard face. It seemed sleep didn't blot out the troubles from her mind.

Kate had been glad to get out of the house. She hoped her mother would at least have a rest. She wouldn't let herself dwell on exactly what had gone on last night between her parents. She wasn't totally naive and thought sex was probably half the trouble. Over the years she had drawn her own conclusions: she thought her mother probably never refused her father but neither did she show him any outward signs of love; more than likely she was revolted at the thought of him touching her; unable to bear the idea of becoming pregnant again after losing David.

The saddest part of it all was they were such decent people. She loved them both. Dearly. Hated having to take sides. Such a pity that the tragedy of losing their young son had embittered them so early on in their married life.

She pushed the loose strands of her long hair back from her face, tossed one end of her plaid shawl over her left shoulder and quickened her pace. There was a very cold nip in the air even though the sun was doing its best to shine.

Not much further and she would be able to see Melbourne Lodge, so called, it was rumoured, because the first gentleman to have lived there had been an Australian. Whether that was true or not, she didn't know and didn't really care. She loved the place. The house was set on a hill, with gardens running down almost to the river. From the top windows you could see right downriver to Appleton's boat yard. Kate smiled at that thought. Her father hoped that she would marry Victor Appleton because the Appleton yard was similiar to his. She was friendly enough with Victor, but no more than that. In Kate's mind he didn't have a lot going for him. A bit of a dull plodder was how she saw him.

From the back windows of Melbourne Lodge there was a great view of the Surrey countryside. Not that I've been over the whole of the house, she said to herself. On hot days Mary Kennedy, who was cook-housekeeper there, always gave her a glass of lemonade and a piece of her home-made cake. In wintertime it would more likely be a bowl of soup taken in that huge kitchen where big shiny copper pans hung from hooks high up on the wall and a great fire burned in the black-leaded grate.

There had been the odd occasion when she had gone upstairs with Mary collecting linen and such like from the various landing cupboards. Her tendency to stand and stare in awe at the beautiful furnishings always brought a smile to the housekeeper's face and she would playfully tell her that curiosity killed the cat. She had never been allowed to enter the main bedroom, but she was truly envious of the washing facilities in all the other bedrooms. Glazed white earthenware wash-hand basins were fixed to the walls, with pretty splashbacks, sporting pictures of pheasants and fruit. Each basin had a brass plug and chain although there was no running water. Large pitchers were supplied to carry it up from the kitchen. Dirty water drained away into large floral pots which were, in reality, buckets but not shaped as such. Difficult to handle when emptying, Kate supposed, but very decorative for all that.

You wouldn't think anyone who lived in a house like

that could possibly be discontented, but that was how Kate saw Mr Collier. Or, to give him his full name, Mr Charles Christopher Collier, referred to by local folk as 'the Squire'. He was a big man in every sense of the word. Held in awe by some, but revered and respected by the whole of Surrey, though there were many who didn't know of the double life he led, and those who did did not always approve.

Kate turned into the long driveway, trundling her wheelbarrow behind her and immediately saw Mary Kennedy, who had the side door of the house wide open and was waving her welcome. She had a plump face, big breasts, and short brown hair which was only just beginning to go grey. Kate waved back, a happy smile spreading across the whole of her face.

'I knew you'd be on time,' Mary said as Kate drew near. 'As I always say, Kingston Kate always reliable, never late.'

Kate laughed loudly. Every time she came to the house she was greeted with the same saying. Mary had known her from the time she had been a shy toddler holding onto her mother's long skirts. She had a lot of time for young Kate and had grown to love her very much. Kate's well-fitting clothes and strong, good leather boots set her apart from the poorer local children. Her innocence and pleasant attitude, not to mention her well-pronounced speech, made her stand out from the badly spoken kiddies one found begging along the riverbanks.

The name Kingston Kate had come about because, as a child, Kate had been unable to pronounce her surname Kearsley, and she could never remember that she lived at Littleton Green, only that her nan lived at Kingston.

So, to a good many folk, she had become known as Kingston Kate.

She propped her wheelbarrow against the passage wall and hurried into the kitchen. The warmth and cheer that greeted her was always a joy. Afternoon tea was set out on the enormous scrubbed table, as Kate had known it would be. The big brown teapot was beside the range to keep warm and Mary presided over her own home-made scones with strawberry jam and a rich fruit cake.

There were two staircases to the house: the main one, broad and sweeping, carpeted all the way to the top; the other, running up from the kitchen, used only by staff. Dark and narrow, the wooden treads were uncovered. At the foot of these stairs there was a door from which Mrs Bates now stepped out.

''Allo, Kate. I guessed there'd be a cup of tea going seeing as it was your day to vist.'

'Hallo, Mrs Bates. You're here late today, aren't you?'

'Yeah, I am an' all. His floozie . . .' she paused and nodded her head towards the ceiling '. . . she's worked herself into a right uppity mood. Seems 'is lordship ain't been near nor by for two days now and though she'd deny it if you were t'ask 'er, I'm telling yer straight that lass is worried sick.'

Mrs Bates was the cleaner who came each day to 'do' at Melbourne Lodge. Try as Kate might she didn't like the woman though she would have been hard pushed to say exactly why. Perhaps it was because she was rather intimidating, a whole head taller than her own husband and more than half as broad. She always wore a man's flat cap, indoors as well as out. 'I bet she even wears it in bed,' Kate had whispered to her mother when once they had met Mr and Mrs Bates in Kingston market. 'An ill-matched pair if ever I saw one,' had been her mother's comment.

'Put your cleaning things away, Mrs Bates, an' come an' sit up to the table.' Mary's voice was sharp. 'We can't be sending you off home on this cold day without offering you tea and a scone – they are still warm from the oven.'

When both Kate and Mrs Bates had been served, Mary sat down at the head of the table and crossed her arms over her ample chest.

'Mrs Bates,' she began and her tone was so serious that Mrs Bates paused, her mouth wide open, half a scone in her hand halfway to being bitten. 'You would do well to remember that there is a vast difference between a mistress and a floozie. Especially if you value your job in this house.' Mrs Bates' mouth snapped shut and Kate, sitting next to her, heard her teeth grind.

'That's nothing to what they say about the pair of them in the Boar's 'Ead,' she hissed in reply. 'You wanna 'ear them some nights an' I can't say that I blame them. Be honest, Mrs Kennedy, he's well over forty, nearer to fifty if you ask me, an' even out in public he treats her ever so gentle like, you'd think she was some kind of a princess. Bet he never treats his wife like that.'

'Will you stop it, Mrs Bates. I've listened to you spout off about Mr Collier far too often.' Mary spat the words out.

The colour drained from Mrs Bates' cheeks and a brief look passed between her and the housekeeper, but it was Mrs Bates who dropped her eyes first.

'Let me put you straight on a few details,' Mary began.

'Jane Mortimer is mistress in this house, no matter what you might think. I agree with you that she is much younger than Mr Collier but I have always found her to be a lovely, shy, young lady. And I mean lady. There is nothing wicked or shameful about her.'

The hostility between Mary and Mrs Bates rocked Kate to the core. She knew quite a lot about Mr Collier and was aware that many people, her own mother included, were curious about him but never had she heard his affairs discussed so openly. She would have like to have told Mrs Bates that she was a spiteful woman and Mr Collier didn't deserve to be spoken about in such an insolent manner. Warning bells were going off in Kate's head. Keep quiet, keep out of it, she chided herself, remembering what her father was always telling her, 'Your tongue's too sharp for your own good, Kate, and one day you'll say the wrong thing to the wrong person.' He could well be right; there were times when he could be so wise!

Mr Collier's main house was a few miles away from Melbourne Lodge, bordering Hampton Court, and it was there that he and his wife hosted grand parties and balls. There were no children and it was perhaps for that reason that those who knew of Jane Mortimer and this more humble house cast no criticism, even though Mr Collier let it be known that she had taken up permanent residence. It was only the likes of Mrs Bates who thought they had the right to comment on matters that were nothing whatsoever to do with them.

'Is there anything else you would like to bring out into the open?' Mary asked Mrs Bates as she reached for the woman's teacup in order to refill it.

'Well, yes, there is, as a matter of fact.' Mrs Bates' expression was one of defiance. 'What about his wife? 'T'ain't the poor woman's fault she couldn't carry a child full term. Who knows what might 'ave 'appened t'cause her to drop 'em?'

'How dare you!' exclaimed Mary.

Suddenly a deep shadow flitted past the kitchen window, and Charles Collier came in through the back door. His entry into the kitchen caused all three women to jump in surprise.

His shoulders were draped with a heavy velvet-collared cape which he quickly removed laying it across the back of a chair close to the door. As usual he was dressed in the height of fashion. Always a fastidious man he was wearing a double-breasted coat, a perfectly ironed shirt with snow-white frilled cuffs, a silk cravat, heavy corded breeches and knee-high polished boots.

Kate liked him. He was tall with a wide chest, brown eyes and dark hair. She thought of him as a strikingly good-looking gentleman. To some folk he was a miserable man. Not so to Kate. To her he was the grand lord of the manor who lived in a mansion with his wife and took his responsibilities seriously, most of the time. The fact that he owned this riverside house which he used for his lady friend only intrigued her. She saw it as a great, romantic love affair, although sometimes she suffered from a tormenting curiosity as to what the outcome might be. Still, you wouldn't get a bad word about him from me, Kate thought, tossing her head and glaring at Mrs Bates. Mr Collier had always been exceedingly kind to her as far back as she could remember.

'A tray of tea and perhaps some of that rich-looking

19

fruit cake would be nice, if you please, Mary.' Mr Collier gave Mrs Bates a friendly nod, and sat down to remove his boots. He smiled at Kate, whose hair had broken loose from the ribbon that was meant to be holding it back. 'Like to give me a hand, young Kate?' he asked, thinking how young and fresh she looked.

'Of course.' She smiled back, crossed to where he sat and cupped her hands around one foot, tugging for all she was worth.

'Thank you,' he said when both boots were off and standing side by side against the wall. 'So, how are you, Kate? And your parents?'

'Fine, thank you, sir,'

'Well, give them both my regards.'

'Phew!' Mrs Bates let out a great gasp of breath as they watched him leave the room, making for the main staircase, in his stockinged feet. 'D'you think he 'eard me talking as he came in?'

'You can thank your lucky stars that he didn't, my lady. If he had, your feet wouldn't have touched the gravel as you went down that driveway. Now I think it is time you were gone. But just remember my warning, Mrs Bates. You have a kind employer who pays you fair wages, doesn't interfere in your business, and does not expect you to concern yourself with his.'

'All right,' she answered sullenly, 'what d'yer take me for? I do know when it's best t'keep me mouth shut.'

'Do you? Well it's a pity nobody ever told you that a still tongue makes a wise head.'

'No need for you to be so nasty,' she mumbled. 'I'll gather up me things and be on me way. See you on yer next visit, Kate.'

'Yes, all right, Mrs Bates.'

Both Kate and Mary heaved a sigh of relief as they watched Mrs Bates pull her cap down hard, put on her coat, pick up her shopping bag and leave by the side door.

Mary came back downstairs, having taken tea up for Mr Collier and Jane. She sighed very deeply and very sadly, as she flopped into a chair.

'I'm blowed if I know what the outcome will be. They're both such nice people. You only have to look at them to feel the attraction and the love they have for each other. It shines through their eyes, it really does.' She held her hands up in the air. 'But I can't stop myself from wondering whether there can be a lasting happiness for either of them.'

Kate didn't know the answer any more than Mary.

Mary glanced up at the clock on the wall. 'I'd better not keep you too late today, it turns really cold as soon as it gets dark.'

'Yes, it does,' Kate agreed, rising and going into the passage to lift the repaired linen out from her wheelbarrow and to collect her heavy cloak from the peg on which she had hung it.

'There's a parcel over there on the dresser. I've put a note inside for your mother. It's a couple of Mr Collier's dress shirts that need new frills for the cuffs, not much else at the moment,' Mary said, as she came back into the kitchen.

'Well they won't take my mum long, so I'll bring them back soon without waiting for the whole month to slip by,' Kate declared, a happy smile lighting up her face.

'Right then.' Mary took her arm as they walked to the side door. 'You know you don't need an excuse to come down and see me. I've told you often enough I'm always glad of your company.' She smiled at Kate, whose face was framed by loose strands of hair blowing in the wind.

Although Mary was called 'Mrs' Kennedy, it was a courtesy title given to unmarried housekeepers in gentlemen's residences. At that moment she was thinking what she had missed; she would give the world to have had a daughter such as Kate.

'I'd better get off then.'

Mary's lower lip trembled as she put her arms around Kate. 'You take care now. Look after yourself.'

'I will. And I'll see you soon.'

At the bottom of the drive Kate turned to wave, knowing full well that Mary would stand there watching her until she was out of sight.

Chapter Three

KATE GLANCED AT the clock as she swung her legs over the side of her bed. It was just five thirty on Monday morning, the day of the week she loved best. For this was the day that she spent with her gran. Grandma Kearsley, her father's mother.

Tiptoeing across the linoleum she gently pulled the curtains open. Outside, the May dawn already held the promise of a day that would be warm and dry.

It was three months since her father had last knocked her mother about. Kate didn't delude herself that he had turned over a new leaf; that was too much to hope for. Still, the last few weeks had been nice: no raised voices, the three of them eating dinner together every night. Conversation had flowed, with her dad telling them of the work that was rolling into his boat yard, which was sited near old Hampton Court Bridge. It was three years now since the war had ended and the yard was back to running normally. He employed three full-time craftsmen, and at the moment he was cock-a-hoop because he had landed an order for a very special type of boat to be built for a local brewer.

Success usually depended on whether or not the coming summer would turn out to be a long hot one. The saloon steamers had already started to run daily between Kingston, Hampton Court and Windsor. Passengers sat on the decks sipping long, cool drinks, eating sandwiches and fresh fruit, squinting over the sides of the boat at the rippling water, thinking how lovely it must be to live on the riverfront.

They should come back and see it on a really bad winter's day.

Kate slipped her nightdress over her head, filled the washing bowl from the matching jug which stood on top of her marble-topped washstand. She shuddered. 'This water is freezing,' she moaned, rubbing Lifebuoy soap onto her pretty face flannel.

She washed her body quickly and when she was dry, sat down to pull on her long-legged bloomers, then her chemise, then her dark stockings and garters. Today she was to wear a dress laid out ready by her mother last night. It was navy blue and one which her gran had made for her, quite plain really, just two rows of pearl buttons down the front and a lace collar, hand-crocheted by her mother.

She brushed her hair briskly, combed and pinned it into a bun at the nape of her neck. Much good all the pins will do, she thought, barbed wire wouldn't keep my mop in place. Taking a last look in the piece of mirror fixed to the wall she wasn't over-pleased with what she saw. 'Dull-looking, that's what you are, Kate Kearsley,' she said out loud. 'Brown eyes, brown hair. Good job you've got those glints of red in amongst those thick tresses otherwise you'd look even worse.'

That wasn't how Hilda Kearsley saw her daughter as she sat at the kitchen table, watching her drink her tea and eat a slice of toast. Kate had crossed her legs causing the hem of her skirt to ride up, almost to her right knee. She had lovely legs, in fact she was beautiful in every way. With the return of the young men from France young ladies seemed to be . . . well . . . not so modest as they should be, and it was rumoured in the papers that hemlines were to become shorter. Hilda hoped not. She liked the way her girl dressed, the way she acted and, most of all, the way she spoke. She herself had talked with a cockney twang when first she had met Fred. Living here, away from London where life was quieter, slower, more gentle, she took the trouble to pronounce her words properly. Well, at least she tried.

There was a catch in her voice as she bid Kate goodbye. 'Give my love t'yer Gran,' she called after her.

'I will, Mum. See you tonight. Bye.'

Kate set out to walk the three miles to Kingston with a lightness in her step. The birds were singing their hearts out, as if by chorusing their songs they were sharing this lovely, bright spring morning. She turned a bend and saw a great carthorse coming towards her, towing a barge. It was brightly painted and was towing another boat, the second one heavily laden with timber. Two scruffy lads about her own age were balanced on top of the timber, one steering with a long pole-like rudder. She knew who they were; part of the Wilson family who she and her parents met up with from time to time, particularly when the river was busy or Hampton Court was holding its annual fair.

The boys, one blond the other dark haired, spotted her and raised their hands.

''Ow y'doing, Kate?' the tallest of the two yelled.

'I'm fine, Mickey. Good t'see you, and you, Bertie,' she called back, laughing at them both. 'Where are you making for?'

'East Molesey, 'Arry Burton's yard, not far from yer father's place.'

Kate resisted the temptation to stand and watch the gaily coloured barges stream down the river. 'See you,' she shouted, waving like mad and walking backwards for several steps before turning to continue on her way.

Alice Kearsley wore a shapeless dress under a long white apron, the front of which was dominated by two enormous pockets. She lived in a house her husband had built himself when they were a pair of starry-eyed newly-weds. It was a flat-roofed, long, low, part-timbered building. She was a widow now, content with her own company and able to live largely on what she grew in her half-acre of land. She also kept chickens, ducks and rabbits.

The very sight of her grandmother wearing a floppy straw hat on her head and brown button-up boots on her feet brought a smile to the face of her only grandchild.

'Hallo, Gran!' Kate called enthusiastically as she opened the wicker gate. Alice covered the ground between them in a few strides. 'Hallo, my luv,' she said, as she gave Kate a hug.

Kate reached up to straighten her steel-rimmed spectacles. 'I don't know how you manage to see, Gran, your

26

glasses are always crooked. Whatever am I going to do with you?'

Alice took the spectacles off and put them into one of her pockets. 'To tell you the truth, I don't know why your father insisted I had them; I can still see the difference in a halfcrown an' a florin, so why should I bother?'

Kate laughed loudly.

'Up an' about early this morning an' sharp with it, aren't you?'

'Well I don't need no alarm clock to wake me these bright mornings, do I? My big cockerel makes sure everyone hereabouts is awake good an' early.'

'So are we going to sell a load of stuff today and make a lot of money?'

'Well, we better, by golly, 'cause I near broke me back digging up a load of new potatoes and there's some tomatoes that I have had under glass, an' if I do say so myself they are real good. Taste lovely they do. Go on out back, will you, luv, there's two baskets ready, one full of ducks' eggs, the other one is me chickens' eggs. I've packed plenty of straw round them because you know how mad Jack Dawson drives his horse an' cart – don't want no cracked ones, do we?'

'You're always knocking Jack, yet he comes week in week out, no matter what the weather, just to cart you and your produce into Kingston.'

Alice had the grace to mutter, 'Sorry,' then quickly added, 'He's going to market anyway and I sees he don't lose by it. I always buys him a pint in the Griffin an' he don't go home empty-handed.'

Kate shook her head, Alice had an answer for everything. She came back through the kitchen carrying the two baskets of eggs just as Jack Dawson shouted 'whoa' to his horse, bringing it to a halt in the lane outside the house.

'Morning, Mrs Kearsley. 'Allo, young Kate. I've left the right side of me cart free, so put those baskets on and I'll give you an 'and to fetch whatever else your gran has got ready to go.' Jack Dawson, looking as swarthy as ever, let go of the reins and jumped down. Grinning at Kate he said, 'An' 'ow's the old lady today? Still giving out 'er orders left right an' centre, is she?'

Alice sucked in her breath, and fixed him with a beady eye. 'I heard that, young man, just pay attention t'what you're doing and stop asking my granddaughter silly questions!'

'I can see for meself, Mrs Kearsley, you're in fine fettle, an' no mistake.'

'Fit enough to keep you in yer place, me lad,' she teased him solemnly.

Kate was thoroughly enjoying listening to them bait each other. Amid much laughter they sorted everything out, making several trips from the house and garden to the cart.

'That's the lot,' Alice told Jack as she led the procession out to the roadway.

In less than a quarter of an hour they were setting up the stall in Kingston market. All about them other stalls were piled high with vegetables and salad stuff, mostly straight from local smallholdings or allotments. What was that gorgeous smell? Strawberries. Nothing like the scent of the first strawberries of the season. Someone must have a greenhouse to be able to pick them so early. And one farmer's wife had had the good sense to bring a bowl of clotted cream. She's sure to sell that quickly today, Kate thought as she watched the woman cover the bowl with a fine mesh cloth, weighted down by dangling glass beads.

The market wasn't populated entirely by well-fed, prosperous-looking people. There were women with painfully thin children clutching at their skirts. For some of them there was no longer a man in the family; so many men had been killed in the War. Those who had come home had soon found out that the promise of a land fit for heroes had been an empty one.

Kate was well aware that in parts of Kingston living conditions were utterly apalling. Streets where back-to-back houses had three or even four families living in a few cramped rooms. In the hot weather they stank; with one shared lavatory out in the backyard and no proper sanitation, the Lord alone knew how these folk kept themselves clean. Most of the men had no jobs to go to, just the endless daily drudgery of searching for work.

Alice finished serving a young mother with an assortment of pot-herbs and held out a great big, green cabbage. 'How will this do yer, luv? Give us a penny an' it's yours.'

'Aw, thanks, Mrs Kearsley,' the neat young woman whispered. 'Every week you're ever so good t'me.'

'Go on with you, t'ain't everybody can be doing with a cabbage as big as that one. An' wait a minute – 'ere, give the kiddies one of these new carrots to gnaw. You'll need to give them a wipe, but a bit of clean earth never hurt no one.'

Small hands reached up quickly and each child's face

had a wide grin as their mother shared out the fresh young carrots.

'Thanks, Mrs Kearsley,' the children chorused.

'You're welcome,' Alice said lovingly.

Kate smiled warmly. 'You're a right old softie, you know that, Gran, don't you? A real right softie.'

'I'll give you softie, Kate Kearsley, if you don't start pulling your weight round here. Those empty boxes need stacking up. Me feet are killing me and me throat is begging for a drink.'

'Humph,' Kate grunted. 'I wondered how much longer you were going to stand there seeing as how the Griffin has been open for the last hour or more.'

'You cheeky young beggar!' Alice cried, swinging round towards her. Then her voice took on a cooing note, 'You don't mind if yer old gran goes for a drink, do you? I'll bring you back a hot pie.'

'No, you go. We've not much left to sell anyway. Only a few eggs.'

Kate set about packing up the stall. As she worked, she mused, 'I'm so lucky to live in such a lovely place as Littleton Green and even more lucky to have a mum and a dad who love me, never mind dear old gran. Can't be many of her sort left in this world.'

Kate was feeling content as she sat at one end of the kitchen table while Alice sat at the other. When Jack Dawson had brought all the empty baskets and boxes through to the backyard and gone back to lift Alice down from the cart she had seen him kiss her goodbye before he got back up and set off home.

Gran was so special. She had always been there for

Kate with hugs and kisses and help when her mum had been so ill that time. Hilda had been struck down with a terrible flu and Alice had moved in, staying for three weeks. Cooking, washing and ironing for her and her dad, making a lovely dinner every night and special broth for her mum because her throat was too sore to eat solids. Many an afternoon she had walked all the way back to her own house just to see that her neighbours were keeping their promises and looking after her animals. She was also the only person who knew that her dad treated her mum so badly at times.

She looked so different now. Since returning from the market she had changed her clothes, had a wash, and combed and fluffed out her snow-white hair until it formed a halo around her face. On her small feet she wore a pair of red velvet slippers.

'How's your mother?'

Kate looked up, puzzled. 'Why are you suddenly asking?'

'Because I haven't seen your father for a couple of weeks and that's not like him. He usually drops in at least once during a working week, more often than not, twice. Has everything been all right between him and your mother?'

'Yes, but it frightens me.'

'Frightens you? What does?'

'The calmness. They're even acting as if they're friends for a change.'

'And what's wrong with that?'

'Nothing at all. But as you know, it isn't normal. Sometimes you can cut the atmosphere in our house with a knife. At the moment it's like the calm before a storm.'

'Oh, luv.' Alice put out a trembling hand. 'Don't say that. For God's sake, don't even think it. Just let's be grateful that things are so much better between them.'

'Can I ask you a question?'

'Since when did you need permission? What is it? Go on, fire away.'

'Does my dad always come and tell you when they've had a bust up?'

'Yes.'

'Always?'

'Well, I'm pretty sure he does. You see, Kate, when he comes to his senses he's absolutely guilt-ridden. I know that's of no help one way or another to your mother, and I feel for them both. Have done for years. Still, I have to say that there are times when I think it's half a dozen of one and six of the other.'

'Oh, no! No, gran. You can't blame Mum! She's the one that ends up with the black eyes, sore ribs and bruises that turn her body black and blue. Surely you can't believe she deserves it?'

'I never said that, lass. Let's go back to the start of all this trouble. You were far too young to remember. It was a terrible out-and-out tragedy them losing their dear little boy. And, of course, it was made worse by the fact that your father saved the life of someone else's child and in a roundabout way caused young David's death.'

Kate sat with her eyes downcast, saying nothing.

Her grandma got to her feet, and poured them each a glass of home-made lemonade.

'Thank you,' Kate said as she took hold of her glass, then quietly added, 'I don't see why you don't have more to say to dad when he tells you about what he's done. I mean . . . well . . . you don't think it's right for a man to hit his wife, do you?'

Alice sighed heavily, crossed the room and perched herself on the wide window sill so that she was facing Kate.

'I'll tell you what I've come to know over the years, because I think you're old enough to hear it, and I'll tell you, lass, as honestly as I can. Most men have their needs, and when two people get married that gives the man the right to expect that those needs will be satisfied by his wife. As far as I know, my son has not gone looking for other women. Your mother is a good woman and I could not have asked for a better daughter-in-law, but what she has seen fit to tell me has lead me to believe that all your parents' troubles started in the marriage bed. Your dad once said it was like sleeping with a stuffed dummy and your mother on one occasion admitted to me that she cringed whenever my Fred came near her.

'To my way of thinking, a little forgiveness on her part wouldn't go amiss. Sixteen years is a long time to bear a grudge. Your dad did what he thought was right when he went into the river to save that little girl. Perhaps he did make the wrong decision. But he wasn't to know that David, left on his own in the boat, would stand up, topple the boat and fall into the water. Your mother has always said he should have thought of that.

'No one blamed her at the time for turning on her husband. She was distraught – as any mother would have been. I can say only now that with hindsight we can all be clever. Your mother has held bitterness in her heart for so long she doesn't know how to forgive any more.'

33

Neither of them moved until Kate let out a deep breath.

'All my life I've hated being an only child, at times it's been very lonely, especially when we went to London, to see Mum's sister, Aunt Dolly. Up there I've got so many cousins yet I can't remember when we last visited any of them. Oh, I don't know. I'm eighteen years old, you'd think I'd have got used to it by now.'

'Kate, luv, there are some things in life that you never get used to no matter how hard you try.'

Look at me, Alice Kearsley almost said to her grand-daughter, but decided against it. Poor lass had enough to cope with already. There was, however, no one more able to tell her that life never went as you wanted or even expected it to. She and her Jack had started out reaching for the moon and Jack, a young man of nineteen then, had promised her the stars to go with it. And he was well on his way to giving her all that when, in the prime of life, he'd suffered a stroke and died. Three children they'd had. A right good little family. Just the one boy and two girls, and both girls had caught scarlet fever and died before they even reached school age. Life could be a bitch sometimes, but these memories didn't help either of them.

As if sensing the sadness in each other, their eyes met and Alice got to her feet and crossed the room, to put her arm around Kate's shoulders.

'Come on, luv. Take it a day at a time. At least yer mum an' dad are doin' all right at the moment. Don't let's start looking for trouble.'

Kate sighed and tilted her lips up to kiss Alice's soft cheek. 'What would I do without you?'

'Silly question, girl. You haven't even got to think about that, 'cos you have got me. Now, how about going through to me scullery, filling the kettle, puting it on the gas an' making yer poor ole gran a good strong cup of tea while I fix us some scrambled eggs and bacon.'

'You don't have to go t'all that trouble.'

'I know I don't, but I am. Eating a meal with you, lass, every Monday, before you set off home, is the highlight of my week. Oh, an' I forgot to tell you, I've made you the biggest bread pudding you've ever seen. It's full of spices and raisins, so what you don't eat you can take home for your mum an' dad.'

When it was time for Kate to go, Alice kissed her and, before releasing her, whispered, 'Take care, an' remember I'm always here.'

'Thanks, Gran. God bless you.'

Alice stood in the lane and didn't go back inside until she'd seen her granddaughter turn and wave before stepping out of sight. Long after Kate had left, her mind was filled with confusion. That lovely girl obviously felt that the burden on her shoulders was too heavy to bear at times. And so it was. She would like to beat the daylights out of her own son when he came to unburden his soul, blurting out how hateful he had been to Hilda.

But there again, he was not entirely to blame. She was not blind to the fact that he had had no reasonable married life for the last sixteen years. There had to be a breaking point somewhere. Her Fred was a man and no man could go on living and suffering the way Hilda made him. Enough ought to be enough for the pair of them. What would the outcome be?

If the way they were acting at the moment, according

to Kate, was anything to go by, perhaps at last there might be some happiness there for both of them in the future. I can't see it though, they've hurt each other too much, she thought.

She dropped down into her armchair, bent and took off her slippers, replacing them with the old boots she wore only in the garden. When she had them laced up, she went through to the scullery, found her sacking apron and tied it round her waist. Then, with a sigh, she went wearily out through the back door to feed and water her animals and see they were settled down for the night.

Chapter Four

KATE STUDIED HER mother, who was standing on the towpath gazing out across the river. Her feelings were mixed. Her father had been away on business for three days, and since his return her parents seemed to be doing their best to avoid each other, as if their brief truce had never happened. At dinner the night before she had felt they were struggling to be polite, glancing occasionally at each other, but determinedly refraining from speaking.

It had been left to her to break the silence. 'Did you have a good trip, Dad?'

Her father had shrugged. 'Did a bit of business, Kate.'

A terrible expression had spread over her mother's face, and she had let out a snarl. 'You're not man enough t'tell her what kind of business, are you?' Then she'd left the table.

Kate's stomach had twisted itself into knots. She had lain awake half the night telling herself that open hostility was obviously going to be the order of the day once again. You'd have had to be blind not to see and feel the animosity between her parents at breakfast this morning.

She glanced over at her mother and found she was watching her. Gran's right, Kate thought, she's so bitter. It's such a shame she's so unhappy. She opened the front gate and crossed to where Hilda stood.

'Do you feel better now?'

Hilda studied her daughter, then did her best to smile. 'I'm fine. There's nothing wrong with me.'

'I lay awake last night, Mum, wondering what's going on now between you an' Dad.'

'Nothing's going on. There's nothing for you to worry about.'

Kate shocked her by replying, 'I wish you'd tell me the truth for once.'

Hilda flushed and quickly turned away, making for the house.

In the kitchen, Kate resisted the impulse to put her arms around her.

'Don't be so hard on Dad, please, Mum.'

'He's hateful to me.'

'I know. You're hateful to him, too. Why can't you both try to be a little more . . . well . . . gentle with each other?'

Hilda reached up and took two cups down from the dresser. 'I'm sorry, Kate, I'm beginning to see what harm your father an' I have done to you by letting you witness our long-standing bitterness.' She set the cups down on the table and sunk down onto a chair. 'All right, I'll speak to your father. I'll try.'

'Thanks, Mum.' Kate smiled broadly, feeling hopeful. 'I'll make the tea and then do you want me to take the shirts back to Mr Collier?'

'Yes, they should go back today. I couldn't get the lace locally as you know, I had to send a special order to London, so what with one thing an' another I've been a long time doing the repairs, though I did write to Mary and ask her to explain to Mr Collier.'

'It wasn't your fault. I'll tell you what. Why don't you come with me to Melbourne Lodge? It's a lovely day, the walk would do you good and you know how pleased Mary would be to see you.'

'No, luv. It's a nice thought, but I'm tired. I'll have a cup of tea and a bite to eat with you now, an' then I'm going to have a lie down.'

Hilda made them each a cheese sandwich while Kate poured out the tea, but it was a sad, somehow lonely lunch with very little conversation from either of them. Kate left as soon as she had finished eating, saying she wouldn't be late back and for her mother to have a nice nap.

When she was gone the house suddenly felt awful. Silent and unfriendly.

Hilda cleared up the kitchen, washed her face and hands and went to sit in the front room. The bright sunshine was dazzling, shining directly through the bay window. She set out her sewing basket beside the sofa and settled herself down to do some work, but found concentrating difficult and finally laid it aside. She had come so near to telling Kate that her father had another woman and that in all probability he and she had been off on holiday together. Business trip! Never in your life!

She shouldn't blame him and there were times when she didn't. Their marriage had been a sham since the day David had died.

She sat stock still, wondering. She was not a person to shed many tears, she knew herself to be too hard for that. It was her own fault that Fred had turned to another woman, and at least he had the decency to be discreet. Even his own mother had never cottoned on, and he would sell his soul rather than let his beloved Kate find out. What made her blood boil was that, when full of drink, he would come home and demand his rights from her. She hated the whole performance: the touch of his hands roaming over her body, his wet lips and beery breath. If he kept to someone else and left her alone she would be more than happy to live a life of routine respectability, put on a show for their relations and neighbours. But that wasn't enough for him. How could he come from another woman's bed and into hers?

Yes, she had been hard, laying all the blame for David's death on him. She couldn't help it, that's how she felt. It *had* been his fault, no one else's. She had lost her first born, her son, because of him. David had drowned because his father was too busy looking after another mother's child.

But still . . . Her thoughts trailed off and she made herself remember that she had promised Kate to try and adopt a more friendly attitude towards her father. God give me the strength, she said to herself. She had her doubts but try she would. Whether she or Fred could somehow put a stop to this wretched existence, show respect and learn to treat each other as ordinary, decent human beings was another matter entirely.

*   *   *

Kate did a little hop, skip, and jump. Now, in sunny warm June, the river was a sight to behold. A passing steamer blew its whistle, folk on board waved and Kate waved back. Everything outdoors today looked and smelled wonderful. The air rang with the squeals of half a dozen children playing down by the river. She stood for a moment watching them. Their bare legs were brown, their hair bedraggled, their feet dirty, but they were having a grand time. Why hadn't her mother made the effort and come for a walk? Perhaps the sight of small boys playing by the water would have brought memories rushing back. Even after all this time her mother could not forget, let alone forgive.

The thought suddenly angered her. Her mother had no right to bear such a grudge against her father and her father had no right to hit her mother no matter what cause she gave him.

'I'm always the one in the middle! I don't deserve to have to live with all this pent-up anger!' she muttered.

She moved on, taking deep breaths as she glanced round her. How could anyone be miserable when they were lucky enough to live in such beautiful surroundings?

A grin spread over her face as she heard the trot of a horse's hooves.

'Morning, Mr Baldwin.' Kate greeted the local miller.

'You daydreaming or something, young Kate? It's almost two o'clock so I think we can safely assume that it's now afternoon,' he said as he pulled his horse to a halt.

Mr Baldwin had iron-grey hair, steel-rimmed glasses and huge hands covered with black hairs. His voice was loud and hearty. He looked well pleased with himself as he added, 'Want to know something else?'

Kate put out a hand to pat his horse. She had known the miller ever since she could remember and liked him a lot; you couldn't have a kinder man. A jolly man was how most would describe him.

'And what would that be?'

'You're looking, well . . . sort of tempting this morning, Kate Kearsley, and I think there should be a law against allowing young women who look as beautiful as you do from roaming the lanes.'

'Still full of flattery, or is flannel the better word? You know, when next I come up to the mill I think I shall have a little talk to Mrs Baldwin about you.'

The miller threw back his head and his roar of laughter rang out loudly. 'There is nothing about me that you or a dozen others could tell my Bessie that she doesn't already know. By the way, lass, how's your mother? I saw your dad yesterday but I haven't set eyes on your mum for ages.'

'Mother's not too well. She doesn't go out a lot, but she sits in the garden and gets the air.'

'Well, tell her I was asking after her and that my Bessie would be only too pleased to see her when she fancies a walk.'

'I will, and I'll try and get her to pay Mrs Baldwin a visit.'

'Good. You take care, Kate.'

He flicked the reins and told the horse to walk on.

'I wonder if the Kearsleys really know what they put that girl through?' Ken Baldwin exclaimed angrily to himself. 'Bad enough that they make life hell for each other, but I reckon it's time that someone told them a few home truths.'

The whole village knew that Fred Kearsley laid into his wife when the mood took him, and one night in the pub when he'd had a skinful the customers had been forced to listen to him wallow on about how his wife didn't understand him. Nothing but self-pity! It had been degrading!

Like a lot of the men who had been in the bar that evening he'd felt the urge to smash him in the face. That wouldn't have done anyone any good – least of all young Kate – but he had been sorely tempted.

The thought of seeing Mary and having tea in that happy household made Kate quicken her footsteps.

She had taken such pains with her hair this morning but still strands had torn free and were dangling down over her ears as she walked up the drive. Never mind, she grinned to herself, Mary is well-used to seeing my hair in an unruly state.

Mary answered her knock dressed in a very nice dress the colour of the clear sky, pale blue with white daisies all strung together round the neck and each cuff. Her hair must have been newly washed; it looked shiny and fluffy.

'Hallo there, Kingston Kate, always reliable, never late, in fact I think you're early today.'

'Something smells delicious,' Kate commented, having planted a kiss on Mary's cheek.

'It's a cherry cake baking in the oven and those fruit pies on the dresser aren't cold yet, but it's not quite teatime, so would you like a cold drink? There's milk in the larder.'

Elizabeth Waite

'Milk would be lovely. I'll get it.'

She felt at home as she cleared a pile of knitting to one end of the dresser and placed the neat parcel containing Mr Collier's two shirts beside a bag of wool.

Mary was busy wiping away all signs of flour from the kitchen table when she came back into the room sipping a glass of creamy milk.

'What's all the white wool for? What are you knitting?'

Mary looked at Kate and raised her eyebrows, her expression cagey. 'That's what I'm dying to tell you.'

Kate propped herself up against the front of the dresser. 'Oh, that sounds interesting. Has Mrs Bates been given her marching orders?'

Mary laughed. 'No, nothing like that. Jane Mortimer is pregnant.'

Kate drew in her breath sharply and her eyebrows shot up.

'Really?'

'Yes, really. The baby's due about Christmas time, and I'm trying my hand at baby clothes.'

'Well, after all this time! Miss Mortimer pregnant! Imagine that. What does Mr Collier think about it? Does he want the baby?'

'Yes, both of them do. Very much so, by all accounts.'

'Bet that was a relief for her and for you, Mary, when you heard. Otherwise it could have been a sticky situation.'

'Don't I know it. But guess what?'

'You mean there's more?'

'Only that it was the squire himself who came and told me. Over the moon he was. Fetched Jane down,

44

brought a bottle of wine up from the cellar, opened it, and here in the kichen, we three together toasted the new baby. 'To my first born' is what he said, an' oh, Kate, you should have seen the look on his face as he stared at Jane. If ever a man was in love, then he is. He adores her. You can tell just by watching him.'

Kate was fascinated.

'Does Mrs Bates know about this?'

Mary shook her head. 'We've managed to keep it from her so far. You can guess at the rumours she'd soon have flying about.'

Kate put her glass down on the table and smiled at Mary. 'I'm so happy for them.'

'Me too. But it won't be all plain sailing. On the quiet, Mr Collier asked me to take extra care of Miss Jane. As if I needed asking! What he really wanted was to hear me pledge that I would remain on here as housekeeper after the baby is born. Even went as far as promising me an increase in my wages.'

Kate went and patted her on the shoulder and giggled. 'No need for you to tell me what your answer was. You'll be like a mother hen with a new chick.'

Mary's face suddenly lost its colour and her eyes glistened with unshed tears.

'What's the matter? You look as if you're going to faint. Are you all right?' Kate asked, full of concern.

'Yes,' she whispered, sitting in an armchair. 'I'm really pleased for them both, of course I am, but I'm not sure how it will affect me. I've been in this house a lot longer than Miss Jane has. Mr Collier engaged me when he first acquired this property. In those days it was hardly used, only for entertaining business gentlemen, and some of his guests were very distinguished, I can tell you. Some even from foreign countries. It remains to be seen what kind of duties I will be called on to perform now. I've come to love Miss Jane, no one could say different, and the baby well . . . just so long as they don't install any toffee-nosed, stiff and starched nurse in this house to give me orders and expect me to wait on her hand, foot an' finger.'

Mary's outburst startled Kate. She wanted to reassure her but wasn't sure how to go about it. 'Come on. It's not like you to trouble trouble before it troubles you. Mr Collier won't let anyone upset you, he values you too much; he's already proved that by coming to you directly and asking you to stay.'

'I know I'm being daft. Pity though, everything here goes so smoothly and now there will be disruptions, bound to be, and that's putting it mildly.' Mary got up and finished her clearing up, rinsed her cloths out under the tap and filled the kettle.

'To be honest, Kate, I don't relish the prospect, but then they do say all babies bring their love with them.'

'Course they do.'

'We'll just have to wait an' see, won't we? Now, my kitchen is all straight an' tidy so I think I've earned a cup of tea and you can save my legs by taking a tray upstairs to Miss Jane.'

Kate made no reply.

'Well?' Mary demanded.

'I will if you want me too,' she said half-heartedly.

'I wouldn't have asked if I hadn't wanted you to.' In fact, it was Jane herself who had asked that Kate be sent up to see her.

Kate laid the table and set out a tray for one, while Mary made two pots of tea. Coming back from the larder Mary set a plate of butter shortbread down onto the tray beside the bone-china cup and saucer.

'Miss Jane likes shortbread. And I think we'll tempt her with a slice of apple pie.'

'You're sure you want me to take her tea up to her? I mean, she won't mind, will she?'

'I'm sure she'll be more than glad to see you. Doesn't get much young company. I expect she will be glad of the opportunity to tell you about the baby herself.'

'I hope you're right,' Kate mumbled as she picked up the tray and went out into the hall.

Outside the first-floor front room, which Jane used as a sitting room, Kate paused for a moment and gripped the handles of the tray more tightly before giving a gentle knock. She had barely taken her hand away from the wood panel when the door was opened by Jane.

'Oh, Kate, how kind of you to bring tea up for me. Here, set the tray down and come and sit by the window.'

Kate swallowed hard. This was too much. Miss Jane was treating her as if she were a friend come to pay a visit.

She did as she was bid and, as soon as she was seated, Jane came to stand beside her, and laid a palm on her right arm. 'Has Mary told you about the baby?'

'Yes, she has. Congratulations.' She was unable to think of another word to say.

'Thank you, Kate. I'll pour the tea.' A moment later she protested, 'But you've only brought one cup, aren't you going to join me?'

Kate felt her cheeks redden, 'Oh, Miss Jane, I shall have tea downstairs with Mary.'

'I see,' Jane murmured sadly. 'You don't mind if I have mine?'

'I'll come back later and fetch the tray, Miss Jane.'

'Will you do two things for me?'

'I will if I can.'

Jane clicked her tongue against the inside of her cheek. 'Please stop calling me Miss Jane; Jane will do nicely, if it's all right by you. And the second thing is, please stay a while with me.'

Kate gaped at her and then nodded, and while Jane busied herself with the tea tray Kate watched her closely. She was such a pretty young woman and her movements were so gentle. Her face had a delicate look, framed by her blond hair, which was swept up into neat curls. Her body was slim. She caught Kate's eye and smiled.

There was something else about Jane that Kate couldn't fathom. She was from humble origins, or so the gossips said. But her affair with Charles Collier had gone from strength to strength, despite that most had warned it would not last. Each time Kate saw them together they appeared to love each other more dearly. The fact that their relationship had lasted so long had become the talk of Surrey. Now a baby was on the way. Well! That would certainly put the cat among the pigeons.

Jane had taken the chair opposite her. The big wide windows were open and the bright afternoon sunshine filtered in through the long lace curtains and shone on Jane's fair hair making it look like spun gold. She was wearing a pale-pink chiffon dress, with a high stand-up collar, the embroidered bodice falling loosely down over her waistline.

Her blue eyes lit up as she suddenly announced, 'Having you here, Kate, calls for a celebration. I have a bottle of wine, I'll open it.'

'No, please don't.'

'Why ever not? I want you to drink a toast to my unborn baby. Say you will, please. You are happy for me, aren't you?'

'Oh, yes, Miss Jane. Really I am.'

'There you go again. You promised you'd call me Jane.'

'It doesn't seem proper,' she said firmly.

'And why not? We can be friends, surely.'

'You're being very kind.'

'Anyway, we're not going to argue about it now. I'll fetch the bottle.'

Kate gazed round while Jane went to the sideboard. It was a lovely room, furnished with sofas, deep armchairs and side tables on which stood small lamps. The colourings were mostly beige with soft peach overtones and the carpet pile was deep enough to bury your toes in. How many happy hours Jane and Mr Collier must have spent here together.

'Here we are,' Jane declared happily, setting down a bottle and two glasses on the small table which stood between them.

Kate had to smile; at that moment Jane looked like a little girl having an unexpected treat. She opened the bottle without difficulty and poured some of the sparkling white wine into each of their glasses.

'You name the toast, Kate. What shall we drink to?'

Kate shot her a sideways glance, got to her feet and

49

held up her own glass. 'Here's to you, Mr Collier, and your baby. May you all three have a healthy and happy life.'

'Thank you, thank you very much,' Jane said softly. 'I'll drink to that.'

They drank their wine in silence and Kate watched as Jane nibbled at her shortbread. When their glasses were empty she rose to go.

'I do wish you well, Jane,' she murmured as they stood together in the doorway.

'I know you do, dear Kate. Will you come and see me whenever you can? Say you will.'

'I will,' Kate promised, and she meant it.

She breathed a sigh of relief as she entered the kitchen.

'Well?' Mary asked even before she had a chance to sit down. 'What d'you think. How was she?'

'Happy and excited. Pleased. Hoping to give Mr Collier the son he has always wanted, she confided to me. And she gave me a glass of wine. I hope and pray everything works out well for both of them.'

Mary let out a deep breath. 'Come on, lass, I've had the cosy on the pot, let's have our tea now.'

They sat opposite each other at the kitchen table. Kate was eating a slice of blackberry and apple pie, over which Mary had poured a generous amount of thick cream, when out of the blue Mary said, 'About Jane and the baby, you sound as if you're doubtful.'

Kate swallowed what was left in her mouth, wiped her lips with a napkin and raised her eyes to Mary's.

'Not everyone in the world outside this house will smile when this news gets out, will they?'

'Oh, Kate, you've got an old head on your young shoulders.'

'Be that as it may, I'm right, aren't I?'

'They deserve some happiness.' Mary's voice had grown defensive. 'They'll soon find out who their true friends are.'

The remarkable day ended with Kate giving her mother a full account of what she had learnt at Melbourne Lodge.

'A baby for his mistress when his wife has never been able to bear him a child. How sad for poor Mrs Collier.'

In many ways Kate agreed, but she did not say so out loud. 'Miss Mortimer and Mr Collier have been together a long time. It isn't as if it's a five-minute fling.'

'That's hardly the point. You mustn't be heard taking sides, not out in the village at any rate. Say what you like, he does still have a legal wife.'

'Miss Jane opened a bottle of wine and she and I drank a toast to the baby.'

Hilda started to laugh. 'It's funny when you think about it. His wife lives in that great mansion, they have every single thing that money can buy and still he turns to another woman, in this case, a young woman. Men! There's not a lot to choose between any of them when it comes down to it.'

Kate sucked in a deep breath and merely shrugged.

If she had spoken at that moment it would have been to tell her mother that she hoped to God the day would never dawn when she became as embittered as she.

Chapter Five

THE HEAT WAS unbearable.

'I think we've both had enough for one day,' Alice complained to Kate. 'We've been standing in this market since half-past seven this morning and I think we should make tracks for home so's I can put me feet up.'

'I'm all for that. But we'll have to walk because it's not yet two and Jack said he wouldn't come back for us until four.'

'Never mind, I'll leave word for him with Ben over at the Griffin, we can take it slowly, anything is better than standing about here in the heat and we've practically sold out what little we had, anyway.'

Kate smiled to herself. Of all the places to leave a message for Jack it had to be in the Griffin!

'Go on, Gran, I'll clear up here. You might as well have a drink before we set off, and I wouldn't mind a bottle of something myself.'

Kate watched as Alice made her way between the stalls. In her long black skirt and white blouse adorned with a narrow black ribbon tied in a bow at the neck, she looked smart, even elegant. On top of her fluffy white hair she wore a shiny black straw hat with a wide brim which helped to shield her face from the sun. She might be small, but she held her back straight and she certainly was not the typical type of old woman who frequented Kingston market.

A huge dray cart, laden with barrels of beer and pulled by two enormous shire horses, barged its way round the corner making for the Griffin, at the same time as Kate decided she might as well join her gran inside. She gave the dray a wide berth and breathed a thankful sigh as she entered the dim, cool saloon bar and headed for where Alice was seated.

'Everyone seems to have the same idea today,' Kate said as soon as she had taken a long drink from the glass of shandy Alice had ordered for her.

'Can't blame them, can you? We're going to have a storm, an' God knows we need it to clear the air. Best we drink up, lass, and start out on our walk.'

'Well, we've nothing to carry. I've piled the bowls and cloths into one of the bigger boxes and I've tied the handles of the baskets together. They're all out in the yard and Mrs Hodgeson said she'll see that Jack loads them up and brings them home for you.'

'Ah, you're a good girl, Kate, and Dolly Hodgeson is a good landlady. It's all the thoughtful little things she does for her customers that help t'make the Griffin such a great pub.'

And the fact that they serve you a great pint of

Guinness, Kate thought, but wisely she said nothing as she helped her grandmother to her feet.

They walked slowly, keeping to the shade as much as possible.

July and August had been lovely months, but as the weeks had progressed, unrelenting sunshine had brought drought. The fields were so dusty they seemed to be shrouded in mist. Cows and sheep searched in desperation for patches of shade and even the birds stayed on the branches of the trees or in the hedgerows as if longing for a breeze. The Thames seemed to have stopped flowing and the water near to the bank appeared still and scum-coated. We'll keep to the tow-path, Kate decided.

Her throat was dry despite the fact that she had had that drink before leaving the market and Alice was sweating visibly.

Her gran was marvellous, the way she had coped during all this hot weather; tending her chickens, and all the other animals she seemed to acquire. Then there were her flowerbeds and the vegetable garden. Cans and cans of water she must lug about to keep the plants from shrivelling up.

Alice let go of Kate's arm and took a deep breath of the dry hot air. 'Let's stop for a minute,' she pleaded.

'Undo the neck of your blouse, that might help,' Kate suggested, as she dragged her hair further back away from her face.

The sky darkened so suddenly it was as if someone had turned off the light. Within seconds a deafening peal of thunder split the sky and blobs of rain, heavy and stinging, fell onto the parched ground.

Kate didn't know whether to look for shelter or to carry

on and get Alice home as fast as possible. Another thing was nagging her; her mother was at home on her own and she'd be terrified of the storm. At the best of times she would tremble at the first rumble of thunder, and lightning would send her scurrying to hide beneath the staircase. For days now she hadn't been well. I shouldn't have left her on her own this morning, Kate rebuked herself.

'Come on, Gran, we've come too far to turn back now. If we hurry we can be home in about ten minutes.'

Forked lightning streaked across the sky. The rain was coming down straight, like stair-rods. They had no choice; to stand beneath trees would be too dangerous. Holding on tight to each other's arm they tucked their heads down until their chins were resting on their chests and did their best to quicken their footsteps, hampered by their long wet skirts.

Alice pushed open her front door. It was never locked, and she stood a moment to thank God that she and her granddaughter had safely reached the shelter of her home.

'Undo your skirt. Come on, step out of it,' she ordered Kate, as she herself did the same thing. 'Everything off, it won't do to leave those wet underclothes on, you'll catch your death. I'll nip upstairs and fetch us some bath towels and we'll see about getting you something to wear home after we've had something to eat.'

More blasts of thunder shook the doors and caused the windows to rattle as the storm grew fiercer by the minute.

With one arm full of towels and a thick woolly dressing

gown draped over the other, Alice smiled at Kate. 'Here, put this on for now. This storm can't last much longer, it will soon pass over,' she said with more conviction than she felt.

But the storm did not pass over. It went on and on for the next hour while Alice prepared some sandwiches and Kate busied herself making a pot of tea.

'I'll have to go home soon, Mum will be half out of her wits by now. You know how she is whenever we have a storm.'

Alice sighed heavily as she went to stand near the window and peered outside. There was no let up in the rain, though it had been some time since sheet lightning had lit up the sky.

'It's been a long time since I've seen anything like this. In fact, I can't remember anything remotely like it and God knows I've seen some storms.'

'All the same, Gran, I'm going to have to go soon.'

Kate was feeling warm and dry now, wrapped up snugly in the enormous woolly dressing gown, which, if Alice ever wore it, must have covered her small frame ten times over.

Looking up, Kate saw an expression of sorrow on Alice's face. 'What's the matter, Gran?' she asked anxiously.

'I was thinking of your mother. I do know how storms affect her. Poor Hilda, she'll be really frightened by this lot I shouldn't wonder.' She shook herself, much as a wet dog might, then pulling her massive fringed black shawl even more tightly around her, she tied the two ends of it in a knot across her belly to keep it secure. 'I'll have a rummage through me cupboards and see what I can find that's fit for you to wear. I know what will cover you an' keep you a bit dry. D'you remember that big black mackintosh cape I keep down in the shed, I'll get that in, that'll cover you from head . . . I was going to say from head t'toe, but seeing as you're lanky, like it will only reach as far as your knees.'

Kate laughed loudly. 'By the time you've finished with me I'll be going home looking like a scarecrow.'

'Better that than a drowned rat,' her grandmother told her sternly.

On impulse Kate bent and kissed her gran on the cheek. 'You're a lovely lady, an' I'm glad you're my gran.'

'And you're a lovely lass,' Alice answered softly, turning away to fetch the dry clothes, thinking as she left the room, and you deserve a far happier life than you've been living these past years. My son and that wife of his! One is no better than the other. They both need their heads banging together, though to be honest I think it's a bit late in the day for that now. Too much bitterness between the pair of them.

Kate didn't feel at all comfortable in the clothes Alice had fitted her out with but she kept quiet. The tweed skirt came barely past her knees and she looked like a bedraggled policeman with the shiny cape hanging from her shoulders. The hat was the funniest. It must have been dug up out of the ark. Still it was close fitting, and at least she had managed to tuck some of her hair up inside it.

'Your mum will be relieved to see you,' Alice observed as she came to the front door to see Kate off. 'You're a tower of strength to her, Kate, she's always telling me that.'

'Really?' Kate asked, feeling pleased.

'Yes, really. Now off you go. Keep your head down and mind you don't slip, 'cos the paths will be treacherous.'

'Bye, Gran.' She turned away quickly so as to hide her amusement. There were times when her gran treated her as if she were eight years old instead of eighteen.

Fate was kind. The skies lightened and the rain ceased to fall so heavily. By the time Kate had left Kingston behind the air was beginning to feel much fresher and she was taking regular deep breaths. It must have been almost six o'clock when she walked by the George and Dragon public house, on the outskirts of Thames Ditton. The doors to both the public and the saloon bars were propped open and Kate could see men grouped together at the bars.

''Allo there, Kate,' a middle-aged woman who had a weekly stall in the market close by her gran's greeted her. 'I've just been inside trying t'persuade me 'usband t'come home for his tea. Didn't have much luck. Can't say as I blame him. Right proper storm, wasn't it? When my Frank didn't come to pick me up I guessed where he was. The men have all got an excuse today, what with all that heavy rain. Bob Bateman says he hadn't the heart to turn them out an' so he let them stay drinking all the afternoon. One way of lining his pockets still further, isn't it?'

Given half a chance Kate would have kept walking; what happened in the George and Dragon was none of her business, plus she felt very foolish, looking as she did.

The stall holder, whose name was Martha, had other ideas. She wasn't finished with Kate yet. Not by a long chalk. 'Your father was just leaving the pub when I arrived here and he wasn't going of his own free will neither.'

Kate clenched her fists, the colour rising in her face. You malicious old busybody, she wanted to yell at the woman, but all she managed to say was, 'Really?'

'Yep, see it all, I did. Bob Bateman helped your dad to the door, not too gently I might add. Yer dad would have fallen flat on his face if it hadn't been for Chris Wilson. She led him away. Or to tell you the truth, she half dragged him down the road, not that he was putting up much resistance.'

'Thanks,' Kate managed to murmur. 'I know where Mrs Wilson lives, I'll see to it my father gets home all right.'

Martha gave her a look of sheer pity, which only served to make Kate feel even more cross.

'Some hopes you got, my luv. It'll take more than a slip of a girl like you to get your dad free if Chris Wilson has got her claws into him, and from what I've heard tell, you're too late. Years too late. Chris is no fool, she knows when she's onto a good thing.'

'Yes, well, thank you.' Kate managed to make her goodbye sound polite, and, deep in thought, she carried on walking.

Everyone knew of Mrs Wilson. Some of the tales told about her were good, others . . . well, as Gran would say when Mrs Wilson came to buy eggs from her, 'Live an' let live has always been my motto. Right common she might be but she ain't never done me no harm, an' until she does I'll mind me own business and leave her to get on with hers.' Dear old Gran saw good in everyone, but she was right about one thing, Mrs Wilson did look common. She was a brassy young widow who had been pampered by her much older husband. Not so well off since his death, she now made a living by filling her house with male lodgers. Not that any of them stayed for any length of time, by all accounts.

Kate didn't have to close her eyes to picture her. Chris Wilson would stand out in any crowd. She was a plump, henna redhead with her cheeks always heavily rouged and her lips brightly painted. Very outspoken. On the other hand, Kate knew her to be kind-hearted. More than once she had seen her buy an extra half-dozen eggs and give them to some old woman or to a young mother with a crowd of kiddies to feed. That was another thing Gran said about her: that if she took to someone there was nothing she wouldn't do for them, but God help anyone that got on the wrong side of her. How she had come to that conclusion Kate didn't know, and she had never yet found the courage to ask.

Kate approached the cluster of cottages with caution, mainly because the pathway was slippery, just as Gran had warned it would be. She was also not exactly sure where Mrs Wilson lived. There were just four cottages, all very old, with stone walls and tiled roofs, very sturdy dwellings in an idealistic setting. Each one detached, set in its own small plot of land, open fields to the back and a wooded area to the front.

What shall I do? Shall I knock at the first door and ask for her by name? Kate was tingling all over, was it fear? She hadn't got anything to be frightened of, had she? Every instinct warned that she had. If her father was in such a state, how was she going to get him home? Oh, for goodness' sake, pull yourself together, she scolded herself.

Suddenly she stopped dead in her tracks. She couldn't believe what she was seeing! It couldn't be happening! But it was! Right there in front of her eyes, in the very first cottage she came to.

The evening being balmy after the storm, the curtains had not been drawn and the sash window was thrown up, open as wide as it would go. There was very little front garden to the cottage and only a low stone wall separated it from the public pathway. A few yards lay between Kate and the two occupants of that small front room. Mrs Wilson and her father were both standing up, arms locked around each other and neither of them had a stitch of clothing on.

Kate watched as her father kissed and fondled the woman. His actions appeared to be gentle, even reverent, and hot burning tears stung the back of Kate's eyes. Oh, dear God, it's not fair. Why in heaven's name didn't he treat her mother like that? She stood as if made of stone and stared. She watched as her father grabbed Mrs Wilson by the waist and swung her round. 'Whoopee! There's never been a better lover than you, my beauty. Fit for any king you are.' His speech was slurred, but Kate heard every word.

When he finally let her feet touch the floor she was giggling helplessly. 'You're my king, yer daft bugger,' Chris Wilson said.

Kate could never clearly remember what happened next. Although she wanted to leave it was as if she were rooted to the spot. Afterwards she supposed she must have screamed. Her father, almost in slow motion, released his grip on Mrs Wilson and took a step towards the open window.

His good humour vanished abruptly. 'Damn you, Kate. What sort of a daughter spies on her father?'

Minutes must have passed and still she hadn't moved, but her father, now wearing a long raincoat, was outside, confronting her. He reached for her, grabbing her spitefully by the arms. She smelt the whisky on his breath. Oh God! Why had she lingered? Why had she watched? Why hadn't she just run? She struggled, using her elbows to try to push him away, all the time pleading, 'Dad, calm down, please, Dad, you'll regret this when you're sober.'

Her words never got through to his drink-fuddled mind. In fact they made him worse. He was wild-eyed as he grabbed her hair and, knocking the ridiculous hat flying, pulled her head back hard.

'Stop it!' She brought the heel of her boot down on his foot with all her strength.

Releasing his hold on her he yelled in pain, 'I'll kill you, you little bitch!'

Kate took a deep breath and ran, stumbling, but he was quickly after her. His clenched fist lashed out, smashing against her jaw, hard. With a piercing cry she pitched backwards, hitting the ground with such force she split the back of her head open. She saw stars and felt sick and dizzy; when she put her hand to her head, she felt warm blood matting her hair and trickling down over the back of Gran's rain cape.

'Serves you right! You're deceitful, cowardly, horrible.

63

You deserve everything you get, and I ain't finished with you yet,' her father bawled at her, shaking his fist in front of her face.

This wasn't her father, it was a drunken madman, and he was going to kill her. Terror gave her strength, made her voice loud, 'Go away, Dad, leave me alone. You don't know what you're doing.'

She managed to get to her knees. On all fours she crawled away from him, then toppled, and rolled over and over down an embankment, into a clump of bushes. Branches lashed her, prickles scratched her hands and face. At last she came to a halt. For what seemed ages, she lay very still.

Where her father was, she had no idea and at that moment she didn't care. He was foul. A drunken beast. She had seen him – him and her. Both of them, naked! She closed her eyes trying to blot out the shameful, unforgettable sight.

Her head hurt and her body felt as if it were on fire, yet Kate knew she had to keep going. If she were to lay down now she might fall asleep and never again wake up.

Home. At last. It took a tremendous effort just to get the front door of the house open.

'What on earth . . . ?' Hilda Kearsley's hands flew to cover her mouth. She had never seen such a sight. From where she stood, in the doorway of the living room, Kate looked filthy. And the clothes she was wearing!

Kate stumbled, putting out a hand towards her, the very gesture was a plea for help. In two strides her mother was at her side. Grabbing hold of Kate's hand she bent and took a close look at her face.

'Jesus! Holy Mary! Were you out in the storm? Did you get struck by lightning? Whatever happened to your own clothes?'

It was beyond Kate to form any answers. Her body sagged and she would have slipped to the floor had her mother not caught her up in her arms. Hilda half dragged her into the living room and laid her down on the carpet, placing a pillow under her head and a blanket over her body, then she fetched a bowl of warm water and some soft white rags.

She was grateful that, for the moment, Kate was unconscious, but terrified when she began to thrash about, murmuring words that at first she couldn't put a meaning too.

'No, Dad. Leave me alone. Dad!'

Hilda was horrified. The state Kate was in was bad enough. The implication of what she was muttering went beyond all else! Huge bruises were showing on her arms, the side of her face was badly swollen and her hair was sticky with blood. Because of the blood and hair it was impossible for Hilda to see how bad the head wound was, but from the dark stains already showing on the pillowcase she knew Kate needed urgent attention.

'Oh, Kate, Kate, don't try to tell me what happened, just lie still, I'll get the doctor.' Hilda's voice was thick with suppressed anger, and hatred flamed in her eyes.

'Well now. You are in a mess, young Kate, and no mistake.' Dr Pearson removed his jacket and handed it to Hilda, saying softly, 'You did right not to move her.'

He dropped down onto his knees, moving his hands gently over Kate's limbs. Looking up at Hilda, he said,

'Thankfully, no bones broken. Must see to her head first. May I have two bowls, one filled with really hot water, the other with cold?'

Hilda nodded and left the room to do his bidding.

Gently raising Kate's head from the pillow, he examined the wound, smiled, and said, 'I'm going to have to cut some of that lovely hair away.'

Kate didn't even open her eyes.

'These bruises and cuts on your face and hands, how did you get them?' he asked.

'I fell and stumbled down a bank into some bramble bushes,' she replied faintly.

'Did you indeed?' he muttered, asking himself what kind of a man would attack such a lovely slip of a lass. 'Well, I'll try not to hurt you.' Taking a gleaming pair of scissors, a pot of ointment and a dark-green bottle of disinfectant from his medical bag, he set to work.

Some time later he helped Hilda get Kate up the stairs and onto her bed. 'I'll leave you to get the rest of her clothes off, just make sure she takes these two tablets – with some warm milk would be best – and I'll look in again some time tomorrow.'

'Thanks, Dr Pearson, I'll come down and see you out.'

'No need, Mrs Kearsley, it's not the first time I've been up and down these stairs now, is it?'

Hilda managed a weak smile. 'All right, but I really am grateful.'

'Kate will be fine,' he hastened to assure her.

Fine! It'll take a lot more than iodine and ointment to make Kate forget whatever it is that has happened to her tonight, Hilda thought bitterly as she straightened the bedcovers and went downstairs to warm some milk.

She never left Kate's bedside all night.

The sky was light and the sun just peeping through a crack in the curtains when Kate turned her head and manoeuvred herself to the edge of the bed until she was able to grasp her mother's hand.

'Mum?'

'I'm here, Kate, go back to sleep,' she whispered.

That afternoon there was a banging on the door and, looking out of the window, Hilda saw her husband. She had been expecting him to turn up and had shot the bolts, top and bottom, on the inside of the front door.

Looking up he saw Hilda. Still very drunk and realising that she had deliberately locked him out, he started to rant and rave.

'It's all your fault, woman. You sent our girl to spy on me. I'm gonna . . . I'm gonna teach her a lesson . . . an' you.'

Hilda looked back to where Kate lay so still in her bed. She must stop Fred from making such a racket. Kate's eyes were closed but her face wore a frown, as if she could see and hear things she didn't understand.

'Your glass is empty, luv,' Hilda whispered, smoothing Kate's hair back from her forehead. 'I'll get you some more water, be back in a couple of minutes.'

She wasn't sure whether Kate had heard her or not, she only knew she had to get herself downstairs and try and talk some sense into her husband. She gave a harsh laugh. A good talking to is the last thing he needs, especially from me. I know what I'd like to do to him, but that would be against the law. But then it isn't exactly lawful what he's done to his own daughter, and come hell or high water he's going to pay for that.

Slowly, she opened the door just a crack. Before Hilda knew what was happening, Fred put his shoulder to the frame and shoved hard. Hilda was thrown back against the wall, hitting it with a heavy thud.

'No one, least of all you, is going to keep me out of my own house. It's my house, I'm telling you, an' don't you ever damn well forget that!' His voice had risen to a shriek, his eyes staring. 'You've made my life an absolute hell and, up till now, I've done bugger all about it. Now you've gone too far. You've set our daughter against me. The one good thing that's come out of my marrying you and you had to make sure that she finished up hating me as much as you do. Didn't you?' He spluttered the last two words thrusting his face forward until it was only inches from her own.

Hilda could feel his hot beery breath; she was rapidly becoming more and more alarmed both for Kate and herself. In the state of mind Fred was in there was no telling what he might do. She made to turn her head to the wall.

'Oh, no, you don't.' Fred was a big man, and today, with his belly full of booze, he had the strength of ten men. He grabbed his wife's chin in a vice-like grip with one hand and wagged her face from side to side. 'You, Hilda, can rot in hell as far as I'm concerned but you'll leave our Kate alone. I love that girl an' I'm not gonna have you turn her against me. Do you hear me?' he roared.

'I should think you can be heard as far away as Kingston, Mr Kearsley.'

Fred lowered his arm, backed away from his wife and turned to look into the face of Dr Pearson who had entered the hallway without being heard.

'What's it got t'do with you?' Fred tried to bluff, but his voice was much quieter.

'We'll discuss that later. For now, you're coming home with me. My wife and housekeeper between them ought to be able to clean and sober you up.'

Dr Pearson was not as tall as Fred but he had a military background and, as he roughly took hold of Fred's elbow, he barked out an order, 'Get in my car.'

Fred hesitated, frowning deeply.

'Do as you're told, man, or I'll send for the police.'

'But . . .'

'No buts, wait in the car. I'll have a word with your wife and then we'll be off.'

Still Fred didn't move. 'I want t'know how my Kate is.'

'She's as well as can be expected,' Dr Pearson replied.

'No thanks to you,' Hilda shot back at him.

Fred clutched the doctor's arm. He swallowed hard. 'She will be all right, won't she? I never meant . . .'

The doctor's manner softened. 'Come along, man. I'll help you.'

Two minutes later the doctor was back. 'He's feeling very guilty, Mrs Kearsley. When we get him sobered up he's going to be full of remorse.'

'That's as may be but him having a guilty conscience isn't going to help Kate, is it?'

'No, of course it isn't. But both of you are going to

have to come to terms with what has happened and get on with your lives. You, and Mr Kearsley more so. It is how you two react that is going to affect young Kate.'

Earlier that day, quite by chance, he had met up with the landlord of the George and Dragon and between them they had pieced together the whole sorry story.

'Now, let's go upstairs and see how my patient is.'

At the foot of the stairs he turned and faced Hilda squarely.

'I will do what I can for your husband because, basically, I think he's a good, hard-working man. One thing though I will promise you, if I can prevent it he will not come back to live under this roof until he is well and truly sober and settled down. One more thing. He's right, you know. You, I, or anyone else for that matter, cannot keep him out if he decides otherwise. It *is* his house.'

Chapter Six

THE DRESS KATE was wearing was one of the nicest she had ever owned, sage-green brocade silk, perfectly simple, fitting really well. Its only trimmings were an edging of beige lace at the cuffs and collar. Her mother had made it for her in the last three weeks, during which Kate hadn't set foot outside the house.

The idea of a new dress to cheer her up had been a kind thought and she was grateful. But the belief that new clothes could make matters better was beyond her. The dress felt good. It made her look good. But it also made her feel guilty. Of what she wasn't sure.

Her father and mother seemed, once again, to have called a truce. The worst thing was that they only spoke to each other when the occasion demanded it. Not one word of regret, sorrow or remorse had her father uttered to her. He was gentle towards her but, somehow, nothing rang true. Kate felt the peace in the household was as fragile as a sheet of tissue paper. It could be blown away at any moment.

The door to the front room opened and Hilda came in pushing a tea trolley over to where Kate sat by the window.

'It's a lovely day out, cold but bright, you should make an effort an' go for a walk, Kate.'

'I've told you, Mum, I don't want to go out, not yet.'

'You're better now, luv. You can't go on burying your head in the sand for ever,' Hilda coaxed, laying out the cups and pouring a little milk into each of them.

'I know that, but do you?'

'It's best forgotten,' her mother muttered beneath her breath.

'Really, Mother! You're no more able to forget it than fly to the moon. You're just waiting for your chance to get your own back on Dad, only you won't admit it.' Kate sounded as she felt: bitter. 'You know what happened, don't you?'

Hilda busied herself cutting a Victoria sponge into sections, making no answer to her question.

'I don't know how you found out what happened to me but you have, I know full well you have. You won't even let me talk about it, never mind tell you the details.'

'I keep telling you, luv. We all have t'live together and it's best forgotten. As soon as you feel able, why don't you go and stay with your gran for a while?'

Kate's head jerked upwards. 'And leave you and Dad to fly at each other's throats again?' A sudden thought flashed through her mind. 'God! Why did it never occur to me before now? Look at me. You know all about Mrs Wilson, don't you? You've known all along! For just how long, Mum?'

'Don't judge me too harshly,' Hilda pleaded. 'I've done what most women in my position would have done. I've turned a blind eye. Your father and me, well, we never felt the same after David died, and a man has his needs. That's the way it goes.'

'You didn't think what Dad was doing was . . . wrong?'

Her mother thought about that for a while. 'When I first found out, I minded.'

At that moment Kate felt something unlock inside her. The sight of her father and that woman together had replayed itself over and over in her mind so many times that she had wanted to scream. Now she wanted to talk, to tell her mother exactly what had happened, how she had felt when her own father had come towards her with hate in his eyes. The words, which until now she had not been able to utter, came tumbling from her lips and Hilda could only sit there, helpless to stop the flow or mend the hurt that was eating away at her daughter.

'I saw him, Mum! Through the open window in that house with that woman! She was . . . she had no clothes on an' neither did Dad. I stood an' watched what they were doing. I should have run. I know I should have but I couldn't move. I don't know why, I just couldn't. Then Dad saw me. He caught me looking in.'

Kate's outburst came to an abrupt end as a sob caught in her throat and angry tears fell from her eyes.

'Oh, my goodness! My poor Kate. Neither your Dad nor me ever wanted you to find out. Certainly not this way.'

'I'll never forget. I keep dreaming of the way he stared at me. He hated me. He wanted to kill me.'

Hilda looked at her sadly. 'No, luv. You've got it

73

wrong. He was so upset because you'd found out. You of all people! He still feels so guilty, I know he does.'

'But he knocked me to the ground. Started hitting me. Said I was spying on him.'

'There now, luv, leave it be. Truly, it was guilty conscience that drove your father to do what he did. And I'm so sorry,' she whispered, 'so sorry you had to be brought into it.'

Tears, unstoppable now, trickled down Hilda's face. She got to her feet, pushed the tea trolley to one side and opened her arms. Kate stood up and went into them. Both were crying softly.

Hilda rocked her daughter back and forth, hushing her, whispering against her hair, 'It will be all right, you'll see.'

When at last Kate seemed to relax, Hilda used her forefinger to tilt her daughter's chin upwards and looked into her eyes. 'Your dad has never hit you before an' he never will again, that I promise.'

'It wasn't the blows that were so awful, not even the pain really. It was . . . well . . . first seeing him . . . like that . . . with her. Then, when he came at me – to see him in that state. He was, I don't know, mad I suppose. I'm sure he hated me.'

'Come on, dear, this won't solve anything. Let's have our tea,' Hilda said.

Kate nodded her agreement and they sat down.

'In so many ways your father is a good man. It's the drink that sets him off.'

To herself she said, but he's overstepped the mark this time. I've taken his brutal lovemaking and, yes, even blows he's struck in anger. I've always told myself that kind of behaviour was my punishment for not hiding the fact that I did not and could not love him. I couldn't pretend feelings that just weren't there. Not after he let David die.

But to hit Kate! That wasn't right. Kate was the one good thing in her life. The only reason she had stayed with Fred. On the day they had lowered their baby son's tiny coffin into the ground she would have done away with herself had it not been for Kate. That sweet dark-eyed little girl, as innocent of evil as an angel. Both she and Fred had been so wrong. They had allowed her to be the invisible cord that bound them, keeping them together even though the hatred had festered and grown with the years. It was sinful what, between them, they had done to their only daughter.

It was true that they had given her a secure, sheltered upbringing; she had been well fed, given nice clothes and had a lovely warm house in which to live. The only real poverty she had ever seen was when she'd been taken to the East End to visit her aunt. It was a vastly different picture up there. The way Dolly and her husband Bert struggled to bring up their children in a small house, which was cramped, dark and squalid. Hilda shook her head at the memory. It didn't bear thinking about, yet it was home to dozens of families, where women fought an endless battle against poverty. Filthy children, tawdry prostitutes earning a few shillings by selling their bodies. Bug-ridden tenements, all in shocking disrepair, inside walls where the dampness ran in rivulets. Kate had only ever had a glimpse of that part of the world.

Had Kate been fortunate? In dozens of ways, yes. But because of the hatred between Fred and herself there had been no brothers or sisters for her to play with or to fight and squabble with, let alone to stand alongside against the rest of the world. I suppose most of the blame for that must rest on my shoulders, Hilda told herself grimly. I hope she finds a decent lad and gets married soon; I wouldn't want her to be on her own when Fred and I die. She'll probably be very cautious and choosy having seen the way our married life has turned out. There was that Victor Appleton who'd come calling on Kate quite a few times and Fred was still doing his best to encourage that match. Well, he would, wouldn't he? And old Jack Appleton, Victor's father, was of the same mind. Amalgamate the two boat yards and they'd have almost complete control of this section of the river.

Hilda shook herself, and sat upright. She looked at her daughter's sweet face. If there was one worthwhile thing she had done in this life it was to rear Kate. She loved her daughter dearly and Kate, in turn, was a credit to her. I wish there was some way I could ensure that she had a happy future, Hilda said to herself.

Fred and herself were doing their best to appear friendly towards each other, but how long would that last? Things between them had been dreadful before and now, since Kate had found out about her father, they'd become desperate. Neither of them willing to forgive the other.

And perhaps the worst thing of all was that Fred was unable to forgive himself. Every time his gaze settled on Kate's bruised face, Hilda was aware of his torment. It'll not be long before he turns to the drink again, she thought sadly, never mind what assurances he's given to the doctor and his wife. Men used to drinking couldn't suddenly give it up, no matter how hard they tried. And Fred was never going to be the exception.

Chapter Seven

'ARE YOU IN, Mum?' Kate called standing in the centre of the empty living room. She had been staying at her grandmother's for the past week.

'Yes, luv, I'm upstairs,' came the faint reply.

Fear rose in Kate's throat as she made for the stairs; there had been something odd in her mother's tone. She crossed the room to stand at the side of the bed. Hilda had the bedclothes pulled tight up under her chin and, as Kate bent over her, she saw tears glistening in her mother's eyes, though she was doing her best to smile.

'Are you all right? That's a silly question. You wouldn't be in bed in the afternoon if you were. Pull the clothes back, Mum, I want to have a look at you.'

Hilda winced as Kate gave the top sheet a tug.

'It's only my arm.' Hilda bit her bottom lip hard.

Tenderly, Kate moved her fingers along the line of Hilda's shoulder; she felt jagged bone and knew it was broken. Very, very gently she took the pillows from the other side of the double bed, raised her mother as best she could, and made a padded seat around her shoulders giving support to her neck. Hilda looked weak and her face was a funny colour.

'I'm going downstairs to make you a hot drink and then I'm going along to Dr Pearson's to find out how I can get you to hospital. Lie as still as you can, I won't be long.' She softly kissed her mother's forehead.

Once out of the bedroom, Kate's mouth straightened into a thin, angry line. This time was once too often. She was going to threaten her father with the police. He couldn't be allowed to use her mum as a punching bag every time he felt like it. She had to find a way to put a stop to it.

Dr Pearson was goodness itself. He quickly confirmed that Hilda's collarbone was broken and, brooking no argument, said, 'Give me about a quarter of an hour and then I can be free to run you both into Kingston Hospital. That will be the best and quickest way of getting you there.'

Following an X-ray, Hilda was admitted to the hospital. She had been given an injection to ease the pain and Kate sat by the bed until, at last, Hilda's eyelids began to droop. Kate looked at her mother's lovely brown hair, free of pins and combs, fanned out over the pillow. Her face was a deathly white, though there were no dark bruises, thank God. She looked desperately tired.

Kate leant across the bed and kissed Hilda's cheek. 'I'll be back to see you tomorrow. I love you.'

As she left the ward she asked herself how it was that two good people, who must have loved each other dearly at one time, could go on hurting each other day after day, year after year, making their lives a living hell.

What had set her father off this time? By the look of her mother it must have been quite a beating. She was probably alive only by the grace of God. One day he might end up killing her and then where would they all be?

The next afternoon, Kate stopped outside the hospital and bought a sweet-smelling bunch of freesias from an old lady who wished her luck. From the next barrow she chose a huge bunch of black grapes and was rewarded with a cheeky grin and a sly wink as the young man pressed her change into the palm of her hand while holding onto her fingers for much longer than he needed to. These friendly gestures told her she was looking nice and it was with a smile on her face that she entered the ward.

'Oh, Mum, you look miles better,' she exclaimed, laying her gifts down on the counterpane.

That wasn't quite true, but Kate felt there was some improvement, even though there were dark rings around Hilda's eyes. The nurse brought her a cup of tea and while she was sipping it her mother suddenly asked, 'Have you seen your father?'

No point in telling the truth, Kate decided. Her mother would only lay there and worry herself sick. 'No, he hasn't been home while I've been there.'

'It was my own fault, you know, Kate.'

'Mother, don't be so daft.'

'It was,' she insisted, 'I shouldn't have answered him back.'

'For goodness' sake, what are you? A dimwit who has to keep their tongue between their teeth?' Anger welled up inside Kate and she didn't know how to cope with it.

'Kate, you know how things are between yer dad an' me. Just as soon as the doctor says I can get up I'm coming home and everything will be all right. You'll see. I won't be in here all that long. A few days at the most.'

Kate turned away, not wanting her mother to see the doubtful expression on her face. The day that everything was all right between her parents was a day she wished she could live to see.

'Are you sure you'll be fit enough to come home so quickly?'

'I'll be fine once I get on my feet again,' her mother replied bravely, attempting a smile that didn't quite come off.

They fell silent. Neither of them able to voice what they were thinking.

When the bell rang to signal that visiting time was over, it was on the tip of Kate's tongue to tell her mother that when she had got up that morning she'd found her father sitting at the kitchen table, eating his breakfast as if nothing had happened to interrupt their daily lives. She fought back the impulse. Perhaps when her mother did return home, things *would* be different – after all, it was the first time that her mother had ended up in hospital, and it might just act as the warning her father so badly needed. Would he take heed of it? He might if he stayed sober, Kate thought dolefully as she kissed her mother goodbye.

*   *   *

It was the second week in October before Kate was allowed to bring her mother home to Bramble Cottage. The front door was closed even though Alice had been staying while Hilda was in hospital; Kate had expected her to be at the door to welcome them.

Both Hilda and Kate smiled as they set foot in the living room. The old lady was sitting by the fire dozing, with her needlework in her lap, her glasses resting on the very tip of her nose. She woke with a start, staggered to her feet, and kissed her daughter-in-law on the cheek.

'Welcome home, lass, I've put a rabbit and loads of vegetables into your big black pot, it's all in the oven, won't be ready for ages yet, but I've made a few rock cakes an' I'm sure you can be doing with a cup of tea.'

'Thanks, Ma, I'm ever so grateful t'you. Kate's told me all you've done an' that Fred has been the soul of discretion.'

'Never mind about all that now, Hilda, I'm only sorry I couldn't get him to visit you . . . but perhaps it's just as well he stayed away.'

Alice pushed her glasses further up her nose sizing up her son's wife. She looked ill, there was no getting away from that. Until now she had always maintained that it was six of one an' half a dozen of the other where right an' wrong was being handed out between her Fred and this wife of his. This time she wasn't so sure. But, she thought as she watched Hilda take off her coat, there's no getting away from the fact that you drove my son into the arms of Chris Wilson, more's the pity, the cold frigid way you've treated him. And if it hadn't been her it would have been someone else.

81

Something didn't seem right, Kate decided. Her gran and her mother were being cagey with each other. When was the atmosphere in this house ever going to feel normal?

Her thoughts turned to her father. When he didn't come home she worried, and when he *was* at home she worried even more. Time was when she had no doubt that he loved her. Always had and always would. She'd have sworn that to be true up until the day she had caught him with that woman. She'd have given anything to be able to turn the clock back, but that was impossible.

Now my father doesn't even like me, she told herself, sadly. Sometimes he looks at me with such a terrible expression. I'm not imagining it – some days there's hate in his eyes. Gran keeps telling me I'm wrong and that time will ease the situation. She says my father is to be pitied because of the shame and humiliation he has suffered.

He should be pitied! All this was of his making!

What about *me*, Gran? she would like to have asked but hadn't dared. I'm eighteen years old! I never go out with young people. I want to dance, be happy, have fun. There's certainly never any fun in this house. And if and when I get married, I want a lad to fall in love with me because he likes me. Not because my dad owns a boat yard.

'You're deep in thought, lass,' Alice said, bringing Kate back with a start. 'You might put the kettle on, and while you're out in the scullery have a look at the copper for me, will you? I put some sheets in t'boil.'

Hilda put out a hand to stay Kate. 'I'll go. I can

82

manage, I don't want you or your gran to treat me like an invalid.'

Alice looked dubiously at Hilda. 'You always were too independent. Still, if that's the way you want it, I'll have a cup of tea with you and then I'll be on me way.'

'Oh, Mum, I didn't mean it like that.'

'It's all right, lass, don't fret yerself. No kitchen has ever been built that's big enough for two women to work in. Besides I want to get off home. Neighbours are very good an' kind but I worry about me animals, and there's no bed like yer own.'

Hilda did her best to smile. 'You're right there. Be a treat for me to get into my bed an' not have to feel a rubber sheet underneath me. Hospital beds are horrible.'

Kate had made the tea and the three of them ate and drunk in an atmosphere that was edgy to say the least.

'I'm going upstairs to have a little rest,' Hilda said, her voice little more than a whisper. 'Kate, why don't you walk part of the way with your gran?'

'If you're sure you'll be all right, I'll do that.'

'You don't like my mum all that much, do you, Gran?' Kate asked as they wandered along the towpath.

'I have my reasons, or more likely you could call them regrets.'

'I don't understand.'

'Don't you?'

'No, I don't.'

'It doesn't matter,' Alice said dismissively. 'Let's just leave sleeping dogs lie.'

They paused to watch two young men carry a small boat down towards the river.

'Peaceful out here, ain't it?' Alice said out of the blue. 'The more time I spend outdoors the better I like it.'

'You're deliberately changing the subject,' Kate accused her but a smile spread across her face.

Alice chuckled. 'True. When it comes to your parents I think the least said between you an' me the better. Unless, of course, there comes a time when you really feel things are getting on top of you and then . . . well, you know where to find me. Day or night you know that my door's never locked.'

'Can I tell you one thing, Gran?'

'What's that?'

'I'll be glad when tonight's over. You know what I mean, the two of them coming face to face like.'

Alice wanted to fling her arms round her grand-daughter, to comfort and reassure her. Poor girl, she thought, she's been robbed of the joy of having brothers and sisters, brought up in a terrible atmosphere and, if I'm honest, part of the blame has to be laid at my door. I should have knocked her parents' heads together years ago!

'When your dad comes home, try to act normal. Dinner's all ready, I told you, nice rabbit stew. So, you lay the table and set a few flowers in a jug and you'll see, you'll have yer dad twisted round your little finger before it's time for bed.'

'Wish I could be as sure as you are.'

'Yes, well, it's about time you turned back an' I continued on my way. Come on, give yer old gran a kiss, and for God's sake don't leave me looking like that. Stop frowning an' let me see you smile.'

Kate hesitated, then said, 'There are times when it seems as if everything is fine and then it all blows up. If you weren't around, I wouldn't know who to turn to.'

'Would you like to move out, live with me?'

'I don't know. To tell you the truth, I've thought about it before now.'

'You've never mentioned it. I think your mum and dad would understand if you should decide that's what you want to do.'

'Thanks, Gran. I'll see how things go. You're a wise old bird and I do love you.'

They spent a few moments enfolded in each other's arms and when they finally turned to go their different ways they were closer than they'd ever been.

Chapter Eight

IT WAS NEARLY midnight on the last Saturday in October, and Kate had been fast asleep for the past three hours.

What on earth was that noise? She half raised her head from the pillow. There was another almighty crash! She shook herself fully awake. Somebody was breaking down the front door. But why? If it was her father he knew full well that a spare key hung from inside the letterbox on a string. Surely he wasn't drunk!

Since her mother had come home he had been very docile. His eyes had often filled with suffering, showing just how much he regretted having hurt both his wife and his daughter.

The days hadn't been easy. Kate still worried about her mother; she always looked so tired and her shiny brown hair, worn in a tight bun at the nape of her neck, was becoming increasingly mixed with grey. Small wonder when you considered what she'd been through.

At times Kate almost hated her father, then he would raise his head and look at her, pleading for understanding and, against her better judgement, she would find herself feeling sorry for him, biting back any angry words.

There was no doubt it was her father downstairs; he was kicking up an awful commotion. What should she do? Go first and see if her mother was all right or venture downstairs to see what he was up to? The living room was probably a right old shambles by now. Suddenly the racket stopped and the silence that followed seemed more menacing than the din. Perhaps he had fallen down. If so he could lay there and sleep it off until the morning.

However, Kate finally reached for her dressing gown, stretching her arms above her head to loosen her shoulder-blades. Pushing her feet into her slippers she glanced around her bedroom. It was a small, square, low-ceilinged room. The walls were papered with a pretty pink paper and on the polished floorboards soft rugs had been placed on each side and at the foot of the bed. It was a comfortable, cheerful little room by daylight; a room where Kate felt happy and safe. Now, with only a glimmer of moonlight showing through the edge of the curtains she suddenly felt terribly afraid.

Someone was staggering up the stairs. The noise was enough to wake the dead. Kate hesitated and that was her undoing; her father must have sensed she was standing behind the door.

He pushed open the door and, scarcely inside the room, he reached out and grabbed his daughter round the throat with one large fist. Kate stared at him, terror and disbelief blazing from her eyes.

'I'm gonna teach you a lesson, you dirty little sneak. You deliberately followed me.'

Fred's face was red with anger and he forced the words out through clenched teeth. His hands now gripped her shoulders, pressing her down onto the mattress. Kate twisted and turned, fighting to get away from him. He wasn't going to give in that easily. He gripped her more tightly, his fingertips digging into her flesh.

God help me, Kate prayed as, now towering above her, he brought his arm back and gave her a stinging blow on the side of her head. His face was inches from her own. His breathing was heavy and his breath hot and foul.

She gave up struggling; gasping with the pain in her head. She knew her father didn't realise what he was doing but she was helpless against his great strength and, with the amount of whisky he must have drunk, he was a very dangerous man.

The only thought going through Fred Kearsley's mind at that moment was that he needed to teach his daughter a lesson. He had to let her know that what he got up to was none of her business. It was bad enough that for years his wife had led him a dog's life, he wasn't going to let a slip of a girl dictate to him what he could do and who he could see. She had humiliated him once. Well, she wouldn't get the chance to do it again.

He clenched his fist. Kate saw the blow coming and flinched from it. His hand struck her jaw but the blow had no force behind it. She felt her father shudder, his fingers opened and his fist uncurled. He reeled sideways, his whole body now full-length on top of her, his arms stretched forward, either side of her head. He made a noise, a horrible sort of groan, shuddered again and then lay still, his full weight bearing down on her.

Kate turned her head to one side and, with amazement, saw her mother standing there, dressed only in her long thin cotton nightdress, her hair hanging free over her shoulders. Her face showed no trace of emotion, but her eyes were gleaming. It was almost as if she were gloating. She heard her mother's intake of breath, watched as she leant forward and with a mighty effort pulled Fred's heavy body to one side.

There wasn't a sound in the room.

Relief flooded through Kate. The removal of her father's weight was sheer blessed deliverance.

'Are you all right?' her mother asked, her voice sounding strange.

Kate nodded. Big tears welled up in her eyes as she struggled to sit up. She took the hand her mother was holding out to her and the minute she was up on her feet she began to cry in earnest.

Hilda took her in her arms, whispering soft words. 'It's all right. Calm down, my darling, he won't hurt you any more.'

'What will we do? We can't leave him there like that, we should call a doctor, shouldn't we?'

It was then, as she turned towards the bed, that she saw the knife sticking out from between his shoulderblades and the dark, sticky red blood staining her bedspread. Bile rose in her throat. 'Oh my God, I'm going to be sick!'

Her mother pushed her aside and bent over her father. Suddenly Hilda let out a weird eerie sound, then, drawing swiftly back, she began to scream. Kate couldn't bear to listen. She covered her ears with her hands. Every bad thing about her father was wiped from her mind as she walked towards the bed. Perching herself on the edge she raised her father's head and cradled it in her lap.

Her mother stumbled from the room, her piercing screams vibrating in the air behind her.

Kate's mind went blank. She didn't speak, just sat there, swaying back and forth.

She only realised that strange men were in her bedroom when Dr Pearson endeavoured to free her hands from her father's body and she heard his soft voice urging her to stand up. There was a steady hum of male voices but the actual words went over Kate's head, until she heard the word mortuary.

'What?' she heard herself scream, but even she knew it was more like a wail. 'Why isn't my father going to hospital?' She directed the question to Dr Pearson, the only friendly face she could focus on.

'Come, Kate, I'm going to take you home with me, tuck you up nice and warm, Mrs Pearson will.'

'I don't want to go home with you. My father has been hurt an' I want to go in the ambulance with him. Please, doctor, let me do that.'

God in heaven! The doctor sighed heavily, he'd had some tasks to perform in his life but surely never one as distasteful as this. He took hold of her hands and firmly turned her until she was standing facing him. 'Kate, listen to me. Your father is dead. I am so very sorry but there is nothing we can do for him now. Your mother is not at all well and she is being looked after. So, please, be a good girl and do as you're told.'

Kate's face was set in a deep frown, she uttered no words, just let out a long, low moan as she withdrew her hands from the doctor's grasp and walked from her bedroom and down the stairs.

Dr Pearson picked up his case, nodded to the police officers, and followed her from the house.

How the hell had this come about? he asked himself. It just goes to show that a woman, if pushed too far, is capable of anything.

Chapter Nine

KATE WAS SITTING with the Reverend James Hutchinson and her grandmother, still feeling bewildered
and shocked. The past three weeks had been a living
nightmare.

She had been given only the briefest information as to
what was happening to her mother, but now Reverend
Hutchinson was taking great pains to make sure she
understood what would take place now that the police
had released her father's body for burial. Kate was only
too willing to let others take complete charge of the
proceedings. She listened, saying nothing, until the vicar
said, 'Do you agree, Kate?'

She looked across to where Alice sat.

'It's the best we can do, Kate, just say you agree,' her
gran instructed.

The Reverend Hutchinson stared at Alice in open
admiration. She had been like the Rock of Gibraltar,
sustaining her young granddaughter day and night.

When you took into consideration that it was her only son that had been murdered, one wondered how it was that the old lady had been able to bear up so well.

'Well, Kate?' The vicar's voice was gentle.

She nodded her head and agreed to the date and time of the funeral. 'Please, Reverend Hutchinson, may we keep it as private as possible?'

With a bleak smile, he said, 'Of course, Kate, the private service will be held in the small chapel.'

God forgive me, he prayed silently. It would take more powers than I possess to keep the sightseers away on that day. The circumstances in which the poor man had died and the date having been set for his wife's trial was enough to bring inquisitive busybodies out in droves. There was also the press! They would have a field day.

Three days to go until they could lay her father to rest.

Kate was in Bramble Cottage, on her own for the very first time since that awful night. Alice had gone to buy black for the two of them to wear.

Despite her gran's pleading, Kate had steadfastly refused to leave the house. Her cup, saucer and porridge bowl remained on the kitchen table and she sat still, staring into space. Nothing but silence. This is how it will be from now on, she thought, just me, no one else. Strangely, at this moment she felt quite calm about it, which amazed her. Perhaps it had all been a dream, simply some horrible nightmare, but the picture in her mind was vivid: her father lying on her bed, she cradling his head while his life's blood trickled from his body, her mother, screaming. It was no nightmare, it was grim reality and the repercussions had hardly started. There was so much more heartache to come.

Of that there was no doubt!

Her feeling of calm gave way to a terror that escalated until it threatened to crush her.

'Mum! Dad!' she called. Her voice, resounding through the empty house, brought no reponse. 'Help me, God! Help me, someone!' she wailed.

A sudden pounding on the front door had her almost jumping out of her skin. Such a racket, she muttered, rising and going to answer it.

As an assortment of voices called, ''Allo, Kate,' she had to blink away the tears.

How good of them all! She hadn't been expecting Aunt Dolly and her three children. Didn't look as if Uncle Bert was with them though.

Her four relations crowded into the narrow hallway and Kate led the way into the living room. Awkward minutes ticked away until Aunt Dolly pushed forward her twin boys, Tom and Stan, now fifteen and already working on the docks. Each in turn wrapped Kate in their arms. It was an affectionate gesture.

''Ow ar yer, Kate?' Tom queried.

'You're gonna be all right,' Stan chipped in. 'Me Dad says t'tell yer he'll be down for yer dad's funeral an' that you're t'remember there's always a 'ome for yer with us.'

Hilda, Dolly's only girl, named after Kate's mother, and almost the same age as Kate, yanked Stan away and she, too, gripped Kate affectionately. 'See! You ain't alone. No matter what, you got family. You just remember that.'

Aunt Dolly squeezed Kate's shoulder and in a voice strong with emotion announced, 'We're taking you back wiv us t'day, luv. But not before you've put the kettle on an' we've all 'ad a cuppa. Jesus, the journey down 'ere seemed t'take forever, an' me feet are killing me. Ye don't mind if I take me boots off, d'you, luv?'

'Stop moaning, Mum,' Hilda rebuked her. 'Yer can take off yer 'at, yer shawl, yer boots, an' any thing else yer like just so long as yer stop complaining.'

'I expect yer want to loosen yer stays as well, don't yer?' Tom threw in for good measure.

A few chuckles eased the strain, more so when his mother's hand whizzed about his head, but didn't make contact as the lanky lad ducked with the ease of a trained boxer.

Hilda went out to the scullery and took charge of making the tea.

Dolly, now comfortably settled in an armchair, leant towards Kate and laid a hand on her knee. "Ow 'ave yer bin really, my luv? We ain't stayed away 'cos we didn't care. It's just bin . . . such a shock. Yer uncle Bert did come down an' 'ave a talk wiv yer gran. You were out for the count that night.'

'I know, Auntie, Gran told me Uncle Bert had been, and you're here now, and it's very good of you.'

'Nonsense, an' you know it. Yer mum is me only sister an' though she went off and left London, we always knew we only 'ad to shout an' the other would be there like a flash. In times of trouble real families cling together. Pity two of me brothers were killed in the war, an' the rest of them married stuck-up bitches.' Lowering her voice, Aunt Dolly said seriously, 'Me and my Bert, we've tried twice t'see yer mum. Nothing doing. They said they'd let us know when we can go.'

Kate's head was lowered; she made no comment.

'Come on, luv,' Dolly pleaded. 'Talk t'me. Let it out. I can be a good listener yer know.'

Kate straightened up and made a decision to tell her aunt the unvarnished truth.

'I think I'm going mad,' she began. 'I can't sleep, I can't eat, everything sticks in my throat and I feel I'm going to choke. I feel sick all the time. Gran keeps telling me, what's done is done, there's no bringing Dad back. I know that's true but I can't look her in the eye. After all, he was her son. Her only son. And my mum killed him. She's a lovely old lady. I love her dearly, she knows I do, but she didn't really like Mum and I can't help wondering how she feels about her now. She doesn't say much.'

'Oh, you poor lamb.' Aunt Dolly whipped a handkerchief out of her pocket and rubbed at her eyes. 'What a mess. What a Goddam awful mess!'

Kate stifled a sob and stared at her aunt. 'I never meant to upset you. I'm sorry.'

Dolly shook her head, hard. 'Never mind being sorry, an' don't you go taking yer gran's troubles on your shoulders. Christ knows it's bad enough for her, but none of it was of your making, so just you remember that. Yer gran will survive it all. You'll see.'

'What about Dad's funeral? That will be bad enough, and then there's everything else to get through.' Kate's voice was little more than a whisper.

Dolly's heart ached for her. Kate was so young, and unworldly. This was a terrible business an' no mistake.

'Nobody seems to be thinking about my mum.' The

accusation came harshly from Kate's lips and once started she couldn't stop. 'Oh, Aunt Dolly, they let me see her. She was worried about me! Can you believe that? It was a nice room they brought her to so we could talk, but what about the rest of the time? Is she alone in a cell? Is she allowed to do anything? Read a book? Talk to anyone? Or does she just sit and stare into space? What's happening to her doesn't bear thinking about.'

Later in the afternoon, when the twins came back from a walk along the riverbank, Dolly said it was nearly time for them to set off for home so Kate had better put a few things into a bag. Kate didn't respond.

'I'll do it for you,' Dolly said, heading for the stairs. ''Cos I'm not taking no for an answer. You're coming 'ome with us whether you like it or not.'

'Kate, let's go outside for a minute,' Hilda suggested and the two cousins put on coats and went out into the front garden.

The wind swept in from the river, tangling Kate's long hair. A longboat glided into view and the man at the tiller, seeing the two girls, tugged hard on a rope sending out a loud whistle from the steamhorn. They waved in answer. Then a strained silence descended.

Hilda kicked at the grass and Kate thought that already the garden had a neglected look.

'You don't mind coming home with us, do you, Kate?' Hilda asked.

'I don't care one way or the other,' was the despondent reply.

'Hell, even our noisy home has t'be better than staying here on yer own. We're yer family, we want you with us, you know that.'

'Yes, I know.' Kate stared at the toes of her shoes.

Unexpectedly Hilda grinned. 'You don't 'ave much choice, Kate. If me mum says you're coming with us, she means it.'

Under her breath Kate mumbled, 'I still can't believe it.' It sounded as if she were still in shock.

'Neither can any of us, luv,' Hilda said sympathetically, 'so I reckon it must be a thousand times worse for you. I've always been jealous of you, did you know that, Kate? I always thought you had it made, living down 'ere in the country, just you, Aunt Hilda an' Uncle Fred. 'Ole 'ouse, by the river all t'yerselves. Everything so clean, nice an' fresh. Wanting for nothing. You've never even had t'go out t'work let alone slave hours on end in a dirty dark factory like I do. I just can't believe it 'as all gone so wrong for you.'

Kate made no answer.

Finally Hilda draped an arm across Kate's shoulders. 'Come on, time t'make a move. Nothing we say or do will turn the clock back. I'll be with you as much as I can. You'll not be lonely, you'll 'ave me mum for company, an' I expect she'll show you bits of London you've never set eyes on.'

Kate knew she had to make a stand and speak up for herself. She said, 'It was really good of Aunt Dolly to fetch you all down here today. I haven't been able to find words to tell her that yet, but I want her to know that I really do appreciate it.'

Impulsively Hilda threw her arms around Kate, hugging her close. 'So you'll come indoors an' get yerself ready t'leave?'

'I didn't say that.' Kate backed away, blinking hard, turning towards the house that no longer felt like a home. 'I need time. I can't leave Gran, not now, not until after my dad's funeral. I will come an' stay with you then. I promise. But this next three days – God how I wish they were over – Gran and I have so many things to do.'

'There's no moving you, is there?'

'Afraid not. I do think at the moment Gran needs me as much as I need her.'

'All right then, luv. I'll tell me mum. As long as you tell her you will come to London as soon as the funeral is over I don't suppose she'll carry on too much at us.'

Linking arms they walked inside, and in the doorway Hilda turned, 'Dad will do everything he can, I promise you that, Kate.'

'I know he will. Uncle Bert's a good man,' Kate answered, all the while asking herself what there was that anyone could do?

They had done her father proud. After all, he was a well-respected businessman and his yard had built boats to order for more than half of the dignitaries who were here to attend his funeral.

The glass-sided hearse and black horses with black-feathered plumes drew the coffin slowly towards his last resting place.

'Throw that rose down onto his coffin,' Alice, standing close beside Kate, ordered in a tight voice.

Kate took a step forward but her legs were shaking so badly they nearly collapsed beneath her.

'Steady. Hold on t'me. There's a good girl.' Uncle Bert was there beside her, his warmth and strength reassuring, as he led her to the side of the gaping hole.

Kate tried to smile at him but her chest tightened. It wasn't possible. Neither could she cry. She was past tears. The father she had adored, who had loved and cherished her, had turned into a man of whom she was afraid. Well, at least that part was over now. He was at peace. Some day soon, if God were good, her mother might also be able to find peace.

As she turned she saw Alice wipe away her tears, and went to her. Dear Gran, she reflected, how hard it must be for her.

Dr Pearson stood at the edge of the crowd, hoping against hope that his services would not be needed. He nodded as Kate's relations passed by, making their way back to the carriages. He stepped forward to shake hands with Alice, then he shook hands with Kate.

There was still Hilda Kearsley's trial to be got through. What a mess, he thought as, shoulders hunched against the cold, he returned to his car. What a bloody awful mess.

Chapter Ten

BY THE TIME her mother's trial came to Kingston Assizes, nearly four months after that terrible night, Kate had become used to people recognising her in the street. When she walked into a shop, folk whispered. She hated the notoriety.

The trial was halfway through its second morning and Adam Wright, one of the Kearsleys' neighbours, had taken the stand.

'I am a neighbour of Mrs Kearsley and live at Tumble Weed cottage, Hitchin Lane, Littleton Green,' he told the court. 'About two in the morning of the last day of October last year I heard a terrified screaming coming from the Kearsley cottage. I ran the few yards along the towpath, and all the while the screaming went on and on.

'The front door had been smashed open and the gas light at the top of the stairs was lit. I entered the house, taking the stairs two at a time. Hilda Kearsley was standing on the landing staring through the open door of the small bedroom. My main concern was to stop her screaming and this I did by taking her by the shoulders and shaking her.

'The daughter, Kate Kearsley, was in the bedroom with her father who was stretched out, full-length, on the bed and I asked her if her dad had had a heart attack but she shook her head. I then asked her to tell me what had happened and if I could help in any way.

'"Don't touch him, don't touch him," she said in a most piteous way. About a minute after that, Jack Seymour, the Kearsleys' neighbour on the other side, burst into the room, he was breathless and panting hard. "The doctor is on his way," he gasped.'

The man dressed in a long black gown and wearing a wig on his head, whom Kate had been told was a barrister, now asked Adam Wright a question.

'All this time Mr Kearsley had not moved?'

'No, sir. He just lay on the bed. I think I knew he was dead.'

'Mr Wright, did you say anything else to the daughter?'

'Yes, I asked if she thought her father had suffered a stroke.'

'What answer did she give you?'

'None. It was Mrs Kearsley who said, "Maybe . . . No . . . I don't know."'

'So, it was quite evident, was it not, that Hilda Kearsley was in a very agitated state at that time?'

'Oh, yes, sir, definitely. In my opinion she was distraught.'

'Thank you, Mr Wright.'

The barrister sat down and Adam was told he could leave the stand.

Next it was the doctor's turn to be cross-examined.

'Dr James Pearson. I live at 24 Oaklands Way, Littleton Green, which is approximately five minutes' walk from the towpath. I was called up by Mr Seymour in the early hours of the morning on October the 31st and I went to the Kearsley's house. Upstairs, in what I knew to be the daughter's bedroom, I found Frederick Kearsley lying on the bed, with his daughter, Kate, rocking back and forth by his side.

'I first felt for his pulse, and found that there wasn't one, the man was dead. I should think that about twenty-five minutes had elapsed from the time I was woken up to the time I actually got to the body. When I examined the man I should say he had been dead somewhere between forty and forty-five minutes. Mrs Kearsley could not give me a coherent version of what had happened, she was totally confused, hysterical almost. When I told her that her husband was dead she nodded her head vigorously, muttering, "He'd gone too far, I wasn't going to stand by and let him hurt Kate. No . . . I wasn't going to let that happen, not again."'

At this point the barrister held up his hand.

'You think Mrs Kearsley was aware of what she had done?'

Dr Pearson turned to face the judge, and asked, 'Do I have to answer that question?'

'Yes, I'm afraid you do,' came the stern reply.

'Then my answer has to be yes.'

'Thank you, Dr Pearson, please continue.'

'I leant over the body and saw a knife had been plunged into his back, just the one wound, no other bleeding points, but the blood had welled out, saturating the bedclothes he was lying on. I did not see any indications of a struggle having taken place.'

Dr Pearson was thanked and told he, too, could stand down.

Next came a gentleman who identified himself to the court as being the Senior Pathologist to the Home Office.

'I made a post-mortem examination of the body of Frederick Kearsley on the 2nd of November last. The body was that of a well-nourished and well-built man. I found one deep cut, delivered from behind. The knife had penetrated deep into the man's chest and that one blow was enough to have caused his death.'

The following day Kate was called upon to take the witness stand. Having given her full name and address she was asked to take her time and give her version of what had happened to cause her father's death.

'. . . I think matters came to a head when my father became aware that I knew he was having an affair with another woman. It was the day we had a terrible storm, my father was the worse for drink and in a terrible rage when he realised I had seen the two of them together.'

'You hadn't known about this association previous to this day?'

'No, sir, I had not.'

'Please go on, Miss Kearsley.'

'My father came racing out of Mrs Wilson's house, accusing me of spying on them. He bellowed at me, saying it was disgraceful that a girl should follow her father to find out what he was doing.' Kate's voice ended on a sob.

'Had you been keeping a constant watch on your father?'

'No, I hadn't. It was pure chance I came upon him and Mrs Wilson as I walked home from my grandma's.'

The barrister gave Kate a smile of encouragement before prompting her by saying, 'And then?'

'My father just went berserk. I'm sure he didn't know what he was doing. If he had been sober at the time he would not have hit me. He seemed to roar like a lion and . . . well, rush at me.'

'Miss Kearsley, are you telling the court that on this occasion, your father actually did you physical harm?'

'Yes, sir. Until I lost my footing and rolled down the bank he just went on hitting me.'

'And?'

She was tired and very near to tears.

'My father was full of remorse. For the next few weeks he was kindness itself to both me and my mother. Kind, but sort of edgy all the time.'

'That was how you would describe his behaviour up until the night of his death? Kind, remorseful, but on edge.'

'Yes, that's the best way I can put it.'

'Very well, Miss Kearsley, at this stage we won't put you through the ordeal of what happened on that fateful night. Thank you.'

Kate turned her gaze to meet the eyes of the grim-faced judge.

'You may leave the witness box, Miss Kearsley,' he said, in what it seemed to Kate was a very kindly manner. 'But please remember you may be required to give further evidence.'

Examinations continued until the name of Mrs Christine Wilson was called. Kate watched her mother closely. Her big frame had lost its firm look and she no longer held her head high. Most of the time her hands lay clenched in her lap, her head so low that her face was not to be seen, only her greying hair which was drawn back severely into a tight knot at the nape of her neck. This was the first time during the whole of the proceedings that she had seen any reaction from her mother.

As Mrs Wilson entered the witness box, her whole frame moved as she shuddered and Kate felt a longing to rise from her seat, rush across the floor of the court-room and throw her arms around her. How long since anyone had shown her the slightest affection? She wasn't a bad person. Of course she wasn't. Frosty, embittered. Yes, both of those things. But wicked? No. What she had done had been in her daughter's defence. Kate was hard pushed to keep back her tears.

Chris Wilson was in fine form.

Her hennaed hair looked as brassy as ever but she had taken pains with her make-up, going easy on the bright red lipstick. She wore a brown costume with a fawn blouse showing beneath it, which Kate thought suited her plump figure very well.

'I well remember the 31st of October,' Chris Wilson began her evidence, her voice strong and very assured. 'Fred Kearsley had spent the whole day with me, took me out an' about and during the late part of the evening we were together in my house. I should think it must have been going on for two o'clock in the morning when he left to go home.'

'Are we to take it that Mr Kearsley was a regular visitor to your home?'

Mrs Wilson drew herself up to her full height, stared straight into the barrister's eyes and took her time before answering his question.

'Mr Kearsley had been in the habit of visiting me at least once a week for the past eight years. I will tell you what his last words to me were. As I let him out of the door, he said, "I'll see you again soon, my love."'

'So, would it be true to say that you entertained men at your house and in return they gave you money?'

The forthright question seemed to shock Mrs Wilson and some few seconds passed before she was able to answer.

'That's not how it was at all,' she replied indignantly.

'You are telling the court there is no truth in that?'

By now Mrs Wilson was a very disgruntled witness.

'No, there's not,' she said, raising her voice to a much higher pitch. 'I'll have you know Fred Kearsley was my only gentleman friend, and God alone knows there were times when he sorely needed a friend and I like to think I was that friend.'

'Very well. Mrs Wilson will you please tell the court something of what you and Mr Kearsley did on that fateful day.'

'Well, I suppose seeing as how I'm on oath I've got to admit we drank far too much. Started at lunchtime we did, had a bit of a sleep in the afternoon, then went on a pub crawl in the evening and at turning-out time Fred bought a bottle of whisky to take back to my place. It was nearing midnight when he started to get argumentative and I annoyed him by taking the whisky bottle from him, going into the scullery and pouring what was left down the sink. That's when he tried to lay into me.'

'Are you telling the court that Mr Kearsley actually struck you?'

'He would have if I hadn't kicked him. The din he set up could have been heard yards away. It wouldn't be the first time he'd belted me, but that's not to say that Mr Kearsley was always violent, cos he wasn't. When he wasn't in drink he was a lovely man. Ever so kind an' generous.'

Just as Kate felt she could bear no more the judge said he was adjourning the proceedings until the next day.

Inwardly sobbing with rage and weakness Kate pushed aside the detective sitting beside her. She wanted to get out of the building, breathe some fresh air into her lungs. This portrayal of her father was absolutely dreadful. No one, least of all the likes of Chris Wilson, should be allowed to stand up in open court and tell the world that her father was a drunken, violent bully. If her mother had never said that much aloud, and she was the one who had cause, it wasn't right that a woman of that sort should be permitted to do so.

Kate hesitated outside the court, her head drooping with weariness. She couldn't go straight home to face her gran, although she asked no questions and had steadfastly refused to accompany her to the court. What the old lady's thoughts were or even her intentions for the future, Kate had not the slightest idea.

She began to cry, as she slowly walked towards the river. No matter how hard she tried there was no getting away from the stark truth. Her mother had killed her father and it seemed very likely that the law of the land was going to decide that her mother should pay the price and die also.

Leaving the pathway, Kate sat down on the ground. Laying the flat of her hands on the cool, damp earth, she wished that all the pain and misery was over and done with.

'Are you awake, Kate?' Alice called softly in the darkness, sensing that she still was. She couldn't sleep either, the guilt she was feeling was stopping her from dropping off.

'Yes, Gran.'

Alice crossed the room to stand beside the bed. 'Are you all right, luv?'

Kate struggled to sit up. 'I keep thinking about tomorrow.'

'Yes, I know. Be all wrapped up, won't it?'

'So I've been told.'

Alice reached out and touched her arm. 'Do you hate me for not having been to the court with you?'

'No, 'course I don't. I've done my best to see your side in all of this. It can't have been easy for you.'

'Come to that, Kate my luv, it hasn't been easy for any of us. I thought it would break my heart losing my son, and it nearly did, but I've tried to keep going for your sake. There was an awful time when I could willingly have killed your mother myself, but now . . .' She started to sob.

It was the first time Kate had seen her cry.

'Imagine me feeling like that. Wanting to kill my own daughter-in-law. Pretty messy state of affairs all round.' Her words were muffled by her sobs.

'Please don't take on so,' Kate murmured, trying to comfort her.

Alice pulled Kate to her, held her tight, and began stroking her hair. 'It's what this mess is doing to you, that worries me. God knows what the long-term effect will be. I love you so much, lass. I would do anything to help you through it all, but I just couldn't bring myself to sit through those proceedings, hear all the details, face your mother. I just couldn't do it. I shan't blame you if you do end up hating me.'

'Stop saying that! You've been wonderful to me all my life. How things got to this pitch we'll never know, but whatever happens tomorrow, well, we'll have to live with it. I don't know how, but somehow I suppose we'll carry on. Have too, won't we?'

Alice had no answer to that, so she continued to stroke her granddaughter's hair. Then she said 'I think perhaps it would be better if I went back to live in my own place. You ought to think about going to stay with your aunt and uncle in London.'

Kate wriggled free from her arms. She knew her gran couldn't stay with her for ever.

'You're right, of course. I've kept you away from your animals for far too long and it is about time I began to stand on my own two feet.'

'Hmmh. We're not going to fall out over this, are we? I shan't be doing you any favours if I stay on here indefinitely. It's some young company you need around you not some old woman like me holding you back all the time. When the dust settles you have to look around you, start making decisions, live your life as you want to while you're still young enough to enjoy it. Anyway, since both of us are so wide awake I'm going downstairs to make us a cup of tea. You tuck down in bed and I'll bring the tray up here.'

Alice still felt very guilty as she made her way down the stairs, ashamed of her cowardice in not going to the court. But she knew her decision had been the right one. Her daughter-in-law had no one to blame but herself for the predicament she was in. God help her. More to the point, God help young Kate, for it was she that was going to have to live the rest of her life with the aftermath of all this hanging over her.

Kate looked up at the stone steps leading to the court and began to feel light-headed. She didn't want to go in there today. Frowning, she stood still and took a deep breath.

The policeman at her side, glanced at her. 'You feeling all right, miss? You've gone very pale.'

Kate brushed a hand over her forehead and managed a weak smile. 'I'll be fine,' she said.

The burly copper nodded his head. He had a great deal of admiration for this young woman. She had stood up to the ordeal remarkably well. He sighed heavily, today would be different. Should be all over and as far as he could tell the outcome was a foregone conclusion.

'Come along, Miss Kearsley,' he said kindly. Taking hold of her arm he directed her towards the side door of the court. The crowds waiting to be admitted round the front seemed even greater today and she could surely do without any more harassment.

They had hardly settled in their seats when an usher called the court to order and the day's proceedings commenced once more.

*   *   *

Closing speech for the defence.

'May it please your lordship, members of the jury, the time has now arrived for me to perform the last part of the duty that has been assigned to me in presenting to you the defence to this charge of wilful murder against Hilda Kearsley. There is, and never has been, any dispute that Frederick Kearsley met his death because of one blow inflicted on him by his wife. That being the case, the facts are straight and simple. The only question for the jury is whether, from the facts placed before them, they are justified in bringing in a verdict of wilful murder or one of manslaughter, or some other verdict.

'Let us return to the night of the murder. I contend that everything points to the killing of Frederick Kearsley being an unpremeditated act by his wife.

'Everything that Frederick Kearsley did and said on the night of his murder indicates that he put his daughter in fear of her life. Hilda Kearsley heard her husband's frenzied attack on their daughter and did what any other mother would have done. She was horrified when she realised that in trying to ward off this drunken man she had, instead, killed him.

'What happened to her husband was a tragedy but it was in no way premeditated.

'This lady suffered intense loneliness and frustration. Her husband spent large sums of money on his mistress, Mrs Wilson, and was frequently drunk and violent. Hilda Kearsley is a lady; not one to complain. Her one aim in life was to see her only daughter happy. She bore in silence her husband's beatings – until he turned on Kate Kearsley.

'That ladies and gentlemen of the jury was one blow too far.

114

'It is for you to say whether the arguments I have put forward for your consideration are well founded. You must decide whether, beyond all reasonable doubt, Hilda Kearsley is guilty of murder. Or was her act unpremeditated, in which case, you must find her guilty of manslaughter.'

A drawn-out silence was followed by a shuffling of feet and a clearing of throats. Then another gentleman rose to his feet to give the closing speech for the prosecution.

'Your lordship, members of the jury, you have listened to an impressive and powerful speech from my learned friend. Now I ask that you treat this case as a straightforward murder. Do not be impressed or swayed by the fact that the prisoner is a woman. It is an indisputable fact that Mr Kearsley was killed in his own home, by his wife. Killed with a knife that she had ready to hand, which she had placed beneath a pillow days before. I have to tell you that it was a case of deliberate, premeditated murder. It will be for each of you to decide whether any of the arguments that have been put before you justify you in finding a lesser verdict than murder. It has been suggested that Hilda Kearsley acted, not with any intention to kill but purely in the defence of her daughter, and, therefore, the verdict ought to be one of manslaughter.

'It has also been suggested that this is a justifiable homicide on the part of Mrs Kearsley, which means that she acted in self-defence.

'Members of the jury, Frederick Kearsley was stabbed in the back. Therefore I put it to you that there is no evidence upon which you can reasonably or possibly come to the conclusion that the prisoner was acting in self-defence when she killed her husband. Your verdict has to be guilty of murder.'

As the judge made ready to sum up, Kate couldn't bear the pain as she looked at her mother. She had made no move to defend herself. Despite encouragement from all sources she had refused to make a single statement. Now she seemed to pull herself up to sit straight and face the judge. Her head was high almost as if it were an act of defiance. But her face was the colour of parchment and her eyes as they met Kate's for the first time since the trial had begun, held a look of sheer despair.

'My charge to you, members of the jury, is that there is only one indictment in this case, and that is the indictment of Hilda Kearsley for wilful murder. If you are satisfied that she intended to murder, then, of course you will find her guilty. You have to study the evidence very carefully, patiently and sensibly and acquit the prisoner unless you are satisfied that the case against her is proved beyond doubt.

'Her whole case is that she did not intend to kill. Ask yourselves then, why take a knife upstairs to the bedroom? Does one need a knife to frighten a drunken man into keeping his distance? She was shocked that just one blow, delivered in the heat of the moment, was enough to kill her husband. Could she have delivered that blow had the knife not been to hand?

'You will not convict unless you are satisfied that there was intent to kill. If you are not satisfied of that it will be your duty to acquit Hilda Kearsley. Will you please retire and consider your verdict.'

How much longer? Kate wondered as she watched the

men standing outside on the steps light up yet more cigarettes. For three hours now she had been in a quandary. Should she or shouldn't she stay to hear the verdict? Whatever the outcome she must hold her emotions in check. On no account must she scream.

'The jury is coming back!' someone shouted.

If her legs could have carried her, Kate would have run a mile at that moment.

'Come on, Miss Kearsley, soon be over now.' She felt her elbow taken in a strong grip and she was propelled back into the courtroom.

Soon be all over! For whom?

Whichever way the verdict has gone, it will never be all over for me, Kate told herself ruefully. This was a nightmare that would go on for as long as she lived.

The twelve good and true members of the community sat upright in the jury box, their faces blank. The clerk of the court faced them, his question directed at the foreman.

'Have you reached a verdict?'

'Yes, sir, we have.'

'And is it the verdict of you all?'

'Yes, sir, it is a unanimous verdict,' he answered, handing a slip of paper to the clerk, which he in turn handed up to the judge.

The judge scanned the paper in silence. Then, looking at the foreman of the jury he asked, 'Do you find the prisoner, Hilda Kearsley, guilty or not guilty of the murder of Frederick Kearsley?'

The foreman cleared his throat before making his reply, 'Guilty, sir.'

As if in a trance Kate watched as someone placed a

square of black cloth over the top of the judge's wig.

'Hilda Ellen Kearsley, you have been found guilty of murder. The sentence of the court upon you is that you be taken from this place to a lawful prison, where you will be held . . .'

Kate could bear no more. 'Oh dear Jesus!' She clenched her hands, tightening them until the knuckles were white. She had to get out of here. She struggled to stand up, her head spinning, her breath coming in short hard gasps. She put one foot forward, the room was spinning. Then mercifully, blackness.

When she came round she was sitting on the ground propped up against the stone wall of the Court House at the top of the steps. Her head throbbed and she could taste blood where she had bitten her lip so hard. She wiped her mouth with the sleeve of her coat and just sat staring into space.

'Come along, Miss Kearsley, we'll find someone to take you home.' The kindly police officer who had carried her from the court would have wrapped his arms around her shaking body if there hadn't been so many people around. It would be a wonder if she didn't lose her reason! First her father was murdered and now her mother was to hang. Just how much trouble could the good Lord heap on the shoulders of such a young girl?

'Come on, let's get you home,' he urged her more strongly.

'Home,' she repeated, parrot-fashion. 'Home to what?'

If only he had an answer for her. What this lass had to look forward to didn't bear thinking about.

Chapter Eleven

ON THE FIRST Monday in April, Kate walked slowly down the aisle of the lovely old Saint Peter's Church holding onto the arm of her Aunt Dolly. Reverend Hutchinson had suggested that she came to church on this morning; the morning her mother was to be hanged.

At this early hour there was no one else there. Alice had still refused even to talk about the outcome of her mother's trial, let alone come to church.

Kate thought it was good of her aunt to have come. No sign of Uncle Bert or her cousins but then she hadn't been expecting them.

'Much as I liked yer sister, you can't expect me t'go to the governor an' ask for time off t'attend me sister-in-law's funeral, now can yer, Dolly? Be fair. It ain't a funeral, is it? God rest 'er soul, it's a bloody 'anging!'

That was how Bert had argued his point.

Kate had half guessed at what had taken place as she listened to her aunt making her uncle's excuses.

Rough-and-ready Joe Blunt was Bert Hopkins. Different as chalk and cheese had been her parents' marriage and that of her aunt's. Time had proved which sister had experienced the happiest years. For all the pinching and scraping to make ends meet you'd hardly ever see Dolly and Bert Hopkins without a smile on their faces. The same could never have been said about her parents.

This morning Dolly looked different. Huge dark eyes in a pale white face. Her clothes didn't help. Thick black skirt, black blouse, black coat, thick black stockings and black button-up boots. On top of her straggly hair she wore a wide-brimmed, black felt hat anchored down by two enormous hatpins.

Kate was wearing a simple fitted dark-grey coat which had a small cape fastened beneath the collar allowing it to flow around her shoulders. Alice had shown good taste when buying it. Kate also had on a black felt hat pushed to the back of her head. It had a broad, high brim with narrow black ribbons as its only adornment. Beneath it, her face was also the colour of chalk. She had tucked her unruly hair tightly beneath the brim of the hat, but as usual odd strands had broken loose and lay on her white forehead and around her ears. A door opening made her look up, and Reverend Hutchinson came to stand in front of the pew where they were sitting. Kate stole a glance at her watch. It wanted just two minutes till eight o'clock.

Quietly the vicar began to pray. 'Though I shall walk through the valley of the shadow of death I shall fear no evil, for thou art with me. Thy rod and thy staff they comfort me.'

Kate put her finger into her mouth, and bit it so hard that she drew blood.

Two days ago they had allowed her to see her mother. Calm, utterly composed, Hilda had not spoken one word. Just held onto Kate's hand, her thumb moving in circles across the back of it the whole time. Not even a goodbye when the wardress had told Kate it was time for her to go. Just one last, long hug and then her mother had gently pushed her away. There had been a smile on her face as she had turned at the doorway to look back. The most sweet and loving smile. It had seemed filled with longing.

And now . . . it was time!

Somewhere, far off, a clock chimed eight.

She was no longer even sure how she felt; it was as if her insides were frozen. There was a sense of loss, of broken promises, of utter, deep despair.

Her mother was dead. She and her father were both gone.

Kate swallowed, stopping herself by force from being sick. Slowly she sank down onto her knees. She was crying now, her tears dripped onto the hassock on which she knelt. She moved her right hand, seeking comfort. Aunt Dolly, herself now crying profusely, took hold and held on tightly as though she too was finding it all too much to bear.

James Hutchinson put his hand on Kate's shoulder. 'The horror will lessen, Kate, the memory will fade.'

'Will it?' she asked pitifully.

Would it ever? She very much doubted it. This day, this hour, this exact minute would stay with her, imprinted on her mind for the rest of her life. A beam of sunlight hit the stained glass window high above the altar, sending down into the well of the church a ray that could almost be called a rainbow. Or perhaps, she thought wistfully, a stairway to heaven. Emotion stronger than any she'd ever previously experienced welled up inside her, rendering her speechless. For a while time stood still and she felt at peace . . .

Aunt Dolly was pulling her to her feet, 'Come on, pet, time t'go.'

Reverend Hutchinson shook hands with each of them in turn.

'God bless you both. I'll remember you in my prayers, Kate,' he said, praying that this young girl would survive the ordeal she had been forced to suffer and that happier times lay ahead.

Dry-eyed and utterly miserable Kate allowed Dolly to hold her close and kiss her on both cheeks.

'Now you promise, luv. Two weeks to sort things out. Listen t'what yer dad's solicitor 'as t'say, then shut the front door an' come t'London. You'll be right surprised as t'what good a change of scenery will do for you.'

'All right, Aunt Dolly. I promise. Two weeks and then I'll arrive on your doorstep.'

'Good girl. Meanwhile, you do yer best to set things right with yer gran. Just try an' remember, luv, it's been damned 'ard for 'er as well. Like every mother she idolised 'er son. Now he's gone an' you're all she's got left, apart from some wonderful neighbours so she tells me.'

'I'll do my best,' Kate promised meekly.

The tram came rattling into view. Dolly kissed her

again. 'Do try an' put the past behind you, luv,' she murmured.

Kate made no promise as she handed her aunt's shopping bag up to where she stood on the outside platform of the tram. 'Bye, auntie, thank you for coming, and . . . thanks for everything.'

'Just get yerself sorted, pet. An' I'll be expecting yer. Two weeks mind, no longer.'

Kate waved until the tram was out of sight. Then, taking a scarf from out of her coat pocket she wound it round her neck, pulled her hat down harder over her ears, and her gloves onto her hands before setting off to walk beside her beloved river Thames.

She didn't have any idea what she was going to do next, never mind with the rest of her life and, more to the point, she didn't really care.

Chapter Twelve

'AUNT DOLLY.' KATE stood at the kitchen door, waiting. 'It's Saturday. You said we were going to the market. If we don't hurry surely we'll be too late?'

Dolly threw back her head and laughed loudly.

'You're in the East End now, my love, the stalls in the markets will be doing business till ten o'clock tonight. They probably do a third of their trade when the pubs turn out.'

Kate had been staying with her aunt and uncle for almost a week now. Try as she would she didn't like being there one little bit. The houses and tenements were horrible, soot blackened and identical, huddled together in rows, front doors opening directly onto the pavement. Her aunt and uncle were better off than most. They lived in a funny little house, which had no inside toilet and no bathroom whatsoever. It was at the end of a narrow street which backed onto a yard belonging to the Sunlight Laundry. The yard was used for the vans that came in and out from morning till night.

The day she had arrived a long-legged young man with a saucy smile had swung down from the back of a white van and actually asked if she wanted to go up to the pub with him to have a drink. She could not believe the cheek of the man. The next day she had been standing in the street, trying to get a breath of air, for it was stifling inside her aunt's house, when the same young lad with the cheeky smile and a mop of brown wavy hair, had come out of the yard and walked up to her. Before she could return his greeting, he had put an arm around her shoulders and planted a wet kiss on her cheek.

'He don't mean no 'arm.' A middle-aged woman who lived next door grinned as Kate pushed the lad away. She looked a kind, cheerful woman. Her top front teeth stuck out over her bottom lip and they were badly discoloured. She wore a sack apron over her flowered dress and what looked like men's lace-up boots on her feet and a man's flat cap stuck on her head. For a moment Kate was reminded of Mrs Bates who did the cleaning at Melbourne Lodge. No, that was unfair, Kate chided herself, Mrs Bates never looked as rough as this cheery London woman did.

The thought of Melbourne Lodge had Kate yearning for those days. It seemed almost another lifetime since she had walked the leafy lanes and taken tea with dear Mary. So much had happened since then! She had received letters of condolence both from Mary and from Mr Collier for which she was very grateful. So many so-called friends and acquaintances had crossed the road rather than speak to her since her father had died. Who could blame them? What does one say to a girl whose mother has killed her father?

Victor Appleton didn't court her any more, which was very funny when she came to think about it. After all, she had never been under any illusions about his feelings. Victor's and his father's main interest had always been in the Kearsley Boat Yard; being on the part of the river that ran so close to Hampton Court made it a very valuable site. Now it seemed she was tainted. Not good enough for Victor Appleton, because of the notorious reputation attached to her by her mother. What difference that made to the business she had yet to fathom out.

Oh dear! Kate shook her head, how could I have been so thoughtless? Thinking of Melbourne Lodge brought Jane Mortimer to her mind. Her baby had been due at Christmas! God, I hope she was delivered safely. Whatever must they think of me never to have been in touch? The very least I could have done was enquire from Mary as to how Jane was managing. Christmas had come and gone in Bramble Cottage with both Gran and me too mixed up to have anything to celebrate.

'You sitting in there daydreaming, Kate?' Dolly's sharp voice made her jump.

'No, just thinking,' she answered with a sigh.

'Never a day passes but what I don't think about your mother,' Dolly shouted from the scullery. 'There's not many sisters got on as well as me an' her did.'

You never came near her for months on end, Kate muttered under her breath. Aloud she asked, 'Where's Uncle Bert?'

'Where he always is on Saturday mornings. Up the

flaming pub. If I 'ad me way he'd take his bed up there an' give me a bit of peace.'

Dolly passed Kate a cup of tea, so strong it looked more like prune juice. That seemed to be the way folk liked to drink their tea in London. Hot and strong, even stewed, as long as the spoon stood up in the cup. That was another thing. She had never seen anyone put so many spoonfuls of sugar into one cup as her twin cousins did.

''Elps it stick to yer ribs,' Stan had teased her when she had passed comment.

'Thanks,' Kate said as she sipped at the tea from the thick, heavy cup. 'Am I stopping you from getting on?'

'No, course you ain't, luv. You don't know 'ow 'appy I am to 'ave you.' She stretched out her arms and Kate went into them. 'You ain't altogether 'appy 'ere though, are you, Kate?' Dolly sounded serious for once as she softly stroked her niece's long hair.

Kate coughed to cover the sudden rush of tears, telling herself she should feel glad to be here. Those two weeks in Bramble Cottage had been so lonely and terrifying. When she did manage to get off to sleep it was never very long before she was sitting bolt upright again, covered in a cold sweat, her chest heaving. To her embarrassment it had happened twice since she'd been here in London. The first time it had frightened Hilda out of her wits. Aunt Dolly had rushed in, telling both girls that it was only a nightmare. Only a nightmare! Her aunt had no idea how unbearably real it always seemed.

Awake or asleep the screaming was the worst. If she lived to be a hundred she knew there would never be a time when she would be able to blot from her mind

entirely the sound of her mother's shrill, piercing, agon-
ised screams which had seemed to go on for ever after
she had struck that fatal blow. And there was always the
image of her father! A big hefty man to be struck down
by one single stab from a knife.

Daytimes, alone in the cottage, had been almost as
bad. No one to talk to, to share a pot of tea with.
No one to give her a bit of a cuddle when she was
feeling down. Here, it was the exact opposite. The little
house was teeming with people, young and old, morning,
noon and night. The boys were on opposite shifts, which
meant meals on the table at all odd hours. Hilda came
home at lunchtime, bringing mates with her everyday.
Neighbours were in and out, calling over the wall, shouting down the passageway from the street. There wasn't
a moment's peace to be had.

The nicest rooms in this funny house were the kitchen
and the scullery that adjoined it. At least that's how Kate
saw it. Whitewashed walls, deep brownstone sink with a
brass tap and a great wooden plate rack above it which
Uncle Bert had made.

'Mind you, that's why the plates 'ave so many chips
out of them,' Dolly complained. 'No one puts them in
the rack gently, in too much of a ruddy 'urry to worry
about being careful.'

The kitchen floor was covered in cracked lino, red in
colour, and the pans hanging from the wall over the
fireplace were enamel not copper as they were back
home. Still, the black-leaded range was lovely. A fire
was kept going all the time and a huge black kettle,
always full, sang away. In the centre of the room was
the kitchen table, the top scrubbed till it was as white

as any butcher's block. Only on Sundays, high days and holidays was it covered with Dolly's best tablecloth.

Many a tale could be told of what went on when the whole family gathered around that table. It was an experience Kate had never known in her life before. And some evenings the loud chatter, the merriment and the jovial teasing made her feel so sad. There was no getting away from it, she was an outsider, she didn't belong here in London and no matter how hard she might try she knew she would never entirely fit in.

'Aunt Dolly, I would like to go home soon. Not that . . . I . . .' Kate's voice trailed off in embarrassment.

Dolly took her hands out of the bowl of soapy water and turned to face Kate. 'Now you don't mean that, luv. You've not given yourself a chance to settle in. There's our 'ilda's wedding t'think about and you know she's put in a word for you to 'ave a job alongside her. You'd like working with a load of other young girls, you'd 'ave a laugh – go out together. Especially weekends, maybe meet a few lads. God knows you've lived a sheltered life for far too long. It's 'igh time you went out into the world, see 'ow the other 'alf live.'

'Oh, Aunt Dolly! Please, I don't want to sound ungrateful but that kind of life is not for me. I don't need to work in a factory. My father has left me well provided for. Our house is bought and paid for and the boat yard is being sorted out.'

'What d'yer mean by being sorted out? Is it t'be sold?'

'No. The solicitor said Dad was very wise when he made his will. Everything would have gone to my mother, but in the event that I was the one to inherit,

I could dispose of nothing until I reach the age of twenty-five.'

''Ow the 'ell can a slip of a girl like you be expected to run a boat yard? It's only men that work there, ain't it?'

Kate found herself laughing. 'What difference does that make, Auntie?'

'A ruddy lot in my book. Can't 'ave you scrambling about in an' out over sides of boats. Wouldn't be decent, not with men looking on.'

'There's never been any intention of me working there. Dad has employed a foreman cum manager for years. Jack Stuart his name is and the firm of solicitors stand by Dad's judgement. They say he's a sound worker, happily married with three kiddies, and that under his management there will be enough income to keep me in comfort.'

'But you'll go barmy! Sitting alone in that cottage, nothing t'do, no one t'look after yer. Never going out t'work, t'aint natural. That's been more than 'alf the trouble with my sister all these years. If she 'ad 'ad t'get up off 'er backside an' do a 'ard day's work she wouldn't 'ave 'ad time t'dwell on all her supposed troubles.'

Kate sighed. She would have liked to stand up for her mother, telling how well she kept the house, all the baking she did, providing wonderful meals and spending time doing exquisite needlework. Better to keep quiet. After all, she was in her aunt's house and as such she should keep her opinions to herself.

'No, I'm not 'aving you going back 'ome, at least not yet.' Dolly flopped down in a chair to sit opposite her. 'You ain't given yerself a chance t'see whether you like living up 'ere or not. Besides you must be 'ere for your cousin's wedding. Our 'ilda can't possibly get married without you being there. Tell yer what, luv, I bet she's just waiting for a chance t'ask yer t'be 'er bridesmaid.'

Kate did her best to smile, touched as always by her aunt's intensity. She knew she was trying to impress on her the fact that she was part and parcel of their family, even if they were only her poor relations.

'It'll be a proper do. 'Onest it will, Kate. A real East End turn out.' Dolly's eyes sparkled with amusement, then suddenly darkened. 'Kate, I 'ope our 'ilda is doing the right thing. Benny Withers is a real catch, there's no doubt about that. You 'aven't 'ad a chance to meet 'im yet, but you will. He's got a finger in more pies than I could ever keep count of, not much in the way of social graces – been too busy making money to take much bother over his manners. There's always rumours going round about him, folk love to gossip, still he swears our 'ilda is the first girl he's ever asked to marry 'im. Suppose that's something in his favour.' Suddenly the excitement in Dolly bubbled up again and she wrapped her arms over her flat chest and grinned at Kate. 'Reckons he's gonna buy an 'ouse up 'Amstead way. Can you imagine it!'

Kate made no reply. She was thinking of the first night she'd been here when Hilda had been getting ready to go out with Ben Withers and Uncle Bert had complained about the amount of rouge she had put on her cheeks. Hilda had said her goodbyes and made her escape.

Once she had gone, Dolly, doing her best to keep the peace, had said to Bert, 'Don't know why you don't like

Benny, he's never done us any 'arm. A bit of a rough diamond maybe, but he's all right.'

'Hmm. He's rough all right,' Uncle Bert had declared, stomping out of the room, muttering fiercely to himself.

Kate had stayed quiet on that occasion, and she stayed quiet now, her head hanging low, her fingers fidgeting nervously in her lap. She didn't want to meet this Ben Withers, and as to being a bridesmaid at her cousin's wedding, the very thought terrified her.

Dolly's conscience came to the fore as she gazed at this lovely niece of hers. Kate wasn't right. Each day she should be getting a bit better, putting the past behind her, but she wasn't. The girl was never at ease. Jittery was the only word that came to mind and, God help her, she felt useless just looking at her. Kate needed help, there was no getting away from that fact. The kind of help that neither she nor any member of her family seemed able to give her. Oh Kate! she thought, whatever is to become of you?

Aloud, she said, 'You miss your mum an' dad.' It was a statement not a question.

Kate nodded her head and sighed deeply.

'Course y'do, luv. But life 'as t'go on.'

'That's all everyone seems to be telling me these days. But what life is there for me? That's what I'd like to know.'

'Why don't yer try and settle down 'ere, amongst yer own family? After all yer mum were me only sister. In time you'd get used to going out to work, once you met up with girls of yer own age.'

Just for a moment Kate felt awful. Why couldn't she be more grateful. Do as her aunt wanted her to? Stay here for ever. She cringed at the thought. This tiny cramped house got her down. Going with Bert to his allotment was the best part. There he toiled endlessly to grow vegetables and even some flowers in the poor dusty soil.

'I'm ever so grateful to you and Uncle Bert, really I am,' Kate murmured in appreciation, 'and I will try a bit harder. Do you mind if I go for a walk now?'

''Course not, luv, I'll be finished 'ere shortly, then I'll get meself ready an' we'll go shopping. Just don't go too far. Hang about up by the corner. You should meet our 'Ilda coming 'ome; she finishes at twelve on a Saturday.'

They smiled at each other, both secretly relieved that Kate had made the decision to leave the house for a while.

Kate had walked a lot further than she had intended. She paused to stare up at several blocks of tenements. How dirty and dingy they looked, she thought. Each level had a corridor that ran right outside people's front doors and was criss-crossed with washing lines. She supposed that the washing had to be dried somewhere, but how awful to have to live like that. She couldn't imagine getting up in the morning and never being able to walk out into a garden. However small, a garden provided so many things to do and see. She lowered her eyes to the entrance of these buildings. Gosh, what a shambles! She could only gape, wide eyed. A long line of what looked to be coal sheds; did folk really have to come down several floors with a bucket and shovel to get their coal? How, for goodness' sake, did they manage to carry the heavy bucket all the way back up to where they lived? Besides that, look at the junk! There were prams, pushchairs, bikes and barrows of all shapes and sizes. The whole place was strewn with litter, cats and dogs roaming free, not to mention the hordes of yelling, grubby-looking children, and hoarse-voiced vendors hawking their wares.

Two old women in tattered coats and greasy felt hats slouched by. They looked dirty and they certainly smelt funny. They never even sent a glance in Kate's direction. At home in Littleton Green no one passed without a cheery greeting and, as for the river folk, well . . . that very thought brought a lump to Kate's throat and tears to her eyes, and with shoulders drooping, she retraced her footsteps.

Come Monday morning, Dolly watched as Kate packed her clothes neatly into the small case she had brought with her.

'Kate, we none of us want you t'go back t'live on yer own.'

'I won't be on my own all the time. You mustn't worry about me. Gran only lives in Kingston, which isn't so far away. And then I've plenty of neighbours, besides I've made up my mind to call in at Melbourne Lodge. Mary Kennedy's always been a good friend, she might even find me some work to do, just to keep my mind occupied.'

Dolly nodded, admitting defeat.

When it came time to say goodbye she had the feeling that her aunt was, in some ways, relieved to see her go. She didn't blame her one little bit; after all she hadn't exactly been the best of company.

Chapter Thirteen

KATE COULDN'T BELIEVE it. She had only been home for four days and here was Mr Collier sitting opposite her in what had been her mother's front parlour. He was the last person she had expected to find when she opened her front door in answer to his knock.

'So how are you, Kate?' he asked.

Kate's reply was a slight shrug.

'You're looking very thoughtful.'

'To tell you the truth, Mr Collier, at this moment I'm feeling very guilty. I haven't enquired as to how any of you at Melbourne Lodge have been faring.'

'That's very understandable. You have had so much to cope with, but you have constantly been in our thoughts and Mary sends you her love and said to make sure I let you know how much she is looking forward to seeing you.'

Kate's face lit up with pleasure. 'Oh, please thank her. And what of Miss Jane, and the baby, did she have a boy or a girl?'

'Jane gave birth to a little boy three days before Christmas. He's doing remarkably well. We've named him Joshua.'

Kate's smile broadened. 'Oh, how lovely, I can't wait to see him. And is Miss Jane all right? She must be very happy.'

There was a long-drawn-out pause and Kate raised her eyes to meet Mr Collier's. She knew straight off that something was dreadfully wrong.

'Jane died . . . of a haemorrhage,' he said quietly.

Kate sucked her breath in sharply. How terrible! What could she say? She had been so wrapped up in her own affairs that she hadn't given these kind friends a thought.

'I am so sorry.' The few words she managed came out as little more than a whisper. 'I just can't find words . . .'

Mr Collier nodded wretchedly. 'There's nothing one can say. No one knows that better than you do, Kate. I found writing that short note to you one of the hardest tasks I've ever had to do.'

'How have you been managing with the baby?'

'Getting by. But only just.'

'Mr Collier, may I ask you a question?'

'Certainly, ask away.'

'You said 'we' named the baby Joshua.'

'Yes. This is a bit awkward. I rather feel I have relied far too much on Mary since Jane died. Mary is more than just a housekeeper, she's become, over the years, a very good friend and it was she who came up with the name. Since both of Jane's parents are dead there was no one else for me to confer with. Mary also helped

138

me to find a daytime nurse for the baby but it has fallen to her to cope with the nights. May I be perfectly frank with you, Kate?'

'Yes, of course.'

'You know the circumstances of my relationship with Jane so you must realise the stigma that will be attached to Joshua. Through no fault of his own, disgrace will inevitably follow him throughout his entire life. I shall do my utmost to relieve at least some of that handicap. With my wife still alive it is impossible for me to acknowledge him as my son. To the outside world that is.' Mr Collier paused, a deep frown creasing his forehead.

Kate groaned inwardly, not knowing how she could help.

'If you will bear with me I will set out the main reason for my being here today. But before I put it to you I would like you to know that the proposal came from Mary Kennedy herself. Would you consider moving into Melbourne Lodge and taking charge of Joshua on a long-term basis?'

'Oh, I couldn't,' Kate protested, 'I've had no training to be a nurse.'

'Training is not what is needed, my dear Kate. Common sense and a loving, caring attitude is going to be of more importance to Joshua as time goes on than all the authoritative approach of an official nanny. Please, Kate, will you consider it?'

Kate nodded but didn't reply. This was a bolt out of the blue.

'I would make adequate and binding arrangements, both for you and my son. You would need have no fear of the future. I am not a young man; chances are I shall not live to see Joshua grow into manhood. His education and his well-being will be provided for and should you do me the honour of taking on the task of bringing him up as if he were your own, you too will be protected.'

Kate was utterly lost and it showed on her face.

'You do like babies, don't you?'

This sudden question made her smile. 'Yes, doesn't everyone?'

'Indeed they do not,' Mr Collier replied and he too was smiling. 'I'll tell you what, why don't you give yourself time to think about my proposal and in the meantime come along and meet Joshua, have tea with Mary. She will be so pleased to see you.'

'I'd like to do that, but I'm not sure I want to give up this cottage and move into Melbourne Lodge.'

'My dear Kate, no one is asking you to give up your home. That would be foolish. If you do agree to take care of my son, you will still have time off, time to lead your own life and Bramble Cottage could be a bolt-hole for you if ever Joshua has a day when he never stops crying.'

'Oh, Mr Collier, you're teasing me now. As if I'd come away from the house if the baby were in a fretful mood.'

He beamed. 'Ahh, so you *are* considering coming to share the Lodge with Mary and taking care of the baby?'

'I didn't say that.' But she was finding it difficult not to be swept along by his enthusiasm.

'Believe me, Kate, I have spent long hours giving this matter a great deal of thought. There will be a number of prejudiced people from all walks of life who will turn against Joshua because he happened to be born out of wedlock. I am doing my best to protect him from such folk.

'Luckily enough, my financial situation is such that I am able, in a somewhat limited way, to ensure that these slights will not affect him too much. Money talks all languages, Kate. You will do well to remember that. But, and it is a very big but, there isn't enough money in the world to provide my son with the love and affection he would have had had his mother lived. I do believe, however, should you decide to become Joshua's guardian, he will be getting the best substitute for Jane that I could possibly find.'

'Oh, Mr Collier! I'm only nineteen years old, surely the law would not allow me to become a child's guardian. Besides . . .' she paused and took a deep breath, 'I still need time, time to come to terms with the fact that both my parents are dead, time to really think about what I want to do.'

'I don't mean to rush you into making a decision, I appreciate what you say and as for you becoming Joshua's guardian let me reassure you.' He leant forward and took Kate's hand between his. 'All the time I am alive I shall be his legal custodian, there's no two ways about that. When I am no longer around . . . Well, as I've already said, ample provision will be made both for you and for Joshua. No one, and I mean no one, would have the power to remove him from your care if you did decide to take him on.'

'You seem to have thought of everything, but what I don't understand is, why me?'

'To be honest, many professional nurses would be reluctant to take on an illegitimate child, more so to take charge when there is not even one parent living in the same house.'

141

'I see,' Kate murmured, sounding very doubtful.

'I don't think you do, my dear. Mary is loathe to have a stranger move into the Lodge, especially as they would be at liberty to leave at will. I owe Mary a lot and my plans have to include her long-term well-being as much as Joshua's. When she put it to me that since the death of Jane she felt very much alone living in that big house and she felt you must also be in need of company, she didn't need to elaborate further. I thought of it as a God-sent solution. You really would be doing me a great kindness.'

Kate made no reply, and a minute or two passed before he added, 'One answer might be for you to visit Mary and meet the baby as we have already decided you would, and then before you commit yourself to any long-term arrangements pack a few things and stay at the Lodge for a few days. A trial run might help you to make a decision, don't you think?' He looked at his watch. 'I have to be going. I've taken up quite enough of your time.'

Time is what I have plenty of, Kate told herself, it's company I lack.

'Just promise me you will give a lot of thought to what I'm asking. There is no hurry. I wouldn't expect you to move in to Melbourne Lodge until you are absolutely sure that it was right for you to do so.'

Kate took the hand he held out. 'I'd hoped to find work of some kind, but . . .'

'Well, there we are. God moves in a mysterious way.'

They left it at that. But it was a very thoughtful Kate who watched as Mr Collier doffed his tall hat to her before walking off along the towpath.

Chapter Fourteen

I DO MISS Mum and Dad, Kate thought, as she dusted the china which stood on the dresser. She missed them more than she cared to admit even to herself. But she wasn't going to let her loneliness influence her decision as to whether or not she would go and live in Melbourne Lodge.

Gran had told her she would be daft not to. Poor Gran! She had aged terribly since they had buried her son. She hardly ever came out to Littleton Green these days, but she was always pleased to see Kate when she appeared in Kingston unannounced.

She reached up to replace a tiny figurine and, as she did so, she smiled. Her father had taken her and her mother to the Derby at Epsom and she had bought the statuette as a present for her mum. Derby Day wouldn't be the same without the Epsom Fair.

Kate sighed. All these memories she was left with.

Whenever she opened a cupboard or a drawer she had to blink back tears. Between her mother's underclothes she had found silver-framed photographs of her parents' wedding and of her brother David. The big old chest on the landing contained stacks of winter woollies, mostly hand-knitted by her mother. In the spare bedroom stood a tall lightweight set of drawers, used by her father as a filing cabinet, full of documents to do with the boat yard going back more than two generations.

I suppose I ought to invite Jack Stuart up to the house and let him go through that lot. She mulled the matter over. After all he was in charge of the business now.

Then there were her father's suits and the lovely dresses belonging to her mother, many of which had hung for so long unworn at the back of her wardrobe. What, she wondered, should she do with all these items? As she went from room to room, sometimes she found something that had her laughing outright, other times she was reduced to tears.

Yesterday she had gone berserk. Scrubbing and scouring the house from top to bottom. Chucking out so much stuff that she'd come to the conclusion she'd have to find a totter with a big cart to take away the mound that was now blocking the back gate.

The trouble was, every decision made had to be hers. There was no one else.

During the days that followed Mr Collier's visit, Kate spent a lot of her time walking by the river. Although May was almost out, the nights were still a little chilly, but it made no difference. Sometimes she did not return to Bramble Cottage until it was quite dark. Wearing a scarf over her head, an old mackintosh and proper walking shoes, she trudged miles.

By the first week of June Kate's decision whether or not

to live at Melbourne Lodge had become slightly easier. She had woken early one morning with a very sore throat and realised that, for the very first time in her life, she was virtually alone. There was no one near who would know whether she was sick or well except Dr Pearson and the Reverend Hutchinson who had repeatedly checked on her. It was then that she made her decision. She would take up Mr Collier's kind offer. Suddenly she very much wanted to go and live at Melbourne Lodge.

I've been very selfish, she chided herself, not giving a moment's thought how Mary feels about all of this. She was a bit long in the tooth to be having to take charge of a young baby during the night, and she must be feeling lonely. Taking care of Mr Collier and Jane had filled her life. Kate found herself wondering whether Mr Collier spent as much time at the Lodge as he used to. Poor Mary's life had been turned upside down.

I really must make the effort and at least pay her a visit before anything is finally decided, Kate rebuked herself, picturing the plump, homely face of her dear friend. Mary was the kindest, most decent person she knew. She did not have a bad bone in her body, was always considerate, and generous to a fault. She had never heard her say an unkind word about anyone, and knew that she spent a great deal of her time helping those less fortunate than herself.

Kate felt she couldn't stand being on her own in the cottage for a moment longer. Abruptly, she jumped up and started to get herself ready. Twenty minutes later, she closed the front door behind her and hurried off down the garden path.

*   *   *

It was a gorgeous morning. The sky was clear blue, without a cloud in sight, and although it had only just turned nine o'clock the sun was really warm. She walked quickly, turning off the towpath into the leafy green lanes which held so many memories – most of them good – and felt she was about to solve some of her problems.

Because it was such a nice day Kate had left her coat at home and was wearing a white dress patterned with tiny blue flowers, with a darker blue shawl thrown round her shoulders. On her feet she had her favourite sandals, made of a wonderful soft brown leather.

As Kate approached the Lodge, she saw Mary setting the baby's pram outside in the sunshine. The moment Kate set foot on the drive Mary looked up and saw her. Kate flew the yards that separated them, straight into the older woman's arms and they held each other tightly, each taking comfort from the other's presence. Kate let out a contented sigh, feeling more secure than she had done for a very long time.

Finally they drew apart, and Mary looked up into Kate's pretty face. 'My God, Kate, you're a sight for sore eyes. I can't tell you how pleased, and, yes, relieved I am to see you.'

'Me too,' Kate managed to murmer, hastily sniffing away her tears.

Nothing much had changed in Melbourne Lodge since she had last been here almost a year ago. The instant Kate stepped inside the large, familiar kitchen she felt at home.

'Take your shawl off, and go and put it in my sitting room,' Mary said. It was on the tip of her tongue to say, you're as thin as a rake, but she thought better of it.

To Kate, Mary's sitting room had always been one of the prettiest rooms in the Lodge, decorated by Mary herself many years ago when she had first come here as housekeeper. The walls were a soft peach, the carpet beige, while the chairs and sofa that gave some bright colour to the room were floral chintz. One wall was covered with white painted shelves which held many books and a stack of magazines. Instantly Kate imagined herself and Mary on cold winter's nights sitting in this room, the log fire blazing in the grate and the two of them peacefully reading.

'What would you like to drink?' Mary asked as she came back into the kitchen.

'Tea will be fine, please,' she answered, smiling because Mary had already set out the tray and a big home-made cake.

'Oh, Kate!' Mary took hold of her arm. 'I've worried myself sick over you.'

It was true, she had longed to go to Kate and time after time she had set out only to turn back again. Now her relief that Kate was safe and well and, more to the point, here in the flesh, so overwhelmed her that she was near to tears.

They sat at the table, drinking their tea and catching up as best they could without going into sad details, so happy to be in each other's company the time just flew by.

'I'm so comforted by the thought that you will be coming to live here. I'm not jumping the gun, am I? You being here today does mean that you have agreed to Mr Collier's proposal, doesn't it? I don't think I could manage the baby on my own during the night time, not for much longer, I couldn't.'

Kate gave her time to get her breath back before looking across the table. 'I'm looking forward now, Mary, to being with you and to taking care of Joshua. By the way, where is he?'

As if on cue, the kitchen door opened and a woman dressed in a nurse's uniform stepped in, a bonny baby, looking every inch a boy, bouncing in her arms.

'This is Miss Parker, Kate. Come along it's high time you two met.' Mary beamed, taking six-month-old Joshua into her arms and leaving the nurse free to shake Kate's hand.

Miss Parker was a tall, thin lady, her back was as straight as a ramrod and she held her head so high, that when she faced Kate, it appeared as if she were looking down her nose at her. It was only when she said, 'Hallo, Kate, I'm Ethel,' and, smiling gently, sat herself down opposite her, that Kate began to think she had been too quick in jumping to the wrong conclusion where Miss Parker was concerned.

Kate rose and went round the table to where Mary was holding the baby. She stared, long and hard, totally captivated. 'Oh, he's absolutely delightful,' she whispered. Her hand sought his tiny fingers and when they curled round her forefinger she stood still, mesmerised by his perfection. Such clear skin, soft blond downy hair and blue eyes the likes of which she had not seen before. 'He has his mother's colouring, don't you think so?'

'Why not let Kate hold him?' Ethel Parker suggested.

'I hadn't better, he's not used to me, he might cry.'

'What could you do to him that would make him cry?' Miss Parker asked, pretending innocence.

'Get on with you, she's teasing you. We both know this is the best-behaved baby there ever was. He'll go to anyone, doesn't seem to give a fig just so long as someone is taking notice of him. He won Mrs Bates over before he was a week old.'

'Is Mrs Bates still working here?' Kate asked, suppressing a giggle.

'Yes, still comes three times a week, still putting the world to rights, as she sees it. Only yesterday she was saying she hoped you were going to come and live here. Mr Collier told her what he had in mind and even he was astounded when she told him she heartily approved.'

Mary gently placed Joshua in Kate's arms and Miss Parker looked on with a smile on her lips. 'There, you see, it's not so difficult. A baby knows how to snuggle up and it also knows when loving care is being showered on it. Joshua will take to you like a duck to water.'

Mary gave Kate a faint smile, and she smiled back. But there was sadness in her smile and Mary thought again of the amount of pain she had suffered. There must have been times when the sorrow had been almost unbearable. Who knew what scars would be left on her? She suppressed a sigh. She would do everything within her power to make Kate's life a happier one. Coming here to live and taking charge of the tiny infant she was nursing so gently, might be just what she needed. A blessing in disguise that's what it was!

'This calls for a celebration,' she declared. 'How about we have a glass of sherry before I start on the lunch?'

'That would be lovely,' Miss Parker answered.

Kate raised her head but still kept her tight hold on the baby. 'Yes please, Mary, I'd like that.'

Handing them each a brimming glass, Mary said, 'Here's to friendship and a long and happy life to this young man.' She nodded her head towards the baby and raised her glass in a toast.

'Friendship and the baby's well-being,' Kate and Miss Parker chorused.

'You two sit there and get to know each other while I prepare a few vegetables,' Mary instructed.

Kate was more than happy to do as she was told just so long as she was allowed to keep hold of Joshua. And after only a short while she realised what Mary had already discovered, that Ethel Parker was a kind woman who only held back because of her shyness.

That wasn't the only reason Kate was smiling to herself. She had the distinct feeling she had made the right decision. She would care for this baby as if he were her own. It would be a hard struggle to put the past behind her, but if she didn't succeed it wouldn't be for want of trying. The past had to be just that. Life was for living and, today, she felt better than she had in a long time. Somehow the future no longer looked quite so bleak.

'I'd better see about taking Joshua for his walk. Would you like to come with me? You can push the pram if you like.' Miss Parker broke into Kate's thoughts.

'Oh, yes, please.'

Mary stared after them as they set off down the drive. Then she gazed up at the sky and prayed, 'Please God let it all work out. Let this house ring with some happiness before too long.'

Then with a mischievous glint in her eye she went back

inside to finish drinking her glass of sherry. Already she was planning what room she would make look fresh and pretty for Kate to move into. It had to be near to the nursery. There was no doubt she would insist on that.

Chapter Fifteen

KATE BREATHED IN deeply. There wasn't a smell quite
like it in all the world. Hay. Newly scythed, lying in the
fields, almost dry enough to be stacked. Security, for the
farmers, winter fodder for the animals.

She looked out once more across the rolling fields.
She had so much to be grateful for. Coming to live here
at Melbourne Lodge had saved her reason, she was in
no doubt about that.

The months following her parents' death had not been
easy, most of the time she had felt crushed, lost. For so
long the daily routine of her mother and herself had
revolved around her father and his needs. His death
had left a vacuum that no amount of hard work could
fill. But she had somehow got through each day, trying
not to show how bewildered she actually was. One thing
puzzled her, and that was how well Alice had coped. She
seemed to have found some great strength which Kate
could not fathom. How lonely she must have been.

After those first few months life had changed so fast that she sometimes felt it was all a bit unreal. She hadn't minded working hard and taking care of Jane's adorable little son. He'd been such a dear and so helpless. The constant attention Joshua had needed had helped to dull the pain of having no parents to turn to. Her dad had always given her a hug when he came home of an evening, encouraged her to talk of the day's events, and it was those good times that she did her best to keep alive. She hadn't realised just how lucky she had been. Her mother had loved her just as much, of course she had, but hers had been a practical love.

Then, after all the turmoil and the pain and the tragedy and the utter despair, Charles Collier had come to her rescue. Moving into Melbourne Lodge, having baby Joshua put into her arms, being with him, feeding him, changing his nappies, singing him to sleep, watching him grow, his first smile, his first tooth, taking his first unsteady steps, knowing that he was hers to care for, that nobody could take him from her had been like slipping into another, much happier world. And that's how it had stayed for the last nine years.

Joshua knew she was not his mother. He had been told the full facts just as soon as he was able to grasp their meaning. No son was ever more loved by his father than Joshua. He was a lively child with Jane's colouring, blue eyes and tight curly fair hair. When he smiled it was often with a wicked grin which would melt your heart to see. Many a day Kate had stood waiting for him at the school gate, watching him come stomping along with his hands in his pockets, socks falling down and the belt of his raincoat trailing down at one side,

and thanked God that she had been given the privilege
of caring for him.

It was by his own choice that he called her Mum and
Mary Nanna. Both women had guessed the reason; it
made it so much easier for him at school.

Now his father was dead and soon Joshua would have
to go to a different school, most probably as a boarder.
In three months' time it would be Christmas and Joshua
would have his tenth birthday. The years would turn him
into a handsome youth, but come what may he would
still be her baby.

'You spoil him rotten,' Mary was fond of saying. 'That
boy can twist you round his little finger.'

'And of course you don't.' Kate would laugh.

Kate found herself wishing that Charles could have
lived just a few more years until Joshua was old enough to
face the world on his own. His wife had died when Joshua
was two years old and from that day he had devoted his
life to his son; taking him to places of interest, spending
time with him, attending every school function in which
he was involved. He was always there whenever Joshua
needed him. It had done Kate's heart good to see them
together. She sighed softly. Charles Collier had been
the dearest, most loving and most generous man in
the world.

Telling Joshua the news of his father's death had been
one of the worst things Kate had ever had to do. She
had taken a deep breath and said, 'Joshua, your father
has died. He didn't suffer, he wasn't ill or anything. He
died peacefully in his sleep.'

Joshua hadn't said a word, but his face had crumpled
and, child that he was, he had reached out and she had

taken him into her arms, smoothed his hair and kissed
the top of his head, rocking him to and fro as if he were
still a baby. With tear-stained cheeks and blurry eyes he
had pulled away and looked into her face. 'I don't want
him to be dead. I love him. The days when he doesn't
come here I miss him an' now he won't ever come here
again, will he?'

'Shh . . .'

'Oh, Mum . . .'

'Shh . . . There now . . .' was all she had been able
to murmur.

Life was so cruel, Kate thought, and perhaps now
without Charles to defend him Joshua was about to
find that out for himself. She would fight tooth and
nail for him, always be there for him. He was her life.
She had made him so and she had no regrets. Would
that be enough? How could she possibly know?

'Come on, son, we don't have to be brave,' she had
soothed him and together they had given way to a bout
of weeping.

The solicitors had sent a message, that they would deal
with the funeral arrangements and would notify her of
the time and place in due course.

'Will I have to go to the funeral?' Joshua had asked.

'Only if you want to,' Kate told him.

'Will you be there?'

'Of course.'

'And will you hold my hand all the time?'

'All the time. You'll be close by my side.'

'Then I shall go and take him some flowers from the
garden.'

And that is what he'd done. Daisies, cornflowers

and roses, hand-picked by Joshua himself and, with the help of his beloved nanna, they had been woven into a tight posy.

Mr Collier had been buried very quietly although quite a crowd of dark-suited men filled the front pews of the church.

Joshua had sat between Kate and Mary, and Mrs Bates had sat on Kate's left. They had taken seats about halfway down the aisle because Kate thought it best to distance themselves from Charles's relations and business friends. Most of the villagers stood at the back of the church.

They heard Reverend Hutchinson praise Charles Collier for having done so much for others less fortunate than himself.

'So moving,' Mrs Bates had sighed, her flat cap exchanged for a wide-brimmed felt hat in honour of her past employer.

'Yes,' Mary had quietly replied, 'nice to hear that people didn't take for granted the fact that Mr Collier toiled endlessly to improve the lot of the poor.'

After the service was over Kate had told Mary she was taking Joshua for a walk, there was no need to put him through the ordeal of standing by the open graveside.

It had been no surprise when, three weeks after the burial, Kate received a letter summoning her to the offices of Hawhurst and Weatherford, Mr Collier's solicitors. The day of reckoning had arrived!

Kate took one more look out over the green fields, then turned away, telling herself she must get ready to keep her appointment. It had been a long night in which she had lain awake tormenting herself, feeling very uneasy as to what the situation would now be not only for Joshua but also for herself.

Could the powers that be take Joshua away from her? What ever would she do if they did?

She gave herself a mental shake. Stop it, she chided herself, you'll get nowhere meeting trouble before you even know what the outcome is going to be. Shoulders back, head held high and with a grim, determined look on her face she left the sitting room and went upstairs to get ready to do battle. Joshua had been her charge for as long as he could remember, to all intents and purposes she had moulded his young life. He needed her and God in heaven knew that she needed him as much, if not more.

She wouldn't give him up! Not without a fight she wouldn't.

Kate wore a tailored pale-grey suit with black velvet collar and cuffs and a matching hat which had a small brim adorned with a single band of corded ribbon. Her hair was still a bother and it had taken her some time to secure it, with the help of many pins, into a tight pleat she could tuck away out of sight. Still, a few curly strands hung down over her ears. Oh well, she shrugged, it will have to do.

She felt apprehensive as she walked the length of Kingston High Street. Over the years, Mr Collier had many times sought the opportunity to reassure her that both she and Mary would be provided for in his will. And, more to the point, that she would always have sole charge of Joshua so long as he was a minor. Well, she was about to find out exactly where she and the boy stood now.

Polite gestures were over and Kate was seated facing a massive desk littered with legal documents. Mr Weatherford was a large man, with iron-grey hair and heavy horn-rimmed spectacles, and in his dark well-cut suit and white shirt with a stiff collar he looked every inch a successful partner of this old, established firm of solicitors.

He cleared his throat, and gazed at the young lady he knew so much about but had never met before today. Her clear dark eyes were looking at him with frankness, she looked fresh and cool, and he noticed the good summer's sun had left her with a lot of freckles. He smiled at her, which made him seem younger, coughed again and began to speak.

'Mr Collier had only a couple of distant relatives and he has left them, and his favourite charities, well provided for,' he began, shuffling a host of papers into some kind of order. Raising his eyes to meet Kate's, he said, 'I presume you knew that Charles Collier was an exceedingly wealthy man?'

Kate made no answer. If she had, she would have told him he had no right to presume any such thing. It was not a matter that had ever been discussed between them. Of course, I knew he had money, Kate indignantly said to herself, how else could he have lived as he did, and run two homes into the bargain?

'Melbourne Lodge he has bequeathed to you, Miss Kearsley, including all the contents therein, together with the adjoining land. This is freehold and outright.' Mr Weatherford ignored the hiss of Kate's indrawn breath and continued. 'He wished to make sure that it would be a safe haven for you and his natural-born son until such time as his son is of age to inherit his own bequests. You, Miss Kearsley, are to be Joshua's legal guardian until he comes of age at twenty-one. Sufficient monies have been invested for the upkeep of the property, and to give you a monthly income that should well meet your needs. You may also set your mind at rest about Mr Collier's housekeeper, Mary Kennedy. A very generous annuity has been arranged and he has also set aside a tidy sum for her which she will inherit outright.'

Kate said nothing. Relief flooded through her veins so swiftly it was making her feel dizzy. She couldn't speak, but her eyes blazed with brightness. Joshua was to stay with her! Still be her son, at least until he became of age. Charles Collier had been as good as his word.

The sheer relief of knowing their strange relationship was not to be undone had her heart thumping with joy. The money didn't matter, she didn't need it. She still owned Bramble Cottage and she and Mary often spent the day there, opening the windows and letting in the fresh air. And the beauty of it was, that all the bad memories had dimmed over the years; only happy memories were allowed to be brought out and thought about. She also owned the Kearsley Boat Yard; under Jack Stuart's management the business had continued to do well and the accountant saw to it that she received an ample income.

'Well,' Kate said at last, 'and how about Joshua?'

Mr Weatherford allowed himself a smile as he took off his glasses. His eyes, without them, seemed to screw up as he peered at her. Across the desk, she met his stare.

'Miss Kearsley, you need never fear on Joshua's account. His father has seen to it that he is a wealthy young man and the icing on the cake is that Hampton Place now belongs to him, together with the remainder of all his father's worldly possessions.'

'It doesn't seem right that I should be given so much.'

'Matters are exactly as Mr Collier wished them to be,' Mr Weatherford said gently.

'I don't need more money, I . . .' She knew that she was behaving stupidly, yet Mr Weatherford was being very kind.

'Does the prospect of money and owning property alarm you?'

'A bit. But not half as much as having to decide what's best for Joshua in the future.'

'Ahh! That is a matter for a great deal of discussion, but it can wait for another day. Our firm will still hold young Joshua's interest as being of paramount importance, and his inheritance will be held in trust and administered by trustees who have been named in Mr Collier's will.'

'Oh, thank you.' Kate really did feel most grateful.

'My partners and I will set up another meeting with you. The first thing to be sorted out will be the question of the boy's education. Again, Mr Collier has set out his preferences so it shouldn't be too difficult.' He started to gather together his documents. 'Mr Collier left a letter in my charge, Miss Kearsley,' Mr Weatherford said, holding it out across the leather-topped desk. 'No doubt you will wish to read it when you are alone. Have you any more questions you would like to put to me?'

'I don't think so.'

'If you do think of anything don't hesitate to contact me, or if I'm not available my partner will be only too happy to help. In any case we shall certainly see each other again before too long.'

'Will you discuss Joshua's new school with him?'

'My dear Miss Kearsley, you are not to worry yourself, I shall make sure that Joshua is present at every meeting that not only affects his education but his entire future.'

At that moment the office door opened and they were joined by a well-dressed man. Younger than Mr Weatherford, he had fair hair, a happy, smiling face and tucked underneath his arm was a bundle of legal documents. 'This is my partner, Mr Hawhurst.' Mr Weatherford rose to his feet as the introductions were made.

'I'm happy to meet you, Miss Kearsley, though I must say your reputation has preceded you.'

'Oh dear, I don't like the sound of that,' Kate told him, her face looking quite stern.

'All good, I do assure you, young lady. According to our late client, Charles Collier, you are a paragon and I am truly pleased to meet you.'

Mr Weatherford coughed. 'Yes, well, I think we have covered enough ground for today. Are you happy with things as they are, Miss Kearsley?'

'A darn sight more happy that when I came in. Oh . . .' Kate's hand flew to cover her mouth; she had said the words without thinking.

Both men looked at each other and burst out laughing.

'I think you'll agree, she'll do,' Mr Weatherford used

a stage whisper to make this statement to his partner as he came round from behind his desk. 'Goodbye then, Miss Kearsley.' He held out his hand, smiling benevolently at her.

'Goodbye, Mr Weatherford, and thank you for everything.'

It was Mr Hawhurst who opened the door for her and, as he said goodbye, he was smiling broadly.

Out in the street Kate stood still, took a deep breath and said a silent prayer. Whether she was thanking God or just Charles Collier she wasn't too sure.

All she had been told! She needed time to sort it all out in her mind.

Wait till she told Mary that their boy, their Joshua, was to stay with them. No one was going to take him away. Even if he did have to go to boarding school, he would be home during the holidays, even weekends maybe.

We'll celebrate tonight. I bet Mary will give Josh all his very favourite things for his tea this afternoon, she thought.

She had stood on this spot for long enough. Her feet started to move then, casting caution to the wind, she began to run. She couldn't wait to get home.

Oh, the future was full of promise.

It was much later that night before Kate, having made sure that Joshua was well settled and that Mary was happily reading a book, finally made herself a cup of cocoa and settled down to read Mr Collier's letter.

The first few sentences had her in tears. What a kind man he was, and so lonely since Jane had died. He too, had made Joshua a great part of his life. What a pity things couldn't have been different between him and his wife.

She put aside her cup and continued to read.

Charles had covered two pages explaining why he had decided that she alone should be the owner of Melbourne Lodge. He wrote that he felt that, whether she married or stayed single, she would keep her promise to bring up Joshua in a just and proper way.

The next part of his letter surprised her even more. He suggested that if she cared to, she could put the unused bedrooms in the house to good use. She could allow needy families from the towns to stay for short periods; sick mothers who needed a rest; children, whose parents would be grateful for a short respite from trying to make ends meet.

Kate's emotions were in a whirl. Was there ever a more caring man? What a wonderful idea! If only he were here to help her get it off the ground. Perhaps he had thought it was a way for her finally to put all the black deeds of her parents behind her. Give back to others a little of the happiness he had made available to her.

Folding the letter and replacing it in the long envelope, Kate lay back in the chair, folded her arms across her chest and was no longer able to hold back the tears. Her grief was for her parents, for Jane, who had never known the joy of bringing up her little son, and now for Charles Collier, who had completely transformed her life.

She cried and cried until there were no more tears left.

★   ★   ★

During the days that followed, Mr Collier's idea never left her. Would she be capable of doing as he had suggested?

She knew that too many children didn't get enough to eat. Whenever possible she still helped Alice on her stall at Kingston market. Going into Kingston was an eye-opener, and on the rare occasion she paid a vist to her aunt and uncle, she always came home counting her blessings and thanking God for the way she was able to live her own life. The East End was awful, at least where Aunt Dolly lived it was. Men unable to find employment. Whole families living in rat-infested tenement blocks where landlords ignored the damp and rotting walls, the leaking roofs and the total lack of sanitation. No wonder so many kiddies had rickets and suffered scurvy. And this was 1931!

From listening to the tales Aunt Dolly told she knew too many young girls had their first baby before they were barely sixteen years old. By the age of thirty they not only looked nearer fifty but were worn out by years of child bearing, producing huge families for whom there was never enough food to go round. Maybe, just maybe, she could provide a holiday and a few necessities that these poor families must yearn for.

Mary was full of approval. 'It will keep us occupied while Joshua is away at school,' she wisely pointed out to Kate.

I'll do it, Kate decided. At least I'll do my best.

A sudden inspiration came to her. Mr Weatherford had said she could call on him for help at any time. Well, he was her solicitor, wasn't he? He knew the law. What rules would cover such a venture and so on. I bet he didn't deal with Charles's estate without getting well paid for it. And for the administration of Joshua's inheritance, he would be getting a fee. She laughed aloud, let's see that he earns those payments.

Chapter Sixteen

JOSHUA CHRISTOPHER COLLIER looked around his room. He couldn't say it was just a bedroom, more a bed-sitting room. Whatever it was, he loved it. It had an open fireplace and on this November day a fire roared halfway up the chimney, the tall fireguard, with its polished brass rail, set firmly in place. He smiled to himself. Nanna, and Mum too come to that, still thought he was a little boy, always telling him to be careful and not to play with the fire. A whole wall of shelves crammed with books and jigsaw puzzles, a big double bed all to himself, two armchairs with flowery loose covers which Nanna was forever taking off for washing. A thick dark-blue carpet, and a table covered with more books, pens and ink, blotters, rubbers, pencils and, best of all, a shiny geometry set, for it was here that he did his homework. This room was entirely his own. Set at the front of the house it boasted a huge bow window and because the house was built on a hill, the gardens ran down almost to the river. He never tired of watching the river. So much went on there and river folk were the most friendly types you could possibly wish to meet. If he had his way he would work on the river when he was older, at least have something to do with boats. And there he was lucky because his mum owned a boat yard and some of his most enjoyable days were spent down at the Kearsley Boat Yard.

He knew his own mother had died on the day he was born, which was very sad. But he loved Kate, she was the only mum he had ever known and the only mum he ever wanted. He had never lacked for anything, not material things, nor for loving people to take care of him.

One of the teachers at his local school had remarked that he was a special and very lucky little boy, even if circumstances had put an old head on his young shoulders. He hadn't really understood the meaning of that statement.

He was happy at home and at school and had plenty of boys with whom he was friendly. His particular friend was Peter Bradley, who knew that whenever he decided to call at Melbourne Lodge or come home with Josh straight from school he would get a fine welcome and good things to eat. His mum and his nan were great like that.

Life would never be quite the same again now his father had died.

He was to stay at home until Christmas, though even Christmas this year was going to be different. Mum and Nanna were having some poor people with children to come to stay for the holiday; he hoped they would be nice and friendly. If they were boys he might even let them have a turn at running his railway set. It went all the way around the walls of one of the spare bedrooms. His Dad and Dr Pearson had set it up. After Christmas he was going to boarding school. The 10th January to be exact. So much was changing in his small world and he wasn't sure that he would like any of it.

For the last two weeks Nanna and his mum had been flying around the house, opening up rooms that were never used, making beds, and a cot, which they told him had been his, was dragged out of a landing cupboard, reassembled and set up beside a double bed in one of the back bedrooms. He'd first heard about these people coming for Christmas when the three of them had been sitting round the huge scrubbed table in the kitchen having a midday meal.

'Josh, are you listening?' his mum had asked in a stern voice, which told him her patience was running out.

'Yes, Mum, but you did say that after we had eaten you were going to take me to Hampton Court and let me spend the afternoon at the boat yard with Mr Stuart.'

Kate had told him she wasn't about to break her promise but that he had to get used to the idea that they were all going to share this house, at different times of the year, with young children and perhaps their mothers, who were not so well off as they were. At first he had listened to this news with considerable alarm. How he wished his father was here. He would be able to tell him whether this was a good idea or not.

'Josh! Josh, will you please answer me.'

His nan, calling him from the bottom of the stairs, brought his thoughts back to today. He bent down, tied his shoelaces, picked up his jacket from where it lay on the chair and made for the door.

Mary watched him descend and, smiling to herself, decided he was a charming little boy. But then that had been her way of thinking from the moment he had been born. To this day it was still impossible for her to see him without becoming emotional. The way he looked, sometimes like a scruffy urchin, other times like a well-scrubbed cherub, but always adorable. The house was never the same when he wasn't in it. The sound of his voice, his laughter, and his tight curly hair which never would lay flat, everything about him filled her with delight and daily she thanked God that she had been allowed to be part of his life. It was just so unfair that his mother had had to die. She had been such a lovely person and so young.

Her thoughts turned to Kate. She had never married herself and now, well into her fifties, she never would. It didn't matter because in her day if one had the chance of a good position that was sufficient.

But Kate was another matter altogether. What a hell of a life she had endured in her younger days! Still, it had all worked out absolutely marvellously with her coming here to care for Joshua. Kate had become a daughter to her, Joshua was a son to each of them and Charles Collier had been their benefactor in, oh, so many ways.

But what of the future? Joshua would be all right. Money wouldn't buy happiness, but the provision his father had made for him would certainly ease his way through boarding school and hopefully on to university. By the time he became twenty-one he'd be a very wealthy young man.

That still left Kate. For the last ten years she had wrapped herself in the role of mother to Joshua. But now what? Every day she hoped and prayed that some nice gentleman would come along and see Kate for the wonderful, kind person she was. So much of her life had been devoted to others; she needed someone to take care of her, to love her, marry her, before it was too late.

'Joshua, for heaven's sake! What have you been doing up there? You know you're supposed to meet your mother in Kingston at twelve.'

'I'd better get going then.'

Mary put her arms about him. 'Have a good time and I'll have dinner ready when you get back.'

'What's it to be tonight?'

'What would you like it to be?'

'Shepherd's pie. And could you kind of burn all the top of the potatoes so that they're all crisp an' crunchy like?'

'Anything for you, sir. You've always been able to get round me and get your own way with your mother. You're not as daft as you make out.'

'Thank you, Nanna. I shall buy you some chocolates for being so kind.'

'Same old charmer. Get off with you, you'll never change.'

She watched him go down the drive.

Yes, that boy had been the best thing that had happened to her. They had been so happy. A good trio. She wondered where their lives would go from here. There was no telling was there.

As Joshua climbed down from the tram he spied his

mother standing with her back against the wall of the chemist's shop, surrounded by brown carrier bags and gaily wrapped parcels. 'Are these all yours?' he asked, disbelief in his voice.

'Well, yes. A bit of Christmas shopping and a few little things for a young man I know who has a birthday coming up.'

'Oh, Mum, what have you bought me?'

'Wait an' see.'

'I can't wait, Mum. Please.'

'Curiosity killed the cat. Anyway, I've finished most of what I wanted to do. Shall we have lunch before we start searching for whatever it is you've decided you'd like to buy?'

'Nanna's going to have dinner ready when we get home this evening so I'd better not eat too much, though I am hungry now.'

Kate threw back her head and laughed. 'I'd like to know when you're not hungry. Hollow legs, that's what you've got. Come on, pick up some of my shopping an' let's go.'

'Where to?'

'How about Bentalls? Isn't that where you say they do the best chips?'

'Cor, that big restaurant upstairs does a fabulous Knickerbocker Glory, can I have one of those?'

'All right then, but . . .'

Josh hadn't stopped to hear any more. He had gathered up his mother's packages and, with both hands filled, made his way towards the kerb. Swiftly, Kate collected up the few items he had left on the ground, and hurried after him.

Kingston's largest department store was only a few minutes' walk. Joshua heaved his shoulder against the heavy glass door and stood waiting until his mother had gone through. Inside he paused, his eyes darting all round. Everything was wonderful. Christmassy. All shiny silver and gold decorations with lots of red balloons hanging from the ceiling.

Kate watched him, her heart bursting with love. Almost ten years old – how the time had flown. He was such a happy boy and it showed. His cheeks were rosy from the wind and his eyes as bright as stars.

They took the main staircase up to the restaurant and looked around for somewhere to sit. A waitress returning to the kitchen with a tray laden with dirty crockery nodded her head towards a window table. 'That table is free now, madam.'

Kate smiled her thanks.

Joshua piled all the packages in a neat pile on the floor and with this done his mother said, 'Take your coat off, hang it on the back of your chair, look at the menu and decide what you are going to have to eat.'

'Mum . . .'

Kate looked across the table. 'Well, what is it?'

'I only had porridge for breakfast this morning.'

'Josh, you're telling me fibs. I left early because I had so much to do, but I know full well your nanna was there to get your breakfast.'

'I am not telling fibs,' he said, doing his best to sound indignant, 'and it wasn't Nan's fault . . . I didn't have time.'

'Aah! Now we're getting to the truth. You, my lad,

173

didn't get up when I called you. You went back to sleep, didn't you?'

Josh tried to look sheepish, his lips twiched and they both laughed.

'All right. You don't deserve it but, come on, decide what you want.'

Joshua never even glanced at the menu. 'Bacon, egg, sausage and chips, please, and please may I have at least a milkshake to follow?'

'You're naughty, you know that, but all right, I give in.' Kate turned to give her order to the friendly waitress who was standing, smiling, at her side. 'And I'll have a pot of tea and two toasted muffins, please.'

'Would you like a preserve to go with the muffins, madam?'

'Yes, please, make it apricot.'

'Bless my soul, you made short work of that,' Kate said as she watched her son clear the plate.

'It was a super breakfast, thanks, Mum. But you're only halfway through your muffins an' you haven't drunk your tea.'

'I'm doing fine, the tea's still scalding hot. Of course, you're waiting for your second course of whatever gooey stuff it is you've decided to have,' she teased him. 'And while you're waiting perhaps you might give me a few suggestions as to what you would really like for your birthday.'

There was no hesitation on Joshua's part.

'I'd really like a boat.'

Kate wasn't in the least surprised by this request. Josh had been mad about boats ever since he could walk. Sometimes, when they were at the boat yard, she would stand back and watch Jack Stuart outlining some intricate part of the boat the men were working on while Josh hung on his every word. Her own imagination would run riot. What if her dad were still alive? What if Josh were her own true son? His grandson. Oh, if only!

Josh was busy drawing strawberry-flavoured milk up from the tall glass by means of two straws and, pausing for breath, he did not wait to hear what answer his mother was going to give. 'I thought as it would be such a big present you could give it to me for my birthday and for my Christmas present as well.'

'Josh, slow down, and take your time to drink that milkshake. The way you're going on you'll choke yourself. Even if I do agree that you may have a boat we certainly won't be buying one. What we could do is rope Mr Stuart in on this, kind of give him a commission to build you one.'

'Really?' Joshua could scarcely believe that his mother had given in so readily. 'When can we go and see him?'

'Oh, don't rush me along so. There's a lot to talk about. Size for one thing. It can only be a small one and Mr Stuart will decide if it's to be just a row boat or whether he thinks fit to add a small outboard motor.' Kate frowned as her thoughts turned to her little brother who had drowned. Sounding flustered, she added, 'And there's the safety angle to be considered. I'm not having you out on the river on your own. Definitely not.'

'Oh, Mum, you're not going to start fussing me, are you?'

'No, but how about for your birthday I buy you all the safety trappings and pay someone to give you lessons on how to take care when out on the river and how to maintain your own boat and keep it in good order?'

'I can learn all that from Mr Stuart, I know most of it anyhow and, besides, when would I get the boat?'

'Just you listen to me, Joshua, if we agree, we'll have all of the arrangements on a proper businesslike footing and, as to when you can have the boat, perhaps Mr Stuart will give us a date. If you're lucky, maybe, and it is only a maybe, he and his men could have it ready by the time you come home for your summer holidays.'

'Mum, you're smashing, honest you are, but couldn't it be ready by Easter?'

In spite of herself Kate was laughing as she told him firmly, 'If I were you, young man, I wouldn't push my luck. I have been known to change my mind.'

'Cor! You wouldn't do that to me, I know you wouldn't.'

He was right. Kate knew she could no more disappoint him than fly in the air. If he had asked for the sky and the stars to go with it she would have done her very best to get them for him.

'A boat of my own! Can't wait to tell Peter,' Josh mused.

Kate couldn't keep the smile off her face as she watched him but she wasn't about to totally commit herself.

'It all depends on what Mr Stuart has to say about it,' she said, forcing herself to be stern. 'If he thinks you're old enough and is confident you wouldn't do anything reckless, then we'll ask him to go ahead and build you a boat that, in his opinion, would be suitable.'

She looked at her watch, gathered up her handbag and pulled herself up onto her feet. 'Is there anything

176

special you want to buy today or did you just intend to have a look round the shops – get some ideas?'

'Nothing really special, except I promised Nan I would buy her some chocolates.'

'Bribery now, is it?' Kate teased him. 'And one more thing, Josh, whatever we decide, you are not to rush Mr Stuart. If he says he could have a small boat ready for you by the beginning of the summer I think that should suit you fine. You won't need it before then anyway.'

No, Josh thought sadly as he loaded himself up with his mother's purchases, you and my father's solicitors have settled that I am to be sent away to boarding school and there doesn't seem very much that I can do about it.

Chapter Seventeen

'UNBELIEVABLE, ISN'T IT? Ten years old today.' Mary wiped her eyes with the corner of the pinafore she was wearing.

'Yes, the years have simply flown by, haven't they?'

The two women were standing in the doorway watching Josh and his friend Peter Bradley tear the wrappings off Joshua's birthday presents.

Peter was short and dumpy compared with Josh, and as dark as Josh was fair. Nevertheless, as Kate watched their open smiling faces she was grateful that these two boys were such good friends.

'I have a present for each of you,' Mary informed them.

'Really?' Josh smiled his thanks. 'May we open them now?'

Peter flicked a strand of dark hair away from his face as he took the bulky parcel from Mary. He grinned. 'It's not my birthday, Mrs Kennedy, but thanks anyway.' Turning to Josh and seeing that his parcel was exactly the same shape and size, he asked, 'What do you think it is?'

'Haven't a clue. Has to be something to do with the boat. Any ideas?' Josh asked.

'I don't believe you two,' Mary said, making a funny face, 'the only way you'll find out is to open them!'

Both lads laughed and raced to see who could get the string undone and the paper off first.

'Good gracious!' Peter exclaimed. 'It's a life jacket.'

Josh had his out of the wrapping paper, and slung the brightly coloured jacket over his shoulder and hugged Mary. 'Thanks, Nan, it's a super present and thanks for buying one for Peter as well. You're wonderful, you really are.'

'Cor yes, Mrs Kennedy, thanks ever so much.' Turning to face her, Peter asked, 'Does this mean that I shall be allowed to go out with Josh in his boat?'

'If your parents give their permission of course you'll go out together, but only with an adult to begin with.'

Josh hugged her a second time. 'You couldn't have given us anything better. I love you. And you, Mum, the waders and everything else you've given me are great.'

'I'm glad you're pleased with your presents. Wait a minute though, you're not to pester Jack Stuart. He'll do his best to give you a good, strong boat but it will take time. Meanwhile, he's going to arrange for both you and Peter to be taken out on the river whenever he gets the chance. If you listen to all the instructions and pay attention to all the rules then, please God, you'll enjoy yourselves and be relatively safe.'

'So,' Mary said, rubbing her hands together, 'we've a hell of a lot to do today what with our Christmas guests arriving this evening. You'd better tell me now what time you would like your tea.'

Josh glanced at his mother. 'Am I getting a cake?'

'I don't know,' she teased. 'You'd better ask your Nan about that.'

'I am, aren't I, Nan? And candles.' Without waiting to hear her reply he tugged at Peter's arm. 'Come on, Pete, let's take all my presents upstairs. If we stay down here you know what will happen, they'll rope us into helping with all the jobs.'

Mary and Kate stood still for a minute listening to the boys' footsteps as they clattered up the uncarpeted back stairs. Suddenly they heard Joshua let out a yell, 'I'm gonna get my own boat!' His voice rang with excitement.

'Does your heart good to see them together, doesn't it?' Mary exclaimed.

'It sure does.'

When the two of them had finished picking up all the torn wrapping paper, Kate straightened the chairs and smoothed the creases from the tablecloth.

'Right then,' she said briskly. 'Let's get ourselves ready for this invasion.'

At the end of Joshua's birthday there were five adults and five children sleeping in Melbourne Lodge.

Kate, despite being tired out, was sitting in an arm-chair in her bedroom. It was past midnight. The curtains hadn't been drawn and the sky was bright with stars. There was no wind and a bright moon showed up the outline of the trees. It was so quiet that when, somewhere in the distance, a dog barked it split the silence. About time you got into bed, she chided herself, the house won't be quiet in the morning; it will be noisy, full of children's chatter.

Kate was never to forget how her visitors had looked when they arrived. First to step over the threshold was Mrs Holt and her three-year-old daughter Peggy. She looked little more than a teenager herself. Pale faced and thin as a rake she was wearing a long, faded dark dress beneath a coat so worn Kate was sure you could shoot peas through the material. Peggy was not too badly turned out, though the coat she wore, while being clean and of good quality, was several sizes too big for her tiny little body. The pair of them looked as if they hadn't eaten a good meal in ages. The other family was a middle-aged mother, Mrs Flynn, her married daughter, Jean Brown and Jean's three sons, Tommy aged five, John aged seven and Stanley who was eight. A terrible sight, those young boys, shocking. Not a decent bit of clothing on any of them. First thing in the morning she would have to go into Kingston and see what she could rustle up. Thank God there were two more shopping days before Christmas.

Wondering what the hell she had let herself in for, she climbed into bed, telling herself there was little to be gained by staying awake and worrying herself sick.

Kate wasn't prepared for the noise that hit her as she opened the kitchen door. Grey-haired Mrs Flynn and her daughter were facing each other like two spitting cats.

'Mrs Flynn! Whatever it is that is wrong, surely there's no need to shout.'

The angry woman shot Kate a look to kill.

'It's 'er eldest boy, Stanley. Cheeky little sod, says he

ain't staying down 'ere where there ain't nuffin t'do, an' no shops. An' my Jean, would yer believe it, is all for giving in t'him, packing up an' clearing off back to London. I told 'er, I'm staying put! There ain't a thing in our 'ouse t'eat, this is the first chance we've 'ad in years to 'ave a good Christmas an' I ain't gonna stand by an' see that little tike spoil it for the rest of us.'

Kate caught her breath and swallowed, taking a minute to make sure she stayed calm. Then, turning, she faced Stanley, all the time wondering how she could ask his grandmother to curb her language. It was difficult to believe that this whole arrangement had been set up with the help of Reverend Hutchinson through the London Church Association.

'Stanley, you haven't given yourself or us a chance, have you? I promise you that after we have all had breakfast there will be lots of things for you to see and do.'

The spotty-faced lad, who acted as if he were years older than he really was, stuck his nose in the air and sniffed deliberately. 'I ain't seen no signs of a proper breakfast. I don't want none of that porridge muck.'

Mary turned from the stove where she was busy frying rashers of bacon. Kate had never seen her look so angry. She heaved a sigh and said, 'If you would all sit up at the table there is plenty of toast ready and your fried breakfast won't be long.' She raised her eyebrows and with a note of pleading in her voice said to Kate, 'Would you please make two pots of tea? Kettle is boiling.'

Standing side by side at the stove, Kate asked in a whisper, 'Where's Joshua?'

Mary tutted. 'No need to whisper.' She nodded her

head to where the seven visitors were now busy stuffing their faces. 'Eating doesn't seem to stop them talking, they all speak with their mouths full. Josh heard the beginning of the rumpus and disappeared. He'll be back when the coast is clear, or at least when he's hungry. Going to be a great Christmas, don't you think?'

Kate was about to answer when Mary lifted the corner of her apron and wiped the sweat from her forehead, in doing so her elbow nudged Kate quite hard.

'Taking it out on me, are you? I'm beginning to think we must have needed our brains tested. I bet Mr Collier didn't know what he was letting us in for when he made this suggestion.'

'I bet he never! And we're only at the start of it. I can't help wondering what the next few days are going to bring.'

Their eyes met and they had to smother their giggles.

'Oh, well.' Mary grinned as she handed Kate a cloth. 'You can be waitress and take their breakfasts to the table. Mind, the plates are very hot.'

'In for a penny, in for a pound,' Kate muttered as she made the third trip from the stove to the table.

'Did you threaten them or was it something you put in their tea?'

Mary gave Kate a sideways look. 'I know what you mean. Funny ain't it, the difference three hours has made. Come to the front door, you can hear more of what's going on from there.'

As Kate opened the front door, the sharp cold air hit them. It was a bright day with weak sunshine. There had been a frost during the night and signs of it still lingered beneath the shrubs. Pulling their cardigans tight round their chests they walked down the front lawn until they were able to view the children in the distance. Kate was surprised at how much noise they were making; it looked as if they were splashing each other and they were certainly screaming with laughter. Thinking back, she remembered the time she had spent in London with her aunt. The awful smell of too many people living close together, their sweaty bodies, the big tin bath hanging in the coal shed and dragged into the house only once a week for each to use in turn. The coalman in his soot-covered clothes and cap, delivering the sacks of coal by walking right through the house, brushing against the walls as he went. No wonder Mrs Brown's eldest boy had wanted to go home. Fresh air was something he wasn't used to, and the silence all around must have seemed frightening.

'I have a feeling we're in for a hellva lot more surprises before this week is out. That poor thin woman, Mrs Holt, doesn't have much to say for herself, but the other lot make up for her and then some.'

'I can't help feeling sorry for them,' Kate murmured as they turned to go back into the warmth of the house.

'Yes, I know what you mean, right bedraggled looking lot, aren't they? They need some warm clothes if it's only a jersey each and scarves and gloves. I could take to that little one, Tommy. The way he looks at me, well . . .'

'He gets to me just the same. He's so tiny and chubby and what with his cheeky face and blue eyes he could bring out the maternal instincts in any woman without even trying. Wonder where the father is?'

'Best if we don't start asking awkward questions like that. I think we've taken on as much as we can cope

185

with now without looking for more trouble that is none of our business.'

'I'm sure you're right,' Kate said with a twinkle in her eye. 'But don't tell me you aren't feeling just a little bit inquisitive.'

'Yes, well, I'll do my best to keep my curiosity under wraps.'

They had reached the house and Mary flung open the door, 'We're so lucky! Everywhere in this house is so lovely and warm.'

Kate didn't answer but a great sense of determination swept through her. 'Can you manage on your own if I pop off into Kingston?'

''Course I can, my love, and I don't need no telling what you're going for.'

Kate gave her a sheepish grin. 'I know we've got several presents for everybody to put round the tree, but I can't stand to see those boys running around in what are little more than rags. I'll be as quick as I can.' With a devilish smile, she added, 'Try not to have a nervous breakdown while I'm gone.'

Mary had gone to the sink to fill the kettle but Kate could hear her chuckling. 'I'll do me best to stop them wrecking the house. By the way, get something pretty and warm for little Peggy and whatever you get for the boys I'll go halves with you. Get yourself ready an' I'll make you a hot drink before you set off.'

'Wanna know something, Mary Kennedy? The older you get the bigger softie you become. Those kids already know you're a pushover and by the time Christmas day arrives they'll have you eating out of their hands.'

*　　*　　*

With her hat pulled well down over her ears, handbag tucked under her arm and clutching a very large shopping bag, Kate set off down the drive at a steady pace. Reaching the towpath she came face to face with the children and was thrilled to see that Joshua was holding little Peggy's hand. He stopped dead in his tracks and pulled his socks up.

'Where are you going, Mum? We're all cold and were coming up to the house for something hot to drink.'

'That's all right,' Kate said, beaming at the funny-looking picture the five children made as they stood shivering in front of her. 'I won't be long, and I'm sure your nan will find you all a big bowl of soup.' Then doing her best to be kind, she smiled at Stanley. 'Found plenty to amuse you this morning, have you? Pity it's so cold. I'll bring you an' your brothers back a long warm scarf to wrap round your necks. That ought to help.'

'No!' Stanley spoke hastily. He was beginning to like this lady but he didn't want to be beholden to her. He hadn't yet worked out what it was she wanted from him and his family or the reason she was having them all to stay in her beautiful house for the whole of Christmas. Nobody did something for others without wanting something in return. He might not be quite grown up but that much he had learnt ages ago. His hand flew to his neck and up the back of his head, apart from his feet, which were freezing, it was the coldest part of his body. 'It's very nice of yer, missus, but me an' me bruvvers don't wear scarves.'

'Well, we'll see.' Kate's voice trembled. The lad had actually been very polite to her and she realised that his tough cockney manner was more likely than not a front he put up to prove how tough he could be. Poor little lad. He couldn't have known many privileges in his short life.

Joshua moved closer to her. 'Don't be too long, will you?'

'No, I promise. Now, go on, all of you. It's far too cold for any of us to stand around here.'

Stanley backed off and gave the order, 'Run!' The laughter echoing down the driveway as the children ran as fast as their legs would carry them did Kate a power of good. She set off on her shopping expedition, facing the prospect of Christmas with a lot more optimism than she had started out with at the beginning of the day.

Chapter Eighteen

ON CHRISTMAS MORNING Kate persuaded Mary to go with her to the early-morning church service.

'It will only be for half an hour. We'll be back before the house is awake and almost everything is prepared for dinner, isn't it?'

'Yes, well, all right. But I'll bet my bottom dollar those boys will be awake, screaming and shouting and most likely wrecking the place by the time we get back.'

'Come on, Mary, you know you don't mean a word of it. It's as I said it would be, those kids have worked their way into your affections and I don't care what you say – it's true.'

'Can't deny that the two little ones have turned out to be really nice kids. Who could resist little Peggy? She's such a shy, sweet little thing, doll-like almost, with her fair colouring and blond curls. And as for that young Tommy, well, you said yourself he'd make any woman feel motherly and I'm beginning to think the little tinker gets away with murder.'

Thick frost crunched under their feet as they made their way along the towpath. The river didn't look at all friendly this morning, but they were both well wrapped up against the cold. Mary wore nothing fussy, her grey hair tucked up under a brown felt hat, her face round and rosy without a trace of face-powder or rouge and her eyes shining. Her long fawn coat, which had a deep fur collar, had been chosen with Kate's help and her high, soft leather boots had been one of Kate's Christmas presents to her.

As they walked, arms linked, she stole a glance at Kate. She looked beautiful. Her dark curls were bobbing on each side of her face though, in the main, her hair was restrained beneath the dark blue, narrow-brimmed hat which suited her so well. Her new coat was a lighter shade of blue, edged only with a narrow strip of fur at the neck and hem. She wore a single string of pearls and her face showed just a light trace of make-up, which was to be expected in this day and age when women were beginning to demand that more notice be taken of them.

The church had that special feel which comes only with Christmas. The altar rail was banked with white Christmas roses intertwined with red-berried holly. Friends of the church had given a great deal of their time to making these floral arrangements. The village children had been involved in setting up the nativity display in the nave and candles burnt brightly at each end of the crib. The rafters rang with the sound of joyful singing and Kate felt she had a lot to thank God for.

On their return, feeling relaxed and uplifted, she put the key in the front door and pushed it open, pausing to stamp her damp boots on the doormat. Sounds of laughter and merriment came to them as they stepped inside.

The door to the drawing room stood open. Mary and Kate smiled at each other, took a deep breath and went in. It felt a bit like walking into one great big happy family. A huge tree had been set up two days ago and decorated by the children with silver bells, tinsel and clip-on candleholders with small red candles. Holly hung everywhere, gathered from their own grounds by Mr White, their gardener and odd-job man. Mary had lit the fire and piled it with logs before they had set out for church. Outside the day was dark and grey, threatening to snow before very long. Inside the pale-coloured walls danced with reflected firelight and the Christmas baubles on the tree glittered. Alice, having been given a lift into Littleton Green by Bob Bateman, landlord of the George and Dragon, and Mrs Flynn, dressed, neatly for a change, in a black skirt, white blouse and grey cardigan, were sitting comfortably, facing each other in armchairs by the fireside, chatting away as if they had known each other all their lives. Mrs Flynn's daughter, Jean, and a smiling Mrs Holt were grouped round them drinking cups of tea.

For an instant there was silence, then the children looked up to see who had come into the room. Joshua laid down the parcel he was opening and was on his feet and by his mother's side. 'Where have you been? All our stockings were filled and you must come and see what we've all got,' he implored, tugging at her arm.

191

Suddenly, they were surrounded by five children their faces flushed with excitement, their voices shrill with enthusiasm, making such a din that Kate laughingly covered her ears with her hands. 'Please,' she pleaded, 'give us a chance to take our coats off.'

Kate and Mary were acutely aware that four of the children had never before known such warmth and comfort, let alone the joy of waking up to a stocking filled with presents. Mrs Holt set down her cup and saucer and crossed the room to face them. She took Kate's hand in her own and looked up into their faces, 'I don't have the words to say to you . . . what you've done for the children . . .' She looked away, biting her lip. There was something so sad about this young mother. She couldn't bring herself to say more, she didn't have to, the look in her eyes said it all.

With breakfast over, the six women sat with glasses of sherry and gave themselves up to watching the look of sheer enchantment on the children's faces as they were each given a present. Little Peggy had them all on the verge of tears as she held up the new dress Mary and Kate had bought for her.

'Mummy, it's so pretty, can I try it on?'

She didn't wait for an answer, her skirt was round her ankles and her jumper pulled over her head before anyone could stop her. That caused a great deal of laughter as she stood among four boys clad only in her vest and knickers.

'As pretty as a picture,' Mary declared. 'Go on, love, give us a twirl.'

Warm and sensible, but still very attractive the dress

was a mixture of shades of pink, both light and dark. It was long sleeved, with a full skirt and a band of rich velvet at the neck and hem. Kate had had the forethought to buy some extra velvet ribbon in a matching shade to be worn in the child's hair. Peggy needed no second bidding. Using both hands she held the hem of the dress wide as she twirled gaily. Everyone in the room clapped and no one more enthusiastically than young Tommy, which caused more laughter. So Peggy twirled again.

Kate left the room to see how the dinner was doing and was not in the least surprised to find that Alice had followed her.

'You know I nearly never came today,' she said holding her face up for Kate's kiss.

'Oh, Gran, I'm so pleased you have, I can't begin to tell you. The times that Mary an' I have sent you invitations and you never even answered our letters. Not that you need an invite, you know that perfectly well, and I also know it's difficult for you to get out here to us. I'm a lot to blame, I don't visit you half as often as I should.'

'For God's sake, Kate!' Alice yelled in exasperation. 'I'm here now, it's Christmas day, so less of yer chat and let's be seeing to this dinner.' So saying she took down an apron from a hook beside the range and tied it round her ample waist.

'Oh, no you don't, Mary and I have everything under control so just take yourself back into the front room. If you really want to be helpful go and check on the dining-room table, see we haven't missed anything, and then make sure that our visitors' glasses are kept charged.'

Alice pretended to sigh heavily. 'Was a time when it would have been me cooking Christmas dinner.'

'And we don't want any of the self-pity. You've done your share of waiting on me over the years, now please let me have my day.'

'All right. One thing I've got t'say. I didn't go much on this idea of yours, having strangers to stay in the house all over Christmas, but since I've met them I've changed me mind.'

'Glad t'hear it. And you don't have to start on about going home because Mary and I have seen to it that there's a room all ready for you. And before you ask, Gran, yes, the sheets are aired and we've had a fire burning in the room for the last three days.'

'Proper old clever clogs these days, aren't you,' Alice mumbled as she untied the apron and made for the door.

'Gran.'

'What is it now?'

'I'm glad you're here, and before you go back to the others, how about a special kiss for Christmas?'

'Oh, lass, I can't tell you how proud I am of the way you've put the past behind you and tackled the job of looking after Joshua. He's turned out an amazing lad. A credit to you.'

Kate wrapped her arms around her grandmother. 'Praise from the highest,' she whispered, doing her best to turn this serious moment into a lighter mood.

'Nothing more than you deserve,' Alice told her, breaking free. At the door she hesitated and looked back. 'One word of advice, my love. With Josh off to boarding school, it's about time you looked round and started to live a life of your own.'

The door shut quickly, giving Kate no chance to reply.

Still a wise old bird, my gran, she thought as Mary put her head round the door.

'Come and have a drink and then we'll get the vegetables on. Everyone is wondering what you're doing out here.'

'Most of it *is* on now, but there is time for me to have a drink before we dish up.' Kate gave in gracefully.

'Hiding away, were you?'

'You could say that. All right, pour me a sherry an' I'll be there in a minute.'

By half-past one everybody was seated around the big dining table.

'Cor, it does look pretty.' Jean Brown and quiet Mrs Holt spoke in unison.

'You can say that again,' Jean's mother chipped in. 'Must've cost a pretty penny, what with all those crackers an' things.'

'If I know my granddaughter, an' I should do by now,' Alice said, with a smug smile on her face, 'I'll wager her and Mary have spent many an evening making those crackers. They'll have good little presents in them an' all, not like some of the rubbish you buy in the shops, all fancy box and coloured paper they are.'

'Mum, may we pull them now, before we start to eat?'

''Course you can. Help the little ones with theirs first.'

'And each of you can put one of these on your head,' Mary said as she walked round the table letting each child and adult pick a party hat from the big cardboard box she was holding.

The noise was deafening; chattering gave way to squeals

of laughter as whistles were blown, mottos and riddles read, and funny little toys exchanged.

'Now, it's time for the feast to begin. Clear away all the paper and sit up straight,' Alice ordered, in her element, as she helped Kate and Mary to bring in the dishes.

Mary had carved the breast of one side of the turkey out in the kitchen, laying the white slices on the plates, but still the bird was caried in on a huge meat dish and set down in the centre of the table amid yells of surprise and delight. Also on each plate was a sausage rolled and roasted in a rasher of bacon.

'Blimey, that looks good,' Stanley declared, as he grabbed the sausage between his fingers and brought it up to his mouth.

'Ain't you got no manners at all?' his gran yelled, clipping him round the side of his head. 'Put it down. Use ye knife an' fork, you ain't at 'ome now.'

'Leave him be, please, Mrs Flynn, it's Christmas.'

'Come on, ladies,' Mary called out, 'help the children to vegetables and pile up your own plates.'

There were roast potatoes, baby Brussels sprouts, carrots and parsnips, and two jugs filled with thick dark gravy made rich with the juice from the giblets. 'Would you like some cranberry sauce?' Josh asked John who was seated next to him.

John, by far the quietest of Jean's three boys, looked into the bowl that Josh was offering him. 'Naw, we don't 'ave jam with our dinner, it would spoil it.'

Josh replaced the dish near the centre of the table and turned to face his mother who was seated on his other side. They both grinned.

'All right, son?' She winked at him.

'Yes, smashing, Mum.'

Kate reached over and patted his shoulder and in a whisper asked, 'You don't feel neglected?'

He laughed, catching hold of her hand. 'No, I've got you, Nan, and my gran today.'

'Good boy, now eat up before everything goes cold.'

Noisy voices buzzed and little Tommy knelt up on his chair as Mary brought the Christmas pudding to the table. 'It's on fire,' he yelled, his eyes wide with amazement as he stared at the blue flames made by the brandy Mary had poured over the pudding before putting a match to it. Brandy butter for the adults, custard for the children and a silver sixpence slipped into each of their dishes. By the time the plates were cleared from the table, the children were sounding over-excited and Alice was chosen as the best person to read them a story. With five women in the kitchen the mound of washing up was quickly done and finally Mary said that her kitchen was back to being shipshape and Bristol fashion and that they could all relax now. The front-room carpet was strewn with toys and books and Alice said there was only one thing she wanted and that was a cup of tea.

'I'll make it,' Jean Brown offered. 'Anyone else fancy one?'

'Yes, please,' came a chorus of voices.

'And I'll see about organising a few games,' Kate said, as she sorted out a record to put on the gramophone. Mary soon had a ring of chairs set in the centre of the room. 'We're going to play pass the parcel, you've all played this game before, haven't you?'

'Let's start then. Each of you find a chair.' Kate turned

her back to the room, lifted the gramophone needle and asked, 'Is one of you holding the parcel?'

'Yes, I am,' Stanley's firm voice announced.

'Right. Ready, steady, go.'

Some ten minutes later, Kate sank down into a chair alongside Mary and the pair of them gratefully accepted a cup of tea from Jean, who laughingly said, 'You look as if you're in need of that.'

'Never more so,' Mary agreed. 'It's a good job Christmas only comes once a year.'

Later that night, when all their visitors had gone upstairs to bed and Kate had seen that Joshua was sound asleep, Mary made some sandwiches and they, together with Alice unwound with a mug of cocoa.

'You did well – remarkably well – both of you,' Alice told them. 'You made those kids really happy, they've had the time of their lives.'

Kate was touched by her praise, and felt full of love for her. She got up, went across, bent over and kissed her soft cheek. 'It was all worthwhile, wasn't it? But you know, Gran, the best part for me and Josh was having you here. One way an' another I think it's been a smashing day.'

'My sentiments exactly,' Mary interrupted. 'And, Alice, it wouldn't have been the same if you hadn't been here.'

'Well, tomorrow's another day. How do you propose to keep them all amused?' Alice asked, getting to her feet.

'We've boxed clever. We're taking everyone to the pantomine in Kingston.'

'Thank God for that.' Alice made for the door. 'I'm going up. How long will you be?'

'We'll be right behind you, just as soon as we've banked down the fire.'

'Well done, Kate,' Mary said as soon as they were alone. She sounded very emotional.

'Couldn't have done it without you, Mary. I'd say it was a joint effort.'

'Yes, well, turn the light out and let's go up to bed. I think we'll both sleep well tonight.'

Chapter Nineteen

IT HAD BEEN a good Christmas, Kate decided. It was a time for families. Sharing their home this year with three adults and four children had been well worthwhile. The departure of their guests had brought tears, but they had been tears of happiness. When they had arrived their faces had been pinched, their bodies far too thin and their clothes skimpy and faded. How different they had each looked as they climbed aboard the station carrier, calling their thanks and waving their goodbyes. She smiled as she remembered the way Jean's three boys had wound their new, long woollen mufflers tightly around their necks. Scarves that brave little Stanley had vowed they'd never wear.

I hope Charles Collier has found his reward in heaven, Kate sighed to herself. It had been his generosity that had made this Christmas possible.

Now she needed to find calm and an inner strength because in two days' time Joshua was off to boarding school in Guildford and she wouldn't see him again until Easter. Take one thing at a time, Mary had told her, and she had done her best to follow this advice, but there still seemed an awful lot left to do. So, Kate muttered to herself, stop all this daydreaming and start getting some of the jobs done.

'Josh, where are you and what are you doing?' she called from the foot of the stairs.

'Trying on my uniform. Nan told me to, just to check that everything is all right.'

'Well come down and let us see you when you're ready. I hope you're ticking everything off the list as you pack them in your trunk.'

'I will, and I have,' came his cheeky reply.

Kate was torn between laughter and tears. Dear God, she was going to miss having him around the house.

When he came into the kitchen it was as if he had been transformed from a child into a grown lad. What a difference a uniform made!

'Oh, my, my, my,' Mary murmured.

'You think I'll do, Mum?' Josh asked, and, as he spoke, he raised his beautiful blue eyes to meet Kate's. They looked at each other, not needing to say a word, both knew that a very strong bond existed between them.

'Oh, you'll do, an' then some. Now you are ready to go out into the big outside world.'

The station carrier was once again outside the house, this time with a flat open-backed cart drawn by a huge black horse and onto this Joshua's trunk and his case holding his sportswear were loaded. Mary, Kate and Joshua stood in a group and watched as Mr White helped the railway man to rope it all securely. Hardly had the cart disappeared from sight than a car turned into the drive.

'Hallo, young Joshua, all ready for the off? I see your luggage has gone on ahead.'

'Good morning, Mr Weatherford. Yes, everything is safely on the cart.'

Josh watched this big man, who was in charge of his affairs, turn and shake hands first with his mother and then with his nan. A sad thought came to Josh: what a pity my father couldn't have lived to take care of me himself; at least until I was grown up. His mum and nan were wonderful, he loved them both dearly. but he missed his father so much; knowing he wasn't around, would never unexpectedly walk through the door again. It made him want to cry. It was these legal men who had said he had to go away to school. Neither his mum nor his nan really wanted him to go, and he certainly didn't want to leave them or his lovely home.

'Come along, Joshua, say your goodbyes and get into the car,' Mr Weatherford ordered.

Kate had never imagined it would be this bad. It was right that she shouldn't go to Guildford with Josh, but to have to say goodbye like this was terrible.

Mary went forward first, putting both her arms around his strong shoulders. 'Goodbye, Josh, I'll send you parcels.' She couldn't find anything else to say, so she kissed his cheek and pushed him towards his mother.

'Bye, Mum. I'll write.'

'Mind you do. And take care of yourself. The weeks will fly by an' you'll soon be home again.'

Then man and boy got into the car.

'Quick, be brave, let him see us smiling and waving,' Mary implored Kate.

Kate did as she was told, though her heart was breaking. She wanted to run after the car, grab Joshua from it and keep him with her for ever and ever. They could see him waving frantically from the back window, and the pair of them went on waving back until the car was out of sight.

A whole month had slipped by since Joshua had gone away to school and still Kate's emotions were in such turmoil that she couldn't settle to anything for more than ten minutes, and she had walked so many miles that her legs had begun to ache. Once a week, regular as clockwork, Joshua wrote her a letter and from what she could tell life at boarding school hadn't turned out to be half as bad as he had feared.

He liked his form master, Mr Holmes, even though he was very strict. Weekends were the best, Saturdays most of all because they played outdoor games. On Sunday mornings they went to church and every pupil had to write home during the afternoon. There were seven other boys sleeping in the same dormitory as he was. He had made friends with a boy named Nicholas Banks and the two of them had been picked for the rugby team. The last sentence was always the most important: I hope you and Nan are both well and please can you find out from Mr Stuart how far the work on my boat has progressed.

Kate knew the contents of each letter off by heart. Joshua wasn't missing her that much. That's as it should be, she rebuked herself, you'd be much more upset if he wrote that he was utterly miserable and very homesick.

It was the letter that Mary had received by this morning's post that had made Kate's restless feeling so much worse. Mary was going to have to go to Wales.

Kate understood that she had no option. Her sister's husband had died very suddenly leaving Mary's sister Blanche in a terrible situation. Struck down with polio at the age of fourteen she had been left with the lower half of her body paralysed. When she was twenty years old, she had met and married George Edwards, a man whom Mary had never taken to.

'Give him his due,' Mary had said sadly, while they were discussing the letter over breakfast, 'he was fit as a fiddle himself but he took good care of Blanche – though I still think the money our father left my sister had a lot to do with his offer of marriage.'

'Did you voice that opinion at the time?' Kate asked, unable to keep a note of incredulity from her voice.

'Well . . .' Mary looked sheepishly at her. 'When you're young it's difficult to keep a still tongue in your head. It was the day after the wedding an' I overheard George setting up a deal to buy some property. I told him what I thought and he had his say.'

'And you've never seen your sister since?'

'Afraid not. I left Wales, came to Surrey and was fortunate enough to find a job with Mr Collier. Over the years, Blanche and I have exchanged letters and birthday cards, but no, I've never been back home. I've no other relatives left and I didn't see the need. I don't know what will happen to Blanche now; I don't think I can stand by and see her go into a home.'

'Oh, Mary,' Kate was shocked, 'of course you can't,

you have to go and see her, only then will you be able to judge what will be for the best.'

'I'll go tomorrow and I *will* do my best, but that's not to say I'll give up my life here with you. Perhaps the best solution will turn out to be for my sister to remain in her own home and have a nurse live in. We'll have to see.'

'I know what I'm going to do!' Kate's sudden outburst made Mary jump.

'What?'

'I've made up my mind. Today I'm going to get on to the GPO and have them install a telephone.'

Mary laughed. 'What brought that on?'

'Well, if I'm to be stuck here in this big house all on my own – you miles away in Wales and Josh at school – at least it will be some sort of a lifeline.'

'I think it's a great idea. I really do. Don't know why we've never given it a thought before now. I'll be able to keep in touch with you – let you know what's happening – an' I wouldn't be at all surprised if Josh's school doesn't allow boarders to phone home from time to time.'

'Mary! That would be wonderful. That's it. We're definitely having a telephone.'

Kate stood shivering as she watched the taxi bear Mary off to the railway station. During the night the wind had dropped and the temperature had fallen. A mantle of white hoar frost covered everything, gleaming and sparkling on the shrubs and grass and making the pathways very slippery. Kate stamped her feet and blew on her fingers, determined not to go back inside until Mary was out of sight. She wished for the hundredth time that Mary didn't have to go away and leave her. It was the first time that she had been alone in this house since she had come here to take care of Joshua. What am I going to do? she asked herself.

She had so often regretted the fact that she had no brothers or sisters. Because her parents had died in such circumstances, most of her old friends had fought shy of her. She did hear occasionally from her cousin Hilda, but she was married and now had three children and it seemed that life in the East End was far too busy for them to find time to come to sleepy Littleton Green.

Thankful to be back in the warmth of the big kitchen, Kate made herself a fresh pot of tea and set the flat irons out on top of the range. A batch of ironing seemed a very good idea on a cold morning such as this, and when she'd finished she would sit down and write to Josh. That decided, she set a blanket out across the table, covered it with a clean sheet and went out into the scullery to fetch the wicker basket.

What was she going to do? Kate asked herself again as she contemplated the long empty days that lay ahead. The reality was that she had no choice but to live alone and fill her days as best she could. I am twenty-nine years old. Good God! Next year I shall be thirty. The thought depressed her even more. She looked back over the last ten years. Had she been happy? She could truthfully answer yes to that question. Joshua had brought love and joy into her life, Mary had become a dear friend. And she had put the terrible nightmare of what had happened to her father and her mother behind her. A child's love was a wonderful thing, but she wouldn't be human if she didn't sometimes wonder what it would be like to be loved by a man: to feel his hands touching her body, his fingers in her hair, his lips on hers. Had she ever experienced a kiss of passion? Only if you counted Vic Appleton's fumblings when they used to walk together along the towpath and hide beneath Hampton Court Bridge. Dear Jesus, you've suddenly got a good memory. She laughed as she spat on a fresh iron, wiped it clean and began to press a linen tablecloth. She had dragged Vic Appleton up from the past! She'd been little more than a schoolgirl and it was hard for her to remember how she had looked then, some twelve or fourteen years ago. In pretty full-skirted summer dresses, her thick mop of curls blowing in the wind that always seemed to come off the river.

If she were honest she'd fancied the lads who lived and worked on the river. They'd always seemed so lively and carefree, with their tanned skins and dark good looks. A good tug on the boats' steam whistle as they glided past, a cheery wave and a friendly shout had always had her wishing that her own life could be as free and easy. Kate caught sight of herself in the mirror that hung over the fireplace. She shook her head and made a rueful grimace. The few river lads that had paid her any attention had been sent on their way with a flea in the ear by her father; he hadn't intended for his only daughter to associate with those vagabonds! Kate's lips set in a thin, tight line as anger and resentment rose in her. Her father had been a fine one to talk! A pillar of the community only when it suited him. The animosity that had for years existed between her parents had certainly back-washed on to her. Thirty next year and still a virgin!

Come on, she urged herself, at least you're well off. You own this house outright, you still have Bramble

Cottage and the Kearsley Boat Yard which brings you in a very nice income. There's many a woman would give her eye teeth to be in my shoes, so I'd better start counting my blessings and maybe someday, who knows, a Mister Right will come looking for me. It was a brave attitude and one Kate would do her best to believe in. All the same she knew she would lie awake at night now that she was alone in the house and every day would seem long and empty.

Chapter Twenty

'NOW WHAT?' KATE muttered, clicking her tongue in annoyance. Somebody had their finger on her doorbell and wasn't going to go away until she answered it. She was on the top landing sorting out the linen cupboard and putting aside items that needed mending. Getting up off her knees she straightened her skirt and went downstairs. She glanced at the hall clock, saw that it was almost half past ten, tucked a few strands of hair behind her ears, and went to answer the door.

'Jack Dawson? What on earth are you doing here?'

As she asked the question fear gripped her heart. It had to be her gran. Nothing else would have brought Jack all this way out on a weekday. He had his stalls on the go every day except Sunday; it was a hard enough way to earn a living without him taking days off.

'Sorry, Jack,' she mumbled, stepping back and inviting him in.

He removed his cap, wiped his boots on the doormat

and followed her down the hallway and into the kitchen.

'Kate, it's your gran. I'm ever so sorry.'

'I guessed as much, do sit down.'

He drew one of the high-backed wooden chairs out from under the table, sat himself down with his elbows resting on the table. The sad look that passed between them was enough and they remained silent for a minute until Kate asked, 'She's not just ill, is she? Not in hospital or anything?'

'Afraid not, she's gone. Died in her sleep. I found her this morning.'

Kate couldn't speak. She was choked. Crossing the room she filled the kettle, placed it on the gas stove and lit the jet. With her back to Jack, she busied herself setting out two cups and saucers on a tray. When she brought the tea to the table and Jack had a chance to look at her he was utterly dismayed. The expression on her face was enough to make a grown man weep. Such sadness and suffering the like of which he had never seen before.

Kate stirred the tea in the pot and passed him a big breakfast cup, brim-full. 'Help yourself to sugar,' she said.

Still a silence lay between them, and Jack Dawson could think of no suitable words to fill it. Why doesn't she ask me questions? Why doesn't she cry? Blame someone? Me if she likes, but for God's sake say or do something! He couldn't bear to watch her. He had known Kate since she was a mere slip of a girl. Gosh, how she had loved to get to Kingston market with her gran, even in her school holidays. Then life had taken a terrible turn for her. Most youngsters would have gone berserk with what she'd had to deal with. But Kate had weathered it all, including the gossip. Christ, there had been a load more newsmongering when Charles Collier had installed her in this house. But she had shown them all! Kept herself to herself and brought Joshua up to be a credit to her. It couldn't have been much of a life for her though, with only Mary Kennedy for company. Never married. Probably never would now. Such a shame. Jack put his now empty cup on the saucer, and shook his head.

'Are you all right, Kate?'

She nodded.

'Shall I tell you what happened?'

'Please,' she said gruffly.

'Well, yer gran hasn't been out an' about a lot since Christmas. Though she did tell me only a fortnight ago that you'd been in and taken her to Bentalls for tea.'

'Thank God I did,' Kate whispered, raising her head and giving Jack a weak grin. 'I asked her then to move out, come an' live here with me, but you know my gran, Jack, wild horses wouldn't drag her from the place my grandad built for her. "I lived most of me life here and I'll die here," is what she kept telling me.'

'Well, my love, she got her wish. Can't ask for more than that. Funny thing, I knocked on her front door this morning, something I never do. Always go round the back. The door's never locked.

'I knew there was something wrong the minute I set foot in the scullery. In the kitchen her fire had burnt very low during the night, but most telling of all, her big black kettle was to the side of the hob. First thing your gran did every morning was pull the kettle to the centre of the range so's it would come to the boil while she was having a wash.

'I went through to her bedroom. Peaceful as a baby she was. Her eyes were closed. Lovely way for her to go if you ask me. I'm ever so sorry to be the bearer of such sad news. I really liked your gran and so did everyone who knew her.'

'Yes. She was such a special person. So very wise.'

'I know you must feel awful but there are a lot of things to be seen to. Things only you can do, being her next of kin. If you like I can wait for you to get ready, take you into Kingston and run you about all day to the various offices. That's if you want me to.'

'Are you sure, Jack? Can you really spare the time?'

'I wouldn't have offered if I didn't mean it. Go on, get your coat and put something a bit stronger on your feet,' he half laughed, gazing down at her dainty slippers.

'Thanks,' Kate said with feeling. 'I'll be about ten minutes. Help yourself to another cup of tea.'

He rewarded her with a grin and, as she went to get herself ready, she vowed that some way or another she would make sure that he would not be the loser for all the trade he was missing today.

Kate felt she had done her best and that the arrangements she had made for her grandmother's funeral were as right as they could be. Mary wasn't coming home from Wales and Kate fully understood her reasons. What a godsend the telephone being installed in Melbourne Lodge had turned out to be. She and Mary had lengthy conversations, so much easier than trying to find the right words to put down on paper.

After several unsuccessful attempts Mary had at last found a housekeeper cum companion and a part-time nurse who were both in harmony with Blanche's needs and outlook on life. 'None the more for that I am going to stay at least until Whitsun,' Mary had said. Kate's heart had sunk, it was four weeks until Easter. 'By that time, if everything is still going great guns in this household I will feel that I have done my duty and be able to leave Blanche in capable hands and have nothing on my conscience.' With that Kate had to be content.

Joshua was being allowed home from school for the funeral, but only for the day. Kate had been hoping that, as the school holidays were so near, he might have been allowed to stay at home until the new term began after the Easter break. 'No such luck, Mum,' he had moaned down the telephone line. Still, at least she was going to get to see him for a whole day.

The church was sweet with the scent of flowers and there were a lot more people sitting in the pews than Kate had imagined there would be. They had come from all walks of life; poor folk who over the years Alice had given a helping hand to, bargees and boatmen and women of the floating river community who had become her friends, and other kindly friends and neighbours she had lived alongside for a great many years. Joshua looked so grown up, wearing his grey school suit with a black armband that matron had sewn on for him. Reverend Hutchinson was looking old himself. He cleared his throat and looked around at the solemn faces.

'Alice Kearsley once said to me that you take what life dishes out and get on with it or you go under. She was a caring, optimistic lady. Her husband, Jack, died at an early age, leaving her with three small children to bring up. Her two lovely little daughters died before even reaching school age, taken by that dreadful disease scarlet fever. Then in the prime of his life, her only son was also taken from her. Today, I would like you all to know that the endless grief Alice suffered did not make her bitter, rather it gave her endless compassion for others. Anyone who paid her a visit, left feeling merrier, knowing that they had a special friend. She will be remembered with love.'

Kate looked around her. There were a good many people wiping away a tear. It was nice, what the vicar had said. It was true an' all! Her greatest gifts had been her warmth and humanity.

James Hutchinson's voice was deep with emotion as he announced the numbers of the two hymns that the congregation would now sing.

Here comes the worse part, Kate thought as they went out into the spring sunshine and walked the few yards across to the churchyard. Joshua slipped his hand into hers and gripped it tightly. Death was so final, and the lowering of the coffin into the dark gaping hole made him shudder.

'Gran's not really there.' Kate lowered her head and whispered, 'Really she's not, Josh. That's only her tired old body, which she hasn't any more use for now; the best part of her is away free and without pain.'

They had to shake hands with so many people who were offering their sincere condolences. Kate thought about Mary and wished, for Josh's sake, that she could have been here. Though the sun was still shining there was a sharp wind whipping round the tombstones and she was thankful when at last she was able to say to him, 'Come on, let's make our way to the car. Let's go home.'

Most of the afternoon, they spent in front of the drawing-room fire. Kate laughed suddenly, feeling more relaxed than she had done for weeks.

'What's tickled you?' Josh was anxious to know when yet again she let out a peal of laughter.

'You haven't been listening to yourself, young man, or else you wouldn't need to ask that question,' Kate said, wiping the tears from her eyes. 'You've got boats and boat yards on the brain.'

Josh looked at her and he, too, burst out laughing. 'Oh, I see what you mean. I have been going on a bit, haven't I? I just wish there was time for me to go down to the yard and see how far Mr Stuart has got. Do you really believe it won't be finished in time for the Easter holidays?'

'Well, there isn't time for you to go, unfortunately, the car will be here for you at four thirty and, no, I do not think your boat will be finished in time for this coming holiday. In fact, I know it won't be.'

'Aw, Mum . . .'

'There's no way you're getting round me on this one. For a start, Easter is pretty early this year and you can bet your life the weather won't be up to much. And for another thing, good workmen never rush a job. But Mr Stuart did say to me that he might let you and Peter do some varnishing on the woodwork.'

'Cor, that would be great! Can't wait for the hols to start, I don't really want to go back to school today, but I suppose I must.'

'Indeed you must, but guess what? I've packed you a special parcel, stacked with goodies. You can share it with your mates when you get back.'

'You're great. No other mum in the world is better than you are. I'm just going up to my room, I might take a couple of my books back with me.'

Kate listened to him humming as he flew up the stairs. At least she had turned the sadness of Alice's funeral around for him. And if she is looking down on me at this minute, Kate thought, she'd say, 'Well done, Kate. I had a good life and a young lad like Josh shouldn't be upset by my going.'

Kate quickened her pace and, when the road was clear, crossed over to where, not one, but two police constables were standing in the doorway of the paper shop.

'Morning,' Kate said smiling. 'I've walked round and round in circles trying to find the offices of Cooper and Dawes. Can you direct me please?'

The youngest constable's face remained straight, but the older man's lips twitched as he smiled at her. 'Lost are you? An' I would have bet a week's pay that you knew your way around Kingston, Miss Kearsley.'

'I would have backed you an' all, that is until today. Fishguard Lane is the address on their letter heading but I can't for the life of me seem to find the place.'

'Understandable. The old firm of solicitors, Dawes it used to be, in the High Street, moved premises when they joined up with Cooper. Tucked in, well back behind the Griffin where the old warehouses used to be. You have to look up to see their sign and then climb a flight of stairs.' He took hold of Kate's arm and walked her briskly to the corner of the road. 'You probably don't remember me, Miss Kearsley, I was on court duty at the time of your mother's trial. May I say it's good to see you looking so well. I often had a chat with your gran and I was sorry to hear of her death. Nice and peaceful way to go though, wasn't it? Bit different from your mum. I bet, for you, that day still doesn't bear thinking about. Really tragic set to that was!'

'Thanks for your help.' Kate gave him a tight smile before turning off in the direction he had pointed out to her.

The policeman stood rooted to the spot. As he watched Kate half walk, half run across the busy road, he reflected, her mother's trial must have been all of ten years ago, so she must be in her late twenties. He remembered her as a shy, bewildered young girl, but now she had matured into a tall, striking figure. Her face was real pretty and her thick hair still glossy and curly. The dark suit she had on fitted her so well, that it was impossible not to notice what a good figure she had.

Kate's thoughts were very different as she hurried on her way. She had no recollection of having known the policeman and, even if she had, she would have done her best to suppress the memory. She was flustered. Memories swirled round and round in her head. The very mention of her mother, the trial, and the awful events leading up to it were enough to make her break out in a sweat. Even after all this time she felt a chill of horror creeping over her body. Why the hell had he had to bring it up? Visiting her mother in prison had been a nightmare, and she had shoved it to the back of her mind. Now because of his remarks the memory was real again:

the long echoing corridors, the grey clothes her mother had been made to wear, the damp dark walls and the fear. She had felt the fear the minute she stepped through the gate.

And worst of all, that last visit; her mother's sad face as she had turned at the doorway to say her final goodbye. In spite of the passing years and the effort of pushing all the facts to the back of her mind, she knew that was one image she would never, *ever*, forget.

Why, oh why, had she had to meet up with that particular policeman?

She turned into the narrow lane, rested her body against the wall and just stood there, dragging great gulps of air into her lungs. She could feel her heart racing, thumping ridiculously fast and a terrifying sensation of panic seemed to tighten every muscle in her body, making her stomach contract. It was no good, without further warning she was bent double, vomiting all over the ground. After a few agonising seconds she straightened herself up and, in doing so, banged the back of her head against the wall. Still feeling sick and trembling all over, she reached into her handbag for a handkerchief with which to wipe away the bile left in her mouth.

Footsteps sounded nearby and she looked up to see a stranger coming towards her. The gentleman threw Kate a questioning look. 'Can I be of any help?' he asked, looking deeply concerned.

She shrank away, looking most uncomfortable. 'Well . . . I . . .' She eyed him, wondering who he was and where he had come from. He was tall with nice soft grey eyes and his wide mouth smiled at her from under a trilby hat.

'The last thing I want to do is embarrass you, but you do look as if you could use a hand.'

'Don't worry, you haven't,' Kate assured him shakily, instinctively adjusting her skirt, 'but I must look a terrible sight.'

'Where were you planning to go? Perhaps you might let me take you somewhere for a cup of tea, you certainly look as if you're in need of a hot drink.'

'Oh, no, I couldn't. You don't know me nor I you, and I have an appointment with this firm of solicitors,' she said, nodding her head upwards towards a flight of wooden stairs.

'Well, this may be of help,' he said, holding out a large clean white handkerchief.

Kate took it, smiling gratefully as she used it to tidy herself up. The gentleman took a step backwards and said, 'Now might be a good time to introduce myself. My name is Bernard Pinfold.'

'Oh,' she stammered, 'I'm Kate Kearsley, I really must go . . . I'm late as it is, but I'm grateful to you.' She looked at his soiled handkerchief and gave him a bewildered look.

'Please keep it. Any gentleman would help a lady in distress.'

'Well, thank you again.'

He tipped his hat. 'Are you sure you are all right?'

'Yes, I'll be fine now. Thank you again for your concern,' she said with sincerity. 'It was kind of you to stop.'

She watched his upright figure as he walked the length

of the lane and, as she climbed the steps that lead to the offices of Cooper and Dawes, there was a puzzled look on her face.

Mr Dawes, who had looked after Alice's affairs, was a short podgy man with a bald head, and the fact that he had a very bad cold and kept blowing his nose very noisily, into a large handkerchief with a wide red border, did not endear him to Kate. As he leant across his leather-topped deck, she found herself drawing as far back into her chair as possible.

'Well,' Mr Dawes cleared his throat yet again, 'as you are the only relative of the late Alice Kearsley everything is very straightforward. No doubt you are aware that the land on which your grandmother's house stood is entirely freehold as is the field beyond. So that's the first part of her will out of the way.'

'Please,' Kate interrupted, 'am I to understand that the field beyond my grandmother's house also belonged to her?'

'You weren't aware of that fact?' Mr Dawes made no attempt to keep the disbelief from his voice.

'I certainly was not,' Kate assured him firmly. 'What with all the ground at the back of the house, where she kept her animals, I never gave the field beyond so much as a thought.'

'Neither did your grandmother it would seem. It has never been cultivated, but it has certainly increased in value since your grandfather acquired it.'

Kate waited, feeling agitated. Things weren't going at all to order today.

Mr Dawes unscrewed the top of his fountain pen

and drew a folder towards him. 'Yes,' he said, half to himself, 'a very straightforward will, but that is to be expected, Mrs Kearsley was a very straightforward lady.' He took off his spectacles that he seemed to need only when reading, and leant further still across the desk and peered at Kate. 'All her worldly possessions, her entire estate, and that includes a tidy sum of money, she has left to you.'

Kate didn't like his tone, it was . . . smarmy was the best word she could think of. It took a moment before she was able to summon the breath to speak. 'I can't believe all this,' she murmured, 'I truly can't. My gran never had a lot of money.'

'For a working-class lady she certainly did,' said Mr Dawes, this time using a gentle tone.

Kate had a job to stop herself from grinning. I seem to be amassing properties and the funds that go with them like other people collect works of art, she thought as she watched him lay papers out in front of her and indicate where she had to sign.

Mr Dawes took off his spectacles, leant back in his chair and rubbed his eyes. 'You seem overwhelmed by all of this, Miss Kearsley. Have you no idea as to what you will do with the property?'

Kate shook her head.

'There will probably be the need for repairs, in fact it might be much better in the long run if the property were to be demolished and the land sold.'

Hold on, Kate almost shouted at him, this has nothing to do with you! Instead, she said, 'That house holds a great many happy memories for me. There's no hurry for any decision. I shall give a lot of thought to this before I come to any conclusion.' She looked away from him, remembering summer days spent with Alice; the chickens and ducks cluttering the backyard, the smell of the rabbit hutches and how she had hated to have to help to clean them out; the great bread pudding they would eat sitting on the grass beneath the shelter of a tree, the lovely brown eggs she would take home to her mother. It all seemed so long ago now.

The solicitor looked at his watch. Kate took the hint. 'I've kept you too long,' she said, rising to her feet and pulling on her white cotton gloves.

'I think,' said Mr Dawes, also standing up and coming round his desk to stand closer to her than was necessary, 'you will need a lot of professional advice when you have had time to consider just what your grandmother's estate entails. You have my telephone number. Please let me know me if I may be of further assistance.'

'Thank you, you've been very kind,' she murmured, stepping quickly towards the door.

As she left the offices of Cooper and Dawes, her head was still aching and she felt too many recollections had been forced on her. Real decisions must wait until later, but if any help were needed she had made up her mind that it would be to Mr Weatherford she would turn, rather than to the firm of Cooper and Dawes. Mr Weatherford was a gentleman of both good sense and charm; she wasn't sure the same could be said of Mr Dawes.

Chapter Twenty-One

COMING OUT OF the solicitor's office into the fresh air, Kate looked down at the ground before gingerly putting her foot on the top step of the wooden staircase. Her insides were all of a flutter, her mouth as dry as a bone and she didn't feel at all well. First having that policeman remind her of the way her mother had died and then to have to sit and listen to Mr Dawes going on about what she ought to be doing with her gran's home. Needs demolishing indeed! That was his opinion, it certainly wasn't hers.

'Can I give you a hand? You don't look at all steady,' enquired a quiet male voice from the bottom of the steps.

Kate raised her head and found herself looking into the kind face of the man who had come to her rescue earlier.

'Well . . . er . . . thank you,' she muttered, feeling somewhat at a loss, but she took her hand from the wooden rail and held it out to the stranger.

'I hope you don't mind my taking the liberty of waiting for you,' he said gently, as he helped her down the remaining steps, 'only I could see you were rather upset, and as you were on your own I was worried about you.'

'That's very kind of you but I'll be all right now.'

'I'd be pleased to buy you that cup of tea, if you would allow me to,' he volunteered, still keeping hold of her hand.

Kate was taken back, but she recovered quickly and found herself saying, 'There's nothing I'd like more at this moment.'

Kate shifted uneasily on the padded chair, which was set near the bay window of the tea shop. Bernard Pinfold sitting next to her touched her arm.

'Would you like anything to eat?'

She shook her head. 'No, thank you.'

'I think you should eat something, it would help to settle your stomach. How about if we both have a toasted teacake?'

Kate smiled and nodded.

The waitress brought their order, setting the cups and saucers beside the teapot directly in front of her. She knew he was watching her as she poured milk into each cup and then the tea. Her hand trembled slightly as she passed a cup over to him.

'Do you take sugar?'

'No, thank you.'

He took a drink of his tea and swivelled round in his chair to stretch his long legs out to the side.

Kate thought, he must be at least six feet tall, fortyish

226

or maybe late thirties, good-looking face, and a fine, firm body. He picked up the dish that held their teacakes and held it towards her. Using a knife she slid one onto her plate and in doing so she touched his hand with her fingertips.

'The colour has come back into your cheeks. You really are a very attractive young lady.'

'Oh!' She was flattered but uncertain. It was a boost to her ego being here with such a nice man, and it made her feel good to be told that she was attractive . . . but should she really be here?

They each buttered their teacake and fell into a comfortable silence until Bernard started talking about his reason for being in Kingston. 'My home is in Bristol, you've probably gathered that from my accent.'

Kate thought only how impressive he sounded but she made no comment. Reaching into his inside pocket he took out a business card and handed it to her. 'Bernard Pinfold, Pharmacist.' His address was also printed there and a telephone number.

'I'm here for the next couple of weeks to help set up a pharmacy within the bounds of Kingston Hospital. How about you, what do you do with yourself?'

Kate hadn't been expecting such a direct question. She stammered for a moment. 'Oh, dear. I've never had a job, not as such. My father said there was no need for me to work. Then . . .' What could she tell him? Certainly not her family background; she had never spoken to a soul about it and she wasn't prepared to do so now.

'Then?' he asked.

To cover her embarrassment she took his cup and poured him some more tea.

'My parents both died and I moved into Melbourne Lodge to care for a baby whose mother had died at birth. That was ten years ago. Joshua is away at boarding school now. I look on him as my own son.'

'And you never married?' He looked directly at her, and she felt something jump inside her. She liked his grey eyes, the soft way he spoke and, now that he had taken his hat off, the brown hair that was turning grey at the sides.

'No, I never did,' she answered, picking up her cup and draining the last of her tea. 'Thanks again for your kindness and for the refreshment.' She smiled, bending to pick up her handbag that lay at her feet.

'I don't know where you live,' he said, 'but I have my car parked just down the street, would you allow me to drive you home?'

'That would be nice, if it's not taking you out of your way.'

Why had she accepted his offer? He was a total stranger and already this morning she had let him take her into tearooms and buy her food and drink. She came to the conclusion that Bernard Pinfold was a nice person; there was something about him, something different that made her want to prolong the time she spent with him.

The stretch of river just outside Littleton Green was less commercial than in Kingston, its green and sloping banks glowed with the promise of spring on this early March morning and Kate thought that, with any luck, by the time Palm Sunday came round all the sticky buds would be bursting out on the branches of the trees.

'It must be wonderful to live here,' Bernard Pinfold

said as she directed him where to turn his car into the driveway of Melbourne Lodge.

'Oh, yes. I've always considered myself extremely lucky to live by the river. The waterfront has a kind of peacefulness about it. Would you like to come in and see the house?'

'If it's all right, I certainly would.'

'It's perfectly all right,' she answered, knowing full well she was throwing caution to the wind by inviting this complete stranger into her home. Half of her was saying that she had taken leave of her senses while the other, overriding half, was protesting that Bernard Pinfold was a sensitive gentleman. He's educated, a man of means, it's written all over him, she said to herself as she put her key into the lock of the front door.

He held the door of the sitting room open for her and, as she took off her coat, he was there at her elbow to take it from her and lay it carefully over the back of a chair.

'Would you like a drink? We have some Madeira, or maybe a sherry?'

'If it's all the same to you, I'd rather have coffee.'

'Coffee's fine. I suppose we always offer wine to visitors because it seems the right thing to do.'

'Can I give you a hand?'

'No, and don't stand there twiddling your hat round in your hands, take your coat off and go and sit in one of the armchairs in the bay; you get a glorious view of the garden from there.' He was doing just as Kate bid him when she turned at the doorway to glance back.

In the kitchen she hummed to herself as she set the kettle to boil, then put a handful of coffee beans into the grinder. She laid a tray, choosing one of Mary's best traycloths, opened the top cupboard of the dresser and took out two of the best bone-china cups which they only used on high days and holidays. Not for Bernard Pinfold, a dainty little coffee cup that held only a mouthful, a breakfast cup would be much more in his line! Now how would you know that? she asked herself, then laughed out loud. She just sensed that she was right. When the coffee was ready she added a bowl of brown sugar, a jug of cream and a plate of shortbread to the tray.

He must have heard her footsteps on the hall tiles, and was again holding the door open for her, ready to take the tray, which he placed on a small table near to where he had been sitting.

'Would you like cream?'

'Yes, please, but no sugar.'

Kate let the thick cream dribble over the back of the teaspoon from where it trickled slowly into swirls on top of the black coffee. She placed a cup before him, and set her own cup on the other side of the table. Leaning back in her chair, she crossed one leg over the other, bent over and took off her shoes.

He took a sip of his coffee and watched her. She was small framed, about twenty-five or maybe a little older, he thought, with a beautiful complexion, big dark-brown eyes and arched eyebrows. But her crowning glory was her hair. Thick and heavy, shiny brown in colour with unusual chestnut glints. He'd lay a pound to a penny that when she had set out this morning it had been combed back, restrained by the use of slides or combs. He loved it as it was now – the sides falling free, dangling over her ears. He found himself wondering what that mop of thick hair would look like spread out loosely over a pillow and what it would feel like to run his fingers through those tresses.

'What is it you do, exactly?' Kate broke the silence because she felt uncomfortable knowing he was studying her.

'Well, I'm legally qualified to sell drugs and poisons, and sometimes I get involved in the preparing of medicines. I'm here to help and advise with the setting up of the hospital's pharmacy. I also travel a lot. The company I work for has irons in the fire in many countries. As soon as this project is up and running I am going to South Africa, Cape Town actually, which is South Africa's oldest city.'

Kate felt her heart sink. What difference will that make to you? she sternly scolded herself. You've only just met the man and when he leaves here this morning you're not likely to set eyes on him ever again

'More coffee?' she asked, more to cover her confusion than anything else.

'Thanks, I'll just have a top-up. I'll help myself,' he said, reaching for the coffeepot. 'How about you, what do you do besides taking care of this beautiful old house?'

Kate felt a little piqued. 'I've already told you, I've never had an outside job.'

'Oh.' He sensed he'd touched a raw spot. 'I am so sorry. It was never my intention to pry.'

He looked so crestfallen that Kate reached over and covered his hand with her own.

'It should be me that is apologising, I'm very touchy about my past and I don't want to go into details. But – 'she hesitated, took her hand away, sipped her coffee,

231

looked across the table at him and finally said, 'I've had a great life here. Looking after Joshua has been a privilege and a pleasure. He's a wonderful lad, the best thing that ever happened to me.' Now she had started, she found that words and thoughts that had been at the back of her mind for years were suddenly pouring out. 'Maybe it hasn't been the life that I dreamt of as a young girl. You must know the sort of thing: boyfriend, get engaged, white wedding in church, children, live happily ever after. Every girl has such dreams. They just didn't work out for me.'

'When you offered me a drink, you said "we" always keep wine in the house. I don't think you meant young Joshua, did you?'

'You're fishing. What you're really asking is, do I live with someone? Well the answer is, yes, I do.' She sat back and let the statement sink in, watching a frown crease his forehead. 'Joshua and I share this house with a lady whose name is Mary Kennedy. Mary was housekeeper to Mr Collier, Joshua's father, long before Joshua was born. His mother, Jane Mortimer, died giving birth to him, and Mr Collier asked me to move in here with Mary and take care of the baby. On his death, he named me as Joshua's guardian. From those few details you will have gathered that Joshua's mother and father were not married. Now you have it all in a nutshell, except that Mary is in Wales at the moment, and won't be home until Whitsuntide.'

They sat in silence for a minute until Bernard cleared his throat and said, 'This is going to sound really awful . . . but I'm glad you were taken unwell in Kingston this morning and that I was able to come to your rescue.' He rose from his chair. 'I've really enjoyed meeting you and talking to you. Life can be very lonely when one moves around as much as I do. I'd better be on my way and let you get on with whatever you had planned for today.'

She watched him walk out of the house, get into his car, and drive away.

It took every bit of her will power to stop herself from shouting after him, please, don't go.

It was turned midnight and Kate was lying awake mulling over the events of the morning and coming to the conclusion that it had been fraught with frustration. First off she and that strange, lovely man had seemed to enjoy each other's company; at one point she had felt the electricity sparking between them. Somehow she had done something wrong. Perhaps she had gone into too many details, giving him the pattern of life here in Melbourne Lodge. Well, he must have gathered that this house had, at one time, been a love nest for Mr Collier and Jane Mortimer. Good job he hadn't probed further! She might have been tempted to reveal the gory details as to how and why she had been on her own and only too grateful to have been offered the chance to come and live here and take care of Jane's baby. That would surely have put him off!

He'd said he was here for another two weeks, yet he had made no suggestion that they should meet again. Perhaps he was a married man. That hadn't occurred to her until now. She was suddenly conscious that she was in this large house all on her own. She had no immediate family, no one in the whole world that she could really call her very own. She became aware of a terrible aching loneliness. Much as she loved Joshua and Mary there was still a need in her that had never been fulfilled.

Why, oh why, hadn't Bernard Pinfold suggested that they meet again? She should have called him back. Offered him lunch . . . what would have been the point? He was leaving the country soon, going far away, to South Africa.

Chapter Twenty-Two

KATE FOUND HERSELF in a discontented frame of mind during the days following her encounter with Bernard Pinfold. The house had seemed empty after Joshua went away to school and even worse when Mary went to Wales. Now the place seemed desolate. After such a short time spent with a total stranger he had woken in her feelings that she had never before allowed to surface. They had hardly had a lengthy conversation when she had invited him in to Melbourne Lodge. She'd thought, after he'd gone, that she hadn't even shown him round the house as she had promised and he hadn't pursued the matter. But there was something about him that had intrigued her and, at the time, she'd been sure it was the same for him. She had felt instantly that he was a man to be trusted, a man she wanted to get to know. It hadn't worked out like that, they'd just been ships that passed in the night.

Kate put down the pile of clean linen as she entered her

bedroom and leant against the wall. Heaving a great sigh she let all the tension drain out of her in one long breath. What was she getting herself in such a state for? A man, a good-looking, fit young man, came along and did her a kindness and she wanted to make so much more out of it. Pull yourself together, for goodness' sake, she rebuked herself. Moving towards the bed she began to strip the covers off. No matter how many times she urged herself to be sensible, she couldn't help wishing that she hadn't seen the last of Bernard Pinfold.

After she had remade the bed with the clean linen and dusted the furniture, she stood in front of the full-length mirror set into the door of the wardrobe and studied herself in earnest. Her figure was good, her breasts high and firm. Well they should be! No babies had been suckled at them and, come to that, no man had ever fondled them. Her waist was small, her belly flat and her legs weren't a bad shape. What was she doing this for? There didn't seem much point to it. Not one real man had ever shown any interest in her and at her time of life she was only deluding herself if she still believed that one day a Prince Charming was going to come riding up on a white charger and carry her off to live happily ever after.

I'd settle for an ordinary man, she laughed to herself, one that worked for his living, got his hands dirty and came home expecting me to wash his mucky overalls. She grinned cynically at her reflection. Who are you kidding? You've enough money and properties to keep a whole family for the rest of their lives, but it still hasn't been an attraction where men have been concerned. Her past had been what had put possible suitors off!

Who in their right mind would want to lie in bed with

me, make passionate love, knowing that my mother had killed my father by stabbing him in the back and had met her own death at the end of a hangman's rope? The whole country had read about it in the daily press and avidly followed the court trial. The various books and articles that had been written about the Thames-side murder had been grossly distorting and there would always be someone like the policeman in Kingston popping up, only too willing to remind her of those awful circumstances. I'd have to live a very long time to live it down entirely. Kate shook her head as she accepted that fact.

'My God, you are morbid this morning,' she said out loud. 'And with good reason,' she answered herself.

Just lately she had hungered for a family of her own. Mary was getting on in years and Joshua wouldn't need her in the future as much as he had in the past. What is there left for me? Who will be left for me?

I could do with some company to cheer me up, she thought, as she bundled up the dirty bedlinen, tucked it under her arm and headed for the stairs. Not being able to think of anyone to visit she decided the next best thing would be to get herself out into the garden and dig up a few weeds.

Once out in the open air, with a scarf tied over her head and gardening gloves on her hands, Kate sank to her knees and started to dig in the earth as if her very life depended on it.

Meeting Bernard Pinfold had unsettled her. But soon it would be the Easter holidays and the house would ring with the laughter of Josh and his chums. Then in only a few more weeks, there'd be another bank holiday,

Whitsuntide. Mary would be home and everything would be back to normal.

Resolving not to be so short-tempered, she loosened the earth around a clump of weeds and tugged until they came away in her hand. If I keep this up for a couple of hours, she mumbled to herself, perhaps I shall feel a darn sight better.

Bernard Pinfold was amazed at the effect Kate Kearsley had had on him. He'd thought he could leave it as just a pleasant chance meeting, but she filled his mind. He stared across the dining room, taking note of the starched white tablelinen set out with good china and crystal wine glasses and at the menu which offered a great choice of well-prepared food. Hotel life was good if one experienced it only once in a while. When it was part of your everyday life it became a bore. He counted himself as being fortunate. Anything he wanted, within reason, he could afford. His friends would say he had the best of all worlds. He loved his job and the travelling it entailed. Did he hanker after a settled home? A family? Well, the other man's grass is always greener. He was a professional man and he had achieved what he had set out to do. His father had been a pharmacist and he had wanted to follow in his footsteps since he was ten years old. At this moment he didn't understand his own feelings.

Folding his napkin into a neat square, he placed it on his side plate and rose from the table. He thought it best to use the telephone box situated in the far corner of the hotel's entrance hall. He picked up the ear piece and asked the operator for Directory Enquiries, when connected he asked for the number of Melbourne Lodge,

Littleton Green. Back to the operator, he put two pennies in to the slot, gave her the number and waited.

The light had begun to fade and Kate was in the garden shed. She was cleaning and stowing away the tools she had been using when the phone rang in the house. She dropped everything and ran. It might be Josh, or Mary ringing for a chat. It had rung several times before she grabbed it and breathlessly said, 'Melbourne Lodge.'

'Hallo, Miss Kearsley, this is Bernard Pinfold.'

She felt the colour flare up in her cheeks.

'Hallo.'

'I'd like to ask you something.'

Kate's insides jumped and a happy smile came to her lips.

'Tomorrow being Saturday, I don't have much to do at the hospital. I could get away by eleven o'clock. The weather looks as if it might be pretty good, so I wondered if you'd spend the day with me?'

Spend the whole day with him! Had she heard him right? Oh, yes please, she thought, but said only, 'Thank you, that would be nice.'

'I'd planned to pay a visit to Hampton Court while I'm here, but as it's not far from you perhaps you'd find it a bore.'

'Not at all,' Kate hastened to assure him. 'If you've never seen Hampton Court Palace I shall be able to point out the interesting parts.'

'Good, that's settled then. What time shall I pick you up?'

'You're the worker, whenever it suits you, I'll be ready.'

'About eleven. I'll see you then. All right? Bye.'

For the next hour Kate sat at the kitchen table with a plate of ham salad and fresh fruit for her sweet. Why in the world had he called her? It was what she had longed for; prayed for.

Now it had happened, that old uneasiness was creeping over her again. It's high time you had a day out she told herself. Live for the moment and let the future take care of itself, she decided, as she made preparations to have a bath before going to bed. Coming up to thirty she might be, but there was a spring to her step as she climbed the stairs and thought about what she was going to wear when Bernard Pinfold took her out next day.

Shafts of bright sunlight flashed across the bonnet of the black Austin as Bernard drove along the main road towards Hampton Court.

'It's a lovely day for our outing,' he remarked to Kate, who was looking extremely elegant in a single-breasted beige suit with a saucy brown-velvet cloche hat which dipped to a point over her right eye and had a colourful feather sewn on the left-hand brim.

'Yes.'

'You wouldn't be able to keep your promise and show me all the interesting parts if it had been raining,' he said, making a brave attempt to draw her into a conversation. 'You really do look very smart,' he added, keeping his voice light.

Why, oh why, did she feel so ill at ease?

'There aren't too many occasions in my life that call for me to dress up,' she answered, doing her best to put a smile into her voice.

'Then I'm flattered that you considered being with me

such an occasion.' He concentrated on the road ahead in silence for a while, then said, 'I thought about you a great deal before I gathered the courage to telephone you.'

'Oh!' His frankness pleased her. 'I thought about you too.'

He glanced at her and they both smiled. Kate felt a whole lot more relaxed and, settling more comfortably in her seat, began to enjoy the ride.

Once Bernard had parked the car he suggested they had coffee before starting to walk, and they chose the first café they came too, which overlooked the Thames. As Bernard gave their order to the waitress, Kate hid her mouth behind her hand to cover her amusement – from where she was sitting she had a straight view of the river and there, nestling low down beyond the great bridge, was a broad sign at the entrance to a yard which said, 'Kearsley Boat Yard. Boat Builders & Repairers'.

Kate stole a glance at this good-looking young man. He looked different today than he had at their first meeting. For one thing he wasn't wearing a hat and was dressed in a more casual way. A lovely navy blue jacket – expensive was the thought that came into her mind – grey trousers, white shirt, top button undone and a plain, pale blue vee-necked pullover. The shoes he was wearing were also casual, black, without laces, the slip-on kind. His hair was not smoothed down – more wiry than anything else – and the grey sideboards were really attractive.

He doesn't know much about me, Kate thought as she stared across at her boat yard.

'Lovely setting,' he remarked, as much to himself as to her. 'A good many ducks and swans on the river and plenty of activity. I didn't realise so much industry

241

focused around this part of the Thames.'

'Why should you? Your home is in Bristol. If I were to visit that town I'd be just as unaware of what went on in that part of the world, wouldn't I?' The warmth of the smile Kate gave him matched her mood. She was feeling happy.

'I nearly came here once, on my honeymoon.'

Kate stiffened. So he was married! She should have known right from the start. He hadn't lied to her. It was only natural a man of his standing would have a wife. She felt sad. She didn't want him to be married.

'Only the marriage didn't last very long.'

'What?'

'Sounds daft, doesn't it? I was twenty-two years old, she was twenty-five. Thought she was the most beautiful girl in the world. She was engaged for two years to my best mate. They had an awful row and split up and she married me on the rebound. He came to the wedding. The same evening she told me she was sorry and went off with him.'

'How awful. I'm so sorry.'

Bernard leant across the table and looked directly into her eyes. 'Don't be. It was only my pride that was hurt and I made up for it by sowing a crop of wild oats.'

Kate tried to stifle a giggle but when he began to laugh so did she.

'The pains of growing up,' he said when their laughter became quieter.

If only you knew! My sufferings were a whole lot more severe than yours, Kate thought as she took a sip of her coffee. But she felt good; knowing that his marriage had been a non-starter was a boost, and she fell to wondering what

242

difference that fact made to her. He was being kind to her; sharing his free time with her. Well, she would make the most of it because that's all there would be to it. Very soon his job would be taking him halfway across the world and they would never set eyes on each other again.

He offered her his arm as they walked. It was as if they were two old friends enjoying a day out together. She showed him the great vine, the old clock and the maze. Then they stared at the parts of the palace which were occupied as residences by private persons.

'I suppose you have to have been on a council housing list for a very long time to get one of these,' he teased.

'Could be.' Kate laughed. 'But I think it would be more helpful if one were a friend of the king, or, in your case, perhaps the queen.'

He squeezed her hand and they burst out laughing.

They found a really old-fashioned pub with a restaurant at the back overlooking Bushey Park, with its avenues of limes and magnificent horse chestnut trees.

'Aren't they graceful animals?' Kate remarked, as they sat at a table in the window watching the deer run across the grass and disappear behind the trees.

'Yes. You really are lucky to live in such a beautiful part of the country,' he told her.

Their eyes met and Kate found it hard to look away.

'You've no room for complaint, you travel the world while I stay put in my little corner,' she said jokingly. She was glad when the waiter brought their food because the interruption eased the tension that had sprung up between them.

Bernard did most of the talking, mainly telling her how the new department was coming along in the hospital.

They had settled for the set menu; asparagus tips to start, followed by roast chicken served with a delicious assortment of fresh vegetables, washed down with a glass of white wine, which he had insisted was a must.

'I think it's really nice of you to have invited me out like this,' Kate said when they had reached the coffee stage. 'It was a lovely meal, I enjoyed it.'

'I did too.' He smiled, lying back in his chair. 'But there is one thing that seems all wrong to me.'

'Maybe you'd better tell me what it is,' Kate said, feeling the colour rise in her cheeks.

'Oh, please, I didn't mean to upset you. It's just . . . well, I can't go on calling you Miss Kearsley. I think we've passed that stage and become friends, don't you?'

She let out a deep breath. 'I'd like it if you called me Kate, in fact I'd feel a whole lot more comfortable if you did.'

'Right, and I'm going to ask you to dispense with the Bernard. I have a nickname that most of my friends use. God alone knows how it came about, but over the years it has certainly stuck.'

'Go on then, tell me what it is.'

'Toby.'

'Toby.' She rolled the name round her tongue. 'Do you know, I think it suits you. It has a warm tone to it, not stuffy like Bernard. Yes, I like Toby, I like it very much.'

'I'm pleased that you're pleased,' he teased her. 'And now that we have that out of the way, shall we make plans as to how we shall spend the rest of this week?'

Kate said hastily, 'I thought you were here to work?'

'Only in an advisory capacity, and if I try hard enough I can usually be free by midday. I wish—' He paused for a long moment, looked down, then cleared his throat

244

before saying, 'You know, Kate, I can't tell you when I've enjoyed someone's company as much as I'm enjoying yours. I feel I'd really like to get to know you better. Will you consider spending more time with me?'

'Oh, Toby.'

She put out her hand to him and he gripped it tightly as he outlined the places he would like to take her to. Kate had not meant her impulsive action to be taken quite so seriously and she withdrew her hand as gently as she could. Nagging doubts crowded her mind. Nothing could come of any of this; he wasn't going to be around. Through the restaurant window she could see a pair of graceful swans gliding upstream. Swans mated for life; it wasn't always like that for people.

'How about a walk along the towpath, nothing too strenuous, just a stroll to help our lunch to go down?' he suggested, signalling to the waiter that he would like to settle the bill.

When Kate smilingly agreed, he was on his feet in an instant, helping her on with her jacket. They crossed the bridge and he tucked her hand through the crook of his arm as they walked down the slope and on to the shingle footpath. The Thames flowed as far as the eye could see, its waters smooth and dark. In places trees grew on its banks, their boughs just tipping the surface. Small boats rode at anchor and the sound of hammering from several boat yards hidden from sight by a bend in the river echoed back up to them.

'It's getting cooler now the sun has gone in. Are you warm enough?' he asked

'I think it might be as well if we made our way back to the car.'

'All right,' Toby agreed. Changing direction, his eyes cast downwards, he said, 'You know you haven't given me an answer, Kate. I asked whether you would spend more days like this, with me.'

She stopped and glanced at him. She really didn't want to start something that was doomed from the start. A few days, wonderful memories, and then what? He'd be gone. On the other hand, hours and hours to enjoy his company! It was just too tempting to refuse, even if she would be left feeling more lonely than ever after he had gone away.

'I'd very much like to,' she said.

'Good. How about tomorrow? I'll be free all day.'

'Fine,' Kate agreed, her heart beating nineteen to the dozen.

'I'll pick you up at eleven again.'

Later that night, Kate frowned into the mirror. What had she let herself in for? Did he really enjoy her company or was he just filling in time because he was in a town where he knew no one? A man in his position could go anywhere, dine anywhere. Yes, but as she knew only too well, it wasn't the same doing things by yourself. Company made all the difference. That's all it was to him. Fate had put him in the right place when she had needed a hand: they had met and liked each other, he had spare time on his hands, in a strange neighbourhood and he was simply being polite, seeking companionship. That's all there was to it.

Getting into bed, she had half convinced herself. Nevertheless, as she snuggled her head down into the pillow, there was a radiant smile playing around her lips. She'd had a lovely day. And Toby was coming to fetch her again in the morning.

Chapter Twenty-Three

KATE WAS READY and waiting when she heard the
car turn into her drive and the single blast from the
horn. Toby was leaning against the body of his car
by the time she had locked the front door. He looked
different again today because he was wearing a grey
suit. She had on a dress and a matching long loose
coat. It was an outfit that suited her very well, the
colour being a soft peach with bindings of dark brown,
her shoes were plain high-heeled court shoes of the
same shade of brown, as were her gloves and handbag.
She had decided against wearing a hat and had pulled
her long hair well back and fastened it with a huge
tortoiseshell slide, leaving a few strands to hang free
over her ears.

'Morning, Kate. The weather doesn't look too promising.'

He seemed genuinely pleased to see her, which set her
a little more at ease. Looking up at the sky she said,

'Probably going to rain. I did think about bringing a picnic hamper but—'

'Certainly not,' he interrupted hastily. 'It's no problem, we'll take our time, decide where you would like to go and later on we'll find a hotel in time for lunch.'

'Sunday tradition, eh? Roast beef an' all that.'

'Well, a proper old stick in the mud, that's me. There's nothing I like better than a good old English roast lunch.'

He held open the car door, making sure she was comfortable before closing it. Minutes later he backed the car out of the drive and drove towards the main road away from the village, turned right, and headed towards Brighton. Kate had hardly spoken a word but that didn't matter to Toby. He took his eyes away from the road and glanced at her. She is so lovely, he told himself, aloof, different to any woman I've ever met. All he cared about at this moment was that she was there, sitting beside him and that he would have her company for the whole day.

This is ridiculous, he suddenly thought. I'm a grown man. A man of the world, and not especially unacquainted with women and here I am, very nearly tongue-tied, acting like some love-sick young lad. He felt awkward and he could tell that she felt the same. He took one hand from the steering wheel and covered hers as it lay in her lap, she smiled and shifted to be nearer to him, and the awkwardness vanished.

'I never asked you, but how do you feel about a visit to Brighton?' he asked, bringing his hand back to the wheel.

'Fine, a walk by the sea will blow our cobwebs away.'

He could smell her fresh perfume and felt her hip touching his occasionally. As the scenery changed from quiet country lanes to the great rolling downs with the sea shimmering below, he asked, 'Shall I park the car and we'll walk a while before we decide where to have our lunch?'

She nodded her agreement.

'What say we take a look at the Royal Pavilion?' Toby asked.

'Of course we must, no one comes to Brighton without paying a visit to Prinny's Palace.'

'Are we both having the same thought?'

'Well, that all depends.'

'On what?'

'On whether or not you had the same kind of history teacher as I did.'

They both burst out laughing.

'Go on,' Toby urged. 'You tell me your version of this fairy-tale place.' Kate lifted her head and stared up at the building that was like no other in the whole of England, with its numerous onion-shaped domes and countless fancy towers.

'Difficult to say which is fact and which is fiction. I grew up believing it was a romantic place and that whosoever entered its doors became enchanted. Whereas now I know the reality.'

'Which is?'

Kate was thoroughly enjoying herself, amused to be standing in Brighton discussing events that had taken place a hundred years and more ago. 'The fact is that the Prince Regent, before he became King George IV, had this place built for the true love of his life, Mrs

Fitzherbert. Can't you just imagine a royal gathering within those walls?'

Toby stared at Kate, who was lost in daydreams. He felt compelled to say, 'I wish it were possible to build such a palace for you today.'

Her jaw dropped and her eyes opened wide. 'Why, you old romantic, I never thought modern men had such thoughts.'

'I mean it, Kate. If it were possible, I would build you a palace without hesitating.'

She became flustered. This was a strange situation, he sounded deadly serious. They'd only known each other for such a short while. Her face lost its smile as she said, 'Normal people don't get to live in palaces.' Then speaking without thinking, she added, 'Besides I already have three houses.'

Toby's face went blank. What was it she was trying to tell him? He should ask her what that had to do with him, how it altered what he found himself feeling for her, and up to a moment ago would have sworn that she was feeling for him? But he said none of these things.

Instead he let her name come out on a sigh, 'Kate! Oh, Kate!'

Kate couldn't believe how upset he sounded. 'Toby, I'm sorry. What I said came out all wrong. It was that . . . your idea was so charming . . . I couldn't take it in. Nobody has ever said anything remotely like that to me.'

He did his best to laugh it off. 'Oh, don't be silly.' He took her hand and tucked it in through his arm, drawing her close. 'It isn't exactly summer yet, is it? Let's walk and decide about lunch. Have you any suggestions?'

Kate took a deep breath as they turned their footsteps towards the seafront.

'When I was a little girl my father used to bring me, my mother, and his mother here to Brighton and on such days we always had a meal at the Old Ship Hotel.'

'And is that a good memory for you?'

'Yes, it is,' she said, without hesitation.

'Then that is where we shall eat our roast beef today.'

They quickened their pace and she glanced across the road to where the sea was rolling in, cutting up a bit rough, its white rollers crashing down between the iron framework that supported the pier. That had been a stormy few minutes in this new relationship. Well it was to be expected really, wasn't it? She knew very little about him and he even less about her. You're going to have to do something about that if you're thinking of seeing more of him, she said silently and answering herself added, yes, I suppose so.

'Keep your head down against this wind,' Toby ordered with his usual show of care and attention as they headed for the hotel.

He opened the heavy door with his shoulder and stood aside until she had gone through, into the warmth and shelter of the Old Ship Hotel. They went towards the lounge, where a bright, cheery log fire burnt in the grate and several people were sitting around having drinks. Toby led her to a chair, placed in a recess, from where she would have a direct view of the sea.

'Will you be all right on your own for a few moments?' He smiled down at her.

'Of course.'

'I'll get a waiter to bring us drinks, but first I'll go to reception and make sure there's a table free for lunch.'

There was a full-length mirror on the wall to Kate's right and turning sideways she saw her reflection. Her hair was a bit windswept, her cheeks rosy from the sea breeze and her eyes bright and shiny. Happiness shows, she said to herself, thinking how much nicer it was to be here in this lovely old hotel on a Sunday morning, with a nice man for company, rather than spending what would have been a long dreary day on her own.

Toby came back, followed by a very smart waiter bearing two drinks on a tray, which he set down on the small round table in front of Kate.

'I took the liberty of ordering you a glass of dry sherry, is that all right?'

'Perfect,' she told him, raising the glass to her lips.

Thirty minutes later, they were being shown to a table for two in the dining room. Toby was used to dining in hotels but, even so, he was impressed, as indeed was Kate.

'This room had been redecorated since I was last here,' she remarked. 'Mind you, it was a very long time ago. It's very elegant, but still in keeping with its old-worldly atmosphere, don't you think?'

'Yes, I do,' Toby agreed as he studied the menu. 'Good, no problem for our main course, but what shall we have to begin?'

Kate was in two minds, wondering whether to have soup or melon. If she were going to have roast beef she certainly didn't want to fill herself up with a heavy starter.

'Seeing as how we're by the sea, I'd say oysters would be a very good choice. Have you ever had them?'

'No, to me, they always look kind of, well, slimy.'

Toby laughed. 'I'm very partial to them, wouldn't you like to try?'

'I won't if you don't mind. I think I'll go for the melon.'

Toby was still grinning broadly as he gave their order to the waiter, who suggested they leave the choice of pudding till later.

It was a long leisurely lunch and by the time they had left the dining room to have their coffee in the lounge, Kate felt relaxed.

'Do you mind if I smoke a cigar?' Toby asked

Kate had been stirring her coffee, she set her spoon down and shook her head. 'Not at all,' she said at the same time thinking, see, that's something else you didn't know about him; he likes to smoke cigars.

It took a minute or two for him to get it going, then, shaking the match out and setting it neatly in the glass ashtray, he looked at Kate. 'Shall we drive up towards the Downs when we've let our lunch digest?'

Kate nodded. What she could have said was, wherever you want to go is fine by me, just so long as you take me with you. The longer she spent in his company the more she liked him. He struck her as being an extraordinarily capable sort of person, ready to take charge, but nice with it. He's solid. Yes, that was the best way to describe him. Solid and warm and, she'd like to add, dependable, but she didn't know him well enough yet to know if it was true. Time would tell about that one.

*   *   *

Elizabeth Waite

It didn't take long for Toby to drive out of Brighton and soon they were approaching Kemp Town racecourse where he brought the car to a halt and wound down his window. Kate did the same to hers and stretched her legs out straight. Toby couldn't take his eyes off her. He reached out with his left hand and rested it on her shoulder, in a very casual way. In a matter of a few days – three meetings – he had come to care for Kate Kearsley. She sat quietly beside him. He looked at her thick brown hair with its distinct hints of copper. She had kept it securely held back and once again he felt the longing to free it, to run his fingers through it.

A strange excitement gripped Kate. She didn't want him to remove his hand, in fact she wished he would take her in his arms. It was exactly what Toby had the urge to do, but caution stopped him. Where would be the sense in it all? He could court her, and more than likely before he had to leave Surrey, he would find the opportunity to make love to her. That was exactly what he wanted to do. She was sitting there, looking dreamy, smiling to herself. Let her be, he ordered himself. Take her home before you do something you'll live to regret; Kate Kearsley is not the sort of girl who is looking for an easy affair with a man she has only just got to know. And certainly not a man who is going to love her and leave her, because, be honest with yourself, that is exactly what you will do; not from choice, he argued with himself. It doesn't make a bit of difference that your feelings are strong, something entirely different from what you've ever felt for any other woman, the fact is that you will be heading for South Africa within a matter of weeks. That's what his mind said, his heart was playing a different tune.

'We'd better head for home,' he said, removing his arm and sitting up straight in his seat.

'I could give you tea when we get back to the house, if you like.'

'I have some paperwork I must catch up with this evening, so I'll drop you off, if you don't mind.'

Kate felt herself blush.

He went on hurriedly, 'And I really do have to work tomorrow, but I will ring you and we'll arrange something for Tuesday.'

The journey back was strained. Had he brushed off her invitation or did he really have to catch up on some paperwork? That will teach you to be forward, Kate rebuked herself.

When Toby drove the car up to the house, he got out, walked round to the passenger side and held the door open for her. Taking a firm hold of her arm he walked by her side to the front door and waited until she had put her key in the lock.

'I've had another lovely day and another meal at your expense. I hope I get the chance to repay you,' she spoke quietly, with almost a hint of an apology in her voice.

Toby put his forefinger beneath her chin and raised her face until their eyes met. 'Kate, it is I who am indebted to you. I would have spent two long, lonely days in a strange town if it weren't for you. I really have enjoyed every minute we've been together, and I shall telephone you tomorrow and see you the next day, all right?'

She made no answer, only looked up at him with those big dark eyes which he now saw were glistening with tears. He pulled her close and she nestled into him, and he kissed her, a long, soft gentle kiss, the like of which she had never experienced before. His hand pressed into the middle of her back and she put her arms around his neck. There, on her own doorstep, they kissed each other as if their very lives depended upon it.

It was Kate who finally pulled away. What she wanted, more than anything else in the world at that moment, was to take his hand and lead him inside her house. What she did was let out a huge deep breath, smile at him and say, 'You have work waiting for you, you had better take yourself off.'

He caught her hand as she turned to go inside. 'One more,' he pleaded.

She needed no second urging, she went willingly into his arms and his kiss left her breathless.

Once in the house she took her coat off and draped it over a chair, then sat looking out of the front-room window. In her mind she went over everything he had said and done during this wonderful never-to-be forgotten day. He was going to ring her tomorrow but more importantly he was coming for her the next day. 'I can't wait,' she murmured, hugging herself. Tomorrow she would wash her hair and sort out a very pretty frock to wear. You're mad, like an excited kid thinking about going to someone's birthday party. Only it was better than that! Loads better!

God willing, she was going to spend another whole day with Toby Pinfold.

Every minute of the previous day had dragged. The hands of the clock had, at times, appeared to be stuck. Kate had done her best to focus on one job after another without much success. The only thought that filled her head was that Toby was coming to see her the next day. Well now it was the next day, and a more miserable day it would be very hard to imagine. It was dark, and the rain was simply lashing down.

The noise as it beat on to the corrugated-iron roof of the shed outside the back door was deafening. Already the gutters were overflowing and, apart from the big kitchen where the coal range hardly ever went out, every room in the house felt cold and damp. He won't come, not in weather like this, Kate said to herself but with her next breath she was spitting forth orders; I'll light the fire in the front room, yes, that's the first job; then I'll see what I can prepare for us to eat because he won't want to go traipsing around the countryside in all this rain; I need to get dressed, can't do any of these things while I'm still walking about in my dressing gown and I'll have to have a bath. She stopped still for a moment and looked up at the old-fashioned clock which had stood on the mantlepiece over the black-leaded range for as long as she could remember. It was twenty minutes past seven. I don't suppose he is even up yet! Why don't you fill the kettle, put it on to boil, make yourself a nice pot of tea and sit down and drink it? Yes, that's what I'll do. No, I'll set the fire going in the front room first so there's plenty of time for it to warm up.

When at last Kate did sit down, it was of Mary she was thinking. I wonder what she would say if she knew I was getting myself all worked up because a man I've known for only a short time is coming to spend the day here with me? One thing's for sure, she wouldn't disapprove. Live an' let live, is the code that Mary applies.

When this house was occupied by Jane, and Mr Collier

257

visited and stayed over whenever he could, Mary was never the one to comment, rather she made all sorts of allowances. It was a happy house then, and it has been ever since. Never mind the weather outside, today is going to be a really lovely day, Kate decided as she rose to her feet. And never mind what would happen when Toby finally had to leave Surrey and go about his business. Today was here and now and she wasn't going to look any further ahead than that.

By ten thirty she had everything ready.

Walking across the bedroom she turned first one way, then the other, looking at herself in the wardrobe mirror. You haven't done badly, she told her reflection. For once not a hair was out of place; she had plaited it into a bun at the nape of her neck leaving several strands free to frame her face. A slight touch of make-up looked perfect and her simple navy blue dress, which had a straight slim skirt, showed her figure off to perfection.

She was at the top of the stairs when she heard him sound his horn. From the landing window, she looked down, saw him get out of the car, turn up the collar of his coat and run through the heavy rain to the shelter of the front porch.

As she flung open the door, he grinned and shook himself, saying, 'God, what a day!' Kate put out a hand, almost dragging him inside. Quickly he undid his coat, unwrapped his scarf from round his neck and, as she took them from him, said, 'That's better, this is a day for the ducks, not for us.'

'That was my thought the minute I got up and looked out of the window, so I've made a few preparations for lunch . . . that is, if you don't mind staying here for the day. Anyway coffee is ready, come on.'

'Sounds fine to me,' Toby told her as she hurried him down the hall towards the kitchen door. When she opened it he gasped in surprise. Cups and saucers, a plate of scones, butter and a dish of jam were set out on the long kitchen table, the iron plate had been removed from the range and the fire was burning brightly, the kettle hummed on the side of the hob and the smell of freshly ground coffee filled the air.

It was all so homely.

'What a lovely welcome!' he exclaimed. 'A sight like this brings home to me what I've been missing all these years.'

'You wouldn't have it any other way, I don't suppose. You must have seen many wonderful things in your travels.

'Come on, sit yourself down. The scones are still warm, though I'm not going to promise that they'll be as good as the ones Mary bakes. It takes me all my time to make decent pastry. This is the first time I've tried my hand at scones.'

'Oh, so I'm to be the guinea pig, am I?'

'I'll nurse you if you become ill.'

Now why had she said that?

'I wish I could believe that was a promise,' he said quietly.

Now who was faking it? What if she said it really was a promise? She could hardly administer loving care if she were here and he was thousands of miles away.

They had their coffee and Toby had said he really liked his scone.

'You sure you wouldn't like another one?'

He laughed, a lovely deep, warm laugh. 'I can see from here that you've already spent time doing a whole host of vegetables for lunch, are you trying to fatten me up?'

'You're only going to get an omelette to go with the vegetables.'

'Fine,' he said, as he crossed one leg over the other and leant back in his chair.

He looked so right sitting there, but there was a strained pause until Kate asked, 'Wouldn't you like to go into the other room? The fire has been alight for ages, so it should be nice and warm.'

'Not unless you're coming with me.' He got to his feet and came round the table and stood looking down at her. Kate felt her heart start to race. 'I have to tell you, I've fallen in love with you,' Toby said, and he meant every word of it.

Every fibre of Kate's being was urging her to tell him she loved him, to grab whatever he was offering. Even half a loaf is better than no bread at all, especially to a starving man. I may not be a man, but I am starving, that's for sure. I've never known love! Never known what it feels like to be the most important human being in any one person's life. I'm tired of being lonely. She said all this to herself as she led the way down the hall, wondering how to manage the rest of the day, and if she had got herself into a whole lot more than she was capable of handling.

They sat side by side on the big sofa and when Toby put his arm around her and pulled her close it seemed the most natural thing in the world. He made her feel very feminine, warm and safe, as if this was how it should be.

She felt wanted. Truly loved. Kate moved into him. She could smell his nice fresh shaving soap, a manly smell. His lips moved over her cheeks, then onto her lips, soft, gentle and warm. She responded until minutes later her kisses were as fierce as his had become.

He raised his head to draw breath and Kate lay curled up in his arms like a well-contented cat. Finally, he slid from his seat, got to his feet and pulled her up. Without saying a word they lay down on the rug in front of the fire and, tucking a cushion beneath her head, he balanced himself on one elbow and stared down into her lovely face. Kate became nervous. She had no idea what to do, how to respond to the flood of strange and wonderful sensations sweeping over her. Would he know that she had no experience with men? Would he mind?

His touch was gentle, pleasing, incredible. She couldn't bring herself to stop him now. She didn't want to. It was as if she was dreaming it all. Her clothes came off, slowly, bit by bit and then both of them were naked. For the very first time in her life she was lying in the arms of a man who was whispering everything she had ever longed to hear. It was the most wonderful sensation she had ever experienced. Toby released her, and held himself just above her and she felt his warm flesh rubbing against hers. As he moved, he first kissed her lips, then her ears, then his tongue licked her bare shoulders moving along down her arm. She was in heaven. Floating.

'Oh, Toby,' she whispered, over and over again.

It was a gentle, tender lovemaking. When it came to an end, Kate could not have described her feelings out loud, not even to save her soul.

More than an hour later they were still lying side by

side, her head on his chest, his hand tangled in her thick hair. Morning had given way to early afternoon. He raised himself slightly and, looking straight into her eyes, said, 'This is what I've been searching for all my life. Someone as sweet and pure as you. After the fiasco of my marriage I became cynical, I trusted no one and I used people. People who had been good friends. I'm not proud of the fact, Kate, I just did not believe that there was any one on this earth like you.' He paused to gently kiss her cheek. 'I was the first! I can't believe that you have gone through life untouched. What of the men in your life? Were they blind? I didn't want to fall in love with you, but I have and I want you to know, whatever happens, it is a deep and lasting love which will stand the test of time.'

'You know so very little about me, there are things perhaps I should tell you.'

'Hush. Hush.' Toby smiled, hugging her tighter. 'Tomorrow we'll talk. I promise. There are things I must say to you and you to me, but they can wait. Today is ours! There is no one else in our world today, just you and me. Does that sound right?'

'Fine,' she agreed, thinking that for once the angels were on her side.

When they were dressed and back in the kitchen the fire had burnt low and the rain was still lashing against the window panes.

'Kate, I have to tell you one thing.' He smiled at her as she fussed with the vegetables and saucepans.

'Yes?' She half turned towards him. Oh, God, I really do love him, she thought. His hair was ruffled, his shirt unbuttoned and he looked so at home here in the kitchen.

'I'm starving.'

'In this household if one works we all work. So, mister, the fire needs to be made up and the table set, for what I fear is a very belated lunch.'

'Yes, ma'am.' He touched his finger to his forehead giving her a mock salute, before striding across the floor to stand at her side.

'Payment in advance please,' he begged.

Smiling, she held up her face to be kissed.

As he held her he was silent, full of thought. God, she is beautiful. She has a freshness about her that I can't explain. It's not only her looks or even her big brown eyes, but somehow the whole of her.

She made to break away, then she hesitated, looked up into his face, and said, 'Thank you, Toby.'

'Oh, my darling, what have you to thank me for?'

Her eyes were bright with unshed tears. 'Because you've made me feel loved, wanted, and so much more.'

'Oh, Kate, Kate.' He pulled her back into his arms, holding her gently, saying, 'I can't believe this, you know, I can't believe it. What if we had never met?'

'But we have, and I, too, am finding it hard to believe.'

'There's only one thing I find wrong with you, Kate Kearsley, you take an awfully long time to feed a starving man!'

Her jaw dropped, then, as she playfully slapped him, they both burst out laughing.

'Move yourself! Make the fire up, and set the table and the food won't be long.'

'Exactly what I was going to do ten minutes ago if

you hadn't distracted me, but I'll get my own back after we've eaten.'

She closed her eyes in anticipation and broke eggs into a basin, all the while sending up a silent prayer of thanks that Toby had been sent to help set up a pharmacy in Kingston Hospital.

Chapter Twenty-Four

TOBY MADE UP his mind to do as little work as possible for the remainder of his stay in Surrey. And except for the necessary jobs around the house, Kate lived only for the moment when he arrived on her doorstep. Wednesday had been spent much as Tuesday had been. The two of them stayed indoors, mostly making love.

On Thursday morning, bright and early they set off in his car to Box Hill, a well-known beauty spot and a favourite with courting couples. Holding hands they stood looking up at the great grassy hill.

'How high do you think it is?' he asked.

'It's about six hundred feet to the top. I've walked this hill so many times with my father. Come on, it's not too steep and the view is fantastic. Besides the climb does have its compensations.'

'Which are?'

'There's a pub right at the top. The Hand-in-Hand.'

'Well, what are we waiting for?'

They took their time, Kate stopped every now and then to pick a long strand of grass which she chewed between her teeth. The ground was too wet for them to sit on, so on reaching the top they made for the pub where Toby fetched her a glass of shandy and a beer for himself. As they were both wearing topcoats and had long scarves around their necks they stayed outside in the fresh air, seating themselves at one of the rustic tables. They could hear voices in the distance but close by there were no other couples.

'Lucky today, aren't we,' Kate said, lifting her face up to let the sun shine on her cheeks.

'Yes, we are. But there's not much warmth in the sun yet. I don't think we'll want to sit still for too long.'

They were silent, yet they knew they needed to talk, although, so far, they had been avoiding it.

'What are we going to do?' Toby asked quietly.

Kate remained silent, torn apart. Then, she spoke in a whisper, 'Before we decide anything you should know about my parents.'

'The first morning we met, didn't you tell me they were both dead and that was the reason you had moved into Melbourne Lodge to take care of Joshua?'

'Yes. What I failed to tell you was the manner in which they died.'

Toby looked concerned. 'You don't have to tell me anything. It won't make a scrap of difference to the love I feel for you.'

'I do have to make all the facts known to you. There is no other way I can deal with it.'

'Kate,' he leant towards her and took one of her hands and held it between his, 'Kate, my darling, there is no

266

longer you and me. There is just us. After what you have given me I would go to the ends of the earth for you. Christ, how can I make you believe that I love you more deeply than I ever imagined it was possible for one person to love another? Whatever you have to tell me, well, it simply cannot alter that fact.'

She believed him, mainly because she so desperately needed to. So, she began to tell him her history. During the telling, there came into her mind distorted and painful pictures of those years. No matter how desperately she tried to put these unbearable memories behind her, there always seemed to come a time when they surfaced.

'I could never have lived with the notoriety that followed if Mr Collier hadn't offered me a haven at Melbourne Lodge,' she ended on a pitiful note.

'My poor Kate,' he murmured, his voice thick with sympathy. 'Sins of the fathers come home to roost on the children, we are taught. Never seems fair to me. My father had been married before he met my mother. He was older than her by fifteen years. When she had me it was his first child and the fact that she had given him a son was something that gave him a new lease of life. He died when I was seventeen years old. My mother never married again. Five years ago I was in Canada when she suffered a stroke and died the same day. I only just made it home for her funeral.'

'A sad story,' Kate said, with feeling. 'But nothing like the horror story my early life turned into. No need for you to wonder now why men have never wanted anything to do with me.'

'Their loss and my gain, my darling. Now I know God

in his heaven has been saving you just for me, and . . .' he stopped talking as he reached out, this time to catch hold of both her hands '. . . If you think what you've told me changes anything then you are wrong. Totally wrong!'

The landlord came out into the grounds at that moment and stood staring up at the sky.

Kate leant into Toby and very quietly said, 'You're a lucky man, because if that gentleman hadn't come out when he did I would have thrown myself at you. And by the way, I would like to make another point clear.'

'I'll keep you to what I think you have just promised me and, as to your point, be my guest, go ahead,' he teased.

'I love you, Toby. I think I'm coming round to believe as you do – we were meant to meet.'

Toby couldn't have cared less if the whole world had been watching at that moment. He got to his feet, almost dragging Kate up and into his arms and placed his lips gently on hers in what she was to think was the sweetest lingering kiss any girl had ever received. Afterwards they held tightly on to each other as they made their way down the sloping path.

He took her for lunch at the inn near Burford Bridge, which stood at the foot of Box Hill, and held her hands across the table. The few other diners on this weekday smiled, there was no disguising the love he felt for her; it was on his face for everyone to see.

Back home, Kate was disappointed when he said he wouldn't come into the house.

'This evening's meeting is a must for me.'

She accepted his explanation but still didn't like it;

she'd had visions of them spending the whole night together. But what could she do?

'Tell you what,' he said, releasing his hold on her, 'why don't I come to breakfast in the morning? I shall be here before you're even up in the morning and after I have told you yet again how much I love you, we have to get down to some serious talking. Agreed?'

Kate stared directly into his eyes. 'Yes,' she replied, smiling thinly.

'Good. It will be easier for both of us when we come to a decision.'

Several seconds ticked by as he kissed her yet again, then as he turned to go, he said, 'You'll never know how reluctant I am to leave you, Kate. And that's the truth.'

He walked to his car. She heard the door click shut, the engine fire, and she was standing alone, staring at an empty driveway.

Kate couldn't sleep. Her thoughts were almost frightening and she wished she could stop thinking about tomorrow and the decisions she was going to have to make. She had suffered before. Gone through hell at times. But this was different. It was a new experience and she was driven mad by the pain of loving Toby, knowing that he was going to have to leave her after such a short time together. It was a hopeless situation.

The damp mists of early morning lay low over the river. She placed the vase of freshly picked spring flowers on the window sill just as Toby turned the car into the drive. He was as good as his word, the time was twenty minutes past six.

They ate a full cooked breakfast, acting just as any married couple might, with Toby getting up to bring the teapot to the table and then returning to kneel in front of the glowing range to make toast, using the long-handled toasting fork to spike the thick slices of bread. Both of them knew they were being overpolite. With the table cleared and the washing up done there was no way of avoiding the inevitable.

It was Toby who spoke first. 'I have just four more days, including today. I have to be back in Bristol next Tuesday, and by the following weekend I leave for Cape Town.'

Kate remained silent, her face a picture of utter despair.

'Kate, you must tell me, what would you like to do?'

'I don't know,' she said softly. Raising her eyes to meet his, she added, 'That's not true, of course I know what I'd like to do, but what I *can* do is something entirely different, isn't it.'

'Look, I do have to go on this assignment, it's a long-term thing which is going to involve a great deal of research, I can't walk away. If you say you'll marry me now I'll set the wheels in motion this morning, get a special licence, see to travel arrangements – and we can leave together. It won't be easy, but I'll move heaven and earth to get it done.'

'Oh, Toby! You've just proposed to me!'

'Well?' He looked dumbstruck. 'Whatever else did you think I had in mind? You will marry me, won't you? Please, Kate.'

'Nothing would give me greater pleasure. But I can't. Joshua has no one but me. He understands that I am not his real mother but he feels and thinks of me as such. If I were to up sticks and leave him now, he wouldn't understand, not in a million years. He'd have no way of dealing with it.'

'Are you telling me that these days have meant nothing to you? You could let me go, just like that?'

'I don't see that I have any option. Josh is only a small boy, his world revolves around me. This is his home and I have to be here when he has his school holidays.'

'Did his father leave this property to him? Do you live here free in return for services to his illegitimate son?'

Kate couldn't believe that she had heard him right! His tone of voice had been so harsh.

'It isn't like that at all,' she declared hotly. 'This house was left to me with no strings attached whatsoever. And Joshua is well taken care of. Charles Collier made me Joshua's guardian, a fact of which I am very proud. As to needing free lodgings, I own a house my parents left me, another house and a plot of ground my grandmother left me and, incidentally, a very prosperous boat yard situated at Hampton Court.'

As Kate brought her outburst to an end, Toby looked at her in amazement. He shook his head, and half smiled. 'My, my! I should have known with all that red in your hair you were bound to have a temper.'

'So you're surprised, are you? You insult me and expect me to take it lying down.'

He started to apologise, but Kate stopped him. 'I'm not finished yet. You coming into my life is probably the most wonderful thing that ever happened to me and I thank God for every minute we've spent together. It seems I've misjudged you, though. I thought you were sensitive, kind, aware of, and caring for my feelings, as well as your own. You live an adventurous life and I shall treasure the fact that you asked me to marry you and share that life until the end of my days. My life must seem lonely to you, boring even, taking care of a little boy who isn't even my own flesh and blood, but I took the job on and Joshua has become my son in every sense of the word. I have a responsibility here. To walk away and leave him is something I could not bring myself to do. It would destroy him. As much as I love you, Toby, and want to be with you wherever you are, I couldn't do it. And you wouldn't respect me if I did.

'Just imagine if we were together in South Africa and I somehow got to hear that Joshua was ill. How do you think that would make me feel?'

Toby was silent. He knew he had overstepped the mark. He understood what she was saying about responsibilities and guilt. He knew she was right. She was good and loyal. It only served to make him love her even more. He got to his feet, walked to the window and, looking out, fought with himself, fought to believe that she was right but wanting to fight to keep her for himself. Never had he expected to find anyone like her. He had loved her from the moment he had set eyes on her. He had to go to South Africa, his job demanded it. How can I leave her? he asked himself over and over again.

Kate had a quiet power that pulled at his heart strings whenever he gazed into her big, dark brown eyes. It sounded daft, even to himself, yet it felt as though she had been secretly waiting for him all her life. She had known great tragedy; it showed in her face at times. She had devoted her life to bringing up a little boy and he was sure she loved the child with all her heart. But what of her own happiness? He would give an awful lot to be able to take her with him into his life, keep hold of her and never let her go.

He turned round to see that her head was lowered and her shoulders shaking. She was crying. In a second he was beside her and they held each other for a long time.

'Kate, I'm sorry, so sorry. I was hateful, I know I was. It's the thought of losing you. It wouldn't be a picnic if you did come with me, I shall have miles of travelling to do, but at least you'd be there. Oh, Kate, Kate, what shall we do? I shall be gone for two years at least, and if the project doesn't prove straightforward, it could be a lot longer. So much can happen in that length of time.'

'I must go and wash my face.' Kate sniffed and took herself off to the bathroom.

He had made a fresh pot of tea and was sitting at the kitchen table when she came back. She went to him and he opened his arms; she buried her face in his neck. They clung to each other for what seemed an endless time.

Kate felt she ought to thank him for taking her to heights she had never known existed, for helping her to discover feelings he had aroused by merely tracing his fingers across her bare flesh, for understanding her ignorance, for being so nice. No, not nice, wonderful. For everything. For being him and for wanting her.

Finally he broke away.

'I think it best if we part now, Kate. I couldn't bear any more days with you, knowing the end was in sight.'

She nodded, beginning to cry again. Although there were tears in his eyes, he kept smiling that lovely endearing smile of his.

'I might even leave for Bristol the day after tomorrow. Tie up all the loose ends and be on my way. Is it all right if I write to you sometimes? Not yet, not until I reach Cape Town and see what lies ahead from there.'

'I'd like that,' Kate said, wiping her eyes on a scrap of handkerchief she pulled from her cardigan pocket. 'Joshua would save the stamps and if you could send him a coloured postcard now and again that would really please him.'

'Kind of keep in with my rival, is that what you mean?'

Kate made no answer and they both smiled.

'I shall be around all tomorrow and maybe the next day – it depends. If you do want to see me or just talk, telephone the hospital.'

She knew she would be tempted a dozen times to ring him while he was still in Surrey but she hoped with all her heart that she would be strong enough to resist.

He wound his scarf around his neck and shrugged himself into his coat.

Don't let him go, her mind raged at her. It's the first chance you've ever had to make a life for yourself. For *you* to be happy. You'll never get another.

Taking her hand, Toby walked through the spacious entrance hall to the front door. He kissed her gently and opening the door, stepped out on to the gravel, then he turned, stepped back inside and held her again for several minutes. Neither of them said a word. Kate couldn't have if she had wanted to. They simply stood there, holding onto each other as if their very lives depended upon it. He released her, holding her at arm's length. Tears were running down his cheeks and Kate's vision of him was blurred because the same thing was happening to her.

He put a foot over the step, and when Kate made to follow him, he whispered, 'Don't come outside, please. Just stay where you are.' Turning, he walked slowly away.

She waited until she could no longer hear the sound of the car, then closed the big oak door.

She had made her decision. But at this moment she wasn't sure it had been the right one.

Chapter Twenty-Five

IT WAS NINE o'clock on Easter Saturday morning and Kate had a smile on her face as she watched Joshua tucking into his porridge.

'What's to follow?' he asked with a grin.

'Grilled bacon and sausages.' Kate's expression was full of love. She felt more relaxed and in a much happier frame of mind than she had for days. Joshua was home and the house had come alive again.

He took his empty bowl and placed it on the draining board, picked up an oven cloth and withdrew his breakfast plate from the oven and took it back to the table. 'Beats a school breakfast any day of the week.'

'Well, to look at you this morning no one would believe you're the same lad who arrived home here three days ago looking so spic an' span. You look positively shaggy.'

'Makes a change,' he replied cheerfully.

He had discarded his school uniform and was wearing

long corduroy trousers and a scruffy, ancient jersey that Mary had knitted for him. His blond hair had grown slightly darker, cut short at the back and sides but kept longer on top, it flopped over his forehead and he pushed the fingers of one hand through it when he realised Kate was watching him. He finished his cooked breakfast and began to spread marmalade onto a slice of toast.

'Would you like a cup of tea, Mum? I'll make a pot if you would.'

'Yes, please, that would be nice. Bring the tray over here by the window, we haven't really had a chance to talk yet. I'm dying to hear what's gone on during term time. Have you made any arrangements to meet your mates?'

'I did invite Nick Banks to drop in if he were over this way, I wrote to you about him. I also phoned Pete Bradley and we've agreed to meet up on Monday.'

'I'd bet a pound to a penny I can guess where that meeting place is going to be. It's all right, Jack Stuart is expecting us on Monday and, yes, the boat yard will be open.'

She turned her chair round to face the window. Joshua drew up a side table and poured tea for each of them, before settling himself down on a low stool. For the next half an hour she listened, as he told her what a smashing form master Mr Holmes was and how pleased he had been with Josh's examination results. Then he got on to the success, or sometimes otherwise, of the school rugby team.

'Heavens! All that energy. You must sleep well at night.'

'I do, an' while I've got your full attention I'd like to ask you a couple of things.'

'Oh, you would, would you? That sounds threatening. But come on, let's hear them.'

'First, before I go back, would you give some thought as to whether I can ask a couple of form mates to stay here during the summer holidays? The lads think it's great that we live so near the river and by then I shall probably have my own boat.'

'That is no problem. It will give me great pleasure to have your friends stay here just so long as they have their parents' permission,' Kate answered. 'Now the other request is?'

'Please may I have two more pairs of long trousers? I know the regulation form stated we required one long pair and two short pairs of trousers for new boys in their first term, but honestly, none of us wear the short grey flannel ones, our knees get cold.'

Laughing, Kate got out of her chair and wrapped her arms around him. Josh wriggled free, a crooked smile on his lips and a mischievous gleam in his eye.

'Can I take it that's a yes as well?'

Still laughing loudly, Kate picked up the tea tray and walked across to the sink. 'Yes, we'll go into Kingston and buy you long trousers but don't give me all that nonsense about cold knees. You just want to make out you're older than you really are.'

Mid-morning, on a bright Easter Bank Holiday Monday, the river was a magic place to be. The early low-lying mist had dispersed, giving way to clear blue skies. Standing beside Jack Stuart, Kate observed the ever-changing scene from the slipway of the Kearsley Boat Yard. She relaxed in the overwhelming holiday atmosphere. She was lucky to have Jack as manager of the yard and, today, she was doubly thankful as she watched Joshua and his friend Peter, together with Bert Lewis, an employee, climb down into the launch, start the engine and set off up the river.

Joshua raised his hand to her, his expression a mixture of suppressed excitement at the prospect of a trip out in a boat and disappointment that his own boat had not yet been finished.

It was great to have Josh at home. She wouldn't want to live through the last few days again, not for a king's ransom. The first day after Toby had left she must have picked up the telephone a dozen times, only to replace it quickly. 'If you only want to talk,' he had said, and she did, so very badly. Tell him she loved him so. Ask him not to leave her. What good would it have done? Somehow she had got through those days until Joshua had come home.

Joshua's Easter holiday break had gone by so quickly. There was no doubt that even one term in the first form of an all-boys school had worked wonders for him. It had changed him from a shy adolescent to a self-assured, interesting young man.

'I can't believe it,' Kate told Mary over the telephone, 'he's grown so much, and you should have seen him working in the boat yard. No half-measures, proper boots, brown overalls, mostly covered in varnish. And I didn't see him at all one day, Jack Stuart took him off to visit two other yacht brokers up river. He came back full of it.'

'Kate, I hope to be coming home the week before

Whitsun. Blanche has made friends with Lily Evans, the lady I hired to be housekeeper. In fact they get on so well together I'm beginning to think that I'm in the way here. Another good point is they both like Nurse Jones so, all in all, it's a load off my shoulders and I feel I shall be leaving my sister in very capable hands.'

'Oh, Mary,' Kate had breathed so sadly down the line that Mary quickly asked, 'Is there something wrong? Has anything happened while I've been away?'

If only I could tell you, Kate thought clutching the telephone receiver so tightly that her knuckles showed white. She wanted to blurt out, I met a man, a man who loved me. A man who taught me what it was like to be a woman. He was kind, someone who didn't think my past made me a freak. Someone I spent only a few days with, just a few days, when what I really wanted was to spend the rest of my life with him. But I had to let him go.

Instead, she said, 'The house is just so big and empty with both you and Joshua away.' Then doing her best to put a smile into her voice, 'You've made my day, Mary. Just telling me it will only be a matter of weeks now before you're home. I can't bring Josh to the phone, he's off round at Peter Bradley's house but I will get him to ring you before he goes back to school.'

It was a horrible day, even for March. Mr Weatherford honked the horn of his car to announce his arrival then tactfully busied himself out of earshot.

In the front porch, away from the drizzling rain, Kate and Joshua faced each other.

'This is it then. Back to the grindstone for you.'

'Yes.' Josh seemed happy enough. 'I know the rules now, I'm not stepping out into the unknown like last term.'

'You would tell me if you had any problems, wouldn't you?'

'Yes.' He was quite adamant. 'And, Mum, I do feel better knowing Nanna will be home soon. I didn't like to think of you here all on your own.'

Oh, he was such a loving little boy. Only she hadn't better air such thoughts to him. Grown up now, he considered he was, and the very thought brought tears to Kate's eyes. Still, I'm allowed to be sentimental today of all days, and I'm not the only mother, I bet. Children returning to school left an empty house and an ache in one's heart.

'Bye, Josh.'

'Goodbye, Mum.'

'I love you.'

'I love you too,' he told her, holding up his face for her kiss.

Then he stood back, staring at her with that funny little grin of his, turned away, and ran towards the car.

Kate wept a little as she went back inside the house, telling herself not to be such a fool. It was right and sensible for Josh to be away at school, enjoying the company of boys of his own age. She was lucky to have had him for as long as she had and come what may she mustn't ever make the mistake of trying to hold onto him. There was a great big world out there and the more his mind was stimulated, the more he would want to get out and discover what was on offer for himself.

Kate made tea, and when it had stood for a few

minutes she poured herself a cup and carried it to the windowseat from where she could look out at the garden sloping down from the back of the house. It was hard for her not to feel empty and bereft. For once she allowed herself to wallow in self-pity. Everybody wins but me, she decided sadly.

Chapter Twenty-Six

KATE HAD SAT up late thinking. She'd had another letter from Cooper and Dawes asking what she intended to do about her inheritance. It appeared that they had a client willing to purchase the ground on which her grandmother's house stood, and the land beyond. Bit of a cheek considering she had never expressed any intentions of disposing of Alice's property. Ideas about what she might do with it had been rattling about in her head for ages now. She would have liked someone, especially Mary, to have sat down with her and let her air her thoughts, get another opinion. She smiled to herself. Would someone else's views have made any difference? She very much doubted it.

She had sat at the kitchen table, her chin resting on her elbows. All round her were sheets of paper covered with scribbled drawings and lists of suggestions. She wasn't going to give up until she had come to some kind of a decision. There were at least three options.

She could sell the old property and the land, invest the money and carry on life as usual. But didn't she have more than enough money already?

She could sell up and invest the money in Joshua's name But again, his father had left him very well provided for.

She rather thought she'd have to take advice on the third option. If it were at all possible this was the one she'd like to go ahead with.

I'll not go back to Cooper and Dawes, she'd decided. That fellow gave me the creeps.

First thing in the morning she'd telephone Mr Weatherford and make an appointment to go and see him. Yes, he'd know what to do, and he could also have the job of notifying the other firm that in future he and his partners would be acting on all matters concerning her gran's estate.

Mr Weatherford listened, without once making a comment, to all that Kate had said. He glanced across his deck to where she sat. He couldn't for the life of him put a finger on it but there was no mistaking the difference in her. She was smartly dressed, in a business-like tailored suit, but then when hadn't she dressed well for the appropriate occasion? No. It was more than that. She had a new air of self-confidence, she held her head up higher. He had always admired her. The way she had coped with the adversity life had thrown at her when she'd been little more than a slip of a girl had earned her a good reputation – at least in the minds of people who mattered.

'Kate, let me run the outline of your proposition by

you one more time. Just to make sure that I have the facts right.'

'Please do, Mr Weatherford. I'd like to hear some-one else voice them out loud. These plans have run through my head so many times that even I wouldn't give odds against their survival, always supposing that we do eventually manage to get them off the ground.'

'Your wish is to create something worthwhile from your grandmother's estate. Something that others less fortune than yourself might benefit from.'

'Yes, that's the rough idea.'

Mr Weatherford sorted the sheets of paper on which he had made notes into some kind of order. 'You'd like to set up a mission, to be consolidated and strengthened under a united management of both men and women, the idea being primarily a dwelling place for the handi-capped and poor people of Kingston. You would seek other investors and fund raisers for the financing of such a project. Is that correct?'

'Partly,' Kate agreed in a solemn voice. 'It wouldn't only be for residents of Kingston, all deserving cases would be considered. And not all cases would need to be residents. I'd like to see a kind of family place, offering all sorts of services and facilities, to both the young and the old. Not an asylum or an institution, not even an old folk's home.'

Mr Weatherford concealed a smile. She was aiming not only for the moon but the stars and the sky to go with it.

Kate uncrossed her legs and leant forward. 'I thought that if we attracted enough money we could have the main building erected at one end of the field that lies beyond the house, which would be for long-term residents; at the other end, perhaps a small block of dwellings where needy folk or maybe people who had been ill could holiday or convalesce. Then, rather than demolish Gran's house, renovate it and possibly use it to house the matron, because we would need a matron or maybe two, someone on duty at all times, wouldn't you think?'

The stern-faced solicitor, flung down his pen, threw back his head and roared with laughter.

'Kate. Kate!' For a long time now he had dropped the Miss Kearsley and if he weren't so hide-bound by his profession he felt, at that moment, he would be on his feet, round his desk, sweeping this adorable lass up into his arms. She was something else and then some! 'In theory it is a great and worthwhile idea. One that would, without a doubt, persuade many businessmen to contribute. However, the amount of hurdles you would have to overcome and the shackles that would have to be shed . . .' he paused '. . . you don't have any idea!'

'But it is feasible?'

'Oh, it's feasible all right. All we need is several rich benefactors and God on our side.'

They both laughed.

'You've hooked me, young Kate. I'll throw my hat in with you. But the first thing we have to do is convince the council that the idea is so good that they dare not refuse us planning permission.'

'You think they might?' Kate asked in disbelief.

'Nothing's for certain where the council is concerned.' He paused again, smiled knowingly and tapped the side of his nose, 'I've just had a wicked thought. There's more than one way to skin a cat and what we'll do is practise being a little bit devious, how does that sound to you?'

'Just tell me what I have to do.' She was beginning to enjoy herself.

'Well, I have a young friend who is an ambitious reporter on the *Surrey Comet*, and I think you should invite him to visit you one morning. Then, should it so happen that while you were drinking coffee together you were to make known to him what generous plans you have in mind for the property and ground left to you by your grandmother, he might feel he could make use of that item of news, which would be all to the good. And incidentally, it would do no harm for the young reporter to learn that Mrs Kearsley lived the whole of her life in Kingston and was a well-known figure in the market, braving all weathers right up almost until the day that she died. Well . . . what do you think?'

'Mr Weatherford! I think I'm going to enjoy being devious. If the whole town is showing approval of a plan for which there is not yet an architect or an application for planning permission . . . well!'

'So, shall I ask my friendly young reporter to telephone you?'

Kate's eyes twinkled. 'Please do, I shall forward to his call.'

'By the way, I've been meaning to ask you, how did your Christmas experiment go?'

'It got off on a shaky footing but, as a whole, it went well. Everyone appeared to have a great Christmas. With hindsight it was asking a lot – those children were like fish out of water to begin with.'

'So, you won't be asking more families to stay at Melbourne Lodge?'

Kate looked a bit downcast. 'I'm still thinking about that. Seeing as how it was partly Mr Collier's suggestion I'd feel guilty if I let the whole thing drop, but on the other hand I'm not sure it was fair to Joshua.'

'Did the lad not fit in?'

'Oh, it wasn't that,' Kate hastened to assure him. 'Joshua was fine. He did his best to set the boys at ease and was particularly good with the little girl. No, I just felt that it *is* Joshua's home and, especially at holiday times, he shouldn't be asked to share it with strangers. More so now he is away at school. He has already asked me if he may invite some of his friends to stay with us during the summer holidays.'

'And have you agreed?'

'Of course I have. It will be great. I had thought that maybe I could use Bramble Cottage as a holiday home for needy families. Seems a bit selfish to keep it for myself when I have so much, though Mary and I go there often together. What d'you think?'

Mr Weatherford took off his horn-rimmed glasses, rubbed his eyes and, for a minute or two, sat quietly staring at Kate, wondering if she felt she had a price to pay for what her mother had done?

'Kate,' he said at last, 'if you get this scheme off the ground, I think you will be making a great contribution to the community. Leave it at that for the time being, let's see how things go. In the meantime, I want you to know that I'm here at any time. Any matter, large or small, come and discuss it with me. I would like to feel that you can look upon me not only as a trustee for

Joshua's affairs but as a friend to you both. Will you promise me that?'

'Thank you,' Kate murmured. 'I can't tell you how grateful I am for all you've done for me.'

'I'm delighted that Mr Collier saw fit to leave his affairs in my hands. Have you had news of Mrs Kennedy recently?'

'Yes I have, we speak on the telephone frequently. She will be coming home quite soon now.'

'That is good news. Give her my regards, I'm sure we shall meet up again soon.' There was a twinkle in his eye as he added, 'Mrs Kennedy will want to be involved in the matter of utilising your grandmother's property, don't you think?'

Smiling happily, Kate got to her feet. 'When I outline our plans to Mary it will take an army to keep her out of the front line. Goodbye, Mr Weatherford, and again, thank you.'

'Goodbye Kate. I'll seek out a good architect and get some plans drawn up, and I'll keep you posted. Take care and remember what I've said.'

Mr Weatherford watched as Kate set off down Kingston High Street. What a remarkable young lady, he thought as he went back inside his office.

All the way home Kate felt optimistic. Mr Weatherford had been so encouraging. If all went well she would have plenty to occupy her mind for months to come. If even half her plans got off the ground she wouldn't be bored, and she felt that Alice would approve wholeheartedly. She kept that thought uppermost in her mind as she took off her jacket and carefully hung it inside the wardrobe. Closing the door, she caught a glimpse of the bed reflected in the full-length mirror.

Oh, Toby! In this very bed she had lain in his arms, and had feelings that she still couldn't describe, even to herself. It was five weeks now since they had said goodbye and there wasn't an hour of the day when she didn't think about him. Where was he? What was he doing?

He hadn't called her before he'd left Surrey or written so much as a postcard since. Every time the phone rang she prayed that it might be him. What if it had been? What would he say to her or she to him? She thought he had understood her feelings about Joshua, but had he really? She couldn't have agreed to share his life because of the complications it would cause. She had taken the only possible decision, but it didn't stop her yearning for the one man who had made her feel a woman. God, she loved him so!

She went downstairs and sat at the kitchen table. There was no food on it. Not even a tablecloth. If Mary were here things would be different. At this time in the afternoon, tea would be set out with a plate of scones, warm from the oven, home-made jam and dainty sandwiches. On her own she never bothered; there didn't seem much point cooking and baking just for one's self.

The jangling of the telephone made her jump. What if . . . oh, don't be so daft, get up and go and answer it or whoever it is will hang up.

'Melbourne Lodge,' she said, her heart hammering so hard against her ribs she thought the caller must be able to hear it.

'Kate, it's Mary. I'm ringing to tell you I'm catching

a train first thing in the morning. I shall be in London by twelve thirty. I don't know about connections down to Kingston but I'll ring you from the station.'

'Oh, Mary love, that's wonderful! The best possible news. Don't worry, I'll be at Euston to meet you. It's been so long I can't wait to see you.'

The sound of Mary's laughter came down the line. 'Hang on, Kate, I'm thrilled to hear you're so pleased I'm coming home but there's no need for you to travel up to London to meet the train.'

'Oh, yes, there is. You'll never know. I'll be there. And, Mary, I'm going to buy you the biggest and the best meal that London can provide. See you tomorrow.'

Kate was laughing as she put the phone back on its hook.

What a place, Kate exclaimed to herself as she walked towards the destination board at Euston. The walls were grimed with soot, the very air smelt of smoke and endless pigeons swooped down to gather up any morsel of food they could find and then flew over people's heads to land high up in the metal girders that supported the roof. Everyone was in such a hurry. The clatter and the clanging and loud voices shouting for porters!

Where we live is another world. I'd go so far as to say that there's not a dozen Londoners who have even heard of Littleton Green. Perhaps that's a reason for me to feel grateful. Kate made her way to the platform where Mary's train had already pulled in. She quickened her steps, scanning the passengers, and spotted Mary walking up the platform, lugging her two suitcases. She hurried to meet her.

'Mary! Over here. God, I've missed you,' she said, hugging her friend close. 'I can't tell you how glad I am to see you.' They broke free and Kate held her at arm's length. 'I can't believe it. Wales must have suited you. You look terrific! You've had your hair done – it's all wavy – and a smart new coat!'

'Don't go on so,' Mary said. 'And come to that there's something different about you, young lady. You're turned out as if you were paying a visit to Buckingham Palace.'

'Better than that. I've come to fetch my friend home. The best friend it's possible to have. I mean that. I really have missed you and so did Josh. He sends his love and said you'd better be at home for his next holiday or he'd come down to Wales to fetch you himself. He even told Peter that the reason there weren't any home-made cakes was because his nanna was away.'

'Oh, bless his heart. Was he well? Was he happy?'

'Yes, to both questions and I think it's about time we made a move, we're getting some dirty looks because we're blocking the platform.'

They each picked up a case and started to walk.

'Catch a train straight home or go to a posh restaurant where we can have lunch first?' Kate asked.

'What d'you think?' Mary said. 'I seem to remember you promised me the best lunch in town.'

'Right. You're on. Let's head for the taxi rank.'

Chapter Twenty-Seven

MARY WAS IRONING. Although the April morning was overcast, threatening showers, the big kitchen was cheerful, with the coal fire burning brightly and the table covered with a red chenille cloth, a vase of fresh flowers placed in the centre.

'It's rough out there,' Kate said, coming in the back door. She had been hanging out more washing and Mary smiled at her as strands of her hair blew across her glowing cheeks. 'You sounded happy, Mary. I heard you singing as I was wiping my feet.'

'I am happy. Glad to be home with you,' she replied as she lifted a blouse from the ironing board and hung it carefully on a coat-hanger.

Kate stared at her and lifted her eyebrows. She could have sworn that Mary's mind was far away. She kicked off her garden shoes and watched as Mary took another blouse from the pile in the ironing basket and spread it out. Dipping her fingers into a basin of cold water, she sprinkled little drops up and down the cotton material and began to swish the flat iron gently to and fro. All the time she was humming to herself.

'It's more than you just being glad to be home. You're positively glowing, and I'd like to know why.'

Mary dithered and Kate watched her with growing puzzlement. She was blushing! 'Mary! You're keeping something from me. You've been home two days now and thinking back you've been hinting and smiling knowingly all the time. Are you going to tell me what you're up to?'

'While I was at my sister's I met a man,' Mary blurted the words out, and looked at Kate in alarm. 'Oh, bother! I wasn't going to tell you. Not yet.'

'Why ever not?' Kate cried indignantly.

'Oh, Kate! Dear Kate!' Suddenly Mary looked so sad. 'I shan't blame you if you tell me not to be so ridiculous.'

'Why ever would I do something as cruel as that?' Kate asked impatiently.

'He's sixty-five. Just retired. And I'm sixty-one . . .'

Kate went to her and tenderly kissed her cheek. 'What's that got to do with anything? Put that iron down and tell me how you met.'

'He does voluntary work. He came to the house to repair Blanche's wheelchair. His wife died three years ago, they never had any children and he seemed a bit lonely. I went out with him a few times. I don't think my sister entirely approved.'

'And,' Kate prompted.

'And not much else. We have promised to write to each other and he said he'd like to pay a visit to this part of the world when the weather gets better.'

Kate almost ran from the room, and into the front room. Opening the door to the sideboard she seized a bottle and was back in the kitchen within minutes.

'We must drink a toast,' she declared. 'We can't let this moment pass unrecorded.'

Mary fetched two glasses from the dresser, giggling like a schoolgirl as she watched Kate pour sherry into each glass. 'What's the toast?' she asked.

'We're drinking to friendship. No one should be lonely in this world. Here's to . . . you haven't told me his name.'

'Michael, Michael Kendall. He prefers to be called Mike.'

'Raise your glass then. Here's to you and Mike, may you have a long, lasting, happy time together.'

'Don't rush things. We're not as you put it "together", but it would be nice if later on we could find him a small hotel nearby, just let him visit for a few days, meet you and see what you think of him.'

'Oh, Mary, love, we can do better than that. If you'd rather he didn't stay here in the house we can always let him sleep at Bramble Cottage and have his meals here.'

'Thanks, Kate.'

'You're welcome,' Kate told her, taking in her bright eyes and her new hair style. She looked no more than fifty.

For the rest of the day Kate did her best to smile as she listened to Mary tell her what a wonderful man Mike Kendall was. She felt guilty for feeling so envious when Mary was so happy.

Elizabeth Waite

Late that night, when she'd kissed Mary goodnight and they'd each gone to their own bedrooms, Kate marvelled at the change in her. She had known her for so many years and had always presumed she was quite content to be without a man in her life. Today she had seen another side to her character, a side that made her seem so much younger than her years and certainly a great deal happier. What a difference love could make!

Kate wrapped her dressing gown tightly round herself and opened the window wider to let in the cold night air. Why couldn't it have been as easy for her and Toby as it was for Mary and Mike? Why couldn't Toby's job have taken him to somewhere like Wales. Anywhere, just so long as it could have been within the British Isles. As she stared up at the stars, South Africa seemed even further away.

Melbourne Lodge was a hive of activity. It was the Saturday morning of the August Bank Holiday weekend and there were a number of people staying in the house. Three of Joshua's schoolmates, plus Peter Bradley and Mike Kendall, Mary's friend. Even though the windows and the door leading out to the garden were all wide open, the temperature in the kitchen was rising by the minute.

In the dining room, the five boys and Mike Kendall were tucking into a breakfast cooked by Mary. Kate was busy making endless pieces of toast.

Mary now stood at the kitchen table slicing ham from a gammon she had boiled the day before. She was red in the face and perspiring freely.

'Aren't you glad we don't have permanent boarders?' Kate asked.

'I suppose we should have realised that whatever the season, and however hot the weather, men and boys alike enjoy their food. I must say I'm glad it's been agreed that we all spend the day at Hampton Court, at least there should be a breeze coming off the river.'

Kate came back from taking more toast into the dining room and glanced at the wicker backets Mary was putting food into. 'Good God, are you preparing to feed an army?' One basket held savoury rolls and sandwiches, veal and ham pies, Cornish pasties, hard-boiled eggs and enough salad to feed a large family. There had to be a pudding, Mary had declared last night, but Kate wasn't prepared for what she was now looking at: two glass dishes, one containing raspberry trifle, the other fresh fruit, sliced and set into jelly. There was also a Madeira cake and a Victoria jam sponge.

'Just so we don't forget, be a dear and fetch the apple tarts – they're on the slate shelf of the larder. They should be cool enough to pack now. And while you're there bring in the napkins and the cloth that we use for outdoors, will you, please?'

Kate shook her head in disbelief and out loud called over her shoulder, 'What would we have done if Mike hadn't driven up from Wales? As it is, he'll have to make two trips. He can't get us all in his car at once.'

'Don't worry, Josh has already asked Mike to take them first, which I'm grateful for. It will give us time to clear up and get our breath back.'

The kitchen door opened; Mary looked up and immediately smiled her delight as Mike came into the room. Kate also smiled and asked, 'Have the boys driven you mad or just deaf?'

'They're all right, just acting as they should, boys on holiday an' all that. I'm just setting off with them once they've finished stacking all their gear into the boot of the car. I'll be back for you two ladies as soon as I can.'

Mary crossed the floor to stand in front of him. 'Don't hurry on our account, we're glad of the time to freshen ourselves up a bit.'

'All right. I'll leave you to it,' he said, his smile taking in both of them as he went out of the back door to where his car was parked.

Kate looked across at her friend. Mary obviously really liked him. And she was already beginning to think of him as an old friend. He had been remote and stilted when he had come down and stayed at Bramble Cottage for a week at Whitsuntide, but once he had realised that she was not opposed to him and Mary going out together he had mellowed, treating her with as much friendly courtesy as he did Mary. He was a well-turned-out man, fit and lean, about five feet ten inches tall, with dark hair and eyebrows, speckled with grey. Kate had come to believe that he had great feelings for Mary and she wished them both well.

A real holiday feeling was everywhere when they finally arrived at Hampton Court. The water dazzled blindingly in the sun and heat shimmered on the towpath. Only Bushey Park on the opposite side of the road offered shady, cool places. Kate and Mary, with Mike following, picked their way slowly down the steps to the Kearsley Boat Yard. All three were carrying folded deckchairs, the idea being that they would set up their resting place on the hard standing above the slipway rather than struggle for space on the riverbank which, today, was thronged with people.

Jack Stuart and his wife came out to meet them, greeting Kate with the information that their own three children were already on the river in their boat. Jack helped Mike set up the chairs while Mary and Kate stood watching swans back-paddling to catch the bread some small children were throwing to them.

'I love all the seasons on the river, the continual cycle of life,' Mary exclaimed.

'Yes, I know what you mean,' Kate answered. 'We think it's all so familiar and then we find the pattern of it all does change.'

They strolled to the edge of the hard standing where the boats came alongside to tether to the wall. To their right was Joshua's dinghy, newly varnished and resting upside down on two planks of wood. He had been as pleased as punch when he had come home at Whitsuntime to find it ready and waiting for him. This holiday Jack had put a large cabin cruiser into use for a trip downriver with the assurance to Kate that both he and Mike were in charge and the five boys were to go along only as passengers. The river was extra busy, as it always was at holiday time, more so when the weather was as good as it was today. More of the local boats were back in the water and a pleasure steamer was chugging along in mid-stream on its way to Richmond.

Kate became aware of a gentle splashing and looked to see Josh, with Pete Bradley seated behind him, rowing a dinghy peacefully up stream. She watched the water rippling away from the dipping oars, marvelling at how effortlessly the boat moved, and saw Josh hesitate for a second when he glanced over his shoulder and saw her and Mary leaning on the wall. As they came abreast, Peter yelled, 'Lovely day,' and Josh shouted, 'Hope you've brought loads to drink.' Their voices carried easily across the water and it was Mary who answered them.

'Yes, we have. Soft drinks as well as tea and coffee.' Turning to Kate, she said, 'I'm right pleased to see the pair of them are wearing their life jackets.'

'No fear on that score. Jack knows my dread of the river. He wouldn't let anyone go afloat from our slip-way without one.' Kate continued to lean on the wall, regarding the two boys with a mischievous smile, until Mary asked, 'What are you smiling at?'

'I was just thinking how much Josh's standing will have risen by the time he goes back to school, look at his three friends out there.'

Mary looked towards the cruiser at which Kate was pointing. Joshua's three school mates were sitting on the cabin roof, each of them had a mug in their hand. They looked such healthy lads, wearing only shorts and sleeveless cotton vests, their brown legs bare and on their feet rope-soled deck shoes.

'Ahoy!' they shouted in unison, waving frantically at Kate and Mary.

'Are you having a good time?' Kate called.

Nick Banks knelt up, cupped his hands to his mouth and shouted, 'Brilliant, absolutely brilliant. Mr Stuart and Mr Kendall are below. We'll be setting off as soon as Josh an' Peter come aboard.'

Kate and Mary could almost hear the lad sigh with excitement.

'Fancy a coffee?' Mary asked lightly, as she and Kate settled back in their deckchairs.

'Do you want the bother? We could walk up to the shops.'

'Don't talk so daft, the whole place will be teeming with day trippers. Besides I filled two flasks with coffee; we can't let it go to waste. Here you hold the cups while I pour.'

They were sipping the hot coffee when Mary frowned and said, 'It's been some weeks now since I came back from Wales and I feel shaky inside about bringing it up but . . .'

Kate wrapped both her hands round her cup and avoided looking at her friend. 'It might be better if you say what's on your mind.'

'Probably not, but I have to get it off my chest. You know I love you, Kate, I couldn't feel more for you if you were my own daughter. Something happened to you while I was away; I don't know what it was, but it has left its mark on you. Oh, you try hard not to let it show, but in your unguarded moments you look so sad and it breaks my heart to see you. Can't you tell me? Is there nothing I can do to help?' She twisted round in time to see Kate hastily brush a tear from her eye. 'Oh, I just knew there was something!' She leant to the side of her seat, stood her cup on the ground and placed her hand gently on Kate's arm.

For ages Kate had wanted to tell Mary about Toby but hadn't been able to summon up the courage. Mary was her best friend. More than that she was her family, and for years had been her trusted confidante. She didn't want this to change, but it would if she continued to have secrets from her. Mary had given her an opening, so why was she hesitating?

'In some ways it was much the same as happened to you,' she said at last. 'I think I might have got round to telling you if you hadn't come home so happy with the news of how you had met Mike.'

'Oh!' Mary's jaw dropped as she pondered this astonishing piece of news. 'You mean you met a man! Oh, dear Kate, how selfish I've been. I am so sorry.' Without waiting for her to form an answer and, mostly to cover her own embarrassment, Mary gabbled on, 'What a coincidence! I didn't think things like that happened to people like you an' me. I thought they were just romantic stories in women's magazines.'

Kate did her best to smile but wasn't very successful. 'I couldn't believe it either. However, my episode hasn't turned out as happily as yours.'

'Oh, Kate. I feel a bit ashamed—'

'Why? Because you've been so lucky? Don't spoil it for yourself. I like Mike, I really do, and I'm happy for both of you.'

'Couldn't you try and tell me about him? What went wrong? It might make it a little easier.'

'Nothing went wrong. He didn't ill-treat me or anything like that, but I will tell you.' She began, right from the moment she had asked directions from the policeman in Kingston. 'Bernard Pinfold, that's his name, but he prefers his nickname, Toby.'

Sitting with the hot sun beating down on them and the noise and laughter from the folk who were out to make the most of the last bank holiday of the year, Kate relived every second she had spent with Toby. Parts of the story she refrained from telling Mary; they were moments that belonged entirely to her and to him. By the time she got to the telling of his proposal of marriage, the offer to obtain travel documents and whisk her away to South Africa, it was Mary who was crying softly.

'I suppose you did the right thing,' she ventured, dabbing at her eyes with her handkerchief. 'You couldn't have gone off at a moment's notice and left Joshua.'

'No. Knowing that what I did was right hasn't made it any easier though.'

'Have you heard from him since?'

'Not a word. Sometimes I think that's a relief. Anyway I'm too old to start thinking of going halfway round the world.'

'Don't be so silly. Too old indeed! You won't be thirty until January!'

Mary obviously was intent on pursuing the subject. But, even with Mary, Kate did not want to share any more memories. Her stomach was churning madly as she fought for some way of steering the conversation into safer channels and she was saved by the sight of Jack Stuart's wife.

'Would you two like a trip? We could get one of the riverboats; they'll be fun today, music and singing, though we'd probably have to queue for ages before we got on.'

Kate could have hugged and kissed this homely woman whose whole life was wrapped up in her husband and three children. 'Perhaps we ought to wait until Jack brings our boys back – they'll be starving. We've brought a picnic, plenty for everyone . . .'

Mary could see that Kate was upset and hastily stepped into the breach. 'Have a coffee with us now,' she said, rummaging in one of the bags for the flask and another cup. 'Maybe it's not the best day for us to try and get a river trip, far too busy. After lunch I think I'd like a walk in Bushey Park. It will be nice and cool under the trees.'

All the while the three of them sat looking out over the water Mary was saying to herself, if only there was something that could be done to bring Kate and this man together again. But there wasn't. And even if there was, it would just be interfering. She must remember not to flaunt her own happiness; it wasn't fair on Kate. She would do her best to help her friend over this, for Kate had acted in the only way possible. But she realised only too well that being in the right hadn't made her decision any easier.

Chapter Twenty-Eight

KATE RAN A hand through her hair and tried to concentrate on the papers in front of her. Further meetings had to be set up, projects needed so many people's approval, and letters demanded answers. She needed two pairs of hands, she thought irritably, and a lot more hours in the day. The paperwork never seemed to diminish, no matter how long she stuck at it, and she sometimes wondered whether she'd been right to offer her grandmother's house and land for this charity home. For certain she had never envisaged the amount of work that would fall on her shoulders or the number of hurdles the trustees would be confronted with. She had been up since six that morning and working in the dining room by seven thirty, eager to have some suggestions to put forward at the next meeting of the trustees and desperate to clear some of the accumulated papers. She threw down her fountain pen. Her mind was not on her work. The doorbell rang and that, too, irritated her.

Mary put her head round the door, 'It's Paul Richards. Shall I show him in?'

'Might as well, seeing as all the papers are here.'

'Right and I'll bring coffee for you both. You want to ease up, take a breather. You shouldn't take everything to heart so much.'

'Thanks. I could use a cup of coffee. Bring three cups an' come and join us, whatever Paul has to say I'm sure will be of interest to you.'

Kate leant back in her chair, letting her thoughts dwell on Paul Richards. He was the borough surveyor and had been involved with this venture from the beginning, in June 1932. Good God! More than nine months ago. Kate's first impression of him had been of a sharp, slim young man with thinning hair and glasses. Over the months she'd come to know him well. Behind his business-like exterior was a warmth, an impression that he liked his job and this project in particular, which was enough to make her take to him. But not enough for her to agree to go out with him, despite his frequent requests.

Mary pushed the door open with her hip, crossed the room and set the tray down on a side table. Paul came in after her, his arms full of packages and folders, which he dropped onto the end of the table where Kate was sitting.

'Morning, Kate. I've got some good news for a change.' He beamed at her.

'Let's hope your good news will help solve a few of these problems, because I can't for the life of me see how they're all going to get sorted.'

Mary sniffed. 'Take no notice, Paul, she got out of

bed the wrong side this morning.' Paul Richards' eyes gleamed with amusement. 'If you promise to smile, Kate, I'll take you away from it all. This afternoon I promise both of you a tour of the first finished stage of the 'Alice Memorial Homes'.

Kate cleared most of her papers to one side to allow room for Mary to set down two cups of coffee, one for her and one for Paul. Having done this Mary went to the far side of the room, seated herself near the bay window, and poured coffee for herself. She was always pleased to be kept informed about the progress of the building work and she was grateful that Kate always made sure, at least as much as she was able to, that she wasn't left out of things.

Mary was full of admiration for Kate. She had put her heart and soul into getting this scheme off the ground. She looked across to where Kate and Paul were engrossed in conversation. By golly it hadn't been easy! Right from the start there had been many businessmen only too willing to be part and parcel of the venture, but there had been some who were thinking only of the publicity and the limelight that would come their way because of it. Not everyone did charitable work or gave funds simply from the goodness of their hearts.

These men would have excluded Kate if they'd had their way. But she had held her ground like the fighter she was. In the end it had been agreed that a trust would be set up consisting of eight prominent businessmen, Mr Weatherford had been voted the trust manager and, with some deal of reluctance, Kate had been appointed chairman. It seemed to Mary that the title of chairman was a faint disguise for secretary and general dogsbody, but as this was now 1933 and women hadn't had the vote for any length of time she supposed Kate had to put up with what crumbs men sought to throw at her.

Mary's attention was momentarily distracted by Paul, who was perched on the edge of the table, leaning across and holding Kate's hand. Noting the look of devotion on his face, she began to feel rather sorry for him. One didn't have to be a crystal-gazer to know that he had been taken by Kate's good looks from the moment he'd set eyes on her. Kate could do a lot worse; admittedly, he was a bit of a clever clogs and he'd had a good many lady friends in his time, but Mary had made it her business to find out that although he was thirty-two years old he had never been married. But Kate just didn't want to know. There were times when Mary felt she could shake the life out of her. A few days, that's all it could have been, just a few days in which she had known this Toby and yet she was wasting her life hankering after him. He was never going to come back into her life. It had been a year now. Surely if he had any such intentions he would at least have written to her from time to time. Poor Kate! She felt so sorry for her.

Me having Mike hasn't made matters any better, she thought, though Kate, being the generous person she is, always makes him welcome. She and Mike had no intention of getting married but their friendship did mean a lot to both of them and it had become quite expected that he would come to stay with them in Surrey every so often. Mike would take her to London for a few days; they'd visit museums, see a show, go shopping, but although they always brought presents for Joshua and for Kate, it didn't stop Mary feeling guilty that she'd gone away leaving Kate on her own. Whichever way you looked at it, Kate had drawn the rough end of the stick all through her life. It just wasn't fair.

'I'm going now, Mary. Thanks for the coffee. I'll pick you both up about two. Don't forget to wear sensible shoes – there's still a load of rubble to scramble over.'

His long legs took him to the door in three strides.

'I'll just see Paul to the front door, I shan't be a minute,' Kate said.

More's the pity, Mary thought to herself. It would be great if I were to come out into the hall and find that young man had you in his arms and the pair of you were kissing.

'I'll make us a sandwich for lunch, shall I?' she asked, as Kate came back into the room. 'We'll have our main meal tonight. I think it's ever so sweet of Paul to include me in the invitation for this afternoon, I've been dying to see inside the building for ages now.'

'Suits me fine.' Mary's high spirits were infectious and Kate felt her own heart lift. 'I knew the builders were going great guns, but it is nice of Paul to suggest we have a tour. I'll tidy all these papers away. There's just one letter I must reply to, then I'll go upstairs and get ready.'

Left alone in the dining room Kate turned her mind back to business. Taking matters all in all it hadn't been too hard a struggle, not that it was over yet, not by a long chalk – at least another year before the whole site would be completed. However, God had been on their side. Good things as well as setbacks had come about since the first overgrown shrubs and bushes had been cleared from Alice's land and the first army of workmen

311

had moved onto the site. The house, which hadn't had anything done to it for years, had been attacked with vigour and plans drawn up. Restoration and necessary alterations had transformed it to a greater glory and it could now accommodate as many as four staff, each with their own private bed-sitting room. Another set of builders had dug and laid the foundations that enabled them to start on the first of the new buildings only weeks after the trust had been set up.

To make the scheme even more viable, an old derelict property, which adjoined her gran's holdings, together with the surrounding land, had been purchased, and to enable the trustees to pay for this six-bedroom house and the land on which it stood the local newspaper had sponsored an appeal. Socials, sales of work and collections had been organised by Kate and Mary with a band of willing workers. Under Mr Weatherford's leadership, large sums had soon been raised for the financing of each new stage of the work. He had set his sights beyond Kingston to attract funds by letting Kate's wishes be known that the Alice Memorial Homes would be for the benefit of old and young people alike no matter what part of the country they lived in. The Depression made it a daunting period for any campaigner, however, Mr Weatherford was a well-respected businessman who could empty pockets and please at the same time.

Charles Collier had certainly acted wisely in leaving his son's affairs and those of Mary and herself in the safe hands of this kind solicitor, Kate concluded as she dated a sheet of writing paper and settled down to answer an important letter.

⋆   ⋆   ⋆

Paul Richards was back at the house just as the hall clock struck two. With his usual gallantry he held the door of his car open while Mary settled in the passenger seat, then holding Kate by the elbow, he assisted her into the back of the car. They drove through the small villages with their riverside cottages and homely corner shops, which were open all hours and stocked anything and everything. Soon they were in Kingston and Paul took the turning that led to the site.

Kate gasped. It was only a month since she had been there yet the difference was amazing. She would have been hard put even to recognise the smart house they were approaching as the place where her gran had lived.

As Paul drew the car to a halt the front door was opened by Harriet Tremaine. Kate had wholeheartedly agreed with the trustees' decision to offer the post of house matron to her. Although she was a single lady, aged fifty-two, she could have passed for anyone's grand-mother. Homely and jolly was how Kate would have described her, not very tall, dumpy, with short grey hair, set in waves above her forehead. She wore glasses and showed a suspicion of a double chin, but it was her broad smile that had at once endeared her to Kate. Wearing a grey silk dress, which hung loosely from her shoulders, she had adorned the neck with two rows of dark red glass beads, which twinkled every bit as much as her eyes did behind her glasses as she came down the short path to greet them.

After they had greeted Harriet, she led the way inside. Despite all the renovations, Kate still felt it was her gran's house. It was a warm feeling that pleased her enormously.

They were in the second of the bed-sitting rooms when Mary nudged Kate's elbow and nodded to the fireplace, and for the first time she noticed that there were no gas brackets left on the walls.

'Surely electric light hasn't been installed? Not in this old house?' Kate asked, staring at Paul in disbelief.

Grinning broadly he nodded his head. 'This is only one of the many wondrous things you shall see before the afternoon has passed and, in the coming months, we, meaning myself, the builders and craftsmen and, by no means least, your board of trustees, hope to astound you with.'

'Well, if charm has anything to do with it you'll ease your way through without blinking an eyelid,' Mary informed him, and before he had a chance to reply, Harriet Tremaine added, 'I see someone else has cottoned on to you, Mr Richards.'

Paul threw back his head and laughed out loud, but it was to Kate that he said, 'Just so long as you sweet talk the trustees into finding the money, I can easily remove any small obstacles that appear from time to time, thus enabling your dedicated craftsmen to perform what some would describe as miracles.'

'Cut his tongue out an' he'd still have the last word,' Mary said, in a stage whisper.

All three women were giggling as they continued with their tour of the house. There were several pieces of furniture left that had belonged to Alice, old-fashioned, but made by experts of the trade they would last for years. Some furniture had been bought, mainly beds, and some had been donated. Harriet was the first member of staff, so at the moment she was the sole occupier of this fresh, bright, clean house.

Mary, with Kate following, stepped gingerly up the planks of wood placed over a newly laid path leading up to the front entrance of the new main building. It would be completed 'soon', a burly looking workman informed them. This wing was to house twelve adults for short-term stays, each in a single bedroom with a washbasin with running hot and cold water. At each end of the two landings there would be a bathroom, which would also serve as treatment rooms for residents who might need care. On the ground floor there was to be a communal kitchen, a large dining room and a lounge, part of which would serve as a small library.

Back outside, Paul pointed to the other end of the site, where another three-storey building appeared to be in the final stages. This, at the moment, was being referred to as the residents' wing. Plans were for six flatlettes, each to house a single long-term resident and six double units for long-term elderly married couples who would, in the main, be able to cook and care for themselves.

Hearing Kate and Mary discussing the future tenants, Harriet Tremaine stepped forward. 'Residents in this wing,' she nodded her head to the front opening that hadn't as yet any door, 'will be completely independent but with practical help, advice and guidance at hand as and when it is required. I think, at future meetings, it is to be considered whether it will be practical to offer these residents the choice of a prepared main meal delivered to their door or whether they could join those on convalescence in the dining room of the other wing. We shall have to feel our way, some may even prefer to cook all their own meals. It is a tall order for people to settle into a whole new way of life, and we mustn't expect everything to be a great success from the word go.'

'A very sensible lady, that Harriet Tremaine,' Mary remarked as they got back into Paul's car. 'If anyone can promote neighbourliness and thought for others, she's the one to do it.'

Paul settled himself into the driving seat, and twisted his shoulders round until he was able to see Kate. 'Well now, let's hear from you, since you were the one to instigate this scheme. How do you feel about it now?'

Kate felt overwhelmed by the enormity of the project and was asking herself how she could ever have been so reckless as to set out on such a task. Her voice was low as she said, 'Whichever way the Alice Memorial site develops in the future, I have to convince myself that I started it all with the best of intentions.'

Mary was shocked. How sad and despondent she sounded!

Paul got out of the front of the car, opened the back door and slid in beside Kate. Without saying a word, he put his arms round her and pulled her to him. They stayed like that, silent, for a full minute until Kate drew away.

'Too much mess on the site,' he said. 'A bit daunting, wasn't it? Made you wonder if the project will ever be finished. I promise you, Kate, it will be. And a tremendous success it will turn out to be. Honestly, I'm not joking. In a few weeks' time the garden specialists will move in, shrubs and plants, even trees, will appear overnight and, as if by magic, there will be curtains at the windows, residents in both wings and every person from that day forth will bless the names of Alice and Kate Kearsley. Now, wipe your eyes, stop crying, and tell me you're going to invite me into Melbourne Lodge for tea when we get back.'

Kate looked up at him. 'I'm not crying,' she muttered, brushing quickly at her eyes. 'And seeing as how you've given your afternoon up to driving us about, I suppose the least we can do is give you tea.'

'That's my girl.' He playfully punched her shoulder.

Then as he once again settled himself in the driving seat and switched on the engine he winked saucily at Mary.

I wish he were right Mary thought and Kate was 'his girl'. What a pity it wasn't the true state of affairs.

During the lovely months of spring that followed, Kate gave her time to the trustees without complaint, but when Joshua was home on holiday it was a different matter. The house rang with the sound of happy and, more often than not, grubby-looking boys.

Before she knew it it was July and Mr Weatherford drove Mary and herself down to Josh's school for the prize-giving and sports events that signalled the end of term and the beginning of the long summer holidays. Mrs Weatherford had also come with her husband. She had become a great friend to both Kate and to Mary, very much involved with their schemes to raise funds. She was as gentle in her ways as Mr Weatherford was vigorous.

During the summer holidays Kate allowed Joshua and his friends to spend a lot of their time at Bramble Cottage. There were several advantages to this, the main one being that because it was within walking distance of Melbourne Lodge the boys didn't have to keep pleading for lifts down to Hampton Court. The fact that the cottage fronted straight on to the towpath was a source of delight to them. One of the sheds in the garden served as a changing room when they went swimming in the river, the other shed housed their life jackets and other boating equipment, while the front lawn, at times, held as many as three boats. Each day Mary and Kate would walk the short distance, carrying baskets that held hot and cold food and drink. Beneath the big oak tree was the picnic table that her father had built. Over the years she had gone to great lengths to see that this one reminder of happier days had remained in good repair.

Mike Kendall was a frequent visitor, spending almost as much time in Surrey as he did in Wales. He was like an overgrown schoolkid where the boys were concerned. Mary was thrilled that he was definitely part of the family now. It was a wonderful time.

And then, suddenly, it was September. The boys went back to school and Mary foretold gloomily that they were in for a very hard winter because the hedgerows were already covered in red berries and that, she said, was a true sign.

Two-thirds of Kate's project was to be up and running before Christmas. To a man, the trustees agreed that Kate should be asked to perform the opening ceremony, which was to be held on the first Monday in November at eleven o'clock.

It was bitterly cold. The wireless had broadcast that

early snows had reached North Devon and up on Dartmoor everything was white.

Mary was, as always, sensibly dressed. She was wearing a double-breasted camel coat, with a long scarf, gloves and a woollen hat, all of which she had part-knitted and part-crocheted herself. The scarf was wrapped twice around her neck and shoulders as she came out of the house and walked towards Mr Weatherford's car. Her short fur-lined ankle boots gripped the icy surface of the path preventing her from slipping.

Kate, too, was warmly dressed, but what a different picture she made, Mr Weatherford remarked to his wife as they watched the two women approach. His wife, a fashion-conscious lady at all times, readily agreed. Kate was certainly well turned out! Her calf-length coat was the colour of a rich dark plum, fitted at the waist to swirl out into fullness beneath her knees. The two rows of buttons that ran from beneath her chin down to her thighs were criss-crossed with heavy braid. The collar and the turn-back cuffs of the sleeves were made from the same braided material, which was a deeper shade than the actual coat. On her head she wore a black-velvet hat. At first she had paraded before the mirror wearing a cloche hat but had decided it was too tight fitting. The one she now wore had a wide brim which turned back, giving a full view of her creamy complexion and big brown eyes. Most of her hair she had managed to restrain out of sight, only a few strands lying across her forehead and one long coil covering each ear, which she had deliberately arranged so that they would not feel so cold. Her high button-up boots were of soft black leather, as were her gloves.

*   *   *

What a turn out! So many people! Even Mr Weatherford was surprised.

Three of the trustees had had their say, now it was Kate's turn. She rose from her seat at the back of the platform and walked forward. All she could see was a sea of faces, none of which, at that moment, looked to her to be friendly.

She began by thanking everyone who had helped the cause. 'Without the generosity of so many kind people I would not be standing her today, because my idea would never have got off the ground.' She paused, took several deep breaths and in a much firmer tone, wound up her speech by saying, 'My desire was, and always will be, that the Alice Memorial Homes should be a home in the strictest sense of the word. I hope the trustees and those who work here will never lose sight of this crucial objective. My grandmother lived a long and mostly happy life on this site. I wish the same for all who come here to find rest and shelter.'

Kate cut the royal-blue ribbon tied across the brass plaque to the sound of tremendous applause.

Chapter Twenty-Nine

KATE WAS EATING crusty bread and cheese on the grass just outside the back door. There were so many things she could be doing but, for the moment, they would have to wait. She wasn't in the mood. And, after all, she had no one to please but herself. Mike had taken Mary back with him to Wales for a short holiday. It was a good opportunity for Mary to see something of his home town and to visit her sister Blanche. Mike had promised they would both be back in time for Easter.

Kate pulled a wry face. She couldn't blame Mary. Mike hadn't come up for Christmas and there had just been the three of them on Christmas Day, which had been very enjoyable but not much fun for Joshua. On Boxing Day they had ordered a taxi and dropped him off at Peter Bradley's home. Peter had two elder brothers and a sister so the invitation to Josh to join their family party had been most welcome. Mary and Kate had carried on in the taxi to the Alice Memorial Homes, where they had helped with the Christmas party for all of those who were now in residence.

Why was she feeling so down this morning? Because she was entitled, she told herself. It was two years to the day since she and Toby had parted. She sat, her head tilted slightly forward, staring at the garden. She hadn't so much as one photograph of him yet she only had to close her eyes to see his tall figure, his kind face and soft grey eyes; even the funny grin which she had traced with her fingertips. He might be the only man who had ever made love to her but he'd left her with enough memories to last a lifetime. Through these two long years he hadn't written once. If she'd had an address for him, would she have written to him?

She heard a motor coming up her drive. The postman had already been and she wasn't expecting anybody. Puzzled, she walked through the house and heard the bell ring for a second time just as she was about to open the door.

'My goodness!' she exclaimed, as a smart young man handed her a long white box tied across with a handsome dark green ribbon. Lettered in gold were the words MOYSES STEVENS. What was such a smart London florist doing making a delivery to her?

She signed for the box, asked the young man to wait a moment, laid the package on the hall table and fetched two half-crowns from her purse, which he accepted with a smile.

The box was so beautifully wrapped that she hardly dared to open it but curiosity was killing her. She placed it on the kitchen table and undid it carefully. Inside there lay sprays of red berries, twelve long-stemmed red roses and several sprigs of fern. She bent her head to smell the roses and saw that on the inside of the lid a large white envelope addressed to her was taped.

As she tore the tape away and opened the letter, her hands were shaking. It was a long letter with no return address.

3rd March 1934

Dear Kate,

I hope this finds you well. I am taking a chance that these flowers won't upset your life in any way. I am gambling that you haven't got yourself married, but if you have I shall try to be happy for you. It's asking too much that a lovely girl like you should have remained single.

There is something very important I need to say to you. When I left England I knew I would be away for two years and I came to terms with that. There have been times, many of them, when I just wanted to throw in the towel and come and fetch you. I have never written you a letter or tried in any way to find out what you were doing because, if I had, the temptation would have been too great. Not a single day has gone by when I haven't thought of you, loved you with every fibre of my being. In my imagination I have been there with you; taking you out to dinner, sitting in your lovely garden, walking by the sea at Brighton, even climbing Box Hill. You see, I remember everything. The feel of you, the smell of you. Your unruly hair which would tumble free no matter how much you tried to confine it.

From the moment I met you and you weren't

feeling well, all I wanted was to take care of you and for those few days we had together the wish grew so much that I knew I wanted the commitment to last for the rest of my life. I wanted to share my life with you, to be able to watch you move, to hear you talk – especially to hear you say that you felt the same way about me.

There was a vague sense of tragedy about you, and I wanted to erase all the bad things from your mind. I could not believe that a man had never loved you and claimed you for himself. After we had made love together I was overwhelmed by your emotion and sheer physical beauty. You were a gift from God.

The most wonderful days of my life were those I spent with you. Please believe me, Kate, I came to love you desperately. I love you still and I will until the day I die.

So, why am I writing now after all this time?

I made a pact with myself when I was forced to leave you. I would respect your wishes; that your duty and your love, albeit an entirely different kind of love, lay with Joshua. I had signed an agreement for this South African trip and I would see it through and, as difficult as I knew it would be, I would not contact you in any way during those two years. I would leave you free, maybe to meet another man who could make you happy. But, Kate, my dearest Kate, believe me when I tell you there have been days when I've said, 'I can't wait any longer. I'm going to write and beg her to come and join me.'

But I remembered how strong your feeling of

duty was and how much you loved Joshua. The decision you made was right. I know that. But I also know that leaving you standing in the doorway, getting into my car and driving away was the hardest thing I've ever had to do.

At last my time here was coming to an end and come hell or high water I was going to land on your doorstep.

Then six weeks ago fate stepped in. In the laboratory, where our experiments have been carried out, there was an explosion. One technician, a married man with two children, was killed and several of my colleagues were badly injured. Some of our work, including a lot of our records, went up in smoke. It was heartbreaking, because we were working on a drug that would have been of great help to a lot of suffering people. One day we hope it still will be. For now it is a matter of sorting through what we are left with and getting on with the job. That isn't to say that I am going to stay the course, not this time. However, I cannot desert now and as you, my dear Kate, said to me, you wouldn't respect me if I did.

I am still not going to put an address to this letter. I don't know which would be worse, to receive a letter from you saying that you were no longer free, or to hear that you were longing to be with me as much as I long to have you here. As soon as I am able I shall come home to England. I will first and foremost make it my business to find out how you are and if my returning will not in any way disrupt your life. Being away from you has not kept me from wanting you, loving you, every minute of every day. These two years have been the longest of my life.

Perhaps our having to part, has been some kind of test. If that is true, it has not changed my feelings for you one jot. I love you, Kate. And I always will.

Toby.

P.S. I will be back. I promise.

Kate lowered her head and pushed her face into the box that held the flowers, sniffing hard to inhale the heavy perfume of the roses. Then, holding the pages of the letter close to her chest she went into the front room where she settled herself in an armchair. Wiping away the tears that were blurring her sight, she took a deep breath and began to read the letter through once again.

Toby had not deserted her! He loved her every bit as much as she loved him.

How had he got the letter to England? Had he written direct to Moyses Stevens? How had he paid for the flowers and for the special delivery?

She thought about it for the next half-hour. Finally, she got to her feet, took the telephone number off the box and asked the operator to connect her with the florist. Her heart was thumping against her ribs as the phone began to ring. When she heard the receiver being picked up she almost put hers back on the hook. A young woman's voice said, 'Moyses Stevens.'

Kate swallowed hard before she could explain who she was, thank her for the delivery and ask her questions.

'We are so pleased you like the roses, madam. No, we don't have an address for the sender. If you'd like to wait a moment, I will check in our files as to how and when the order was placed, if that will be of any help to you.'

Kate said gratefully that it would. Her call was transferred and, this time, a gentleman's voice came down the line. 'I am sorry, madam, we have no address or telephone number for the sender. I myself took the order, it was over a week ago and I well remember the elderly man; I dealt with him personally. He was a foreign gentleman and he had instructions written on a sheet of notepaper. The flowers were to be red roses and the date of delivery together with the name Miss Kate Kearsley and the address were all printed in capital letters. Most explicit, I do assure you.'

'Please, would you remember the name and branch of the bank the cheque was drawn on?'

The man coughed discreetly. 'I can understand that you want to thank the sender, madam, but really I can be of no help. The flowers and the delivery charge were paid for in cash.'

Kate thanked him and slowly replaced the receiver, staying exactly where she was for at least five minutes.

Toby really didn't want to have any direct contact with her until he was ready.

She went back into the kitchen, found a tall glass vase and filled it with water. Almost reverentially she lifted the roses out of the box, one by one, grouping them with the branches of berries and the fern until she was satisfied that the whole arrangement looked wonderful. Then, standing back, she blinked several times. 'Oh, Toby . . . Toby . . . Toby,' she said his nickname softly and very sadly, and with that she perched herself on the edge of the table and let herself remember everything that they had said and done in the short time they had had together.

Chapter Thirty

UNLIKE AT MELBOURNE Lodge, meal times at Bramble Cottage were, by necessity, irregular affairs. The last day of the summer term at Josh's school, as always, had been the end of the first week of July. With three lads coming home to stay with Josh for two weeks it had seemed a good idea for the whole family to move to Bramble Cottage for a while.

Breakfast was very much a do-it-yourself meal, with the three boys away to the river long before Kate and Mary were even out of bed.

Now Mary stood at the sink peeling pounds of potatoes in readiness for the evening meal, and Kate whisked eggs in a bowl ready for the cake she was making. The day was far too warm to think of serving soup to the boys at midday so Kate decided that her next job would be to make a batch of salmon and cucumber sandwiches and a few cheese rolls. Independent and bright as buttons Josh and his mates might be, but when it came to feeding time they were only too willing to flop down on the riverbank and allow Mary and herself to wait on them hand, foot and finger.

'A few days time an' we'll be wondering what to do with ourselves,' Mary said to Kate.

'Yes, I suppose we will. You do think I've done right in saying Josh could go off with Nick to France, don't you?'

'Oh, you're not going to start in with all those doubts again, are you? We've been over it enough times already and we agreed we weren't left with much choice. He so obviously wants to go.'

'I know. But it will be the first holiday that he has gone away. And to France! I can't help having my doubts.'

'Well look at it like this, Mr and Mrs Banks have let Nick come and stay with Josh on several occasions, perhaps they think they are repaying our hospitality by inviting Joshua to go with Nick. After all they are not going to strangers. They'll be staying with Nick's aunt an' uncle.'

'You're right, I know you are, and Mrs Weatherford said almost the same thing. Evidently she knows the village where the boys will be staying – it's only a few miles outside Paris.'

'Well, there you are then. All tied up good an' proper. And you'd have to be feeling very brave to turn round and tell Josh that you'd changed your mind and weren't going to let him go.'

'I'm delighted, really, that Joshua is so popular. It's extraordinary, the way he's made friends, right from the first day he went to school. I remember being terrified when Mr Weatherford drove off with him, seeing him kneeling on the back seat of the car, his little face so white and drawn.'

'Me too. I thought my heart would break that day. Suppose I felt a bit guilty. Maybe we had mollycoddled him a bit more than we should have done, but then again he'd never known what it was to have his own mother, and he wasn't very old when his father died. Good job he did have us, all children need to know they are loved and wanted. I've often wondered whether you owning the boat yard had anything to do with Josh being so popular at school. Did that never occur to you?'

'A bit, I suppose. Though not from the money point of view. Most of the friends he's made have rich parents. More likely living so near to the river has been the main attraction and perhaps Josh did boast a bit about having a boat built for him and, as time has gone on, the fact that he has the use of several different motor vessels. Thanks to Jack Stuart we've never had to worry about their safety, he's always found one of his workmen to go out on the river with the boys.'

Mary changed the water in the sink and began to cut the potatoes into small pieces ready for the saucepan. 'Can I ask you something?'

'Sounds pretty daunting, you asking permission.'

'It's not really, but from time to time I have wondered why you've never sold the boat yard. You could have, when you were twenty-one, couldn't you?'

'Yes. Under the terms of my father's will I had to retain it until I became of age but after that I could have sold it.'

'But you never have.'

'What would have been the point? I don't need the

money and it's Jack Stuart's livelihood. He wouldn't have been able to afford to buy the yard and it would have been cruel to sell it over his head. He's a good manager. The staff respect him. He makes money for me as well as for himself.'

'And Josh loves the place,' Mary said, her tone full of merriment.

'Exactly. And he's not the only one, is he? We've had some great times there. Still do. And Mary, to be honest, I did love my parents, each of them in a different way, and when I see the Kearsley Boat Yard sign up over the slipway I think of my dad with a great deal of love. He was a good tradesman and a hard-working man. I've tried to blot out the last months of his life – you know what I mean – tried to remember only the good times. He left me a wonderful legacy, which not only gives me a good income but gives a great deal of pleasure to a number of people.'

'Lovely sentiments, Kate. I have to admit I love going to Hampton Court and I feel pretty special when we use the hard standing outside the yard to set ourselves up for the day. Especially when the riverbanks are crowded. It's like we lord it over ordinary folk by having our own spot.'

'Why, Mary, I didn't know you were a snob!'

'Well, you said yourself it was nice that Josh has rich friends. And even if it is a bit sad for us he's going to France, hopefully the weather will still be good and there'll be some of the summer left when he comes home.'

Kate did mind him going but wild horses wouldn't get her to admit as much. She was looking forward to seeing him come home again. And that wasn't the only person's homecoming she was looking forward to. But she wasn't going to say a word about that. Not yet. Not even to Mary.

That was her secret, to cherish all to herself. Each evening, before she got into bed, she opened her photograph album, filled mainly with pictures of Joshua from his baby days, and gently stroked the two red roses which she had pressed between the pages. She also read the postscript of Toby's letter. 'I will be back. I promise.'

Duty before love. It had turned out to be that way for each of them. There were days when she felt she had secretly been waiting for Toby all her life. In the ten years prior to their meeting she had accustomed herself to living her life through others. But once they had met, it had been magic just being near him. The top of her head barely reached his shoulder yet he made her feel ten feet tall! They had walked and talked, slept together, eaten together, crammed so much into those few days. It had, at the time, seemed so . . . normal.

Now he was coming home. Home to her. She didn't know when, but she did believe it was going to happen. Every night before she drifted off to sleep she would say the words out loud. 'Toby will be back', and then happiness would begin to spread right through her. At times she was so happy it was almost frightening.

Mary came across from the house bearing a tray that held two jugs of lemonade and a bowl full of rosy apples. It was a constant source of wonder to her the way Josh and his friends adapted to life during the holidays. After the strict regime of boarding school it was as if they felt free to do exactly as they liked and especially to dress in any fashion they pleased. Or rather undress, she laughed to herself. About all she ever saw them wear on these warm hazy days were shorts and even they would be discarded at a moment's notice to reveal skimpy swimming trunks before they dived into the river. Not one of them needed any persuasion, they were like river rats, totally at home in the water. These friends of Joshua had all been well raised and indulged by doting parents. But ever since their first visit to Melbourne Lodge, when they were in their first year at boarding school, they, just like Josh, had been entranced by the river folk and the way whole families with many children managed to live on one longboat, some even on working barges. They loved the novelty of going aboard such vessels, being made welcome by the old folk, most of whom had spent their entire life on the river, of diving off the side straight into the water, playing football in the fields beyond with these nomad boys who scarcely ever saw the inside of a classroom. They certainly enjoyed their holidays to the full.

Thank God the weather always seemed to be good, though cool breezes didn't deter the boys. Mary knew full well how much Kate loved having Joshua home and was thrilled to bits when he asked if he might invite his mates once again. Mind you, although the lads teased Kate, she gave as good as she got and she laid down rules. Be it at the big house or Bramble Cottage Kate saw to it that they made their own beds and helped with the washing up after the evening meal was over. The same rules applied to Mike. But then why shouldn't they? Mike was just as big a kid as the boys when the chance presented itself.

Mary was pouring lemonade into several glasses when she heard Josh calling. 'Can you hear what he's saying?' she asked Kate, who was busy clearing away the remnants of the lunchtime picnic.

Kate raised her eyebrows and strained her neck to see what was going on. 'No, but he seems to be pointing to a car parked up there at the corner.'

'Probably someone annoyed that they can't drive along the side of the river. No consideration some of these town folk.'

Josh was now pointing in their direction. They stood still and watched as a woman and a man walked slowly towards them.

'Odd kind of couple,' Mary muttered, 'dressed to kill on a hot day like this, wonder they didn't suffocate in that car.'

As Kate opened her mouth to agree, perhaps laugh at the ridiculous sight this pair made, she was caught by her memory. It was her cousin Hilda and, she supposed, the man was Hilda's husband, Ben Withers.

From ten yards away they could hear Hilda's loud voice, 'Fank God we've found yer. We've bin t'that big 'ouse of yours an' couldn't get any answer. A man with an 'orse an' cart told us you'd be 'ere, an' Christ am I glad he was right. Me feet are burning and me throat's that parched I couldn't spit sixpence.'

Kate forced herself to step forward and submit to being hugged and kissed by her cousin.

'I'll take this tray in and put the kettle on,' Mary said tactfully.

'You sounded just like your mother. Whenever Aunt Dolly arrived here she complained of her bad legs and feet. Here,' Kate pulled two wicker armchairs into the shade of the big tree, 'kick your shoes off and sit yourselves down, there's still a little lemonade left and Mary won't be long with the tea.'

'Don't suppose ye run to a bottle of beer, do yer?' Ben Withers asked.

'No, Ben, sorry, but I'll send for some for you as soon as the off-licence opens,' she said handing him a glass that was half filled with lemonade. 'Have you had a terrible journey? The hot sun couldn't have helped, not while you were driving, and then to find that we weren't at the house, I am sorry . . .'

Kate rambled on to cover her confusion. She only remembered meeting Ben once and he had seemed quite dapper then. A real Jack-the-lad. He certainly looked a lot different today. Kind of flash, and a lot older.

Hilda had gulped her drop of lemonade down and was now rubbing furiously at her feet.

'I knew I never should have bought these basket shoes, the straps are cutting in t'me flesh something chronic.'

'What d'yer expect? Nineteen an' eleven off the market!' Ben groused at his wife. 'I'm always telling yer t'buy one good pair of shoes at a decent shop instead of a dozen pairs of cheap rubbish but will yer listen to me? Oh no, might as well save me breath as talk t'you.'

Kate could feel trouble brewing and was glad that the boys were off out of the way. She didn't know how to calm this pair down, so she didn't try, she just waited.

Mary appeared like the good Samaritan she was and poured tea into a dainty cup with a matching saucer for Hilda and into a large breakfast mug for Ben, then she cut slices of the fruit cake Kate had made that morning and handed a plate to each of them.

'I'm not sure that either of you have ever met Mary Kennedy, she used to be housekeeper to Mr Collier. I know I did talk to you, Hilda, about Mary and Mr Collier, when I stayed with you all in London.'

'Pleased to meet yer,' Hilda said, giving Mary a kindly smile. 'I do know a lot about you, Mary. Me mum gives me Kate's letters to read when I go round there, not that she's written very much lately.'

'Oh that's not fair!' Kate interrupted. 'I never ever got an answer. I don't even know whether Aunt Dolly and Uncle Bert still live at the same address.'

'Didn't mean t'upset yer, Kate. Sorry, luv.' Hilda managed to look contrite. 'You ought t'know better than t'expect any of our lot t'write t'you. Never 'ad the same kind of schooling that you did. But me mum and me dad still live in that grotty end-of-terrace 'ouse which backs on t'the laundry and is a stone's throw from the shipyards. Well, me dad does.' Hilda sniffed and Kate could see that she was having a hard job stopping the tears.

Ben Withers got to his feet, unbuttoned his chalk-striped jacket and threw it over the back of his chair. 'All right, luv,' he said, patting his wife's shoulder. 'There's no need to get yerself all worked up. I'll tell yer cousin why we're 'ere.' He drained the rest of his tea down in one big gulp, placed the empty mug down on the table and faced Kate squarely. 'There's no pretty way of telling yer this so I'll come right t'the point. Yer Aunt Dolly's bin put away. She's gone off her rocker.'

Hilda let out a squeal which had both Mary and Kate

rushing to her side. 'Come on, Hilda, up on your feet,' Mary ordered sensibly. 'Let's get you inside the house. I think you and your husband could do with something a little stronger than tea.' With her arm round Hilda, as if she were an old friend come to visit, Mary led the way and Kate was left to follow on with Ben who was holding her arm so hard it hurt.

He cleared his throat, before gruffly saying, 'It's the truth, Gawd knows it is. Dolly went so bad Bert had no choice. She'd 'ave ended up driving him as batty as she is if they 'adn't taken her away.' He paused in the porch and looking very serious, went on, 'I'd better come to the reason we're down 'ere t'day. Dolly can't 'ardly talk, but when she does make 'erself understood it's 'er sister she wants. An' 'er only sister was your mother, that's right, ain't it? Every minute she's awake, which ain't too often from what I'm told, 'cos they've got her drugged to the eyeballs, she keeps on an' on about 'ilda and we thought at first it were 'er 'ilda she wanted, but it weren't. It were your mum she was on about. So Bert said you was the next best thing an' we ought to ask you t'come an' see yer aunt. Well what else can we do? I'm asking yer, luv, what else is there? We can 'ardly sit round her bed and tell 'er your sister can't come 'cos she killed her 'usband and the law said she 'ad to be hung, now can we? And if not that, what the 'ell do we say? You tell me. 'Cos I've just about 'ad enough of the 'ole tribe of 'opkins. Bert's got the two boys, Stan an' Tom, both doing well, but they and their wives don't wanna know. Well, neither do I fer much longer. I do me best for my 'ilda and our three kids and I don't mind 'elping Bert out now an' agin but I tell you straight, after today I'm washing me 'ands of Dolly. I've tried me best, an' nobody can say I ain't. But now it's going to stop. Did your mate say she'd got a drop of the 'ard stuff? 'Cos if she did, lead me to it fer Christ sake.' And with that he stomped down the passage and into the front room.

Kate was utterly devastated. How dare he talk about her mother like that!

Mary saw that Ben was given a good tot of whisky and Hilda's measure was topped up with ginger wine. Then, with the table quickly set with freshly made tea and hastily prepared sandwiches, together with crusty rolls and great hunks of cheddar cheese and pickles, she motioned silently to Kate that she was going to slip out and wouldn't be long.

Back outside in the sunshine Mary stood still for a minute and caught her breath. Why had that strange pair decided to descend on them now of all times? It wasn't fair on Kate. Coming here when she hadn't seen any of them for years. Raking up the past that poor Kate had tried so hard to live down. Oh well, she sighed heavily, God gave us our relations but it's a jolly good job he allows us to pick our own friends.

She followed the sound of laughter, and there were the boys and with them were several others, lads and, wonder of wonders, three or four girls, all playing with two balls in a kind of criss-cross netball match. She stood still until Josh saw her and he immediately said something to Nick, climbed the bank and was at her side in seconds.

'Is something wrong, Nanna? Who were those people? They asked me if they were in the right place for Bramble Cottage.'

'It's all right,' she hastened to reassure him. 'The lady is your mother's cousin.'

'I've never heard Mum speak of her,' he sounded astonished. 'Are you sure Mum's all right?'

Mary knew he was going to have to be told a lot more about his mother's background but now was not the time. On the other hand she couldn't fob him off with any old story, he was too intelligent for that. 'I promise you your mother is fine. She's more than capable of dealing with the situation. But there is something you could do for her. You and your mates could make yourselves scarce later on. Come into the house, wash and change, and say you all fancy going into Kingston to the pictures or something. That will give your mother time to talk to her relations, we'll give them a meal and they'll be gone by the time you boys get back.'

'Oh, Nanna,' he said, as he punched her shoulder lovingly, 'anything for you, but . . .' he made a face '. . . who's gonna feed us growing lads?'

'If it weren't for the fact that your mates would call you a cissy I'd hug you Joshua Collier. I'll give you some money and you can all have fish and chips, but mind you sit down properly and eat it at a table in the shop, no walking about the streets of Kingston eating out of the paper.'

'As if we would! There are times when you still think I'm a small boy.' He smiled roguishly at her expression of surprise.

'Yes,' she answered quickly, 'and there are times when your mother and I wish we were flies on the wall so that we could see what it is that you really do get up to!'

'Heaven forbid,' he muttered as he turned away.

340

Mary watched him join his mates and then walked slowly back to the house.

Kate wasn't sure exactly what it was Hilda and her husband expected her to do. She was sorry to hear how poorly Dolly was. Shut away in hospital. It didn't bear thinking about.

When she had needed someone, Dolly had not let her down. She had stuck with her through her mother's trial and the horror of the weeks that followed.

Hilda and Ben had forgotten their troubles for the moment. They had drawn their chairs up to the table and were making short work of the hastily prepared meal Mary had set out for them. Looking at her plump cousin, with her dyed hair and bright red lipstick, Kate found it hard to believe she looked so different. She had always thought of Hilda as pretty, but now her face looked a mess. The fact that she had been crying hadn't helped. The mascara she had plastered her eyelashes with was all smeared. When she had stayed with Aunt Dolly and Uncle Bert she had liked Hilda's good humour and straightforwardness and the fact that she never let anything get her down. She had been kind to her, even offered to get her a job, saying they could work together and go out and about together. Kate couldn't help wondering how her life might have turned out if she had accepted Hilda's offer, settled down and made her home in London with the only relatives she had.

She wanted, quite desperately, to be left alone to live her life in this lovely quiet village and wait and hope, even pray, that Toby would come back to share that life with her. She knew she wasn't going to be let off the hook as easily as that!

It was a relief when, much later, Ben drew a paper from his pocket, leant across the table and gave it to Kate. 'On there is the name of the 'ospital, their telephone number and the special ward that your Aunt Dolly is in . . . I realise that this 'as come as a shock fer you and I'm sorry. Yer need time t'think about what yer gonna do but I wanna get back 'cos tonight there's racing at White City.'

'Oh, Ben! Did yer 'ave t'say that. What will Kate think of us?' Hilda shouted.

The look Ben gave his wife was aggressive, to say the least, and Kate felt a bit alarmed.

'Your mother's been a good woman, I ain't saying she ain't,' Ben continued to glare at Hilda, 'but what's 'appened ain't nobody's fault an' there's nothing more that me, yer dad, or the blinking doctors, for what I can see, can do about it. Life 'as t'go on and whether you like it or not I'm going to see the dogs race t'night, so if yer want a lift 'ome you'd better get yer feet in them ridiculous shoes and come an' get in the car.'

'Hilda, I will come up to London just as soon as I settle things here. Tonight I'll telephone the hospital, ask about visiting times and . . . well, we'll see.'

Hilda rubbed her eyes, came to stand beside Kate and put her arms around her. 'Oh, Kate . . . you're . . . you're . . .' she sighed, cross with herself because she couldn't find the words to express her feelings, 'such a kind, gentle person.'

Kate held her cousin close and said over her shoulder, 'I will come to see Aunt Dolly, I promise.'

'Will yer stay with Ben an' me or with me Dad?' Hilda asked, with a sob in her voice.

Kate was silent, digesting the fact that Hilda didn't expect her to go up just for the day. 'I'll talk it over with Mary, get Josh settled an' I'll let you know.'

'We're on the telephone an' all yer know. Ben did yer put our number on that bit of paper you gave Kate?'

'No, I never give it a thought. Give it 'ere, I'll add it on the bottom.'

It was bright early evening when a solemn foursome walked along the towpath towards the car. The sun was much lower in the sky, there weren't the children about now and most day trippers had packed up and gone in search of something to eat. Kate had persuaded Hilda to go upstairs with her and wash her face and freshen up before setting off on the journey back to London. While they were in Kate's bedroom, Hilda had opened up and told her a lot more details about her mother's illness.

'My Ben means well but he's like me dad,' she began, her voice thick with despair. 'Can't be bothered with women's ailments an' when me mum got real bad they were out of their depth. But they can say what they like she's not mad she's . . . oh, I don't know, Kate, I just don't know, but I do know there's times when I'm there on me own with her an' she talks away almost proper like. Mind you, it is all about what 'appened years ago, but that don't mean she's crazy, does it?

'Old Granny Wallace what lives up the road an' 'as known me mum all 'er life, says she's just going through the change of life. I 'ope t'God she's right.'

Kate had gently hugged her cousin. She felt at a loss what to say and even less confident about being able to help in any way. Now, as she stood beside the car, just looking at Hilda brought tears to her eyes. Even though she had her husband with her, Kate felt she was a lost lonely soul.

'You could have stayed longer, Hilda. It wouldn't have taken Mary and me long to have got you both a proper meal.'

'I know, but I 'ave to go, see t'the kids. It took a lot of arguing to get Ben t'bring me down 'ere t'day. Best not push me luck, eh?' she finished with a remorseful grin as she kissed her goodbye.

Kate held onto Mary's hand as they watched Ben drive off. Mary was quietly telling her that it wouldn't be so bad to have to go and see her aunt in hospital. But it was not Mary who was going to have to make the journey, probably stay a few days in her Uncle Bert's little house and see her aunt in the awful state she was in. She was going to have to do all of that.

Chapter Thirty-One

Nick's parents, Joyce and Frank Banks, had collected their son and Josh ready to set off for France the
following day. Well into the night and for the next two
days Kate had talked and Mary had listened, only giving
her advice when asked. They went about their various
tasks, the main one being the turning out of Joshua's
bedroom and giving the rooms that his friends had used
a jolly good cleaning.

Whenever Mary suggested that they stop for a meal
or just to have a cup of tea the subject they talked about
was always the same: whether or not Kate was going to
go to see her Aunt Dolly.

Kate had phoned the hospital and been relieved that
the report, while not explicit, was encouraging. 'Mrs
Hopkins is under sedation, but if you are a close relative you may visit on Wednesday or Sunday afternoons
between two and four. No, I am sorry, I cannot discuss
a patient's illness over the telephone except to say that

the doctors are very pleased with your aunt's progress. Her condition has certainly improved.' And with that Kate had had to be content.

Although she had not yet come round to admitting it, Kate was well aware that sooner or later she was going to have to go to London. The fear of what she might find when she got there was not the only reason making her waver. What if Toby were to arrive and she wasn't here? If Kate made the decision to visit Aunt Dolly, Mary would have to return to Melbourne Lodge, where Toby would go, if he came at all! Now, don't start in with all your previous misgivings, Kate chided herself, then found herself quickly questioning, why would he turn up now? It had been so long. Half the time their meeting didn't seem real, it was as if she had dreamt the whole affair. But then, if she needed reassurance she had only to open the photograph album and take out his letter and the two roses she had pressed. Did she ought to warn Mary that there was a slight possibility he would be calling at the house? Not necessarily, she answered herself.

She had toyed with the idea of telling Mary about the flowers and letter many a time; now was the right time to do it. Earlier than usual Kate went upstairs, got undressed, put on her nightdress and dressing gown and came back downstairs.

Mary looked up in surprise as she entered the front room with her large book tucked underneath her arm.

'When you were in Wales seeing your sister some flowers were delivered to Melbourne Lodge,' Kate began. 'Perhaps I should have told you before . . . somehow I couldn't bring myself to. A letter was taped inside the box.'

Mary pushed her down into an armchair saying, 'Wait, I'll get us a nightcap.' When they each had a glass she drew her own chair nearer to Kate's and urged, 'If you feel like telling me now, why not start at the beginning?'

She didn't pass the letter to Mary to read for herself. Some parts of it were too personal, so she read most of it aloud. When she had finished, Mary reached over, allowing her fingers to touch the heads of the two dark red roses gently. Her eyes glistened with tears and her voice was filled with emotion as she murmured, 'Oh, Kate! How wonderful! What a kind, considerate man your Toby must be. I shall pray with all my heart that he does return to England and that the two of you find the happiness you deserve.'

The next day they called Jack Dawson, who now owned a small van in addition to his horse and cart, and with his help they transported themselves and all essential articles back to Melbourne Lodge. Then they spent the weekend being thoroughly lazy, enjoying each other's company as only true friends can and finally settled that on Wednesday Kate would make the journey to London.

It was Tuesday evening and Kate was ironing one of her favourite summer dresses, telling herself that it would be muggy going up on the train and it wasn't going to be cool and breezy in London, not if this spell of scorching hot weather continued.

Mary looked up from reading the evening paper, 'Have you decided whether or not you're going to stay up there for a few days?'

'Well, the very thought of having to stay in Uncle Bert's house, just me and him, doesn't feel right, and when he goes to work what am I supposed to do with myself? The only other alternative is to stay with Hilda and Ben.' Mary made a face and Kate shuddered, 'Yes, you know right enough what that means!'

'Well, you did call me to the phone on Sunday morning to listen to the racket that was going on in their house. I thought Ben was trying to kill his children. Job to tell who was making the most noise, the kids screaming or their father shouting.'

'The only thing that is making me feel better about this visit is the good reports we've been getting both from the hospital and from Hilda about Aunt Dolly.'

'May I make a suggestion?' Mary got to her feet, folded the newspaper neatly and came to stand near the table. 'Why not make this a reconnaissance trip – just go up and make a visit, see how the land lies.'

'Don't think I haven't given that idea some thought, but I didn't know how to broach the subject to Hilda. I don't want to hurt her feelings.'

'Why don't I phone her now? I won't tell her a lie, just a half-truth. I'll say you have to attend a meeting on Thursday morning, that you are coming up just the same, but only a flying visit this time. I could suggest she meets you at the hospital, and at four o'clock when visiting time ends you could take her somewhere nice for tea before you catch a train back.'

'Would you? Don't let on that I'm here, then she can't insist that I come to the phone.'

With a resolute step and her eyes glinting, Mary went out into the hall to make her call. In a very short time she was back. 'All settled. Hilda will meet you in the front entrance to St Thomas's Hospital at a quarter to two tomorrow.'

'Thanks, Mary,' Kate said, letting out a great sigh of relief.

The guard walked the length of the train making sure that all the doors were safely closed. He watched admiringly as Kate put her foot on the narrow step and got into the carriage.

Kate's dress was lovely, a pale shade of green with long sleeves, a cross-over bodice that was very flattering to her bust, a trim white belt to encircle her waist and a full skirt that swirled down to reach her calves. The neck and hemline of the dress were trimmed with white daisies. Her thick hair was tied well back off her face and on her head she wore the daintiest of straw hats, the brim of which was trimmed with the same white daisies. White gloves and shoes worn with silk stockings gave the total effect, which at a glance said, cool and fresh.

'Need any help?' the guard enquired, holding onto the door handle of her carriage.

Kate murmured something appropriate and settled down in her seat. The journey took less than forty minutes and as she walked the length of the platform at Waterloo Station and came out into the dusty, hot air, she once again thought how different this world was from the one in which she lived! Great buildings, half hiding the sun, people scurrying past, so many motor cars, creeping along, hooting at pedestrians who endeavoured to cross the road in front of them. A gentleman, seeing her failed attempts to hail a taxi, took pity on her. He

349

stepped out into the roadway, waited until a cab came into view, then raised his silver-topped cane and waved it frantically. The cab driver pulled up right in front of them. The gentleman opened the rear door, helped Kate onto the back seat and asked where she was going.

'St Thomas's Hospital, please, and I am very grateful to you,' Kate replied giving him one of her most charming smiles.

He stepped back, raised his hat and murmured, 'My pleasure, young lady,' before giving the driver instructions.

Kate's first sight of this most famous hospital was a bit daunting. It had steps up to the big main doors and a wide hall that one had to cross to get to the enquiry desk. Kate stood aside watching and listening to the receptionist. She was about fifty years old with brown hair set in rigid waves, and appeared to be as stiff as a board. But as the minutes passed, Kate realised that the poor woman needed to be efficient, and certainly firm, to deal with all the people, many of whom seemed set on demanding that they be attended to right away. Suddenly she felt a hand on her shoulder and jumped almost out of her skin. Relief flooded through her as she turned to see Hilda standing smiling at her. They kissed each other's cheeks and then linked arms. Kate was pleased to see that Hilda was dressed more suitably today: she wore a floral dress, with a cream background and her high-heeled shoes were beige. Still, to Kate's mind, she had far too much make-up on but she sensibly decided that it was none of her business. She even found herself feeling pleased to see her cousin and when she suggested that later on she would like to treat Hilda to a slap-up tea, Hilda squeezed her arm to show her appreciation.

'Cor, that would be smashing. Come on now, it's a long walk through to the annex where Mum's ward is. I told her on Sunday that you would be coming and I think she remembered who you were.'

'That is good news, Hilda. Have the doctors told you any more?'

'Well, yes an' no, yer could say. One doctor told me that Mum had suffered a stroke and that it was because she was having trouble stringing her words together that the conclusion had bin drawn that she was losing her mind.'

'Well, that's not very satisfactory, is it? How terrible Aunt Dolly must have been feeling.'

'Yeah, I thought that an' all. Then another day I gets to see a different doctor, much younger than the other geezer and he tells me that me mum might 'ave 'ad a fall, knocked 'er 'ead, and suffered some loss of memory an' that's why she could recall what 'ad 'appened years ago but wasn't with it at all when it comes to living day by day. So, I suppose yer takes yer choice and 'ope fer the best. I 'onestly don't see what else we can do.'

Kate stopped walking. The smell of the corridors wasn't at all pleasant and looking at Hilda, she knew her cousin was frightened. Despite putting up a brave show Hilda was terrified of what was going to happen to her mother. 'I hope she does recognise me,' Kate said, her voice little more than a whisper. 'I've brought her some biscuits and boiled sweets and in the bottom of my bag is a bowl of fruit that Mary put together for her. Is your mum allowed these things?'

''Course she is, though you'll get a shock when yer see 'er. She's as thin as a rake.'

'I meant to stop and buy her some flowers but I got straight out of the taxi and came into the hospital.'

'Good job too. Waste of money. Flowers don't live five minutes in the wards. Nobody bothers t'change the water an' the nurses ain't got the time. 'Ere we are. Look, the sister's just taking the screens away from the door so that means the visitors can go in.'

They had to walk the whole length of the ward because Dolly's bed was the last of a very long row. Hilda stood at the end of it and, having stared at her mother for a couple of minutes she turned to face Kate and pulled a very odd sort of face, giving her a kind of warning. Why should she warn her? What could she be trying to say?

They moved up to the head of the bed and, as Kate got nearer to her aunt, she knew immediately. Dolly was sitting in an armchair, a tartan rug laid across her legs. She could have been an old woman of about ninety, so thin and wrinkled did she look. Her eyes had a terrified look as if she had no idea where she was or what was happening to her. Kate felt so upset and shocked that she had to force herself to stand still, when all she really wanted to do was turn and run. Hilda put down the bags she had brought and knelt down in front of her mother and very tenderly took hold of both her hands. 'How are you today, Mum? You know I told you me cousin Kate was coming t'see you, remember? Well, she's here. Are yer gonna give her a kiss?'

Kate moved alongside Hilda and she too bent her knees so that her face was on a level with that of her aunt.

'Hallo, Aunt Dolly,' she leant forward and placed her lips gently against Dolly's thin cheek. 'How are you feeling?'

It was as if someone had flicked a switch. A moment ago she had looked as if she couldn't move an inch and was consumed by fear, now she slowly unclenched her fists, lifted her face until she was looking straight at Kate, and appeared to recognise her. As the two women waited, sweat broke out on Dolly's face and she began to shake; from her mouth came small sounds of distress.

'I've brought her a new bedjacket,' Hilda said, getting hastily to her feet and rummaging in one of her bags. It was very pretty, the palest baby blue with a swansdown trimming around the neck and cuffs. She draped it around her mother's shoulders, so gently and with such care that Kate was amazed.

'I'll fetch two chairs,' Hilda said, 'they keep a stack of them over there by the wall.'

By the time the two cousins were seated, Dolly was moving her feet which were encased in cheap scuffed black shoes. Hilda seemed to know what she wanted, because she laughed out loud. 'Mum, you do remember!' she cried. She dived once more into her bags and came out with a neat pair of dark blue velvet slippers. She took the shoes from her mother's feet and replaced them with the new slippers. Straightening up, she looked down at her and said, 'Well?'

Dolly's pale, wrinkled face crumbled and a single tear slid down her cheek, but very slowly a thin smile came to her lips. Hilda could scarcely see, for her own tears were blinding her, and she threw her arms round Dolly's shoulders, this time not stopping to be gentle, and rocked her thin frame back and forth, all the time saying over and over again, 'You *are* with it, Mum. You are. You are. See, Kate, I did get through t'er. It was days ago, but she remembered. She did, she did!'

Hurried footsteps sounded and a nurse appeared at the foot of the bed. 'Whatever's going on? Mrs Hopkins must be kept quiet. Visitors must not be allowed to excite her.'

'Sorry, nurse,' Hilda mumbled.

'Very well. You do have chairs, I see. Sit down and try to be calm.'

'Soppy cow,' Hilda muttered under her breath as she watched the stiff back retreat down the ward. 'Seeing us two is a proper tonic, ain't it, Mum? Better than all the pills they've bin stuffing yer with.'

Kate laughed as she lifted her own bag up onto her knees. The sweets and biscuits she had brought she packed tidily away in the locker. The bowl of fruit Mary had sent she placed where her aunt could see it. Then she held up a banana but got no reaction from Dolly. She tried again with an apple and then grapes; no flicker of desire. Then she tried an orange. Both Kate and Hilda smiled broadly as Dolly's feet started to tap. 'An orange it is then,' Kate declared. She peeled one, broke it in half and then into sections placing them one at a time in her aunt's bony fingers.

'See,' Hilda said quietly to Kate as they watched Dolly suck the juice from each piece of the fruit, 'she can not only feed herself, she can make herself understood if people would only persevere and show a little patience.'

'I agree with you,' Kate assured her cousin. 'I suppose

354

in a place like this they just don't have the time to give to individuals.'

'That's no reason that they should 'ave said she was . . . well, you know. And it weren't only the staff in 'ere. It were me dad and that dopey 'usband of mine. They're all right when everything's going fine and me mum is running round after everybody like a blue-arsed fly but when she gets sick they can't wait to shove 'er off into some bloody 'ome. Well it ain't gonna 'appen. Tonight I'm gonna go an' see me bruvvers. Perhaps it ain't all their fault. It's more than likely their stuck-up wives that's kept 'em away.'

Kate leant forward, wiped her aunt's mouth with a clean handkerchief, and gave her another section of the orange. Hilda seemed glad to have someone to talk to and the best thing she could do for her cousin at the moment was sit back and be a good listener.

'Funny, you know, Kate, me mum was talking t'me not so long ago about 'er own bruvvers an' 'ow she 'adn't set eyes on 'em fer years. Know what she said? A daughter's a daughter all 'er life, a son's a son till he takes a wife.'

Dolly's feet were tapping like mad.

'What is it, Mum?' Hilda turned to give her her full attention, saying to Kate, 'I bet she's 'eard every word I've said.'

Dolly dropped the piece of orange into her lap, hunched her shoulders, stretched out her hand and touched Hilda's cheek. Her mouth opened and she dribbled a little. 'Mm . . . mm . . . my . . . girl.'

Hilda looked at Kate in amazement, but before they could say anything, Dolly had twisted in her chair to face

Kate. Again her hand came out and her fingers lay across Kate's wrist. Once again she was trying to say something. Kate sat very still, feeling scared, for two bright spots of colour had appeared in her aunt's cheeks. 'Mm . . . mm . . . my . . . sis . . . st . . . er's . . . girl.' The three words were out. Dolly laid her head back against the chair, and there was no mistaking, she was definitely smiling! Both girls were choked.

'Mum! You clever ole gal!' Hilda whispered into her ear, because her face was pressed up against her mother's cheek.

Kate took one of her aunt's hands and held it firmly between both her own; she had to blink several times to keep her tears from falling. It was some time before any of them moved and when they finally did both women laughed as they each brushed a hand over their eyes.

'Daft pair, ain't we?' Hilda said, as she unpacked her bag.

'Look, Mum,' she now spoke quite normally, 'I'm putting a clean towel and face flannel on the middle shelf of your locker and here's a new tin of talcum powder I'm putting in yer wash bag, I got yer lily of the valley this time, I thought yer must be fed up with English lavender. A clean nightdress an' two pairs of drawers are on the bottom shelf and all the goodies that Kate brought yer are on the top, an' that's where I'm putting some coppers an' a two-bob bit just in case you wanna buy anything from the 'ospital trolley what comes round.'

As Hilda straightened up the bell began to ring.

'Does that mean visiting time is over?' Kate asked, glancing at her watch.

''Fraid so. That's yer lot till Sunday.'

Kate gently hugged her aunt and placed her lips first on her cheek and then on her forehead. She moved away a little so that Hilda could say her own goodbyes to her mother. It had been an emotional couple of hours but nowhere near as bad as she had feared. She would come back.

'I expect we'll have a terrible job to get a taxi,' Kate remarked as much to herself as to her cousin as they stood outside the hospital and watched the streams of traffic pour by.

'A taxi?'

'Well, we agreed that I would take you to tea, didn't we? And I think we both deserve it, if only to wash the smell of disinfectant away. I can actually taste it, can't you?'

'Every time I come 'ere it gets worse. So, where we gonna 'ave this tea.'

'The choice is yours.'

'In that case,' Hilda began, simulating Kate's posh voice, 'why don't we try the Ritz?'

'Why not indeed? That is if we ever manage to stop a cab.'

Hilda threw back her head and laughed. 'You mean it, don't you? I was only joking, 'onest. Can yer see me 'aving tea at the Ritz?'

Kate laughed with her. 'You should always mean what you say. I'm dying for a cup of tea and seeing as how I hardly ever see you, or London come to that, today you and I are taking tea at the Ritz. If we ever get there.'

'If that's all that's stopping us, watch this.' Hilda put two fingers in her mouth and whistled loud enough to

357

wake the dead. It worked, though, and as she held open the door and allowed Kate to step in first, it was she who smiled sweetly at the cab driver and said, 'May we go to the Ritz Hotel, please?'

Their tea was a great success and Hilda insisted that she come to Waterloo Station to see Kate safely on to the train.

'I can't begin t'tell yer what this afternoon 'as meant t'me, Kate. Not a soul encouraged me to think that me mum would ever come out of this lot fit an' well. Mind you, I was always determined to fight her corner, but God above knows it was an up 'ill task trying t'do it on me own. You bin marvellous. Can't believe me mum knew who you were, but she did, didn't she? And we never 'ad t'prompt 'er, did we?'

'I'm just so very pleased that I came,' Kate replied, giving Hilda's arm a squeeze. 'I'm certainly going to keep in touch with you from now on. I'll ring you and let you know when I'm able to make the journey again and, meanwhile, I'm going to make some enquiries about Dolly having a holiday when she's fit enough to travel.'

'Aw, Kate! You won't lose by it. I'll see yer right somehow, don't you fret. I'll go on Sunday, an' as soon as I get 'ome I'll be on the telephone t'you. Let yer know 'ow she is by then.

'Now you take care, an' give me love to that Mary Kennedy, a real nice lady I thought she was. Ain't many around like 'er.'

'I mean it, Hilda, about your mum having a change of scene. I'll see what can be done, and when I see you next I hope to have all the details and I'll fill you in on the whys and wherefores.'

'All right, luv. Look, yer better get in 'cos the guard is going to blow his whistle. Goodbye, Kate.' They hugged each other close. 'God bless yer. Fanks for me tea, it was smashing.'

'Goodbye, Hilda.'

When she could no longer see her cousin Kate drew her head back in from the window. She felt utterly exhausted, but she was so glad she had made the effort – as much for her cousin's sake as for her aunt's. Poor Aunt Dolly! And poor Hilda as well! She was right, she had been fighting a battle for her mother's well-being on her own. Everyone else had been ready to give up and what that would have meant for Dolly didn't bear thinking about. Well, now Hilda wouldn't be on her own. I'll do anything I can. Just as Aunt Dolly helped me when no one else wanted to know, I'll do my best to help her.

It would be like repaying a long overdue debt.

Chapter Thirty-Two

THE LONG-AWAITED MOMENT had arrived, Aunt
Dolly was very much better and Kate was about to
ask permission from the board of trustees that a place
be found for her in the Alice Memorial Homes. She had
already sounded out Harriet Tremaine, who had turned
out to be a thoroughly popular matron, and she had been
wholly in favour of Kate's suggestion. Some weeks had
slipped by since Kate had paid the home a visit. The
whole of her time had been taken up with visiting her
aunt and seeing that Josh enjoyed what remained of his
summer holidays.

They were a little early so they decided to do a bit of
a tour. Kate walked with pride. Every floor she trod and
every public room they peeped into was there because of
her gran. Alice had loved this spot and, without a doubt,
she would be proud that Kate had given it up to be used
for such a worthy purpose. So many people had been
kind and generous and the finished buildings, now fully

operational, were a credit to each and every person who
had been involved. The main rooms were beautiful, right
down to the smallest detail, well proportioned, bright
and sunny. A small rosewood piano, a gift from the
local traders, stood in the lounge facing French windows, which led onto what had once been an overgrown
field. Now the grass was clipped short and rose bushes
lined the borders. This was the largest of all the public
rooms. It was used not only by the sick folk who were
housed for short stays in the main building, but by the
permanent residents who occupied the purpose built
flats. Coffee mornings, bring-and-buy sales, afternoon
card games and occasional evening entertainment were
among the many uses this large lounge was put to. In
the main dining room, vases held fresh-cut flowers, the
curtains, chair covers and cushions, all hand sewn by
willing volunteers, were as pretty as any picture. There
were three tables each seating six people, the chairs
were wooden ones with wheels, the seats covered with
a quilted pad.

Mary looked at her watch. 'Best make our way to
the kitchen, if Harriet is about we're sure to be offered
coffee.'

'All right,' Kate agreed, giving one last loving look
through to the gardens.

The kitchen was unbelievable, so big yet so homely.
There was a huge cooking range with the fire-front
open and the bars already glowing red at this time of
the morning. A dresser took up the whole of one wall.
There were rows of white and red banded cups hanging
from hooks and piles of matching plates tidily stacked
at one end. A rack held pots and pans ranging from

enormous to very small, some were copper, some cast iron; all were scrupulously clean.

'Morning, Kate, morning, Mary, come away in.' The beaming, rosy face of Mrs Burton, the resident cook since the home had first opened, peeped out from the open door of the pantry. 'I've trays ready to be sent up to the office but you're welcome to a coffee or a cuppa before the meeting starts. State your preference. I shan't be a moment.'

Kate and Mary looked at each other and quietly giggled. 'Doesn't alter, does she?' Mary whispered.

'Wouldn't want her to, would we? Mrs Burton is about the only person I've ever met who can tackle half a dozen jobs at once, and still talk nineteen to the dozen while she's doing them.'

'True. Turns out the best bread and cakes that I've ever come across.'

'I heard that, Mary Kennedy, and if you're trying t'butter me up there's no need.'

Mrs Burton was quite the opposite to most people's idea of how a cook should look. Tall and lean with a reddish face and an ever-ready smile, she banged her hands against her bony thighs to shift some of the flour that was clinging to them and grinned at Mary and Kate. 'Knowing the pair of you were coming here today I made an extra couple of cakes. They're in that blue tin on the end of the dresser – don't forget to take them when you leave.'

'You sure they're for us?' Kate asked, smiling knowingly.

'Well, you've done more than enough to help this home get under way, generous to a fault I'd say, and it's nice sometimes to be able to show appreciation in return. The date an' walnut one I did do for you and Mary, but I must admit me mind was on master Joshua when I put in the slab of gingerbread.'

'I knew it. Why is it that everyone who comes into contact with Josh wants to spoil him?'

'That's a daft question if ever I heard one.' Mrs Burton sniffed. 'Hark who's talking! Then again a bit of spoiling never hurt no child, an' you have to admit that young boy of yours only has to smile and with those great big blue eyes there ain't a lady worth her salt that wouldn't try to please him. He's a great lad and a credit to you, but then you don't need me to tell you what you already know.'

Mary, having taken down two cups from the dresser and helped herself to coffee from the enamel pot to the side of the hob, was about to hand one to Kate when the kitchen door opened and Mr Weatherford came in. He smiled at the trio of women. 'Ah! Just in time, am I?' he asked, walking towards Mary.

''Course you are. Here, have mine I'll get myself another,' she assured him.

'We'll have to drink up quickly, I saw a couple of the trustees making their way to the office. What made you two girls arrive so early?'

'Oh, I like the girl bit,' Kate cried. 'I haven't been able to give as much attention to this place as I would have liked just lately, so Mary suggested we treat ourselves to a bit of a tour.'

'And what have you found? Everything to your satisfaction?'

'Everything is absolutely splendid,' Mary cut in and

Kate quickly followed with, 'Couldn't be better. The whole place is a credit to all members of the staff.'

Having drunk their coffee and told Mrs Burton that they would pop in and see her again before they left, they followed Mr Weatherford up the short flight of stairs to the first floor where the office was situated. It was a fair-sized room; a pleasant place with comfortable chairs arranged around three walls. Against the far wall stood an oak desk with a swivel office chair set behind it. The floor was covered with a plain brown, hard-wearing carpet. Two windows looked out onto a section of the garden which was hedged in with small-leafed, close-growing shrubs. Kate immediately thought what a lovely quiet place it would be for people to sit and maybe read a book, especially if the person were recovering from a recent illness.

There were four men already in the room when they entered. The only gentleman who Kate felt she had not got to know well in all her dealings with the trust was Mr Belmont, who had taken on the task of treasurer. He was a lively looking man in his fifties, with very brown eyes and thick dark hair. He was the first to cross the room and shake her hand. Mr Weatherford took his seat behind the desk, looked at everyone for a moment and then smiled, his craggy, serious face changed and Kate thought to herself that he ought to smile more often.

'Gentlemen,' he began, 'no introductions are necessary were Mary Kennedy is concerned. You are all aware how tirelessly she has toiled to accrue funds for the Alice Memorial Homes, and she is here today at the invitation of our benefactor, Kate Kearsley. Between them, these two ladies have a request they would like to put forward and I propose that we hear them out and deal with it quite informally, before we get down to today's business. Naturally Miss Kennedy, not being a member of the board, will withdraw before I officially open the meeting.'

This statement brought the men's gaze round to rest on Mary and in unison they nodded their approval.

'Thank you very much,' she stammered.

At a signal from Mr Weatherford, Kate got to her feet and began very timidly to explain what had happened to her aunt. 'My biggest worry is that St Thomas's Hospital feel that everything possible has been done for her as a patient but that she is not, in the opinion of the doctor, fit to be discharged unless there was someone with her at all times. As that is not possible, I would like your permission to have my aunt stay here so that she may recuperate in far better surroundings than any the hospital could provide.'

It was the treasurer who spoke first. 'I take it, then, Miss Kearsley, that your request is not for your relative to be offered permanent accommodation.'

'Oh, no.' Kate answered Mr Belmont quite forcibly. 'It is more a matter of convalescence while she is recovering from having been so poorly.'

'So what's the problem? There obviously is one.'

Kate relaxed a little. 'I didn't want to be seen as taking liberties.'

A couple of the men coughed and nodded, dismissing the fact that any such idea would have entered their heads.

'Have you spoken to matron about vacancies, Miss Kearsley? I do know our list is not overloaded at present,' Mr Belmont spoke kindly.

'Yes, Mr Belmont, I have,' Kate admitted, somewhat shamefaced, 'and she does know that I am making this request to you gentlemen this morning.'

'And you, Mary, have you anything to add?' Mr Weatherford asked.

'Only to say that we would be doing Kate's aunt and her family a great kindness. I know Kate's relatives and they have done their best, but they all have their livings to earn and there is no one person able to be with Kate's aunt at all times. There is another fact to be considered; the family home is in the East End, not exactly a good area in which to find peace and quiet, which we are led to believe would go a long way towards helping her recovery.'

As Mr Belmont stood up, his lips were set in a kind smile and he made a gesture of finality. 'Gentlemen?' There was a rustling of papers as each man got to his feet, all nodding their agreement in the most hearty of ways.

'Kate,' Mr Weatherford beamed, 'perhaps you and Mary might like to go and find matron, ask her to join us and at the same time tell cook we are ready for our refreshments.'

'Willingly,' Kate said, smiling her thanks to each of the trustees as she and Mary made for the door.

She was bursting to get on the telephone to tell Hilda. Aunt Dolly was coming here to Kingston where, God willing, she would soon get her health back and once again be the lovable, lively, reliable lady that she had always been.

Chapter Thirty-Three

THESE NEXT FEW days were going to be extremely busy ones, Kate thought as she stood staring out of the window, wishing like hell that she knew where Joshua was. It was almost the first weekend in September and that meant Harvest Festival, before all the children went back to school. As usual, both Mary and herself had been roped in to help with the activities that were taking place. Neither of them minded helping to decorate the church, make cakes, pies, and scrub big potatoes ready to be baked in the bonfires that would be lit up and down the towpath one little bit. But besides all that they would have to eat lunch almost as soon as the morning church service was over because they had promised to be at the Alice Memorial Homes when Ben and Hilda arrived with Aunt Dolly. At the moment though, Kate's mind was on other things. The weekend was the least of her worries.

When she had peeped into Joshua's room at seven

o'clock that morning and found he wasn't there she hadn't been too surprised, but for him not to have put in an appearance when breakfast was on the table was another matter. Josh could smell food a mile off. Now it was three o'clock in the afternoon and she was worried sick. Mary had telephoned the parents of all his friends but Josh wasn't at any of their homes. 'I've walked the length of the village and along the side of the river almost into Kingston, I just don't know where else to look,' she was muttering to herself as Mary pushed the door open and came into the room carrying a tea tray. 'He's never ever gone off without telling us before or at least leaving a scribbled note on the kitchen table,' she mumbled.

'I know,' Mary replied softly, 'and I'm kicking myself because, now I come to think about it, that boy has been very quiet ever since he went out to lunch with Mr Weatherford. I thought perhaps it was because he knows this is to be his last term at prep school. What do you think? It's been some hours now, maybe we ought to call the police.'

Kate looked indecisively at Mary for a moment. 'I know what you mean about Josh being quiet and I feel a bit guilty too. I've been meaning to get him on his own and have a good long talk about so many things. Then Mr Weatherford said he wanted to answer all sorts of questions that Josh had been asking, so I thought I'd better wait until after they talked an' then, what with one thing an' another, I've never got round to it.'

'You mustn't go blaming yourself.'

'I know, but I do. Weeks ago, when Hilda turned up, he remarked about me having relatives that he'd never heard of and when he came home from France he went

on and on about Nick's father and uncle all the things
they'd done together. I kind of felt at the time that Josh
was . . . well, jealous. Once or twice since I've heard him
put out the odd remark about his father as if he were his
enemy.'

'His enemy? You can't be serious.'

'Well, perhaps enemy is not the right word, but there
was something, and I should have made time to sort it
out there and then and I didn't.'

'With all the arrangements Mr Collier set up for
Joshua, not a soul could dispute that he loved that boy
dearly. Let's face it, Kate, he made more than ample
provision for his son. Josh will never want for anything.
All the same it's understandable, him being envious of
other boys with fathers and male relations, when as far as
he knows you and I are all he's got. I suppose it is about
time that you told him, not only about his early life, but
about your own as well. That might help. Sit him down
and tell him the truth, Kate. You won't regret it.'

'I'd go down on my bended knees and answer any
questions he cared to put to me if only he'd walk in
here this minute . . . I wish to God I knew where he
was.'

'Mum, Nanna, I'm sorry if you've been worried about
me,' Josh whispered, poking his head round the door.

Kate almost fell off her chair. Mary blinked and the
cup in her hand rattled as she put it down on the saucer.
She crossed the room and put her arms around Josh's
shoulders. 'You all right, love?' she asked giving the boy
a smile.

'Yes, Nan. I walked much further than I meant to
and when I thought I'd make for home and catch a bus,

I remembered I hadn't any money with me, so I had to walk back. Nan, I'm starving.'

'Go and tell your mother you're sorry,' she advised. 'I'll see about getting you something to eat.'

Joshua took a step towards his mother, then a step back. He looked exhausted and he was really grubby. She began to wonder how he had got in such a state.

'Mum? Please? I should have left you a note . . . I just want to tell you I'm sorry.'

'Oh, my love!' The words burst from her and she flew to him, touching his pale face and his thick blond hair which was flattened to his skull with perspiration. 'Why on earth didn't you wake me up if something was bothering you? Or you could have telephoned – reversed the charges – I'd have got a taxi and come to find you. Oh, son, don't you trust me? I know it's more than half my fault – I've had my mind on other things just lately – and you must have felt I'd shut you out. Why, oh why didn't you speak up?'

'Couldn't. I just thought you'd think I was raking up the past. Mr Weatherford told me things. Most of them I kind of half knew about. For a start—' He stiffened and moved out of the circle of her arms. 'I don't know very much at all, do I?'

Kate straightened up. He looked beaten and exhausted. 'Joshua, listen to me. Go up to your room, have a wash and change that shirt and pullover. By then your Nan will have your meal ready, and after you've eaten and had a drink, then we'll talk.'

He bent his head. He made such a sorry sight that Kate's heart ached for him. 'Go on then, upstairs and freshen up, then you'll feel heaps better.'

He nodded and went out meekly as she held the door open for him.

Mary had taken herself off on the pretext that she had to walk into the village to fetch soap flakes and corn plasters from the chemist. Kate smiled to herself. Corn plasters indeed!

'Shall we stay in the kitchen?' Kate asked looking directly at Josh. He shrugged. He had even washed his hair and changed into a short-sleeved white shirt and sleeveless pullover. He looked tons better now that he had eaten, no longer so ill at ease. Kate poured home-made lemonade into two glasses then carried them over to the table. She sat down on one of the pine chairs and, after a moment, Josh took the seat opposite her.

Kate looked steadily at him across the table. 'You'd better begin by telling me what upset you so much that you felt you had to get out of the house.'

'I don't quite know where to begin,' he said guardedly. 'Did you know Mr Weatherford was going to tell me all the arrangements were made for me to go to Eton and that this would be my last term at prep school?'

'Yes, I did. Is that what you wanted to talk to me about?'

He heaved a huge sigh and put both elbows on the table, staring steadily across at her. 'No. I wanted to ask why *you* didn't tell me and – well, that if all my education has been arranged in advance by my father, why aren't you involved more? Only then I started to think some more. I know you aren't my real mother, but I don't want anyone else. Only you – you and me – an' Nanna, only she's not really my nan. I love you . . .

373

but why is there so much secrecy about me? And about you an' all. One fellow at school said your parents were criminals. I gave him a bloody nose, but then . . . I just started to wonder . . . well . . . what made him say it in the first place?'

Kate reached across the table to catch hold of his hands. He was twelve years old, thirteen come Christmas, but he looked at this moment a sad, lonely little boy. The pain in her heart was almost more than she could bear.

'Joshua, from the moment you were put in my arms, you'd have been about six months old then, I made up my mind that I would always tell you the truth and to the best of my ability I've stuck to that resolution. Your mother was a lovely, kind lady who died the day you were born.'

Josh tugged his hands free from her grasp. 'Maybe, but she wasn't married to my father, was she?' he said stonily.

Kate waited a full minute before she took his shoulders gently between her hands and brought his face close to hers. 'Until this moment, Josh, I never thought what happened between my parents had any bearing on you. Now I see that it does. It was because of them that your wonderful father came to my rescue and I ended up living here at Melbourne Lodge, taking care of you.' She released her hold on him and sat back. 'Come on, we'll go into the front room, get comfortable and I shall start at the beginning, and I think you'll realise that most people have some sort of cross to bear.'

'All right,' Josh agreed sheepishly, 'we do seem to have a lot to talk about.'

'More than you know,' Kate said, as she led him

towards the two comfortable chairs that were set in the bay window.

Before starting, she kissed him. 'Just to let you know you mean the world to me, son.'

He didn't answer, just flung his arms around her waist and buried his face in her chest, and she held him tight for what seemed ages. At last they settled in the armchairs.

'A lot of the trouble started when I was only about two years old and my little brother was drowned in the river. My mother blamed my father and things were never the same between them after that, although they were marvellous, loving parents to me.' Kate paused, lost in thought. This was going to be very hard for her. Very hard indeed.

'Is that why you always insist that I wear a life jacket?' Kate nodded. Then slowly and painfully she recalled every minute of what had, at the time, been a ghastly nightmare. There were times when her voice was little more than a whisper, other times when she protested, 'You're too young to have to listen to all of this.'

Eventually she got to the time of the trial.

'My mother was found guilty of the murder of my father and the law decided that she had to pay for that act with her life. That was when I found out how dearly we need good friends in this life.'

Josh was crying quietly, yet Kate felt that she could not comfort him at this point, for if she were to stop now she would never have the courage to continue again.

'My cousin Hilda, who you met a few weeks ago, and her parents were as good as gold to me throughout the whole time. Hilda's mum was my mum's only sister.

Now you know why I had to go to London recently to find out what I could do for her now that she so badly needs a friend.'

Josh sniffed and rubbed his knuckles across his eyes but made no comment.

'After I lost my parents, my aunt and uncle persuaded me to go to London to live with them and I accepted, but it wasn't the kind of life I was used to and I came home. It was one morning soon after, when I was at my very lowest, that your father paid me a visit. The rest you know.

'I have thanked God every day of my life for the kindness and generosity of Charles Collier for allowing me to take care of his only son, Joshua Collier, whom he loved so dearly. And that is a fact that you, young man, would do well to remember throughout the whole of your life.'

Kate let out a deep breath and sat back. That was the first part of it over.

'Be a good boy and take those glasses to the kitchen and refill them, my throat is parched. Then you can tell me what you think is so wrong about having to change schools and anything else that is worrying you.'

Josh went around the end of the table and perched rather uncomfortably on Kate's knee. 'Poor mum, I didn't know . . . I always thought you were ever so happy.'

Kate did her best to stop herself from crying, picked up his hand and held it against her cheek. 'I am happy as long as I know that you are. Now, fetch us our drinks and then it's your turn to talk.'

When they were both once again sitting opposite each

other, Josh blurted out, 'Mum, you still haven't said why my father never married my mother. There must be a reason, or didn't he love her?'

'If only I had the words to tell you, Josh. He adored your mother. The pity of it was that they met late in his life. As a young man he married a lady who was always in poor health and they never had any children. When he met Jane, your mother, they fell in love. His wife never suffered because of their association, she was well provided for and both your father and Jane were very discreet. Jane lived here, in Melbourne Lodge, for years before you were born. Your nan took care of her and your father visited almost every day and stayed whenever he could, just the same as he did after you were born and right up to the time he died. You were the apple of his eye. More so because he had given up the hope of ever becoming a father; both he and your mother thought their prayers had been answered when they learnt that they were to have a baby. He was so proud of you, Joshua, but devastated by your mother's death.'

Josh touched her hand solemnly. 'Thank you for telling me.'

Kate could hear the tears in his voice. It was all too much for such a young boy, and it was a long time before he spoke again.

'Mum,' he began quietly, 'do you think I shall like it at Eton?'

That simple question broke the ice. They sniffed back their tears and grinned at each other. 'Oh, Josh, is it any wonder that I love you so much! You are going to sail through life. You and those big blue eyes of yours

377

will melt the hearts of all the ladies, you know that, don't you?'

'I don't want any ladies, only you and Nan. Mr Weatherford said I had to grow up now, because Eton is a big boys boarding school, but that doesn't mean that I can't get a cuddle from you two now an' again, does it?'

'I'll kill anyone that tells you different. No matter where you go, how tall you grow or how old you are, to me you will always be my baby, and the day you don't want to kiss me or cuddle up to me will be the day that I'd want to die.'

'Eton sounds so grand and so far away.'

'Don't be so daft. It's neither of those things. First off, you want to remember that it was your father who chose which schools you would go to, not Mr Weatherford or his partner. They look after your affairs very well and they care about you, but they are carrying out your father's orders. In his will he set out what he wanted for you in explicit terms. As you grow older you will begin to realise just how much you meant to him and the full extent of the legacy he left you.' Kate paused and took several deep breaths. Joshua was looking puzzled so she gave him a moment to let everything she had told him sink in. 'Your father went to Eton. I'm sure Mr Weatherford told you that, and then he went on to Cambridge University, just as you will in time.'

'Yes, he did tell me, but he said I will have to take the common entrance exam.'

'Is that all that is worrying you? Your housemaster told me at the end of term that you'd sail through. There is one thing you may not be aware of; you were registered to go to Eton almost on the day you were born. All you have to tell yourself is that you are there because your father wanted it. No one else. You will be walking in his footsteps and, though he couldn't make your mother his legal wife, he has done everything within his power to announce to the world that you are his son and heir. He has made sure that his own social background will secure a place for you at a school that takes pride in its historic role of educating the sons of gentry.'

'Do you have any idea what the uniform looks like?' Josh wailed.

Now Kate really did laugh. 'Not really,' she teased him, 'do you?'

'Mr Weatherford showed me a photograph. Black tail-coat, a waistcoat, pin-striped trousers, and you should see the daft winged collars that you have to wear with white bow ties.'

At the sight of Joshua's woeful face the tears trickled down Kate's, but they were happy tears now. 'Pity you have two more terms after Christmas to serve at Guildford. I can't wait to see you all dressed up. Still, as I was about to tell you before you started moaning about the uniform, Eton College is situated on the north bank of the Thames. Opposite Windsor. The castle stands just above the town. I shall be able to visit often. Besides seeing you I shall treat myself to a tour of the castle as I've never been inside it. That's another thing I'll have to do; inform Jack Stuart that I shall need a launch at my disposal so that I may cruise up the river to see how my son is faring at one of the best-known schools in all the world.'

'You're tormenting that poor boy!' Mary cried, as she came into the room.

'You're dead right, Nan, you've arrived back just in time to stop her.' Josh giggled and got to his feet to relieve her of some of the parcels she was carrying.

'I thought you were only going to the chemist,' Kate said, looking at the bags that were now spread out on the hearthrug.

'I called in at the farm to buy some tomatoes. They taste so different when they're picked straight off the vines, and guess what? They were just putting out a few punnets of strawberries, they'll more than likely be the last we shall see this year, lucky to find them so late. I thought they'd make a nice treat for tea and I got a lovely tub of thick cream while I was there.'

'Cor, great, Nan. What else is there for tea? I've only had one meal today,' Josh said, seeking sympathy.

'That's one more than you deserve, my boy,' Mary told him, pulling him close and giving him a hug. Over his shoulder Mary looked across the room at Kate and raised her eyebrows. Kate gave her the thumbs-up sign and a winning smile to go with it. If there was one thing that these two women, of very different ages, had in common it was the love and well-being of this young lad. They would go to the ends of the earth to ensure his good welfare and woe betide anyone who ever tried to hurt him.

Chapter Thirty-Four

JOSHUA'S HIGH SPIRITS were infectious and Kate felt her own heart lift as she watched him and Peter Bradley sort through the box of fireworks they were taking to the harvest celebrations. The frankness with which she had dealt with all his questions seemed to have worked. His anxieties and anguish appeared to have receded, and all at once Kate was filled with happiness, suddenly sure that the future was going to be right.

The evening was all that anyone could have hoped for: dry and quite warm with very little wind.

'It's the hustle and bustle of these occasions that I like, takes years off me,' Mary said as she helped several women to spread thick paper cloths over the trestle-tables the men had set up.

'They're going to light the first bonfire!' a young lad shouted and the cry was taken up all along the bank.

'Keep an eye on our fireworks, Mum,' Josh called

over his shoulder as he and Peter ran as fast as their legs would carry them.

Soon the air was filled with laughter and noisy singing as the scout master organised the children into groups. The smell of burning wood and the appetising aroma coming from various braziers helped to get folk into a party mood. Sausages by the dozen, rissoles, faggots and thick rashers of bacon were all sizzling away. Shrieks from excited kiddies sounded every now and then as great showers of sparks shot up through the air lighting up the dark sky. Farmers and farm labourers had all turned out with village residents to celebrate the bringing in of yet another harvest.

'Here, have a glass of cider,' Mike's voice cut into Kate's daydreaming.

She smiled her thanks as she took hold of the glass he was offering.

'Great turn out.' He beamed. 'We have a great many dos like this in Wales but there's something special about the whole affair when it's held right beside the river.'

As if in agreement with his comments, several tugs, barges and longboats that were anchored along the whole stretch of the towpath sounded their steam whistles and hooters at the same time and were greeted by loud cheers from the crowds. Kate smiled across at Mary. 'It's fun, isn't it?'

'Yes. Worth all the hard work that has gone into it. Yes, it's great fun.'

After a very late night everyone in the household, with the exception of Mike, was loathe to get out of their bed.

It was only after Mike had knocked on bedroom doors offering cups of tea and urging them to hurry otherwise they'd all be late for the special church service that Mary and Kate finally crawled downstairs.

'I shall never, as long as I live, touch another drop of cider,' Mary declared, holding her hand to her throbbing forehead. 'I hope I don't look as bad as I feel,' she continued, looking for sympathy that was unlikely to be forthcoming. 'Mike, did you wait to make sure that Josh was out of his bed?'

'No need, Mary, love. He was up and out as soon as he heard me about and he's eaten quite a good breakfast.'

'Thank the Lord for small mercies,' Mary declared, not feeling at all like cooking. 'Will toast be all right for you two?'

'One slice will be enough for me,' Kate replied.

'How about you, Mike?'

'Don't fret yourself, Mary, you'd probably pass out if I said I felt the need of bacon an' eggs. No, no, don't get flustered, I'm only teasing. I had all I wanted when Josh had his.'

Mary heaved a great sigh of relief.

Josh came in through the back door, all smiles as he said, 'It's a lovely morning, Peter's been round to say that his parents are having people round today and don't want him about, so is it all right if we clear off after we've been to church?'

'And where were you thinking of going?' his mother asked.

'Hampton Court,' Josh said eagerly. 'We can buy something to eat at midday – save us trailing back here

– 'cos if we wait until after lunch there won't be any of the day left to enjoy. You don't really mind, do you, Mum?'

Kate was sensible and understanding as always. 'You're doing the right thing, Josh, making the most of the weather before it breaks. I'll give you enough money to buy something decent to eat. Now, fifteen minutes and we must set off for church.'

'While you ladies sort out which hat you're going to wear I'll bring the car round to the front of the house. Come on, Josh, you come with me and then they won't be able to complain that it was us men who made them late,' Mike said, laughing loudly as, with his arm round Josh's shoulders, the pair of them went out through the back door.

The church looked beautiful. A credit to all the women who had worked so hard to achieve this final result. Each station of the cross was decorated with ears of corn while the steps to the altar glowed with floral arrangements, consisting mainly of Michaelmas daisies and sunflowers. Tables set to each side were laden with gifts of food which the children had brought and which, after the service, would be distributed among the poor. Three local bakers had each baked a huge loaf of bread, the top layer of dough having been intricately woven to form a sheaf of wheat. The service, taken by the Reverend Hutchinson, was one of thanks for the bountiful harvest which had been safely gathered in.

The last hymn of the morning was chiefly for the children and as the first chords of the organ rose up to the high rafters the congregation hastened to its feet.

*We plough the fields and scatter the good seed on the
   ground,*
But it is fed and watered by God's almighty hand.

No hymn books were needed the words were so familiar.
Then, a few minutes of silent prayer, each person alone
with their thoughts, and on out into the autumn sunshine.

'This lamb is very tender,' Kate remarked looking across
the table to where Mary sat.

'Yes, it was a good job I put the joint in the oven
before we set off for church.'

'Don't I get any praise for having done all the vegetables before either of you were out of bed?' Mike asked,
feigning hurt.

'Oh, you big baby,' Mary teased. 'You seem to be
eating your fair share of them, only right that you should
have done some of the work.'

He laid his knife and fork down on his plate and put
his hands up in the air. 'All right, I can see I shall get
nowhere by starting an argument with you two. Instead,
I shall offer to drive you out into the countryside this
afternoon and, to show my appreciation of your kind
hospitality, I shall buy you both the best cream tea we
can find. How does that sound?'

They looked at each other in dismay, but it was left
to Kate to answer. 'Have you forgotten, Mike? My
cousin and her husband are bringing my aunt down this
afternoon. I promised I'd be there when they arrived.
Somewhere about two o'clock is what Ben told me on
the telephone.'

Mike looked apologetic, thinking to himself that there wasn't much difference between hospitals or convalescent homes and he couldn't bear the thought of spending this lovely Sunday afternoon sitting around talking to an invalid.

Mary read his thoughts and Kate was quick to see disappointment show on her friend's face.

'Mary there isn't any need for you to be there.' And as she started to protest, waving her hand in the air to emphasise her intentions, Kate went on, 'Now don't be silly, Aunt Dolly will be here for a few weeks and you'll have ample opportunity to visit her, and if we think about it, it's probably much better that there's only me there when she arrives. She's sure to be tired after the journey and won't want a lot of company. No, you do as Mike says. Let him take you for a nice drive. I'll see you back here tonight.'

'I'll drop you off at the home, Kate, and we could come back for you later, if you're sure you don't mind.'

'I'm quite sure. And I will accept your offer of a lift into Kingston but, please, don't even think about coming back for me. I've no idea what time I shall leave. It all depends on how quickly Aunt Dolly settles in.'

Mary got up from the table.

'I'll fetch the tarts. I made two yesterday, one gooseberry and one apple,' she said, signalling to Kate with a nod of her head to follow her out. Once inside the kitchen Mary kicked the door closed and turned to face Kate. 'I know you're being considerate. Are you sure you can manage to settle your aunt in on your own?'

'I'm positive. Besides I won't be on my own. There's plenty of staff on duty and I don't suppose I shall stay that long myself. Aunt Dolly will need all the rest she can get. So, please, Mary, go off with Mike and have a nice afternoon. You deserve it. Both of you do.'

'Thanks, Kate,' she said, gently planting a kiss on her cheek.

Kate was getting worried, Mike had dropped her at the home at a quarter to two, almost an hour ago and still there was no sign of Aunt Dolly. Just as she was about to go to the front of the house the lounge door opened and Harriet Tremaine poked her head round the door.

'They're here.'

'Thank goodness for that,' Kate answered with relief.

The car was drawn right up to the entrance and Kate watched with mixed feelings as Hilda and Ben climbed out of the two front seats. Kate sighed to herself. Neither of them looked pleased and both were more than a little dishevelled. Bending her knees Kate peered into the back of the car and saw her aunt lying full length on the back seat, her head resting on a pillow. Her eyes were closed and she looked very hot. Kate introduced Harriet to Hilda and Ben, telling them she was the matron of the home.

'How do you do, Mrs Withers, Mr Withers? Pleased to meet you both,' Harriet said. 'I will be helping to take care of your mother. Hopefully a nice rest will have her feeling much better.'

Hilda cleared her throat and in what she thought was a posh voice said, 'I'm ever so grateful. It's really very good of you t'ave me mum like this.'

'Do we 'ave to stand 'ere on the blinking doorstep?' Ben asked, his voice sounding really rough.

Kate took a good look at him and came to the conclusion he was in a filthy mood and hoped to goodness he wasn't going to be rude to all the staff.

Harriet stepped back. 'I think the first thing is for me to get two nurses to help Mrs Hopkins up to her room.' Turning to face a well-built man who had been hovering in the doorway, she asked, 'Bob, will you take Mrs Hopkins things up to her room, while I show her relatives through to the lounge.'

'Certainly, matron,' he said, looking down at the small tattered case and brown paper parcel that Ben was taking from the boot of the car. 'Is that all there is, sir?'

Ben nodded as he stared at the two nurses in their smart white uniforms who were already gently assisting Dolly from the car and settling her comfortably in a wheelchair.

'You're very sleepy, aren't you, pet?' the taller of the two nurses remarked. 'Never mind, we'll soon have you tucked up in bed. Rest is what you need today, time enough tomorrow for you to get your bearings.'

'The doctor gave us a couple of pills to give 'er,' Hilda whispered to the nurse, 'she's been out like a light ever since we left 'ome.'

Good job too, Kate thought wryly to herself, as she watched the nurses wheel her aunt inside the building. With Dolly gone they stood around looking as if they weren't quite sure what to do next.

'Off you go, all of you,' Harriet said. 'I'll have some tea sent in to you and you can go up and see your mother once the nurses have made sure she is comfortable.'

Kate pulled her chair up close to the one that Hilda had plonked herself down on. Ben was standing with his back to them, staring out of the window.

'Now we're alone,' Kate said, 'you can tell me what's upset Ben, and why you have got dirty marks all down the front of your dress.'

'You wanna ask 'im,' Hilda loudly retorted, pointing a finger in the direction of her husband. 'We 'ad t'push the bloody car 'cos he was too mean t'put enough petrol in the tank.'

'Hilda, love, please don't shout and don't swear. You don't want to give the wrong impression on your first visit, do you?' she chided her cousin, but only half-heartedly for, to tell the truth, she felt really sorry for her.

'You 'aven't told 'er why I didn't put petrol in the motor,' Ben shouted angrily. 'Oh, no, you're the goodie an' I'm the baddie. I didn't 'ear you offering to pay for any an' after all it is your old lady, not mine, that I've given up me Sunday for, and what thanks do I get? Nothing but an ear bashing from you all the way down 'ere. Nag, nag, nag. Just you going on an' on about money.' Red in the face, Ben stuffed his fists into his trouser pockets and if looks could kill his wife would have fallen down stone dead. 'I can't 'elp it if I'm skint,' he mumbled.

'Hmm, I'd like to know whose fault you think it is then.'

Ben mumbled something else.

'I didn't hear that,' Hilda snapped.

'I said I had a good tip, risked a bundle, an' it didn't come off,' he retorted.

389

'How much is a bundle?' she snapped at him, her voice louder than before.

'None of your business. I never 'ear you complaining when I come 'ome with me pockets bulging, then it's let's buy this or the kids need that. I thought I could win last night,' he shouted back.

'Stop it, the pair of you. This is neither the time nor the place for you to air your differences.'

Hilda muttered, 'Sorry.' She sounded bitter.

Kate looked directly at Ben, but he steadfastly refused to meet her gaze. She leant across and squeezed Hilda's hand. Speaking softly so that Ben would be unable to hear from where he stood, she said, 'Before you leave I'll slip you some money. You needn't say anything about it to Ben.' Then seeing Hilda start to cry, Kate had the urge to leave the two of them alone. It wasn't any of her business. She excused herself hurriedly saying, 'I'm going to see what's happened to our tea.'

The next half-hour dragged by. They had drunk their tea, eaten the dainty sandwiches and fancy cakes that Harriet Tremaine had so thoughtfully provided with hardly a word passing between them.

'Right,' Kate said eventually, with a lot more determination than she was feeling, 'I'm sure it will be all right for us to go up and see Dolly now.' Looking directly at Hilda, she added, 'There's a bathroom at the end of the corridor, I'm sure you'd like a wash and brush up before you set off home.'

'Well, don't take all day about it,' Ben muttered sullenly. 'I wanna get on the road soon as I can.'

Neither Hilda nor Kate answered him, nor did they look in his direction as they made for the door, they took it for granted that he didn't want to come up to Dolly's room to say goodbye.

A nurse was just coming out of a front bedroom as they reached the top of the stairs. She smiled and held open the door. 'Mrs Hopkins is very comfortable but I'm afraid we haven't been able to rouse her properly. She's still very groggy, but she has had a long drink and drifted off back to sleep. Probably the best thing,' she added brightly.

'Thank you, nurse,' Kate answered.

'Sorry, but I've got to go t'the lav,' Hilda exclaimed and as soon as Kate raised a finger and pointed, she was off at a run heading for the bathroom at the far end of the landing.

Kate was so pleased that Dolly had been given one of the nicest rooms in the home. It had a beautiful view. The round bay window looked out across a well-kept lawn and further onto the quiet leafy area that Kate had come to know so well. For a moment she laughed to herself, for the image that was uppermost in her mind was that of Alice in her old coat, floppy felt hat and lace-up boots, her workworn hands scattering corn for her hens where now there was such smooth green grass. She turned from the window and sat down in the wicker armchair that had been placed beside the bed. Oh dear, she sighed softly, how small Aunt Dolly seemed lying in the high wide bed, but at least she looked comfortable, her shoulders and head were resting on a mound of snow-white pillows which were, in turn, supported by a metal bedrest. Her arms lay on top of the bedclothes and Kate took one of her hands between both of her own. She was still sitting whispering soft words of comfort when

391

the door was pushed open and a much cleaner, tidier looking Hilda came into the room.

'Cor, ain't this nice,' Hilda breathed almost reverently. 'If being 'ere don't make me mum get better I don't know what will.' She looked across at Kate, then at her sleeping mum and more to herself than to her cousin she mumbled, 'I wish t'God I could stay 'ere with 'er for a while. Do me a power of good t'get away from my lot.'

'She does look comfortable, doesn't she? There's not much point in either of us staying here much longer today. I'll come back in the morning. In fact, I shall visit her most days and I'll ring you each evening and let you know what progress she's making.'

'Aw, Kate,' Hilda cried, quickly crossing to her side, 'I'll never be able to thank yer for all you're doing. You're a brick, you really are.'

'You're not so bad yourself,' she told her cousin, slipping a five-pound note into her pocket.

They stood each side of the bed and quietly said their goodbyes to Dolly.

'Poor ole Mum, 'asn't she suffered enough?'

'Being here will make all the difference, you'll see. She'll soon be her old self.'

'I 'ope you're right,' Hilda said as the two of them linked arms and went back down the stairs.

Ben was standing only a few feet away from the front door. 'I thought you said you weren't going to be long,' he snapped, facing Hilda angrily across the wide hall.

'I wasn't. Anyway, you should be glad that Kate has got my mum in such a lovely place as this, rather than keep on complaining all the time.'

392

'Yeah, yeah, just get in the car, will you? And for heaven's sake, let's be on our way. I've stood more than enough for one day.'

Kate said goodbye and watched until the car was out of sight. Listening to them bickering had made her realise what a comfortable, quiet life she led. Sometimes a bit too quiet, she thought as she went back inside to have a chat with Harriet Tremaine.

But if Hilda and Ben's life was anything to go by she wasn't going to complain too much. Instead she would count her blessings.

Chapter Thirty-Five

THE AFTERNOON WAS still lovely. Kate had left behind
the hat she had worn to church that morning and now the
breeze coming off the river blew her hair across her face.
She had decided to walk home, but then asked herself,
Why? There's nobody there.

Presently she realised she had turned away from the
towpath and was heading for the town centre. Across
the road, standing outside Kingston bus depot she saw
a green double-decker bus. The conductor was just
changing the destination blind and out of curiosity she
stopped to see where it was heading. DORKING came
up, and this surprised her; it being a Sunday she hadn't
known that the buses ran on that route.

She hesitated, then shaking herself, she said out loud,
'Why not?' and with that, she ran across the road and
boarded the bus. Her foot was half on the lower deck
when she changed her mind, turned about and swung
herself up the stairs. There were few folk on the top

deck and those who were had chosen seats at the back. She walked the length of the gangway and settled herself in the very front seat which would give her a splendid, clear view throughout the journey.

Having paid for a return ticket she settled back to enjoy the late afternoon sunshine wishing that the driver was allowed to slow down whenever a particularly beautiful place came into view. Couples joined and got off the bus at various stops. She envied them each other's company and fell to wondering if they were going to visit parents or friends or perhaps have tea together. Be nice to have someone to talk to. Then she grinned, scolding herself at the same time. You were glad enough to see the back of Ben and Hilda, now you're feeling sorry for yourself because you're on your own. You can't have it both ways.

Now the area seemed familiar and Kate knew they were nearing the end of the journey, but suddenly she had no intention of going as far as Dorking. She pulled on her white gloves, picked up her handbag and made for the top of the stairs.

The conductor looked upwards, 'Not there yet, love.'

'I realise that, but aren't we nearing Box Hill?'

'We are indeed. Next stop. D'you want to get off there?'

'Please,' she said, descending the last few steps to stand on the platform, making sure she held on tightly to the handrail.

She stood at the foot of the hill. It looks a long way up she mused to herself, oh well, never mind, I'm here now and I've nothing better to do. She walked and, as the footpath became steeper, she paused, breathing heavily, thinking, it's beautiful. Further up still, she gasped, oh, the air is like wine. She rested three times before she finally reached the top where the footpath petered out. A track continued under leafy trees that had mossy, gnarled trunks, the grass was sweet and green, and there was a bank covered in cow-parsley and buttercups. 'Mmm,' Kate said drowsily, 'I'm going to sit myself down under this tree and have forty winks.'

The last time she had been here was with Toby. Just for a moment his face came clear to her mind, the soft grey eyes, the wide smiling mouth, the way his hair was flattened down when he took his hat off and he would run his fingers through it. She let herself recall every detail of that rainy day when he had first made love to her. The day he had taught her what it felt like to be loved. To be a real woman. She looked across to where, in the distance, the pub lay where they had sat outside and enjoyed their drinks, and he had never stopped telling her how much he loved her. Two years ago. Two hard, long years with never a word or a sign that he had meant a word that had been said. But had she ever doubted him? Not really! An odd moment when she had felt utterly alone, longing to feel his arms around her, with his body close to hers, but only momentarily. Toby was a good man. It was unfortunate that the time hadn't been right when they met. But they had met! Coming together in just a few days to experience such a deep love that many couples never encountered in a whole lifetime together. Of that much she was absolutely sure.

And two years to the day her faith had been justified. Red roses, a letter and a firm promise had come. I will be back.

She had believed it at Easter when the package had arrived and although it was now September she still believed it.

Could she bear to go to the pub and buy herself a drink? No, that would be too painful. The sun was going down, already it was much cooler, but she would stay for a few minutes more. Presently she got to her feet, brushed the leaves and grass from the skirt of her dress and began to descend the great hill.

One day she would come back here again with Toby. He would take her hand to make sure she didn't slip. He would again tell her how they had been destined to meet; that he had loved her from the moment he had come to her rescue that day in Kingston and that he would go on loving her for the rest of his life. She would feel whole again. Just as a woman in love with a man who adored her should and would feel. She stood still for a long moment. Kate closed her eyes and prayed with every fibre of her being, 'Please God, let it be soon. Bring Toby back to England and grant that we may never be parted again.'

She was still silently saying that prayer as she boarded the bus that would take her back to Kingston.

Chapter Thirty-Six

KATE DECIDED THAT she had to live for today. She longed for the time when Toby would be back in England, but the months were stretching out. It couldn't possibly be another two years before she was able to set eyes on him again.

She did her various tasks: mended Joshua's sport kit, sewing name tags inside all the new items, took him to London twice to select books for his last term at Guildford. She helped Mary pick the Bramley apples, which had grown in such abundance this year, and then they'd bottled them, stored them and also made lots of pies. She took bags of these lovely cooking apples with her when she went to visit Aunt Dolly, which was at least three times a week. It was a wonder to the patients and the staff just how many various tasty puddings cook managed to turn out from them.

It was also a wonder to Kate the remarkable change in her aunt. In the few weeks that Dolly had been staying

399

at the Alice Memorial Homes, she had put on weight, her cheeks had filled out, her hair looked thicker and certainly had more shine to it. Best of all, her eyes were brighter and her speech much improved. Hilda, in that typical cockney way she had of putting her finger right on the heart of the matter, had summed her mother up by saying, 'She's more with it now than she's been for ages.'

Since that unforgettable day when Ben had driven his wife and mother-in-law down to Kingston he had never put in another appearance. But Hilda had never missed a Sunday, coming only once by train. Her twin brothers, Stan and Tom, both now car owners had taken turns to drive her down to visit their mother, even bringing their father with them, though he had vowed he would never visit her while she was in a home. Seeing Bert and her boys had been as good as any tonic for Dolly.

This morning Kate walked along beside the high stone wall until she reached the black, wrought-iron gates which were always open during daytime. Her feet made a crunching sound as she walked down the clean, weed-free gravel driveway and up towards the main entrance of the convalescent block.

A big ginger cat came slowly across the lawn and stood looking at her out of large, green eyes. It brushed against her legs and stayed close until she reached the front door, then it miaowed loudly.

'So you want to come inside, do you, cat?' she asked. 'I don't blame you, the weather is not so nice this morning, is it? In you go then.' She held the door open, allowing the cat to go by.

She popped her head round the door of the lounge and

was greeted by several ladies calling, 'Good morning, Kate.' She answered them, smiling at each in turn. Although it was still quite early, some were reading the morning papers, others were knitting or sewing. Two men, both seated in wheelchairs, whizzed across the room and came to a stop in front of her.

'Come in, come in,' Joe said pleasantly.

Edward, Joe's companion, grinned. 'I'll give you two guesses where your aunt is at this moment.'

Kate leant forward and in a conspiratorial manner whispered in Edward's ear, 'Then I had better get upstairs quickly before she drowns herself.'

Both men laughingly agreed.

She climbed the stairs to the first floor and was met by Molly Symonds, who had been working as a daily cleaner from the first day the home had opened. Kate felt they had become good friends.

'Morning, Kate,' Molly greeted her, nodding her head towards the end of the corridor.

'Morning, Molly. I guessed as much. My aunt will never get used to the luxury of running hot water.'

'Can't say as I blame her, wish we had it in our house. Anyway Nurse Davison saw Mrs Hopkins safely into the bath and there is a bell in there if she needs help, though she's come on like a house on fire since she's been here. Proper under the weather when she arrived, wasn't she?'

'Yes, she certainly is better,' she agreed, before walking down the corridor to the bathroom.

'It's only me,' Kate called, pushing open the bathroom door. Dolly stood leaning against the white tiled wall with a bath towel wrapped round her body, enveloped in a cloud of steam.

401

'Are you all right?' she asked cautiously.

'Never better in the whole of me blooming life,' Dolly answered as she began to rub her hair vigorously. 'D'yer want t'know something, Kate, luv, I was scared witless the first time those lovely nurses lowered me down into this bath full of water. Thought I was about to drown and that was no joke, I'm telling yer!'

Kate laughed loudly and, taking a small towel from the rail she helped finish drying her aunt's hair.

'Where's your talcum powder? I'll do your back for you. Sit down on the stool. The way you're weaving about you're going to fall over.'

'Well, I'm trying t'get me knickers on before that lass comes back.'

'Oh, Aunt Dolly, you are a one, and no mistake.'

'That's as may be,' Dolly retorted, wriggling her long bloomers up over her ankles. 'It's all right for those that are used to all these newfangled luxuries but when, like me, you ain't never 'ad the whole of yer body dunked into 'ot water before, it comes as a bit of a shock t'yer system.'

'Now you're stretching it a bit. I know for a fact you have regular baths at home. Don't forget I lived with you for a while.'

'And you think our tin bath in front of the fire amounts to the same thing, d'yer? Well, young lady, let me tell yer this. Four or five kettles of water, yer knees propped up under yer chin and yer bum stuck to the ridges of a tin bath don't exactly compare to what I'm fast becoming used to 'ere. And . . .' Dolly paused and grinned wickedly . . . 'more's the pity that my Bert ain't 'ere wiv me, Gawd knows what capers we could 'ave got up to in that tub there. More than enough room for him.'

'Aunt Dolly! Behave yourself!' Kate had a hard job to keep a straight face and was quite relieved when Nurse Davison put in an appearance and took charge.

'Don't suppose you've got a spare pair of stockings in yer bag, ave yer, Kate?' Dolly asked.

'No, but I'll slip out to the shops presently and buy you some,' she called back.

At the foot of the stairs, Harriet Tremaine was waiting. 'Been experiencing your aunt's bath session first hand?'

'You can say that again. I'd say she is almost back to normal, which rather poses a problem, don't you think? We can never be sure what Dolly will say or do next and I dread the day when I have to tell her the time has come for her to go home.'

'Come and have a coffee with me,' Harriet suggested, 'and don't let it worry you. Nobody, staff and patients alike, wants to see the back of Mrs Hopkins. She's liked by everyone and that includes the doctors. And as to going home, you'll see. This peace and quiet and sitting around with no chores to do has suited her just fine while she hasn't been feeling so well, but come the day when she has her full strength back, that's when family, friends and familiar surroundings will begin to call. What do they say about East Enders? Never happy for long away from the sound of Bowbells. Your aunt will let us know when she's had enough of us.'

Kate put out a hand to rest on Harriet's arm, 'You've been a saint. I can't begin to thank you. I mean it. You've done a lot for my aunt.'

'Ever thought that without your generosity these premises would never have come into being?' Then without waiting for Kate to reply Harriet hastily added, 'Come through to the kitchen, Cook will no doubt find us a morsel to have with our coffee.'

Kate did as she was bid. Following Harriet down the corridor she thought that what goes round comes round. It wasn't only the patients who had gained. The homes had provided jobs not only for professional people but for lots of ordinary workers such as cleaners, maids and gardeners. They have meant a lot to me too, she prompted herself. They have given me and Mary a new interest in life. Something useful with which to occupy our time, and we both really do enjoy the fund raising. When it came to boiling it all down, the main people responsible for all of this had to be her grandparents. None of this could have come about if her grandfather hadn't been prudent as a young man. To have bought the first plot of land and built his own house had shown foresight but the purchase of the field beyond had increased his investment no end. Add all that to the fact that Alice, although widowed early in life, had never felt the urge to sell up and live on the proceeds. She had worked, out and about in all weathers, and finally left the house and all the land to her only granddaughter. I hope you can see what has been done with your home, Gran, she murmured to herself and, most important, I hope you approve. She smiled. I wonder what Dolly would say to my gran if she were to appear now. Gawd bless yer, more than likely!

Kate stayed the day with Dolly, taking the opportunity to pop to the shops while the patients were being given their lunch. And about four o'clock, when she took her leave, Dolly was busy helping three other ladies to set up the card table for a game of whist.

By the time Kate got into bed that night it was raining hard and a fierce wind was blowing the rain against the window panes, causing then to rattle in their wooden frames. She huddled down in bed and pulled the sheet high up over her head, thankful she wasn't out on a night like this.

Suddenly something made her stir and she immediately felt that someone was there, in her room. She sat up, stretched . . . and saw him.

Was she dreaming? Charles Collier was dead! But he looked real enough as he stood staring at her from the foot of the bed. He looked well. A fine gentleman, dressed as she remembered in the height of fashion. Lovely jacket, corded breeches and knee-high boots.

She tried to slide back down, her hands flying to cover her mouth; she didn't want to scream, but she was having a hard job stopping herself. He smiled at her.

In little more than a trembling whisper, she asked, 'Why . . . what . . . ?'

'I don't mean to scare you.' His voice also was just as she remembered. 'First I have to thank you. Your efforts on my son's behalf have been extraordinary. He is a credit to you and to my name. I chose well.'

Kate couldn't find words to answer him. This wasn't happening! It couldn't be. She felt apprehensive but not scared, well, not very.

'Please, go up into the attic. Find my small leather

attaché case. It has my initials on it.' His tone of voice turned the request into a plea.

She said nothing, but drew in a deep breath. Suddenly the room felt awfully cold.

'I have used up my allotted time,' he said sadly. 'Thank you so much, Kate.'

And before she could say any of the things that were racing around in her head his outline became misty, he dropped his arms to his sides and slowly vanished from her sight.

To go back to sleep was impossible, she tossed and turned, got out of bed and stood staring out of the window. The wind seemed to have died down; the garden looked peaceful. Everything was in order except for her thoughts. Had she imagined it? She knew full well she hadn't. Would she tell Mary about the visit? No! And certainly not Josh! She got back into bed, longing for daylight to break. She made up her mind that as soon as a favourable time presented itself she would be up in the attic. If I have to move every piece of old junk up there then I will, she vowed. If a case with the initials C. C. C. was there then, by golly, she was going to find it and see for herself what the significance of Charles's ghostly appearance would turn out to be.

When, at breakfast next morning, Mary said she thought she really must go into Kingston and get her hair cut Kate felt like getting up from her chair and throwing her arms around her.

'Why don't you call a taxi, go in early, look round the shops, treat yourself to lunch – make a day of it,' she gabbled, trying to use her powers of persuasion.

'If I didn't know you better, I'd say you were trying

to get rid of me,' Mary said, giving Kate a funny look. 'Why don't you come with me?'

'I don't feel like it. Not today. I've several jobs I've been meaning to do for ages and with the place to myself I think today will be the day to sort them out.'

Mary stood up, not totally convinced. But thinking that Kate really did want some time on her own, she nodded. 'Well, if you're sure, I'll get dressed and then I will phone for a taxi.'

Oh, thank you, God, Kate breathed softly, wondering just how she was going to get herself up into the attic with no one else in the house to assist her.

She stood at the door, waving to Mary as the cab driver closed the passenger door, climbed into the driver's seat and drove away.

She felt guilty. She knew that Mary was aware that her excuses for not going with her had been only half-truths. But what else could she have done? Told her that a man who had been dead for more than three years had come to see her last night and asked her to fetch down a case he had left up in the attic? Mary would think she had gone mad. And who could blame her? She wasn't sure herself that it hadn't all been in her imagination. Now was the time for her to prove that Mr Collier had appeared in her bedroom last night, and the quicker she got herself up in the attic the better she'd be able to do just that.

First things first. From the cupboard under the stairs she fished out a wraparound overall with long sleeves and once she had it on, with the tapes tied securely around her waist, she rummaged for a mop-cap, pushing her thick tresses well in under the brim because there would be layers of dust for her to contend with. She climbed to the top floor of the house, thankful that a pair of stepladders was kept up there.

She set them up immediately below the trapdoor. Climbing to the top of the steps wasn't too bad, but balancing herself and at the same time reaching up and using both hands to force the square door upwards and inwards was a job and a half, and she was quivering from head to toe by the time she had managed to do it. She reached in, laid the torch down and switched it on.

'Good gracious me,' her cry was one of exasperation when she finally stood up straight between the rafters and looked around, 'half this stuff must have been here from the day the house was built.'

Instinct told her that a small case would probably be on a shelf and seeing a number of them set between the supporting beams to her left she turned and went in that direction, moving several tea chests and a couple of old trunks out of her path as best she could. There were three cases of sorts and she felt someone must be guiding her to have found them this quickly. With a great deal of trepidation, she reached up, pulling the top one towards her, which was a mistake. 'Good God,' she muttered, dropping the soft leather case and bowing her head as low as it would go. A thick cloud of dust encircled her. She sneezed and waved her arms trying to disperse it. She had expected dust, but this was beyond anything she had imagined. It was choking her. She wished she had thought to bring some wet cloths up with her. She felt in the pocket of the apron. A duster, that would do to tie around her nose and mouth. Having done just that she grinned, what a sight I must look and what a good job Mary isn't here to see me. She drew in a deep breath, causing the duster to suck in between her lips. It tasted awful.

The case she had lifted down was not an attaché case, more like a music case, soft with a bar that slipped over the handle. She didn't bother to pick it up from where it had fallen, just moved it aside with her foot.

Learning from her first mistake, Kate gently wiped some of the dust away from the second case, using the sleeve of her apron. It was a cheap papier mâché case with a tin handle.

'Third time lucky? I hope so,' she said out loud.

She wasn't enjoying being up here, not one little bit. All she managed to do with the aid of her other sleeve was smear the dust enough for her to realise that this third case was one of good quality. Somehow she had to get it down from that shelf. Closing her eyes tightly and lowering her head she reached up, groped for the handle, and grabbed it, at the same time taking a step backwards, thus avoiding the worst of the swirling dust. Still grasping the leather handle she banged the case once on the floor, loosening some of the still clinging dust. When she brought it up to eye level she could not believe what she was seeing. Faint, yes, but they were there.

She pulled the duster from her face, wrapped a corner of it around her forefinger and spat on it. With the case flat on the floor she rubbed furiously at the embedded dirt and grime, and got her reward. C. C. C. The initials were there, just as Charles Collier had said they would be.

Two hours had sped by but still Kate was being cautious. With great difficulty she got herself safely down from the attic, the only casualty being the big

torch she'd taken up with her. Having dropped it as she
climbed through the hatchway back onto the stepladder
the glass had broken and she'd hidden it away in the
cupboard under the stairs. She didn't want Mary asking
awkward questions. Not yet anyway.

Are you by any chance being a coward? Kate asked
herself. She had cleared away all traces of a disturbance
from the top landing, had a bath and washed her hair
but still she had not looked inside. Well, she couldn't
put it off any longer. With newspapers spread all over
the kitchen table she sat herself down with the case in
front of her and her heart in her mouth. She slid back
the locks and opened the lid.

Some fifty minutes later she sat back and rubbed away
a tear from her eyes.

'Joshua,' she breathed, 'your father was indeed a true,
kind gentleman. If I were offered a pot of gold I could
never explain how, when or why he came to me last
night. But I am totally convinced he did! He must be
watching over you, Josh. He somehow knew the fears you
had about going to Eton and the unanswered questions
that lingered in your mind about your parents. In here
is the history of your father's life; at least all his early
years until his coming of age and starting out into the
world, just as you are about to do.'

Kate rose from her seat, filled the kettle and placed
it on the hob to boil. She badly needed a cup of tea.
She felt now that she would be able to tell Mary what
had taken place. After all, she had been with Mr Collier
for years and she would probably be familiar with a lot
of the events that the documents in the case referred
to. She wouldn't write to Josh about her find. Neither

would she tell him over the telephone. She'd wait until he came home at half-term and then he could take his time, going carefully through each and every document, tracking his father's younger days. There wasn't an item missing as far as she could tell. Right from his baptism at the age of one month, until the day he had left Cambridge University. It was all there: school reports, awards for swimming and diving, dozens of certificates for all manner of sporting events. Even school photographs, which over the years had turned brown with age but from which she and Mary would have no difficulty in pointing out his father from among his colleagues.

There was one photograph in particular that she felt would thrill Josh more than the ones taken as a group. It was of his father and a friend walking beneath the portals of Eton, each wearing wing collars, the kind Josh professed to hate so much, their arms full of books. It was a great gift that Mr Collier had somehow seen fit to give to his son. One that she was sure Joshua would really appreciate.

Chapter Thirty-Seven

SEPTEMBER HAD COME and gone and more than half of October with it. In the early mornings the air was sharp and filled with the smell of burning wood as folk lit their fires and the smoke curled upwards out of the tall chimney stacks. The trees had shed most of their leaves, making a carpet on the earth of reds and golds. Why was it that sometimes time sped by so quickly but whenever Kate thought of Toby days seemed like weeks and the weeks like months?

It was half-term and Josh was home again. Before she had settled down to sleep the night before Kate had made up her mind that in the morning she was going to collar Josh before he went out. It was difficult. For the short time he would be home he had so much he wanted to do, so many friends to see and, of course, he never came home without paying a visit to his beloved boat yard. Come what may, she had to tell him about the case, get him to sit down and go through it for himself. Despite her determination it hadn't worked out that way. She was still in the bathroom when she heard Peter Bradley arrive at the house and minutes later Josh called up the stairs that they were going to Hampton Court to see Jack Stuart.

Kate had told Mary of everything that had happened, resulting in her finding the attaché case. Mary had been wonderful, never once did she ridicule any part of what Kate had said. Only when she described Charles Collier standing at the foot of her bed, did Mary risk an interruption.

'I have always believed that there is more goes on not only in heaven but on this earth than we mere mortals will ever fathom.'

Kate nodded her head at this comment, for she now knew it to be true.

'Come on,' Mary eventually said, 'let's clear the table. I'll wash up and you can wipe.'

A little later she spoke again, 'Kate, you've wiped that saucer so many times it's a wonder there's any pattern left on it. I'm not daft, I know what's bothering you; it's that you haven't got round to telling Josh yet.'

'It isn't that easy,' Kate said indignantly. 'How can I possibly say to a young boy that his dead father paid me a visit?'

'Nobody's asking you to do that.'

'So you tell me, what do I say to him?'

'Keep calm. Tell him the truth, that you were up in the attic, sorting things out and you discovered the case with his father's initials on it. There's no need to go into any more details than that.'

'I suppose you're right.'

414

'I know I am. Now get yourself ready, go to Hampton Court, get Josh on his own and tell him what can only be good news. This find will be worth a lot to him. I for one can't wait to see his face when he gets a look at some of those photographs.'

'I wish I could be as sure as you are that he will be pleased, and most of all I hope he won't start asking awkward questions.'

'There you go again, meeting trouble before it troubles you.' Mary gave her a little push. 'Go on, get yourself ready. And while you're doing that I'll pack you some food, luckily I made some pasties first thing. If you show up with some food and drink you're sure to get a welcome from Josh.'

The river was not all that busy but as Kate walked down the slipway she paused at the entrance to the Kearsley Boat Yard and stood staring upriver. What she saw brought a smile to her face and revived good memories. A brightly painted longboat, its sides covered with intricate pictures, was being loaded with timber. Two great carthorses were tethered out on the grass.

''Ow yer doing, Kate?' Mickey Wilson yelled from where he was precariously perched on top of the load.

'I'm fine, Mickey. Good to see you,' Kate responded. 'We missed you and your family at the harvest festival party this year. Where's Bert? Don't often see one of you without the other.'

'I'm 'ere.' A tousled mop of dark hair appeared over the side and within seconds Bert had jumped down onto the bank and was coming towards her. 'Luverly t'see yer, gal.' He threw his arm round Kate's shoulders and held her close. 'Seen that lad of yours this morning, my he can 'andle a craft, you'd think he'd been born on the river.'

Kate laughed. 'He practically was. And how's all your brood? Is your mum with you this trip?'

'No, she's the reason we didn't turn up for the end-of-the-season do. One of me sister's had another baby. Me mother's twenty-third grandchild. She wasn't going t'miss that. Anyway, must get cracking else Mickey will be saying I'm skiving. See you, Kate,' he shouted, waving like mad as he walked several paces backwards before turning and breaking into a run.

Kate had more than an hour to wait before she heard Josh hailing her. She turned to look upriver, my God those two boys had some energy. Josh and Peter were rowing with a steady rhythm. Knees up under their chins one minute, then legs outstretched, shoulders hunched forward then straightened, elbows bent, arms out full-length. Their actions never altered; perfectly in time with each other, their oars skimmed the water as they steered into the bank. Both lads were wearing thick white polo-necked jerseys, which accentuated the tan they had acquired during the summer months. With the boat securely moored, Josh grinned at his mother, and asked, 'And what's brought you out here so early in the morning?'

'I just thought I'd like to see what the two of you were getting up to.'

He looked unconvinced. 'I was going to see if there was anything I could do in the yard, Peter has to go home, his grandparents are coming for lunch.'

'See you. Bye,' Peter called, as he trotted off down the towpath.

'Come on now, Mum, tell me why you're really here. Do you have something important to tell me?'

'Why is it you always seem able to keep one jump ahead of me?'

'It's because you have such an open face, it's easy to tell when you have something on your mind.'

'Well, we had better find somewhere out of the wind where we can have a picnic, and I think I can safely say that you'll be pleased to hear my news.'

'You've brought food with you?'

'Now, would I come without? Or, more to the point, would your nan let me leave the house without a basket filled with good things for her favourite boy to eat? I've left the basket back in the office. I didn't see Jack Stuart about anywhere.'

'No, he was leaving just as Pete and I got here. He's taken the biggest launch up to the Port of London Authorities. I think he said they wanted a demonstration of some kind. Most of the other men are working in the yard. Did you want Jack for something particular?'

'No, I knew he couldn't be about or he would have come out to see me the minute I arrived. So, where are we going to have this picnic?'

'Let's fetch the basket first and I'll bring a chair out for you to sit on,' he said, running on ahead.

As always it's first things first with Josh, she thought as she sat eating a sandwich while he munched away on pasties and sausages, still warm thanks to the way Mary had wrapped them. When he had finished with the savouries and was winding up with an apple, he suddenly said, 'All right, let's hear it.'

417

'A few days ago,' Kate began, 'I made a rather interesting discovery.' She hesitated and Josh gave her a puzzled look. Sure now that she had his full attention, Kate told her story and then patiently answered several questions he carefully put to her. Satisfied that his mother had said all she was going to on this strange matter, Josh leant back on the rug, resting on his elbows, and stared up into her face.

'This case you've found must have been up in the attic even when my father was alive,' he murmured thoughtfully. 'Directly after dinner tonight, if it's all right by you, I'll take the case up to my room and go through it.'

'Good,' she said, knowing that his head was still full of unasked questions.

'Can I ask you a personal question?' Josh broke into Kate's thoughts, catching her unawares.

'Of course.'

'A little while ago you told me all about your parents and your relations in London, but you never said whether there had ever been a special man in your life. Didn't you ever wish there was?'

Kate held her breath and hesitated.

'Come on, Mum, no lady as pretty as you can have gone all this time without at least a few men showing interest.'

'Flattery won't get me to tell you all my secrets! I suppose there have been a few. When I was a young girl I had a boyfriend and when we first started the scheme that resulted in the Alice Memorial Homes being built, the borough surveyor took me out a couple of times.'

'And?'

'And nothing. I liked him but it went no further than that.'

'So you're telling me there's never been anyone else. Was it because you had me to look after that you hadn't time for a life of your own?'

'Oh, Josh! You mustn't think that. I've had a wonderful life, there's not a moment from the day I set eyes on you that I would have changed.'

'I know how much you love me. But you still haven't answered my question. Was there ever anyone?'

Kate sighed, thinking that this adopted son of hers was wise beyond his years. 'All right,' she said softly, 'there was and, hopefully, is someone.'

Josh let out a whoop of delight. 'Tell me. Come on, tell me.'

Kate began to tell Josh the bare outline of her meeting Toby just before Easter in 1932. He was still staring at her spellbound when she wound up her story by giving him an account of the day the roses and the letter had arrived, two years from the day that he had left her to go to South Africa. When Joshua remained silent Kate found herself praying desperately that he wouldn't read more into the story than she had seen fit to tell him, and also that he wouldn't blame himself for the fact that Toby had gone and she had stayed.

Quite suddenly he raised his head and, looking wistful, said, 'I hope he does come back to you, and I hope he likes me.'

Kate looked at him feeling totally bewildered, asking herself if she had heard him right. 'Josh, you just said you hoped he would like you. How about whether or not you would like him?'

419

Josh gave her one of his special boyish grins. 'I shall like him. If you like him so much that you've waited all this time, I'd say he has to be a really special kind of chap.'

'Oh, Josh! You're a very special lad yourself,' she told him in a voice trembling with emotion.

During dinner that evening Joshua appeared happy, not in any way upset or anxious because of the attaché case.

It was just eight o'clock when Kate went out into the hall and came back with the case, holding it out to Josh and smiling at him. He stood still for a moment, staring at his father's initials and Kate knew that he was feeling more apprehensive about the contents than he was letting on.

'Goodnight, Nan,' he said in a strangely quiet voice. Then turning to his mother he took the case from her, kissed her cheek and said, 'I'll see you in the morning.'

'You can come down and ask me questions if there is anything you don't understand,' she said, finding it hard to refrain from offering to go upstairs with him.

'Yes, perhaps I will,' he agreed cautiously.

Kate and Mary sat reading. The evening seemed endless and as soon as the hall clock struck ten, Mary closed her book and got to her feet. 'Well then, I'll leave you to it, Kate. I'm away to my bed.'

Kate rose and they kissed each other goodnight. She watched while Mary crossed the main hall before closing the door behind her. Then she stood with her hand pressed against her mouth, listening to Mary's footsteps as she climbed the stairs. She so badly wanted to call

out to Josh to come down and talk to her and it took
great willpower to stop herself from doing so. She waited
another two hours before she decided that he wasn't
going to put in an appearance that night.

A little after six o'clock next morning Josh opened the
door and stood regarding his mother. She was curled up
in the armchair, her head on one side, her eyes closed
and her hair uncombed and tangled. As if she felt his
presence she wriggled her body until she was sitting up
straight and only then opened her eyes.

'You've been there all night,' Josh said, sympathetically. 'I'm going to make you a pot of tea. It's my fault
you didn't go to bed, isn't it?'

Kate struggled to her feet, glanced at him anxiously,
and said as briskly as she could, 'Of course it's not. I
just fell asleep. We'll go to the kitchen and make some
tea together.'

It was Josh who took the poker and rattled it between
the bars of the grate, letting the grey ash fall though to
the cinder box. When a red glow appeared he opened
up the top and threw on some dry wood and a shovelful
of coal.

'Come and sit over here by the fire and get yourself
warm.'

Kate was so completely unnerved by the way he was
taking charge that she meekly did what he asked. When
they were both seated with a large mug of hot tea,
Kate tried to gather her thoughts. First she had to
know what Josh's reaction to the contents of the case
was. With two hands round her mug, she took a sip,
cleared her throat nervously, and then said in a voice
that quivered, 'Josh, did you . . .' She stopped again

and then blurted out quickly, 'Tell me what you're thinking.'

He looked across at his mother and smiled his own special smile which lit up his face. 'Will you stop worrying? I can't believe it all. I am just so glad that you went up to the attic and found the case, I wouldn't have missed it for the world.' He looked beyond her and spoke as if to himself. 'When I started reading I felt my father was nearby and as I picked up each sheet of paper and each certificate the feeling grew stronger.'

Kate stared at him. Afraid to say what she was thinking. Something had changed in Joshua. He was sitting up straight in the chair, tranquillity showed in his face and his eyes were clear and comprehending.

'You learnt a lot about your father?'

'Didn't I just!' He made a funny face and laughed. 'It won't seem half so bad going to Eton, not now that I've taken the grand tour mapped out by him. Wasn't it great that he made a kind of catalogue, listing books, pictures, university courses with detailed descriptions and, best of all, those photographs. They're fabulous! Wasn't it lucky that you chanced on that case?'

Kate swallowed hard; her heart felt as if it were turning a somersault. In her mind's eye she could picture Charles Collier smiling at her as he mouthed, 'A job well done, wouldn't you say?' There was no luck connected with that find, she said to herself.

'Josh, I'm so glad you are pleased, you don't know what a relief it is to hear you say so. Shall I cook you some breakfast now?'

'You worry too much. Please could you make it an extra big breakfast, I'm starving.'

As Kate laid rashers of bacon into the frying pan and broke an egg into a bowl she said a passionate thank you to Charles Collier. She was certain he was keeping a watchful eye on his only son, and with that kind of care being lavished on Joshua, Kate felt that she would have no qualms about sending him off to his big boys boarding school.

Chapter Thirty-Eight

'IT'S NO GOOD arguing with her,' Harriet Tremaine said when she telephoned Kate. 'Your aunt has made up her mind. Ever since her husband came down and stayed two days with us she's let it be known that she intends to be back in London with her family in time for Christmas. What do you want me to do?'

'What can we do if, as you say, she's made up her mind?'

'Help her to pack her bags and wish her well. At least she's a lot healthier than when she arrived. The problem now is she's restless and bored.'

'I know what you mean, when I was there three days ago she was hinting that she could rest just as well at home. Anyway, thanks for calling, I'll be in this afternoon and have a talk with her.'

Harriet waived aside Kate's thanks and said to be sure to pop in and have tea and rang off. Kate replaced the receiver and stood still, a thoughtful look on her face.

It was only natural, she supposed, now that Aunt Dolly was back to her usual jolly form that she would want to have her children and her grandchildren round her. Especially with Christmas coming up and half the fun were the weeks before the festivities actually began. Buying presents, stocking the larder with food. Making mince pies and Christmas puddings. She pondered for a few more minutes, telling herself that she seemed to be pretty good at straightening out everyone else's lives, but what of her own?

Mary was well settled with Mike; Kate felt a little envious. There was talk of his coming to stay at Melbourne Lodge over the whole of this coming Christmas and she sincerely hoped he would, because a man in the house made all the difference and he was great with Josh.

Thinking of Joshua had Kate smiling a satisfied smile. He was all right, she was convinced of that. Come next July his prep school days would be over. Then in September he'd be off to Eton. There were no more fears or doubts where he was concerned. Two other boys from Guildford had also been granted places at Eton and one of them was Nick Banks, which had thoroughly pleased Josh, even causing him to show off and produce the photograph of his own father taken with a friend at Eton College.

'Are you going to stand out in the hall all day?' Mary called from the kitchen. 'You said you'd make the pastry while I made a start on the ironing, but we can swop if you prefer.'

Kate stared guiltily at her, having been miles away and being close to self-pity, because everyone, with the exception of herself, seemed to have tidied up their lives very nicely. And where does that leave me? she asked herself. The only answer she could come up with was either playing gooseberry or being around to make the numbers up. Not a very encouraging thought!

She still had no idea when Toby was going to return to England or if he ever would. There were times when she imagined herself ending up a dry old spinster clinging to the memory of a long-lost love. That would be awful, but it could possibly happen. I shall just have to wait and see, I suppose. Keep on hoping that the work Toby is occupied with in South Africa will come to an end and that he will come knocking on my door like a knight in shining armour and we'll be able to spend the rest of our lives together. She sucked in a deep breath. For goodness' sake stop being such a romantic old fool, she chided herself. If he does return, all well and good, and if he doesn't . . . well, I'll just have to get on with my life and stop dreaming about things that happened in the past.

When Kate arrived to visit Dolly she found her waiting in the entrance hall and the minute she saw Kate walk down the hall her expression changed.

''Allo, Kate, luv, what d'yer think? I'm going 'ome,' she said excitedly.

'Well, that is good news,' Kate responded. 'If you're sure that's what you want.'

''Course it is, luv, got all me kids' presents to get for Christmas, ain't I? Been sitting around 'ere long enough. Not that I ain't grateful t'everyone of these luverly people what's looked after me so well.' She stood looking thoughtful for a minute then hastily added, 'And I ain't ever gonna forget that it was you what set about bringing me down 'ere and seeing I was looked after. We won't say too much on the matter, 'tis water under the bridge now, but it'll be a long time before I forget that some members of my family, and I'm sorry t'say that includes my Bert, would 'ave give up on me, 'ad me locked away like I was some bloody geriatric. It's only 'cos my 'ilda and you persisted that I got better.'

'Oh, Aunt Dolly! I don't think there's a person in this world who could manage to keep you down for long. And you mustn't blame Uncle Bert, he was frightened, out of his depth; he's so used to you taking charge and seeing to everyone's needs that he couldn't cope with you so ill.'

'What you're telling me, luv, is me 'usband thinks of me as a right loudmouth bossy boots.'

'I never said any such thing and you know it,' Kate laughingly rebuked her. 'By the way you haven't said when you're thinking of going home.'

'Termorrer night. Sam is gonna come and fetch me when he knocks off work.'

'Don't you feel nervous?'

'A bit, I suppose. Be noisy, won't it, after this place? But I'm excited an' all. Me neighbours will be in an' out of the 'ouse before I've 'ad time to take me 'at off. They'll all be wanting to know the insides out of a donkey's hind leg.'

'And you'll be just the person to tell them. I almost wish I were coming to London with you. Be an experience, your homecoming, I bet.'

'Kate, luv, I don't 'ave t'tell you, do I? There's no one on this earth that I'd love more to see walk through my front door, day or night, an' I mean that. You want a change or just a cuppa and a chat, you can always count on my 'ouse as your 'ome. And, gal, down or up, don't you ever forget it. I think of you as being as much my daughter as my 'ilda is and I thank God everyday for the pair of yer.' Leaning forwards, she gave Kate a resounding kiss on the cheek. 'Thanks, luv. 'Ow about taking me into Kingston now? I've been cooped up 'ere far too long.'

'That's a lovely idea, and you know what? I'm taking you to Bentalls. You can have a look round, choose something nice, because I'm going to treat you.'

Dolly threw back her head and laughed loudly before saying, 'An' I'm gonna let yer, gal, 'cos I ain't never bin one to look a gift 'orse in the mouth, but I can't 'elp wondering if you ain't palming me off with a present 'cos you're glad to see the back of me.'

They both started talking at once.

'Come on, let's fetch your hat and coat,' Kate said, reaching out to grasp her aunt's hand, holding it tightly in hers, all the while thinking to herself just how much she was going to miss this splendid lady who had such an indomitable spirit.

There were just four weeks to go now to Christmas.

Kate lay in bed, in the quiet darkness, staring at the ceiling, and decided that, in a strange way, finding Charles Collier's attaché case had marked a new era. Not only had the contents of the case helped to give Joshua more confidence with which to face the future, it signified that he would no longer need her as much in the future as he had done in the past. Also, now that her aunt had decided to return to London, she was left with more free days, which she sometimes found hard to fill.

Her thoughts returned to Toby. She had been experiencing an uncanny feeling for days now; it was as if she felt him near her. She only had to close her eyes to imagine the way he had kissed her, she could clearly remember his arms round her, his hand fondling her breast, the weight of his body on hers when they had made love. The pain they had each suffered when it had come to their parting.

She was suddenly consumed with the pain of wanting him. She turned on her side, tugging the bedclothes up tightly around her body, telling herself not to be so silly. Just because Charles Collier had made himself visible to her didn't mean that because she now felt Toby to be close he also was unexpectedly going to appear at the foot of her bed. Wishing didn't make it so!

Alone in the darkness, Kate cried as she hadn't done for years. She not only felt lonely she felt rejected.

The hall clock was striking nine when she walked slowly down the stairs. Her thick hair was damp and curly after her bath, quite uncontrollable. She had dressed casually, pulling on a loose skirt, a high-necked blouse and a v-necked jumper over the top. She had dallied with the idea of tying a multi-coloured scarf around her neck but had then discarded it. She sighed. When the Christmas holiday is over and Josh is settled back for his last two terms at Guildford, she promised herself, I shall go away. Leave Mary to have some time alone with Mike. I will, I mean it. I'll have a holiday. It's something to think about. Something to look forward to. They say the journeying is always better than the arriving; well I'll see. Cheered by the prospect, she opened the kitchen door to find Mary sitting in the big chair by the fire, reading the morning newspaper and enjoying what was probably her second or even third cup of tea.

'Morning, Kate, you've slept late,' she said, putting the paper down and getting to her feet. 'That is a fresh pot of tea, pour yourself a cup and I'll cook you some breakfast. What do you fancy?'

'Please don't get up. I don't want anything to eat, not yet. I lay awake for ages and then when it was getting light I fell asleep. Sorry.'

'Nothing to be sorry for, time's our own. I was wondering what you'd like to do today. Anyway let me get you that tea.'

Mary bustled about, not sitting down again until Kate was seated at the table. A brimming cup, a tray which held milk jug and sugar basin, with the small silver teapot being kept warm with the aid of one of Mary's hand-knitted tea cosies. Hardly had her bottom touched the seat of her chair than the doorbell rang. 'I'll get it,' Mary offered. 'You sit still and drink your tea.'

Some minutes ticked by before she returned and when she did her face was so blank that Kate could read nothing from her expression. Without saying a word, she stood beside Kate and held out a small, flat parcel.

Kate took it, saw it was addressed to her, turned it over in her hands twice, then stared up at Mary, her eyebrows raised in question.

'Why don't you try opening it?' was all that Mary said, which bewildered Kate even more because she thought she detected a chuckle in her voice.

Mary took her seat by the fire and sat back, contentedly watching while Kate removed the brown paper from the small package. Inside she found an oblong white leather box measuring approximately three inches by two inches, which she laid on the table and just sat there staring at it.

'Open it. Go on,' Mary urged.

Kate undid the gold clasp, and raised the lid. Her eyes almost popped out of her head. The leather box was lined with cream satin; cradled between a slot that ran through the middle lay two rings. One, a single diamond, set with intricate gold shoulders, dazzled her with a twinkling of sparkling rainbow colours. Beside it lay a plain gold wedding ring.

Tears blurred her vision, but not completely. She didn't allow them to stream down her cheeks until she had removed the small card that lay inside the lid of the case. Six short words that would remain vivid in her mind for the rest of her life. Six short words that would erase the long wait. The lonely days and the nights that had seemed even more lonely. Six short words that could mean only happiness.

Please, will you be my wife?

She sat silent, for a full two minutes before she sniffed and rubbed at her eyes with her handkerchief. Then she frantically grabbed up the brown paper the box had been wrapped in. There were no stamps, no postmark. She turned round to face Mary.

'Who brought it? Did you get the name of the delivery firm? Oh, why the hell didn't I answer the door?' she yelled, her voice filled with desperation.

Mary rose slowly to her feet and said gently, 'Kate, it

432

was delivered by hand. The gentleman is outside waiting for an answer.'

'What? Are you sure?'

'Yes, I'm sure. Your Toby is in the garden. I did ask him to come in, but he said he preferred to wait outside.'

'Oh, Mary,' Kate's voice was little more than a sob, 'what shall I do? I look an absolute mess. My hair is all over the place. I can't let him see me looking like this.'

Mary smiled her understanding. 'You've both waited this long – you think he'll care that you aren't neat and tidy? You're wasting time. If I were you I'd have been out there by now. My feet wouldn't have touched the ground.'

Kate released the leather box, which she had been holding in a tight grip, and laid it down on the table. She ran her fingers through her hair, got to her feet and walked slowly to where Mary stood. 'Mary, oh Mary,' was all she could manage, her voice sounding as if she were once again a small child.

'Just go, Kate,' Mary urged, pushing her towards the door. 'He really is out there waiting for you.'

Kate fumbled with the front door and paused a moment before stepping out into the sharp fresh air. After all the years of waiting she couldn't believe this was happening.

There he was!

Taller than she remembered, the same good figure, hair with more strands of grey, his complexion fresh but certainly not pale. Just a glance and one could tell that he had recently lived in a hot climate.

He strode towards her. She was rooted to the spot.

Stop being so daft, she muttered, move, let him know you're pleased to see him. Still she couldn't lift a foot. He was within yards of her, she staggered forward and his arms wrapped round her, holding her body close to his, so tightly she could scarcely breathe. Minutes passed before he loosened his hold and, when eventually he did, they looked into each other's eyes before he lowered his head and covered her lips with his. Their first kiss was long and tender, and when it was over he still held her close to him, as he murmured, 'God I've waited so long for this. Kate, my own dear Kate, say that you still feel the same about me, say it quickly, tell me you will marry me. You haven't changed your mind, have you?'

He raised her face and then his lips were on hers again and she knew she was not dreaming. Toby had come back. Just as he had promised he would. He was here. We shan't have to be parted again, she promised herself.

When he finally released his grip he kept one arm around her waist. 'You came back,' was all she could think of to say.

'Did you doubt that I would?' he asked and, without waiting for an answer, added, 'I came back as soon as I could. I still feel exactly the same about you as I did on the day we parted. I want you to be my wife.'

She badly wanted to fling herself at this man who had meant so much to her from the moment they had first met, yet something held her back. She was afraid. Supposing she didn't come up to his expectations? He was a man of the world. She had lived such a quiet life, could she be a suitable companion for him? More to the point, would she be a good wife?

Kate said anxiously, 'Toby, it's been more than two years.'

'Two years and eight months to be exact. Thirty-two wasted months. We've got a lot of catching up to do.' He drew her into the shelter of the porch and proceeded to try to show her just how much he had missed her.

It was a long time before Kate had enough breath to say, 'You don't know anything about me now.'

He leant his tall body back against the glass wall and laughed, 'I know a great deal more about you than you imagine and I'm afraid there I have the advantage over you, but I'm willing to spend the rest of my life making sure you find out everything there is to know about me and everything we do in future we shall do together. That's a promise, and I think you know now that I keep my promises.'

Kate loved the sound of that. Her heart sang with happiness.

'How do you know such a lot about me? How did that come about?'

He grinned sheepishly, in fact Kate was sure he had a guilty look about him.

'Shall we go inside the house? I don't want you catching cold before I have time to get you to the church.'

'Toby Pinfold, is there something you're not telling me? I asked you a question and you're shilly-shallying about giving me an answer.'

'All right. I've been back in England for two weeks. There were a lot of matters that I had to settle. But the main reason for my not contacting you earlier was in your interests. I am absolutely sure of my own feelings, I bought the two rings while I was in South Africa I was that certain. But, as I said in my letter, I had to be sure that I wasn't coming back and treading on any toes. It was a lot to ask of you to wait so long, Kate, and I couldn't have blamed you if you had found another man. If you had and you were leading a happy life I would never have let you know that I was back in this country. I would have gone away and left you in peace. I had to find out how you were and how life had dealt with you, in all fairness to you. Do you understand?'

'Yes,' she agreed half-heartedly, 'but how . . . ?'

'With the help of your lovely friend, Mary Kennedy.'

'What? You've met Mary? She's met you?'

'One could hardly have happened without the other.'

'Oh, you know what I mean.' She punched his shoulder playfully.

'Yes, my darling, and I'm sorry, I shouldn't tease you. I was outside the house one day, just sitting in my car wondering what to do, when Mary came out and I took my courage in both hands and introduced myself and since that first time we have met regularly. She has been an absolute gem.'

'I bet she has! You'll be telling me next that you've met Joshua as well.'

'No. But I have learnt a lot about him and I sincerely hope it won't be long before I have the pleasure.'

Kate didn't have an answer to that. Things were bowling along and she was feeling utterly bewildered.

'Come along then,' she said shyly. 'Welcome home. Let's go inside and see if your friend Mary will feed us both because I haven't had any breakfast yet. And besides, there're a few questions I think I need to ask her.'

'Not so fast, young lady,' he exclaimed holding on tight to her arm. 'There's something I haven't had yet and neither of us is moving out of this porch until I get it.'

'And what might that be?'

Toby turned her round until she was square with his own body. He cleared his throat, looked straight into her eyes and said, 'My question is, Kate, will you marry me? Please? I've waited so long.'

'Yes,' she answered holding up her lips for him to kiss.

Chapter Thirty-Nine

ON THE LAST Saturday of March 1935 Kate Kearsley woke up at five o'clock feeling full of the joys of spring. Today was her wedding day.

By the time Joshua helped her out of the car and up the steps of Kingston church she felt sure no one in the whole world felt happier than she did on this beautiful afternoon. She linked her hand through her son's arm, then proceeded slowly down the aisle to the sound of the organ playing the 'Wedding March.' She paused for a moment before taking her place beside Toby at the foot of the altar steps, to smile first at her Aunt Dolly and Uncle Bert, her three cousins, Hilda, Tom and Stan, who were all there with their families, seated in the front pew; then, at Mary and Mike, Mr and Mrs Weatherford, Harriet Tremaine and most of the staff from the Alice Memorial Homes, who sat together in the second row.

After all those months of waiting, three years almost to the day, the service seemed to be over very quickly.

439

Elizabeth Waite

'You may kiss the bride,' Reverend Hutchinson said, smiling broadly, for he was thinking to himself that performing this ceremony had been one of the highlights of his career within the church, and that no bride had ever looked happier or, indeed, deserved happiness more than today's bride.

Kate and Toby left the church to a thunderous peal of bells and a shower of colourful confetti. Their hands clasped tightly as they sat in the back of the chauffeur-driven car, quietly smiling. Arriving at Hampton Court where a large marquee had been set up at the back entrance to the Kearsley Boat Yard, they were surrounded by their guests. Trying to welcome every one of them was proving to be a hard job and Kate found herself separated from Toby.

'You're looking very thoughtful for a new bride,' Jack Stuart touched her arm.

'Yes,' she agreed, looking up at the sign over the wide double doors of the boat yard that had been in her family for four generations.

'Are you thinking of changing the name now?'

'Oh, Jack! No. Never in a million years. My father deserves better than that. When it came to this boat building business he was held in great respect, as were his forefathers. Wouldn't you agree?'

'Yes, indeed,' he hastily assured her.

'The name Kearsley still carries a lot of weight up and down the Thames and I take this opportunity to say thanks, Jack. The yard couldn't have carried on without you and, seeing as how we're having this chat, I also want to add my thanks for all you've done for Joshua. It's down to you that he is safe on the river and so well versed in the art of handling so many different boats.' Seeing that Jack was looking slightly embarrassed Kate continued hurriedly, 'I mean it Jack, you've been a godsend to me in the bringing up of Josh.'

Before he had a chance to reply, Toby's arms came round her neck and in a teasing voice he muttered, 'Trying to swop me for another already, are you?'

Jack Stuart laughed. 'She wouldn't want an old crock like me.'

'That's not exactly true, I still need you badly, Jack, but . . .' she paused and twisted her body round '. . . you, Toby Pinfold are stuck with me for the rest of your life.'

'That is what I've been waiting to hear from the day we met.'

'Well, you'll have to wait a while longer before you can have me all to yourself. We must see that our guests are fed and watered.'

'And you'd better think about getting on with your speech,' Jack told Toby, adding, 'Good luck to you both. And I'd like to say on behalf of my wife and children and all those that are employed here at the Kearsley Yard that we think you two make a smashing pair.'

Toby, having shaken Jack's hand, was about to move off with Kate beside him when they saw Josh, Peter Bradley and Nick Banks, still in their wedding attire, standing gazing longingly inside the main shed to where a new motor launch was perched up on blocks.

'Josh,' Kate shouted. Her son turned and waved. 'Don't even think about it. Not even a rowboat! Not today.'

All three lads laughed, and gave her the thumbs-up sign before trotting off in the direction of the food tent.

★   ★   ★

441

Later that night, the length of the towpath was lit by dozens of coloured lanterns. Owners of vessels that had been specifically made to order from the Kearsley Boat Yard, jostled with barges and longboats for a position on the river. Steam whistles blew, barrel organs, concertinas and accordions bellowed out melodious tunes. Free ice creams and drinks were available for old and young alike.

Folk, having heard that Kate Kearsley was to be married, had come from far and wide. Most had known the suffering and notoriety that Kingston Kate had endured without complaint when tragedy had struck. But that was all in the past. She had survived the long ordeal and over the years had earned respect. Those close to her knew she had proved herself to be a wonderful substitute mother to young Joshua Collier.

Today, however, was Kate's day! She had found herself a man she loved and who in return loved her and, against all the odds, they had been married.

'Happy, Mrs Pinfold?' Toby asked Kate, as Joshua urged their guests to raise their glasses and drink to the happiness of 'Kate and Toby'.

'Happy, beyond my wildest dreams,' she whispered. Then, clutching his hand and squeezing it tight, she said, 'Nothing can hurt me now, because I have you.'

He lowered his head until his lips were close to her ear. Gently he moved aside the soft white veil that shrouded her shoulders and in a voice full of tenderness he said, 'Oh, Kate. My own dear darling, it is even better than that. Every day for the rest of our lives we have each other.'